BREATH TO BEAR

BLOOD & BONE SERIES
BOOK 2

PAULA DOMBROWIAK

Dark Angel Publishing

Breath to Bear
By: Paula Dombrowiak

Copyright © 2022 Paula Dombrowiak
First Edition, November 2021

This is a work of fiction. Names, characters, places, brands, media, and incidents are either the products of the author's imagination or are used fictitiously.

Cover Designer: Paula Dombrowiak
Editor: Katy Nielsen

www.pauladombrowiak.com

For all the 'Jack's' out there who need to find their way out of the darkness. There is a happily ever after waiting for you.

CONTENTS

PLAYLIST

Album

1. Layla - *Eric Clapton*
2. Free Bird - *Lynyrd Skynyrd*
3. Pride and Joy - *Stevie Ray Vaughan*
4. Come Undone - *Tove Lo*
5. Gimme - *BANKS*
6. Jolene - *Ray LaMontagne*
7. Such A Simple Thing - *Ray LaMontagne*
8. Shameless - *Sofia Karlberg*
9. Bad Ones - *Tate McRae*
10. Wallflower - *Kimberly August*
11. Bad Drugs - *King Kavalier, ChrisLee*
12. Maria - *Two Feet*
13. Division - *Killstation*
14. Premonition - *Killstation*
15. Even Stevens - *Sorry X, Original God*
16. Enough's Enough - *Paris Shadows*
17. Hurt So Good - *Astrid S*

18. Prisoner - *Raphael Lake, Aaron Levy & Daniel Ryan Murphy*
19. Keep Me In Your Heart - *Serena Pryne and the Mandevilles*
20. Love Me or Leave Me - *Little Mix*
21. Watch Me Burn - *Michele Morrone*
22. Devil in Me - *Halsey*

The Lamplight

JACK

The neck of the guitar is balanced on my knee while I sit in front of the sound board. I couldn't tell you what half of this shit does, but I know enough to turn on the playback. Wade is the equipment nerd but he's not here most of the time. I usually come alone. I prefer it that way.

The headphones fit snug against my ears, and they drown out whatever noise might be beyond the studio door. But it's late and I'm guessing no one is here anyway. I listen to her songs over and over again. Her voice cascading over me like a clear pool of water I want to wash myself clean in. The sound of the piano with all of its imperfections feels as though it's being played in the same room as me. Her voice is a powerful beacon, burning through me, threatening to tear me apart and like the masochist I am, I revel in it. Here I am, staring at this board, knowing that her voice, her music is still alive, but *she* is not. It's grossly unfair. But nothing in life is fair, and certainly not for me.

I wearily run my hands through my hair, tearing the headphones off and lean forward, closing my eyes. It's unclear if I have the nerve or the will power to finish this album, and God knows I have tried. It deserves to be heard, but writers block consumes me every time I get in the studio. All I know is that I lay awake at night thinking about it. This album is personal. Not only is it the last music Mia would ever make, but it is the last thing we made *together*. I want to hold onto this as long as I can because it is all I have left. Every year, memories fade, and the feel of her loses its sharpness in my mind. I should let those memories go, but I hold on fiercely to retain them.

I have every reason to go home right now, but I can't bring myself to do it.

I am too deep inside my own head.

I am no good to anyone right now, least of all Erin. She would understand but that doesn't mean she should have to.

This is my process.

This is my darkness.

The pen starts to slide off the notebook as I drag it towards me, but I grab it just before it tumbles off the edge. It's a simple composition notebook you can get at any drugstore, but it contains notes, chords, lingering thoughts, ramblings, and drawings that I've transferred from my head onto those pages. If anyone were to look at it, I'm afraid of what they might think.

This album was left unfinished. Like so many other things, I intended to leave it that way, file it away like I've tried to file away that part of my life, but it's begging me not to.

Maybe if I finish it, I can finally sleep.

Sometimes I can't stand to be inside my own skin. I think too much. My mind never stops and I'm exhausted. I thought writing a book would help ease this pain I feel inside, but it hasn't. There are over a hundred thousand words in those pages that people will read, but I lived them, and they are etched inside my soul forever.

Absently, I hit a few minor chords on my guitar, hoping it will provoke a spark of something that resembles creativity, but I come up empty. Calluses on my fingertips prevent me from feeling the strings but I don't need to feel them to know I'm hitting the right chords. There was a time when I didn't feel right in the world without a guitar in my hands. Now, it feels like a strange weight pressed to my thighs and against my torso. Writing songs was never easy, but it was never this hard. There were times when it felt like I was bleeding ink from my veins just to get lyrics onto paper.

Now, I can't even bleed.

I'd smash this guitar to pieces right now if it wasn't a '56 Strat. Not the kind of guitar you obliterate unless you're insane, and I'm not quite there yet. Although I couldn't seem to cure my writers block tonight, I have this Strat in my hand, and it is begging to be played. Cash acquired this at an auction and because he knows what a guitar snob I am, he offered for me to check it out. He's putting a lot more trust in me than I deserve. It has the signature dark brown-to-golden yellow sunburst pattern made from rosewood. It's the perfect guitar to play because of its body design and balance. Even though so many guitars have emulated this style since its inception, there's nothing like the original. I can tell this guitar has been well played, and each scuff mark and ding in the body tells a story.

I need to get the fuck out of here before I do go insane. I pull the master tapes from the analogue machine and secure them back in their case. Some people prefer digital, but to me, the analogue sounds better. I know I'm not the only one; a few artists recently have released an analogue album or a single. Maybe I'm just old school, but technology has removed a certain human element to the process so it's nice to see some going back to their roots. The downfall of these reels is that if something happened to them, it is the only record of this album. That is why they are kept in fireproof cases and locked in a safe in the storage room.

There are rows and rows of reels just like this one. Some have been remastered and stored on digital, but a lot of them haven't. It's what makes them special. They are one of a kind. This room is a museum of sorts for the musicians who have come before me, and the ones that will come after. It's like the dinosaur collection of music. All of my albums are stored here, and for safety reasons, once the album was completed, they were recorded on digital. But not this one. I won't let them touch this one. I hold the metal case in my hands. This one has yet to be finished, and it the most precious one of all.

I lock up the studio and head outside to where my car is parked. I hate driving in LA, but Paul has finally had enough of me. He realized the need to put family first and moved back to Michigan. I have yet to replace him, simply because there is no replacement. So now I'm stuck driving myself around.

Even though it's late, the city lights are like a million stars cast from the sky. I know they say New York is the city that never sleeps, but I feel like LA in general is a kindred spirit. There is always an open club, cars cruising the streets and tour buses chugging by because everyone wants to catch a glimpse at one of those stars. A few kids kick off their skateboards as they ride by with their converse and beanies. I realize LA isn't all that different from when I first came here. It's apparent in how many homeless kids roam the streets at night. The only difference is that the cops have cracked down on the squats, taking back the city and casting out those that need a home. But every time they clear one of the buildings out, people always find their way back in.

I set the guitar on the passenger side and head over to the *Lamplight*. It's a small club in the Venice neighborhood where I like to play sometimes and blow off steam. The owner is a friend, and whenever I've needed to test a song or just play for fun, he makes room for me. I need to get my head straight before I go home and release some of this nervous energy, because if there's one thing I've learned over the years, it's when to self-isolate.

When I pull up outside of the club, the valet comes around and takes my keys. The *Lamplight* is far from anything fancy, and the only reason there's a valet is because there's never any fucking parking around here. The club sits on a corner lot. A large wooden door painted an imposing black, beckons in the front. A warm glow comes from the wide windows flanking the door. Dramatic red curtains hang, tied at each side. Inside is a long wooden bar stretching the length of the building. At the back is a riser big enough for a full band. Can lights are placed in the ceiling to illuminate the stage. Round tables are scattered in the middle of the club. The front of the stage is cleared for dancing or mosh pits, depending on the night. The club is known to host a variety of local bands and special appearances on certain weekends out of the month.

It's a weeknight and the jukebox is playing an old rock tune. The club isn't crowded which suits my purpose. I just need to play and not necessarily for an audience. I spot Benny, the owner, as I enter the club. He loves to hang out with the regulars, greeting everyone at their tables. That's what makes this place special. It's like coming home. He greets me with a wide smile.

"Jack, good to see you." One of his large meaty hands clasps my arm in a gentle squeeze while the other slaps me on the back. Benny has an unruly mustache, and bushy eyebrows. He wears a button up shirt and his belly hangs over his slacks. He always smells like whiskey and sawdust.

He sees the guitar I'm holding and nods in appreciation. "That's a beauty." He comments admiringly. "You here to play then?" He walks me over to the bar and waves at the bartender to get me a coffee. I shake my head and chuckle inside because I think it's well known that I have a substance abuse problem, and Benny is not an enabler. He's a good person. For me, it was never the alcohol that was the problem, although it attributed to my style of self-medicating. It was more the drugs that I couldn't handle. Even after all of these years, I know my addictive personality, and I wouldn't be able to stop at just one drink. I don't hang out in bars, but if I'm up on stage playing, I can block it out, and that's exactly what I will do tonight.

"Thanks, Benny." I grab the cup of coffee, which isn't going to help me sleep, but it does help me stay straight, trading one drug for another. "You got space for me to play?" I ask.

"Sure, sure," he says. "You see anyone playing here tonight? It's fucking dead." His head tips back and he lets out a boisterous laugh.

A couple at the bar look over at us curiously, and based on their whispers, they recognize me. I've lived in Venice for so long I feel like I've become a fixture, and the shininess of celebrity has dulled. The paparazzi are everywhere though, but these days, they seem to be focusing on my kid more than me. Before she turned 18 years old, there was more I could do about it. Now that she's 21 and of legal drinking age, it's out of my control. Although she'd have my head if she thought I was meddling in her life. She's a tough kid, but she's still a kid. She has lots of learning to do, yet, especially in this business.

I wrap my fingers around the warm cup of coffee and head up to the stage. There's already a couple of stools, and I place the cup on the one opposite me. Benny has one of the guys hook up my equipment which consists of simply plugging the amp into my guitar, although, I can play acoustic with an electric guitar just fine. The sound is obviously different, and tonight I want the reverb and the squeal, even if there's no bass or drums to back me up.

People start to take notice as I warm up with a few chords. I am in a wicked mood, fire running in my veins, sorrow in my heart, and these people don't know what they're in for because I am going to play the fuck out of this Strat.

"Thanks for having me tonight," I say into the mic as I dip my neck to place the strap of the guitar over my head.

"We love you, Jack!" I hear a woman yell from the back who I recognize as a regular.

"Thanks, darlin'." The cheap microphone causes my voice to sound more gravelly than usual.

"I hope you don't mind if I play a few covers for you tonight," I say, looking out into the small crowd. "I have this gorgeous guitar here that I got from a friend, and, well, I gotta take it for a test drive."

The single coil sounds so sweet as I warm up with an old Tom Petty song, *It'll All Work Out*. Maybe it's foreshadowing or simply looking back, but this song, a less popular of Petty's, seems appropriate tonight. The soft melodic tone and the beautiful lyrics of a legend taken from us way too soon speaks to all of us in the room of our youth and loves lost. They don't write songs like this anymore, and it's a shame we'll never get another one. I close my eyes and let the muscle memory take over, remembering when I was a teenager and I first learned to play the guitar. It took time for my fingers to become flexible enough to get the placement on the strings just right, and it was a challenge to master the coordination of singing and hitting the right chords at the same time

Now it's like breathing air.

If not for the air in your lungs, you would die.

That's how I move effortlessly into Lynyrd Skynyrd's *Free Bird*, without even having to think about it. I lean into the guitar and the melody envelopes me like the ocean, gently pulling me into its depths. This song is easily one of the greatest songs ever written, and I love performing it, especially the guitar solo at the end. When I open my eyes and look out into the crowd, I see Benny leaning against the bar, watching me with a faraway look in his eyes. It's this kind of nostalgic song that resonates with people, bringing them to a place of solemn remembrance.

When the demons come calling, this is how I chase them away.

I get on stage, and I play.

It's all I know, and if I didn't have music as my guidepost, I would truly be lost.

2
Layla
ERIN

H eat from the fire pit warms my legs as I look out at the waves. The glow from the moon on the cloudless night casts light on the ocean's surface, mimicking tiny glittering diamonds. Nights like these remind me of growing up near Lake Michigan, back when I was young enough to think it was an ocean because it was so big you couldn't see the other side. That was when life was much simpler, and the only thing I had to worry about was getting a flat tire on my bike too far from home.

The expensive headphones I splurged on play some alternative music I added to my playlist recently, a band I've been following lately. Music is one of life's greatest pleasures. It has the power to move you in ways you could never imagine, cause you to tear at your clothes in desperation, see what you need to in the soulful eyes of a lover, make your heart shatter into a million pieces and then put you back together again.

My plane landed yesterday. I've been busy meeting with a festival promoter and ended up covering a showcase as a favor to get the band more media coverage before their tour starts. It ended up being a late night and so I headed over to Jack's place this evening, knowing he'd be finishing up in the studio soon. It should have given him plenty of time, but now it's late in the evening, and I'm still here… alone.

Snuffing out the fire with sand, I grab my shoes and carry them inside with me. Jack's house is dark and uninviting. It's a bachelor pad with minimal furniture and barely any decoration. I used to think it was because Jack wasn't home enough to really enjoy it, but knowing him now for over a year, I know that's not the reason.

It feels odd being here without Jack, like I'm an intruder, not really belonging. It could be the ghosts that linger, or the moon that casts shadows across the wood floor that make it feel unwelcoming. My fingers run over the back of the leather couch as I walk barefoot through the living room. I can see the small dent in the plaster that has never been repaired. I want to touch it, to feel the violence that caused it, but it's impenetrable… like the walls around Jack's heart.

I know the story behind this dent.

The problem is, *I know the story behind a lot of things*.

They say ignorance is bliss, and sometimes I wish I didn't know so much.

When I look around, I can't help but notice this house is bigger than my apartment in New York, but it's considered small by L.A. standards, with only two bedrooms, one bathroom, a small kitchen and cozy living room. I understand why he keeps it, why he loves it, when he could afford a bigger place. Not to mention the view is to die for, and to wake up to the ocean every day would be a dream. Instead, I wake up to the garbage truck rattling down the street, an occasional domestic violence situation, and a neighbor who likes to crank *Journey* at weird hours. Don't get me wrong, I like a good *Journey* song, but there are only so many times you can listen to *Open Arms* without wanting to kick someone in the balls.

Pulling my laptop across the counter, I sit on one of the kitchen stools and contemplate working on an article. I need to get a draft of the showcase I covered this weekend to the editor by tomorrow night. I look at my phone again, but I know Jack hasn't called or texted me back. Accustomed to his idiosyncrasies by now, I know he's turned his phone off while in the studio, but I still worry about him. We finished the book months ago, and he's slowly become more reclusive, inside his head more than usual, and spending a lot of time in the studio. While I try to be understanding, my patience is running thin.

Since I quit my job at *Edge*, I've hopped from one magazine to another. I used to like the stability of a nine to five, not that journalism was always that way, but it was steady pay even though I lived paycheck to paycheck. With the book deal Jack got, my financial stress has been eased a little bit. I finally became an adult when I put my bills on autopay. Not to mention a convenience because I never seem to be home anymore to collect my bills. I travel between L.A. and New York quite often, but I've gotten to travel many places, covering shows and other music related events. Whichever magazine I work for, I'm the one who can leave at a moment's notice.

As I sit here at Jack's kitchen counter, I can't help but think about where I would be if I had never knocked on his door that day. It's funny the places life takes you. If I had left right away when he shut the door in my face, he'd never have had the chance to hijack my car. So where would I be right now? I think often of when he dropped me off at the airport, parting ways and not knowing if we would see each other again.

"When you get back to New York and you've had some time to think, if you still want to do the book, you know how to reach me," Jack said to me, but I had already made up my mind. I'd spent the entire plane ride writing because I couldn't get him out of my head. When my plane landed, the first thing I did was call him. *"Are you ready to do this?"* I asked. His reply was, *"The question is, are you?"* Imagine my surprise when I got to my apartment and Jack was waiting for me on the steps to my building. His answer to my questioning eyes, *"Private planes are much faster than commercial."* That now familiar cocky grin made my stomach flutter. I smile bringing my fingers to my lips as I think back on that memory.

Jack being on my steps was so jarring and out of place that it threw me off my game, but I was so glad that he wanted to do the book, I naively asked, "So, now what?" not knowing how any of this worked. I remember the wicked grin on his face so clearly, the one I am so accustomed to now, *"You invite me into your apartment,"* he said.

Over the past year, Jack and I worked on his book together, arguments not easily won, and compromises hard to acquire. When you work on a biography about someone's life, you sometimes find out things you don't want to know, especially if you are in a relationship with that person. That is my downfall, my Achilles heel. I can't separate the lines between professional relationship and romantic entanglement, especially when it comes to someone like Jack O'Donnell.

When I finished writing the book, I submitted it to a couple of different publishing houses through some contacts I'd made. Admittedly, we knew the publishing industry would love to get their hands on Jack's story, not only because he was a Grammy winning artist with a long history in the industry, but because he had always been so private about his personal life with the press. Here he was with a tell-all book, and the industry lost their minds. Everyone wanted to know the story behind the music. What we didn't expect was a bidding war.

The decision was ultimately Jack's, and for him it was never about the money. He chose a smaller publishing house with a team of people that understood what this book meant to him. Although they couldn't give a huge advance, we struck a deal to get money on the back end through sales. For me, the advance was more money than I'd ever had in my bank account at one time. There were more preorders than we ever imagined. The book was on the New York Times Best Sellers list, even before Jack had started a press tour.

For two people who had met through unlikely circumstances, we created something extraordinary together, forged through long hours, patience, understanding, and without judgement. It is not a story for everyone.

Most wouldn't be able to handle it.

It is brutally honest, unapologetic, raw, and exquisitely beautiful.

Just like Jack.

My name is not on the book. This is not my story.

That's just one of the problems being with a guy like Jack. The press usually leaves him alone, but with the exposure of the book, it's put a new spotlight on him. These days though, Hayley is in the news more often than him, and I know how Jack feels about that.

I'm having a hard time concentrating on my article as I keep looking at the time on the computer screen. It's nearly midnight, and I can't image he'd still be at the studio. There's only one other place he could be.

I change out of my shorts and hoodie into a pair of jeans, T-shirt and sweater. I slip my feet into the flip flops I carried in from the beach, because it's L.A. and I can wear flip flops whenever I want. I grab my wallet from my bag and lock up. The *Lamplight* is only a few blocks from the beach house, but I call for an Uber anyway. If New York has taught me anything, you can never be too careful walking down the street alone, especially if you're a woman.

The neighborhood is peaceful this time of night. Most of the houses are dark, only the streetlamps illuminate the sidewalk. My Uber driver pulls up and I descend the steps. Ten minutes later I'm dropped off in front of the club, and as soon as I get to the door, I can hear the familiar sound of a guitar penetrating its thick wooden frame. I've heard a lot of musicians in my time, all genres and styles, but there's something so distinctive about the way Jack plays. I would know it anywhere.

While growing up, I had an uncle that was a real motor-head. He loved cars, especially muscle cars. The type with big-blocks and imposing bodies. He used to tell me what kind of car was driving past our house just from the sound of the engine. I could never understand how he did it. I kept thinking it must have been a magic trick, but now I get it.

From behind the large wooden doors of the *Lamplight* is the sound of a '56 Strat. I quietly slip inside, standing just at the threshold. The bar is practically empty, but the people in here are riveted to the stage. As my gaze travels the room to the man with the guitar on the small stage, playing those famous beginning chords to *Layla*, joining in with that raspy, deep voice, I don't blame them. Jack lays into the song like he's playing Madison Square Garden instead of some beach dive bar. All I can do is stand and watch because I can't take my eyes off him. Dark brown locks of his hair fall over his eyes and his lips are so close to the mic they are practically kissing it.

Deft fingers move over the strings of that exquisite guitar like he's not afraid to abuse it. His voice is raw and deep, so full of emotion that I feel it deep in my belly. A small drop of sweat clings to his forehead before dropping onto the scuff marked planks of the stage. When people try to explain stage presence, this is what they mean. He's alone, no backup band, just a hot spotlight and a shitty amp, but I can't take my eyes off him. Neither can anyone else in the room.

The song ends, breaking the spell, and I realize I'm still rooted to the same spot as when I entered. Applause startles me as it spreads among the crowd, and a few people stand, showing their appreciation for his talent. Jack dips his neck as he pulls the guitar strap over his head. The sweat flies from the messy strands of his hair hanging in his face, and it's the sexiest thing I've ever seen. Almost as if he finally realizes there are other people in the room, his troubled eyes look out into the crowd with hesitation. When they land on me, there's a flicker of something visceral and dangerous in his gaze. I didn't know dangerous could look so beautiful. I forget why I came here as the butterflies flutter against the inside of my stomach.

I'm in over my head.

I'm out of my league.

But I am in so deep that I couldn't crawl my way out even if I wanted to.

He hops off the stage, the Strat by his side and moves through the crowd towards me with such purpose that I almost feel like I should be scared. He pushes the hair off his face revealing those outrageously beautiful blue eyes of his. When he reaches me, my knees weaken, as he holds out his hand to me. I gladly take it, mesmerized by him, shedding any anger I may have felt.

"Let's go home." His voice is commanding and rough from singing. *Perfection.*

While we wait until the valet brings the car around, his hand rests on the small of my back causing heat to radiate from that single spot like tentacles spreading throughout my body. He holds the car door open for me as I slip into the front seat of his Audi convertible. The top is down, and when we take off, my hair flies around my face in utter chaos, mimicking the beating of my heart. At this hour the streets are nearly deserted and Jack shifts gears as we move through the Venice neighborhoods. He hasn't said anything since he approached me in the club, but the intensity of his driving says enough.

The powerful way he hits the clutch and downshifts as he turns corners causes me to squirm in my seat. All I can think about is what will happen when we get back to his beach house and I squeeze my legs tighter to suppress the ache. I rub my sweaty palms over my thighs. A shiver runs down my spine, goosebumps giving me away as they form along my arm.

The car comes to a stop in the driveway and Jack shoves the gearshift into park. His hand remains on it, the veins raised as he grips the knob. I lick my lips as my gaze travels up his tattooed arm to reach his face.

"Jack." I whisper, breaking the silence, and gently put my hand over his.

I need to touch him, to feel the connection seep into my skin and race through my veins until it explodes into my heart.

He swiftly reaches over to grip the back of my neck, pulling me over the console between us while his lips forcefully take mine. My stomach tightens at the bruising violent way he takes my mouth. The hiss of his breath causes heat to flow like a river down to my core. There is an invisible hold, a gold thread wound so tight around me I couldn't pull away even if I tried. His tongue slides along mine, dipping in and out, causing me to whimper as he gently bites and pulls at my bottom lip. His erection presses sweetly against me. I am left wanting so much more when he pulls back to look at me.

I lean into his hand like a cat wanting to be petted as he touches my cheek. I grab onto his wrist holding him in place. My eyes refocus on the tattoo covering his sinewy forearm, and through the darkness, I can make out his intense blue eyes staring back at me.

I want him.

I want him to be mine, but he's somewhere else, *someone* else's. Right now, I don't care, the need inside of me tamping down any reservations. I'm ready to give him everything, even letting him take me right here in the car if he wanted.

He has the power to break me.

And break me, he will.

My hand travels up his arm, feeling every muscle and every vein until I grab hold of his shirt, gathering it in the palm of my hand like the desperate, needy woman I am.

I give in to the intoxicating scent of him, falling deeper, stretching farther into the void. He smells of aftershave and sweat that has settled and dried on his skin from exertion. The taste of coffee invading my senses as his tongue slides along my lips and slips inside in the most erotic way, all while his hands declare my body as his. I love the feel of his weight against mine, and I arch further into him like a flower bending towards the sun.

With the top down, I have enough room to rise above him, lifting my hands towards the night sky as he pulls the sweater above my head while trailing kisses along my exposed collarbone. Each one a promise igniting a flame inside me. I grind my hips against him, chasing the sweet release of the building pressure between my legs. With just enough force to expel a breath from my lungs, Jack grips my hair and pulls my head back so he can nip at my hardened nipples through my shirt.

At any moment, I feel as if am about to fall over the edge into the unknown.

How can this man make me feel this good without even entering me?

I whimper like a dog whose bone has just been taken away when he releases me so he can exit the car, pulling me with him. My legs take a moment to process the signal from my brain, and I lean against the car for support watching as he runs the back of his hand across his lips. He tracks my movements as I stumble around to the front of the car, the black shiny paint reflecting light from the lamppost. A slight breeze moves across my heated body like a soft caress as I tip my head to the sky.

The soft sound of Jack's feet against the asphalt of the driveway gain my attention. He stands before me, blending into the darkness of the night, a foreboding presence, a twin flame because the heat radiating off him matches my own. The hood takes my weight as he settles his body between my legs, weaving his fingers through my hair and bringing my mouth to his for a possessive kiss. I press my breasts into his chest, wanting, needing to make any kind of contact with him. His touch is addictive, flickers of flame licking up my sides, across my stomach, over the curves of my ass as his hands travel over my body.

I feel like a teenager as we grope each other in the driveway not wanting to break apart for the few seconds it would take to walk to the front door. A porch light turning on from across the street causes him to break contact with my lips and he rests his cheek against mine, watching and waiting. I smile against the thickness of his hair, breathing it in, the smell of smoke and shampoo. I run my fingers through the thick locks, smoothing down the wild tangles. My fingers trace his jawline feeling the rough stubble knowing exactly how these tiny hairs feel against the tender insides of my thighs.

With my lips close to his ear, I whisper to him impatiently, "Take me to bed." My words cause his muscles to tighten.

As he pulls back to look at me, I am forced to realize that this man steals my every breath. It's not in the beautiful planes of his face, or those gorgeous blue eyes but in his very presence.

With gentleness and ease, he lifts me off the hood, my legs wrapping around his waist, he carries me to the steps and up to the front porch. I am lost in his steel arms feeling every bit protected, treasured and desired. I laugh as he tries to unlock the door, fumbling with the keys and nearly dropping them in his haste to balance me and find the lock at the same time. I can tell he's frustrated and desperate to get me inside.

"Don't laugh. I will fuck you right here on the front porch." He growls and I instantly lose my grin, gulping loudly. I have no doubt he would make good on that promise.

He inserts the key in the lock and drops them carelessly as he lets me down, backing me up against the door to close it shut with a click. Resting his hand against the frame above of my head, he looks down at me with eyes that promise to do very bad things to me. Heat gathers between my legs, and I am screaming inside for release that my body shakes with anticipation. I'm afraid the moment he touches me, the bomb that has been ticking away will detonate.

Before he can reach for me, I drop to my knees slowly and watch as his expression changes from shock to desire. I give a tug to his belt, pulling it free from its buckle. The leather rough and worn but soft to the touch, just like him. His Adam's apple bobs as he swallows, and his breath escapes from his parted lips. I am turned on by his reaction and the control I have over him, no matter how fleeting it is. He treats me to a low growl from deep within his diaphragm as the material of his jeans yawns open for me. My fingers roam that delicious V pointing down into the waistband of his underwear.

When I grab onto his length, he tips his head back and his stomach muscles tighten and quiver. The affect I have on him is euphoric and powerful.

I want him to feel the way I do.

Utterly lost.

My tongue darts out and runs along his silky skin before I take him into my mouth. I feel his hands in my hair, gripping the strands as he tries to dictate my movements.

"Fuck," he rasps, as he fights to control himself.

If there is one thing I know for certain about Jack, it's that he likes to be in control at all times.

His hands loosen their grip, letting me move freely. I use my tongue to tease him as I move up and down his length. His hips move to meet me and just when I find a rhythm, he pulls me up, his cock popping free from my mouth and pins me to the door. His chest heaves with each breath and his mouth is only inches from mine. Through thick lashes, he watches as I run my tongue along my bottom lip in nervous anticipation. The feel of his fingers digging into my waist is the kind of pain that makes me wet. He crashes his mouth onto mine as I run my hands through his thick hair, desperate for him.

Tangled, heated, and breathless, I can't get enough of him as he steers me toward the bedroom. Although, I gladly would have let him take me against the door. As we enter the bedroom, the urgency slows to the same cadence as the blood pumping beneath my skin, slow and steady. It feels as if time slows when I take a moment to run my hands along his rib cage to pull the shirt over his head, revealing the smooth inked skin beneath. My finger nail scrapes across his chest, tracing the black lines that make up the beautiful artwork of a fallen angel, black and broken feathers scattered along his chest like the emotional scars he hides underneath.

I know my touch affects him by the way he breathes in a controlled manner because he is desperately trying not to slam me onto the bed and fuck me. Jack likes to be in control, denying himself quick gratification but instead, savoring in the deliciousness of anticipation, letting the pressure build until it cannot be contained any longer.

I like knowing how much he wants me.

I like feeling his erection against me, hard an unyielding.

He grabs onto my wrist to stop my fingers from tracing along his other tattoo, a smattering of stars, and pulls both my arms in the air as he rids me of my shirt. My jeans now discarded on the floor, his thumb seductively runs over my collarbone down to my breast, dipping into the top of my bra and pulling the material down. My stomach quivers as his lips leave mine to run down my skin, licking, sucking and biting, promises of what is yet to come. I gasp and arch my back when his tongue runs over my sensitive and hard nipple, taking it into his mouth.

I fall effortlessly back onto the mattress as easily as if I were falling into the darkness with him. He crawls over my body in a predatory manner making my pulse race until his face is level with mine, hands on either side of me, pinning me to the bed. All he has to do is move his knees forward to cause my thighs to rise and wrap around his waist as if that's what they were made to do.

He teases me with a kiss and then slowly moves back down my body, the rough stubble sending shivers across my body with the slightest brush to my skin. Locks of hair fall against my body like the tattooed feathers on his chest, as he kisses his way down to between my legs. His thumb moves over the center of my panties against my already throbbing clit and I moan. I've wanted his mouth on me since I saw him at the club.

"Is this what you want?" The roughness of his voice vibrating through the thin material of my panties nearly sends me over the edge.

"Yes." My words come out almost inaudible as I writhe under his touch, craving him as much as I crave air.

I think I will lose my mind when he slides the material to the side, teasing me with a dip of his finger inside me and runs the wetness along my center.

"Mmm, Jack," I pant, arching my back, unable to stay still. I'm so turned on that when his lips make contact, I throw my head back against the mattress. I've already been brought to the edge multiple times without him ever entering me, and it feels like I will explode any minute. The ache is so intense that I involuntarily try to close my legs to stop from going over the edge.

His fingers dig into my thighs. "Don't ever close your legs to me," he growls. I'm not the type of girl who likes to be told what to do, but for him and in this bed, I am oh so willing. I shakily open my legs to let him in, because whatever he wants right now, I'm giving.

He grabs ahold of my ass, roughly pulling me to the edge of the bed. Just his presence between my legs is enough to make my thighs clench. With his hands on my hips, I can feel the head of his cock barely skim the surface of my sex. It's like someone lit me on fire. My hips move in response, rolling against him, wanting all of him in me. With great restraint he continues to slide along my core, the fire growing stronger inside of me.

The sweetness of pleasure turns a dark corner into madness made of pure need to stop the ache inside of me.

"Stop teasing me." I manage to bite out and watch as the curve of his beautiful lips turns into a smirk. I know he wants this just as bad as I do, and it angers me that he has me begging. He's moving the head of his cock along my aching sex in an agonizingly slow pace, and my legs drop open even more.

"You want me to beg?" I ask breathlessly.

He nods, wetting his bottom lip with his tongue.

I've never met a man who likes the chase more than Jack O'Donnell. He wants to see me helpless for him, and I am oh so helpless.

Those blue eyes make me melt inside, and I bite my lip as he peers down at me. "Please, Jack." I whine. In response, he moves faster, rubbing against me, the friction so exquisite. There's an inferno building inside. I reach up and grab his hair, pulling his lips to mine in desperation. I'm so close, rolling my hips to meet him, moving faster, my breathing erratic. I could cum this way and he knows it.

"Not yet," he whispers, sweet like honey but lethal as venom.

Without warning, he pushes in deep, and I look into his eyes, mouth wide, fingers griping his hair, a moan leaving my lips in a broken, breathless tone. His mouth hovers over mine, our breaths becoming one unable to move, the sweet wave of pleasure leaving us both immobilized. When his lips meet mine, the kiss is so slow, so sweet, I want to dissolve into him. He moves inside of me like a slow and sensual dance taking me under his spell.

The whines and whimpers are hard to suppress, and at this point, I am past being self-conscious.

"God, you are so beautiful," he whispers, and I come undone.

My belly quivers, my thighs shake, and the fire burns through my veins as I combust. I ride the wave as he slams into me, filling me, ruining me for every other man.

Holy Fuck, Jack O'Donnell.

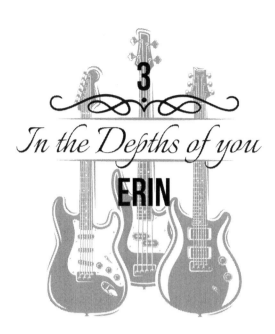

3

In the Depths of you

ERIN

I wake up in Jack's bedroom, wrapped in darkness. I already know without looking next to me that Jack is not there. I move my hand across the cold rumpled sheets beside me. This isn't the first time I've woken up alone. If I keep coming back, it won't be the last.

I look at the clock on the nightstand and see it's almost 4 a.m. As I stare up at the familiar ceiling, I can hear the crashing waves in the distance, and I know where he is. It's where I always find him in the middle of the night.

Wearing only Jack's T-shirt, I get out of bed and make my way into the living room. It's dark and quiet as I head for the back patio.

The curtains flutter in the breeze and I push them aside to see Jack leaning against the railing. He's wearing only his jeans, the button open, causing the material to flare as if he threw them on casually, showing a patch of hair low on his belly. The cherry red of his cigarette temporarily illuminates his face as he takes a drag.

Sometimes when I look at him, I can't help but think what a devastatingly beautiful, broken man he is.

When he turns his gaze to me, I lean against the doorframe, bathed in their intensity. The depths of his eyes, even in this twilight hour, speak to me the most. I know his secrets and his truths, and yet I still feel the wall between us sometimes.

I knew exactly what I was getting into with Jack, but it didn't stop me.

To say that Jack is a complicated man is an understatement. I thought I knew everything about him, but the shadows behind his eyes tell me differently. He's hurting, and I don't know why.

I'm leaving in a few hours to go back to New York, and Jack will be going on his book tour. Maybe a break will help me figure out what it is I want, and what I am willing to give up just to have him.

He flicks the cigarette to the sand but doesn't move. It's as if he can't tear himself away from his thoughts. When I found him at the *Lamplight* last night, I could understand that he needed to blow off some steam, but waking up alone, again, I begin to wonder.

Will I always be the one looking for him?

I move in front of him, wrapping my arms around his waist and placing my cheek against the warmth of his bare shoulder. If I could stay like this forever, everything would be okay, but I can't stop time, and the world is still turning around us. His arms snake around me, the palm of his hand against the back of my head. His touch solidifies the connection we have to each other, and I can feel it like electricity running under my skin.

But is it enough?

"You should come back to bed," I whisper against his skin.

He turns around to face me, letting his eyes settle on mine, and sadly, I wonder who he sees.

"I'm sorry if I woke you." His deep voice vibrates against my cheek. "I know you have to leave early."

"It's okay." The lies we tell ourselves are even greater than the ones we tell others.

I nestle my body against his as he begins to slowly rock me to a song only he can hear. I attempt to decipher the melody while he moves us inside the house. The tenderness of his actions gives me the illusion of feeling content and protected, something I have craved almost my whole life. His movements, the thumping of his heart against my body, speak to me a silent conversation.

I have to leave for the airport in a couple of hours, but right now, I just want him because I don't think I will ever get enough.

That's what scares me.

I could be consumed and lose myself so easily in this man.

"Don't go," he whispers against my neck, so softly that I almost don't hear him.

His kisses are soft like butterfly wings across my neck. Slowly he gathers the material of my T-shirt in his hands, while we dance into the kitchen. A shaky breath escapes from his lips like a soft breeze against my cheek.

Little shock waves run along my spine, sending a tidal wave of goosebumps with it. I can already feel my nipples awaken and harden against his chest. I can't help how my body responds to him, even if my mind knows better.

I let my fingers run the length of his bare back, feeling every muscle, rough edge and scar. Jack is full of scars, not all of them on the surface, and I want to kiss away every single one of them. Familiarity guides our lips together in the darkness.

His fingers trace the sensitive skin of my belly and up my ribs as he lifts the shirt over my head, leaving it to fall carelessly to the floor at our feet. He pulls me towards him to straddle his lap as he sits on the kitchen stool. Rocking my hips against him, I can feel the hardness beneath me. His hair tickles my nose as he makes his way down my neck to my collar bone, his kisses leaving trails of heat on my skin. My stomach tightens and heat pools between my legs at the anticipation of his mouth on my breast as I lean back for him.

My pelvis digs painfully into the zipper of his jeans, chasing the high I am desperate for. That's the problem with drugs, one hit is never enough. He lifts me off his lap, placing me onto the kitchen counter. I smile, drunk on him.

I grab onto his hair and bring him to me. His fingers move between my legs, gently stroking. I close my eyes, my lips hovering over his, but I am unable to move as I let the pleasure take over. His tongue runs along my bottom lip pulling me from my trance, and I open my mouth for him to take what he wants. Slow and seductive, he kisses me like the waves kiss the sand.

He places a hand at the center of my chest and lays me back against the cold granite. My breath hitches as he places my feet on his shoulders. A squeal escapes my lips as he pulls at my hips dragging me closer to the edge of the counter, but it's quickly replaced with a moan.

I can't help the noises slipping endlessly from my lips, the cadence and volume getting louder. I'm helpless and lost like a ship tossed by the sea. The pleasure causes my back to arch, and I'm searching for anything to grab onto because I have no center of gravity.

I've hit the crest of the wave and I can't breathe, my thighs quivering and my insides aching for him. I quake and moan, trying to release the pressure that's threatening to tear me apart. His breath against my core threatens to push me over.

"Your intoxicating," he says, before pressing his lips against me once more. And I'm gone. That's all it takes.

I lift my body up to kiss him. When he enters me, it's not just the feel of him but the sound of him that causes me to fall to pieces. He digs his fingers into my hips as he moves faster, chasing his own release.

He is lost, barely able to kiss me, and I reach for him to pull him back to me.

"See what you fucking do to me," he says against my mouth.

JACK

I wash my face in the bathroom sink, grabbing a towel to dry myself off. The scent of Erin still permeates my senses. I use both hands to brace myself and look in the mirror. Dark strands of hair fall over my face, and I use my wet hand to push them back. There are subtle lines on either side of my eyes and stubble framing my jawline. In the mirror I can see Erin sleeping in my bed, the blanket only covering her lower half as she lies on her stomach. My eyes roam over her bare back. She has no tattoos, her skin a blank canvas I could write lyrics on.

My bare feet pad quietly into the kitchen where I grab a cigarette and take my phone with me to the patio. I scan through a website to find a nearby AA meeting. My hand shakes as I light the cigarette and take a drag. I think about calling Wade when I hear Erin's annoyingly loud phone alarm go off. Grabbing the latte I got for her, I head into the bedroom to see her hiding her face under the pillow, the phone knocked to the floor.

Her morning grumpiness makes me laugh. I know Erin does not function well on little sleep, but I couldn't help myself when she came to me on the patio. Wearing my T-shirt, those long, bare legs and her messy hair, fuck. Looking at her right now as she peeks her head out from under the pillow, squinting her eyes to the sun, my body is already starting to come alive.

I'm used to lack of sleep, either from insomnia or from being on tour. My body has learned to function that way, and, well, coffee helps.

"Here, I thought you might need this." I place the coffee within reach on the nightstand.

"Uggggh." Her groan is muffled by the pillow. "Do you ever sleep?" she grumbles.

I wish. "I have muffins in the kitchen." I took a walk to *Kono's*, a cafe near my house as soon as they opened.

Erin is all tangled up in the sheets, her head still under the pillow and I can't help but run my fingers along the back of her thigh to make sure she didn't fall back asleep. I am treated to a high-pitched squeal as she pulls her leg from my grasp. "Five more minutes!" she grumbles.

I'm leaning against the kitchen counter sipping my coffee when she finally emerges from the bedroom, pulling her luggage behind her. Her hair is up in a messy bun, minimal makeup, distressed jeans, and a T-shirt with white tennis shoes. She's not even trying, and she is sexy as fuck.

PAULA DOMBROWIAK

When I first met her, she called me an aging rock star past my prime, and I knew I had to have her. She wasn't after anything from me, other than my story. She's beautiful, but it was her integrity that drew me to her.

Integrity is something lacking in L.A.

I don't let many people in.

She broke past my armor, saw the person I am inside, and didn't run.

The muffins are sitting in the middle of the kitchen counter, right where Erin's sweet ass was lying early this morning. She raises her eyebrows at me as she pulls her luggage to a stop right in front of the kitchen island. Her cheeks blush as she notices where I've strategically placed the muffins.

"Really, Jack?" Erin rolls her eyes as I give her a smirk.

She settles onto one of the kitchen chairs, her hands wrapped around the coffee cup. "I'm guessing you didn't wipe the counter down, did you?" Erin mimics a wiping motion with her other hand, scrunching up her nose.

I shake my head.

"Hopefully that latte is kicking in." I lean towards her across the counter. "I told the barista to give you an extra shot." I raise my eyebrow.

"Normally I'm a one shot kinda girl," she says playfully.

"That's funny. I thought you liked two shots," I say darkly, causing Erin to clear her throat. It's so easy to get her flustered.

"I'll just grab something to eat at the airport." She narrows those golden-brown eyes at me.

I take one of the muffins and slowly unwrap the paper. She watches intently as I take a bite. Her cheeks turn red. "It's really good. Sure you don't want a bite?" I pull a piece off and hold it close to her lips.

She laughs and swats my hand away.

"Jack?" Her expression changes and she nervously pulls at the sticker on the side of her coffee cup. Pieces of her hair have come loose from her bun. I notice her gaze drop to my hand closed tightly around my coffee cup to keep it from trembling. I tell myself it's the lack of sleep and it will go away, but I know better.

26

"Are you okay?" she asks thoughtfully, but it's the sadness in her eyes that make me uncomfortable. I've already been so vulnerable with her, I don't think I can bare anymore. She doesn't need to take on my burdens.

"I just need to get some sleep," I reassure her.

"My Uber should be here any minute," she says as she checks her phone.

I blanch. "I thought I was driving you?" Even though I hate driving, especially to the airport, I do it for her.

"It's fine. I know you have that meeting with Bret," she says, dismissively.

I settle back against the counter, crossing my arms over my chest.

"I wish you didn't have to leave so soon." It feels like she just got here.

She narrows her eyes. "Why, so you can leave me here alone?"

"You're pissed."

"I'm busy too." She narrows her eyes at me. "My time matters."

I know I haven't been great company lately, and I wish I could tell Erin how I feel, but I don't want to hurt her. This book being released and doing a press tour has brought up some old feelings I thought I had buried a long time ago. I don't want to tell her that I go to the studio just hear Mia's voice, looking for something that I can't even explain. I want to finish this album, but I can't. Seeing Erin in my bed makes me feel guilty, and I don't know how to process everything because it's irrational. My recovery is threatened more and more lately, and I try to hide it because I don't want her to know.

I take her hands in mine. "Erin, look, I'm sorry about yesterday." There is a sadness within her that I never thought I would see. It stops my heart. "I wasn't very good company yesterday, and I just needed to get it out of my system."

"What am I doing here?" Her eyes flash with anger and sadness. "I'm not a pet." She looks down at our fingers that we are slowly inter-twining, and the motion feels as if we are desperate to hold on to each other.

"Erin, of course you're not." I furrow my brow. I hate that she feels this way and that I'm the cause of it, but I don't know what I can do to make this better without admitting the truth. I'm just not ready to release that burden upon her.

"It's just, I don't know if…" She trails off as someone knocks on the front door.

"My ride's here." Erin jumps off the stool, her hands slipping from mine as she grabs her bag. It almost feels like she's running from me.

"Erin," I grab onto her arm to stop her from opening the door. I don't give a fuck if the Uber driver has to wait an hour. I can't let her leave like this.

"Jack." My name escapes from her lips and I want to make it tangible so I can hold onto it for just a few more minutes.

I've never been good at relationships. I couldn't manage to be a good husband and stay faithful to my wife because I was selfish. I fucked up time and time again with the one person I loved more than anything. The guilt I carry is like a chain around my neck, weighing me down, making it hard to breathe. No matter how much I want to be a better person, to be the person Erin deserves, I am shackled in time, unable to move forward.

There's pounding on the door and her arm slips from my fingers. I rip the door open and yell. "Give us a minute," before I realize it's Amber.

Fuck, she has the worst timing in history.

"Wow, is that how you greet all your guests?" Amber saunters in, her eyes wide as she notices Erin standing just behind the door. I scratch the back of my neck in frustration.

"Erin," she nods by way of greeting then turns her gaze to me. "I didn't know you had company."

She places her purse on the kitchen counter.

"Looks like you were just leaving," Amber says as she eyes Erin's suitcase.

Although Amber and I are in a better place these days, it doesn't mean she's going to stop being Amber.

"What are you doing here, Amber?" I eye Erin, trying to decipher what is going on in her mind, desperately.

"Well, if you had a working phone," she swivels only slightly in

Erin's direction, "or weren't occupied, you would see that I've been trying to get ahold of you."

Erin is standing near the door looking uncomfortable, clutching the handle of her luggage. I want to finish our conversation before she leaves, but I can't with Amber here.

"Well, now you found me," I say.

"Are those muffins from *Kono's?*" Amber eyes the display sitting on the counter. Before I can stop her from taking one, Erin jumps in.

"Yes, they're delicious." Erin smiles devilishly. "Help yourself."

I cock my eyebrow at Erin. Sometimes she surprises me.

"I usually don't eat bread products, but I haven't had *Kono's* in forever," Amber grins.

I shake my head at Erin, and she gives me a sly smile. It gives me some semblance of hope.

"I thought you said you had a gluten allergy?" I take the muffin from her.

"It hasn't been officially diagnosed." Amber eyes the muffin.

"Well, this was fun," Erin pipes up, "but I have to get going. My ride is here."

I look out the door and see the Uber pull up in front of the house.

I hold up my finger to Amber. "Just hold on." I follow Erin out the door.

"Hey," I jog down the steps to catch up to her, "will I see you when I'm in New York?"

I have a few interviews and talk shows in New York and then I'm back in L.A. where I can do the rest of the book promotion. I know that she will be covering some festivals this summer, and the thought of not knowing when I will see her again makes me anxious. What may have started as casual has grown into something more, and my heart constricts at the thought of Erin leaving.

"I don't know where I'll be." She doesn't look me in the eye.

I reach out to her, placing the palms of my hands on either side of her cheeks and leaning my forehead against hers. She grabs on to my wrists and I know she's struggling internally. "I'm sorry."

We both sigh.

"Jack! I don't have all day!" Amber calls from the doorway, causing me to groan.

"I have to go." Erin releases my hands.

"Erin, you of all people know I'm a lot to handle." I lean in close to her, my lips a breath away from hers. She doesn't move away and so I press them firmly against hers, hoping to convey that I am in this.

She lets out a breath as I pull away. "Just don't give up on me yet," I ask of her.

4
Killer Legs
JACK

"Look, Amber, I have a meeting I need to get to," I sigh, watching her in my kitchen as she sits with her legs crossed, tapping her heel against the stool.

"I hope I didn't interrupt anything between you and Erin." She sounds anything but remorseful.

"I'm sure you're broken up about that," I say sarcastically, circling the island and grabbing my now cold cup of coffee. I'm getting a headache and it has nothing to do with lack of sleep at this point.

"I didn't come over here to break up your little," she pauses and waves her hand, "whatever that was."

"Why did you come here again?" I scratch my head, sticking my coffee cup in the microwave.

"Have you seen your daughter?" Amber asks, "Or were you too busy with your girlfriend?"

I don't even dignify that with an answer. Amber can still bring the bitch better than anyone I know.

"What's going on with Hayley now?" Knowing my kid has a

penchant for the dramatics, this ought to be good. I mean, look at her parents. It's in the genetics.

"You know how she is." She pushes a few locks of blonde hair off her shoulder.

I'm sure they had another fight which I'm not surprised about.

"What was it about this time?" I cross my arms over my chest.

Amber wants to hold on to that little kid, but Hayley's not a little kid anymore. The more Amber tries, the more Hayley pulls away. When I finally opened up to Hayley, was honest about who I was, what I did in the past, she did start to trust me, trust our relationship. The book gave me an opening, but it was me that had to continue to do the work.

"She treats my house like it's a hotel, Jack," Amber complains. "I don't care if she's an adult. If she lives with me, she lives with me. No in and out, gone for days without telling me, and then coming back like everything is fine."

"Don't you think you are overreacting a little?" As soon as it comes out of my mouth, I regret it.

"I'm not overreacting!" She raises her voice.

"Okay, okay," I motion with my hands for her to stay seated.

My coffee now tastes like shit having been reheated, so I toss it aside. I'll grab something on my way to Bret's later. That's the other issue I'm having today. Bret has been hounding me to come to his office for a meeting. I don't need to deal with Amber and Bret on the same day.

"What is it that you need from me?" I settle in, waiting for whatever it is she has in store.

"She's gone," Amber blurts out.

"And?" I shake my head, confused.

"And she's gone, Jack!" She narrows her eyes at me. "What the fuck do you think that means?"

"What do you mean 'gone'?" I give in and ask.

"We got into a fight and she hasn't come home for a week," Amber huffs. "She's never been gone that long, and she won't answer her phone."

Amber pulls at the neck of her blouse. "Can I get some water?"

I grab a bottle of water out of the fridge and hand it to her.

"I'm guessing that's not normal?" I unwillingly ask. Hayley's an adult and I don't have any reason to worry. I might not like the thought of where she could be sleeping, but she's a smart girl and knows how to handle herself.

"No, it's not fucking normal, Jack," she says, annoyed. "Why would I be here if that was normal?"

After she takes a sip of her water, she rolls up the sleeves of her blouse and I start to wonder if she's having a hot flash or whatever the fuck women her age have.

"Are you..."

"Am I what?" She narrows her eyes at me and I take a step back, but that doesn't stop me from saying another equally stupid thing.

I shrug. "You are in your forties."

"If you are suggesting that I am having hot flashes, Jack, I will kick you in the fucking balls." She pierces me with a menacing gaze that causes my balls to try and retract up inside of me. "I am upset, that's all. I get hot when I'm upset."

"My mistake." I hold up my hands.

"And I am just barely..." she pinches her fingers slightly together for emphasis, "into my forties, as you well know."

"I apologize." I slowly back away from her because I value my nuts. "Let me see if I can get ahold of Hayley." I hope that pacifies her. "Would that make you feel better?"

"I don't know why you are so calm about this. Your daughter is missing."

"I'm sure she's with a friend." I am hoping that's the case anyway. "Don't worry, I'll track her down."

"Thank you, Jack," she says, her voice calmer.

"Soooooo," Amber smiles conspiratorially, resting her elbows on the counter now that she has me doing her dirty work.

"What?" I ask apprehensively.

"You and Erin, huh?" She points at me and then at the door where Erin left not long ago.

I don't answer, instead I wait to find out where's she's going with this.

"Well, it's just things seemed a little, I don't know, tense?" She cocks her head. "What did you do?"

"It didn't help that you showed up," I say.

"I do have good timing," she says sarcastically.

I roll my eyes at her. "And what do you mean by 'what did I do'?"

She narrows her eyes and gives me that 'are you stupid?' look.

"Come on, Jack," she says. "We're friends, right?"

I prop my chin up with the palm of my hand as I lean over the counter.

"Yes?" I say, more as a question than an answer. We have a long history together, and if that makes us friends, then okay. What I really wanted with Amber is mutual respect, but that might be asking too much.

My brain short circuits at her statement. "Does she make you happy?"

I cast my gaze to the ground and focus on the toe of my Converse. It's not that she doesn't; the problem is, she does. I grapple with that feeling all the time. The wanting to be near her, the loss when she's not close, and I don't know what to do with all of it. I'm great at avoiding things, not putting labels on them, just living in the moment. I'm a fool if I think this is just casual.

"We're not that good of friends," I say with an annoyed but playful tone. Amber would not be the person I discuss this with.

Amber rolls her eyes at me and then switches gears. "How is everything going with the book?" she asks.

"Good. I have a promotional tour coming up," I tell her. "Some late-night talk shows scheduled in New York soon."

Amber scoffs. "Oh, to be a fly on the wall for those interviews." Her eyes light up. "Oh wait, I won't have to be because I'll be able to watch it on national TV."

"Why do you say it like that?" I say, offended.

"Because you don't like to talk to anyone." She gets a knowing smile on her face. "Unless they have big brown eyes, pouty lips…" she flicks her hair, "dark hair and killer legs." She raises her eyebrows at me.

"Wade has killer legs?" I chuckle. "I'll let him know you said that."

Amber slaps my arm. "You know who I'm talking about."

Yes, I do know who she is talking about, and she strutted those killer legs right out the door not too long ago.

"I have to admit that I wasn't very nice to her," Amber says guiltily.

I raise my eyebrows. "You? No, I don't believe it," I wink at her.

"I meant when she first came to see me about writing the book." Amber's tone is serious, and I lean away from the counter.

"A woman you don't know comes to tell you your ex-husband is writing a book about his life, and I got apprehensive," Amber continues, "but she has this naive way about her…" she thinks for a minute, seeming to choose her words wisely, "that puts you at ease."

I'm not sure if that's a compliment or not, but I don't say anything and let Amber continue.

"I was very honest." I have the feeling she is trying to tell me something but I'm not quite understanding what. I know Erin did research of her own and spoke with everyone to fact check things in the book.

The intensity of writing songs was nothing compared to writing this book, and fuck if it didn't nearly kill me. Erin and I spent long days hashing out details, making sure everything was portrayed fairly. I smile remembering how she didn't put up with my bullshit. *"If you're going to write a book about your life, at least be honest,"* she said to me. *"Don't be an asshole and give them what you think they want, give them everything they didn't know they wanted."* I trusted her and never looked back. We wrote this book together, created something unique. At times she pissed me off and I know I annoyed the fuck out of her with my whining, but the fact that we survived says something to me about our relationship.

Even after we signed with the publisher, we had to get releases and final signoffs from a few key people, Amber being one of them.

"I'm not sure what you're getting at," I blink.

"Back then, things were…" she pauses, "not good between us." She looks pensive. "I'm grateful for how Erin and you handled my part in the story. It was very gracious."

I nod, an understanding between us. No matter what happened between Amber and I, I would never let anyone talk bad about the mother of my child, least of all me. We may have had our moments of mutual dislike, but I've always protected her.

"Look, Erin helped, but I wrote a lot of it too," I want to make things clear. It wasn't like Erin wrote the entire thing. It was a collaboration.

"Hmmm, did you though?" Amber purses her lips.

"It sounds like you think I'm incapable of writing a book."

Amber stares at me, blinking.

"Do I need to remind you that I can write?" I stare back at her, looking for some recognition. "I write songs, Amber," I say with emphasis.

"Songs, yes," Amber nods. "A book? No."

"Okay, don't you need to get your nails done or something?" I straighten up and usher her to the door.

"Are you trying to get rid of me?" she asks, looking offended.

"And they say models are dumb," I tease, but then I have to evade getting kicked in the nuts.

"Just fucking find Hayley, will you? Jesus, Jack." She saunters out of my front door and down the steps. I mockingly tip my invisible hat and shut the door.

Hidden Hills is full of rich assholes that care more about their expensive cars than their kids. I know this because Glenn Whitney couldn't be bothered to show up to the boarding school where his daughter Beck, along with Hayley, got expelled from in high school. He'd sent a nanny to collect her, not wondering why or what happened. When Beck refused to go with her, we took her home instead. It was one of the few times Hayley was actually glad to see me. Hayley realized that even though I wasn't present in her everyday life, when it mattered, I showed up.

Through some digging and intuition, I deduced that Hayley was probably staying with Beck. I realize it might not be a good idea to just show up at the Whitney's, but I also know that Hayley's not going to answer my call if she's not answering her mother's. I have some time before I need to be downtown, and so I thought I would try my luck.

I pull up in front of the Whitney house, which is an understatement. Glenn Whitney is a Thoroughbred horse breeder, a very pretentious man. I donated a lunch date for a charity auction at the boarding school, and Glenn was the highest bidder. For that, he showed up. I'm not sure what he was expecting, but he probably left the lunch feeling as though he didn't get his money's worth. I spent two hours hearing about the best technique to artificially inseminate a mare and how you can pick a winning foal by looking at their bone structure. I was undeniably questioning my sobriety that day. That was the last time I donated anything to that school, and frankly I was happy when Hayley got expelled, although Amber was not thrilled.

I leave my car in the circular drive and walk up the cobblestone path to the front door. When I ring the doorbell, the housekeeper approaches and opens the massive, frosted glass door. She must have been the same person who let me through the gate when I explained I was here to pick up my daughter. She seems a little too eager to let me in and points to the resort style pool in the backyard.

This house is a modern architectural masterpiece, complete with artwork by someone who no doubt is famous, but it looks as though a child smeared paint on a canvas. The white furniture is covered with fluffy oversized pillows, and shaggy throw rugs are placed throughout the enormous living room. The closer I get to the back yard, the louder the music is. I'm surprised the bass doesn't break the glass doors I have to slide open to step onto the patio. Beck and Hayley are floating in the pool on twin unicorns. Neither one of them hears me as I yell over the music. I stand with my legs apart and my arms crossed over my chest, waiting for one of them to notice me.

Beck's unicorn takes a turn in the right direction and just as she's taking a sip of her beer, she ends up spitting it out and flipping over.

Hayley looks in my direction. "Shit!" She paddles over to the edge and climbs out.

"Hi, Mr. O'Donnell." Beck emerges from under the water, waving at me, her red hair plastered to her head.

I roll my eyes and give her a nod.

"Mom put you up to this, didn't she?" Hayley storms past, grabbing a towel and wrapping it around her waist before going inside the house.

"She's just worried about you, that's all," I say, following her into the kitchen.

Hayley stops in front of the industrial size refrigerator and digs out a fruit platter, placing it on the giant white and grey veined marble island.

"I'm an adult," Hayley huffs.

It doesn't matter if she's twenty-one or forty-one, to me she will always be that little girl who named all of her stuffed animals Pinky.

"She keeps track of me more now than when I was a teenager," Hayley grumbles with resentment.

I give her a solemn smile because I know Amber means well but doesn't always have the best delivery. The events of the past year have changed all of us. Regret and guilt are powerful emotions.

"I didn't need to be taken care of then, and I don't need to be taken care of now."

I scratch my jaw, contemplating that. "Just because you can take care of yourself, doesn't mean you should have to."

"So, what is it you're here to do?" Hayley doesn't look at me. Instead, she continues to fix a plate for her and Beck.

"I told her I would make sure you were alright."

"What are you, her henchmen?"

I shake my head suppressing a smile. "No." But it sure fucking feels like it.

Hayley puts her hand on her hip just like her mother, and I brace myself for a smartass comment.

"You can reassure her I wasn't kidnapped by skinheads and held for ransom."

"I'll do that." I pin her with a stare.

She narrows her eyes at me. "Beck is letting me crash until my tour starts, and then I'm getting my own place."

"You're going on tour?" This is news to me.

She nods.

"What kind of line up?" I try not to sound too eager.

She lifts her eyes to me and squares her shoulders.

"Mostly indie, alt, some Trap and EDM," she explains.

I nod my head as Beck pads into the kitchen, a towel wrapped around her hips, and a bikini top that barely covers her breasts.

"Hey, Mr. O," she says with an emphasis on the O.

I narrow my eyes at her, but she ignores me. Hayley smacks her in the arm.

"Owww!" She rubs her arm mockingly and squeezes past to grab cups from the cabinet.

"I don't suppose you're going with her?" I ask Beck. Personally, I'd feel better if she had a friend to keep an eye out for her, even if it's Beck.

"As her personal assistant." She puts her arm around Hayley's shoulder. "But only to a few because I have to meet my mother in Paris for her show."

"Personal Assistant?" I laugh. "We were lucky if we didn't have to haul our own equipment into the venue."

"That was the '90s. You didn't even have phones." Hayley cocks her head at me like I'm an idiot.

"Some things are still relevant. And don't forget, I still tour," I tell her.

"That's true, your dad's a legend. You could some get some great advice from him." If looks could kill, Beck would be dead.

"I don't need my dad hanging around my shows. It's bad enough that everyone thinks I've gotten where I am because I'm his daughter," she says, agitated.

After contemplating that for a moment, I say. "Fuck those people." Hayley's eyes widen. "Do you think I got where I am because I cared what people think?" I don't pretend to know what it's like for her, but this is what I live by. "Prove them wrong."

Beck raises an eyebrow and nods her head.

"I knew there was a reason I always liked your dad," Beck says as she points at me. "Well, besides being a silver fox and incredibly cool."

"Ew, Beck," Hayley scrunches up her nose in disgust. "A little privacy, please?" She shoos Beck out of the kitchen.

"I have to change anyway," Beck grumbles. "I'm not leaving

because you told me to. I have things to do," she says as she walks down the hall and out of sight.

I place my hands firmly on the counter and look at Hayley. "I do not have grey hair."

"That's not the point," Hayley disagrees as she shakes her head.

I ease back and cross my arms over my chest. "I respect how you feel and I'm not trying to get involved, but just be careful with Bobby Hanson." He's a very well-known manager but he has a bad reputation. "I don't like the guy."

Hayley rolls her eyes. "He's the top manager in the business."

"You think he got there by being a nice guy?" I explain.

Hayley shakes her head.

"Wade's offer is always open." He's offered to put Hayley on his label, but I get why she thinks that would look bad. I just know Adam and Wade would take good care of her, not to mention half a dozen other labels that are not run by Bobby fucking Hanson.

"Uncle Wade, who carries a baby strapped to his chest. That's who you want to manage my career?" I can tell she's half joking.

"He has spit up on his shoulder most of the time, and I don't have the heart to tell him." This at least makes Hayley smile.

"You're not fooling anyone. You just want him to walk around looking like an idiot."

"You got me there," I smile back.

I take the rare bonding moment to get serious. "Look, Hayley, I'm always here for you, if you need anything," I reassure her.

She walks me to the door and stops at the entrance. The fact that she doesn't protest makes me believe she understands it's true.

"How'd you find me anyway?" she asks.

I give her a knowing smile. I'm not giving up my secrets.

"Just text your mom back." Hayley rolls her eyes as she holds the door open for me. I step out onto the front porch and look back at her.

"And stop wearing bikinis on the beach. The paparazzi are having a field day."

"Oh my God, Dad!" She slams the door in my face, but all I heard was the word *Dad*.

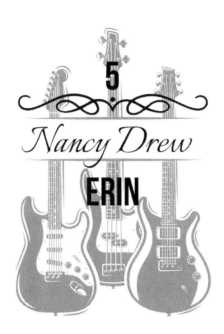

5

Nancy Drew

ERIN

My laptop rests in my lap as I try to get some work done before I head back home to New York. LAX is always busy, and I was lucky to get a seat at my gate. I'm struck by the thought that I spend more time on planes and in hotels than I do in my own apartment these days. The sad thing is that I'm okay with it. I look around at exhausted families waiting to go home with that peaceful look on their faces because they know they are going to be sleeping in their own bed tonight. For me, the thought terrifies me.

My neighbors barely know who I am. The only person who recognizes me by name is Dawn, the mail carrier, and it's only because whenever I see her in the lobby, she berates me about not collecting my mail often enough. I'm a stranger in my own building that visits every once in a while.

Ever since I left my hometown in Illinois for college, I've never looked back, but no place I have lived since has felt like home, no matter how much I want it to. I've been thinking a lot about Chicago lately, and there's an ache in my heart that resembles being homesick. I'm conflicted because when I left, I didn't ever want to go back.

I'm doing a job that I love, and I am well aware of how rare that is because most people go their whole lives punching a time clock like a zombie for a paycheck. I have lived paycheck to paycheck, but I was a journalist. My words are printed in magazines and now in a book. That is something to be proud of. For as long as I can remember, music has been a part of my life. My dad always had a record playing while he cooked dinner when he was home. Barbecues with his band mates and road crew would keep my brother and I entertained until it was time for bed. We would always sneak back downstairs to listen to them play and tell stories. There were so many stories, but I can't seem to remember them. I can only remember a whisper of them, the feeling of hearing something I shouldn't. The sound of laughter and my dad's booming voice echo in my mind. Those are the memories I want to think about, not the ones that haunt me after my brother died.

When I became a ghost.

My mom has been calling me lately, but I avoid answering them. She always phones this time of year, the anniversary of my brother's death coming up soon. Maybe it's out of guilt or sadness, or maybe she finally realized she had another kid, not just the one she lost.

My phone vibrates in my pocket, and I wearily pull it out to see that it's Wade, and breathe a sigh of relief.

"Hello," I say as cheerfully as I can, trying to hide my sadness, although I'm happy to hear from Wade.

I don't think you can meet someone like Wade and not fall in love with him. His unwavering support, friendship, and wit have kept me sane through writing this book with Jack. In all of that darkness there was always hope, and it's friends like Wade that shine the light.

I became too close with all these broken and flawed people in Jack's life. Yes, even Amber in a weird sort of way. I held them close and made them my own because I was desperate for something more in my life. I spent many weeks with Wade, Cash, and Amber, on the phone or in person. There were some unpleasant times and confessions I didn't want to hear, but they were all components of the story that made it whole.

"Nancy Drew!" Wade yells into the phone, his funny nickname for me.

I roll my eyes. "Hi, Wade."

"Solve any mysteries this week?" he jokes.

I laugh. "Oh, you know, same old story, a rich distant uncle thought he was being haunted, and just as he was about to sell his mansion for a very cheap price to a railroad company, I discovered there wasn't a ghost after all. It was the railroad executive who was trying to scare him into selling," I say, taking a long breath. "How are you?" I rest my head against my forearm as I try to relax in the very uncomfortable plastic airport chair.

"Exhausted, actually." I can hear the baby in the background making cooing noises.

"Dylan still not sleeping through the night?" I ask sympathetically. Adam's voice is in the background, soothing and whispering nonsensical words to the baby.

There is no other couple I know that make better parents than Adam and Wade, even if they don't see it yet.

"It's like a scene from the exorcist every night," Wade scoffs. "There's vomit involved, and I swear, sometimes I think he might levitate in his crib."

I chuckle. "Oh, come on, it can't be that bad." Wade likes to exaggerate, but sometimes I wonder.

The last time I was in L.A. I got to hold the baby. Of course, I had to wear a hazmat suit and wash my hands fifty times first, but I can still feel how light and soft his little body was against mine. I should have enjoyed it more, savored that little life I had in my hands and felt joy for Wade and Adam, but I was so lost in my own tragic past that I couldn't feel it.

My little brother was three years younger. I have a picture of me holding him. When he got older and started walking and talking, I remember thinking that someday I would like to have a baby of my own. All I could think of after my brother died was how stupid I was to have ever wanted a baby, because babies grew up and they died.

"No, but close." I can hear him making shushing noises. "I know I complain a lot, but Erin, I am in love. I didn't know it was possible to love someone so much." His voice is so full of emotion that my heart swells.

"Listen, I wanted to know if you'll be in town next week," he asks.

"I'll be covering a festival in Austin," I tell him. "Why?"

"We had to move up the Christening." It sounds like he's covered the phone with his hand because his voice is low and muffled. "Because Adam's mother booked a cruise and won't be in town next month for when we originally planned it."

"I heard that," Adam says in the background.

"Well, I'm sorry, but your mother is impossible." Wade's voice moves further away from the phone as he addresses Adam.

"She really is," Wade whispers to me. I hear shuffling and then a door closing. "Where are you?" he asks, no doubt hearing the boarding announcement of a nearby gate.

"I'm at the airport, on my way back to New York."

"Okay, I've locked myself in the bathroom."

"Ew."

"For privacy."

"Even more ew."

"God, the more you hang out with Jack, the more you sound like him," Wade jokes, and I know he's saying it in the most loving way possible, but I'm just not in the mood right now.

I sigh into the phone.

"What did he do?" Wade's voice is more serious now.

"What makes you think he did something?" I scoff, because Wade is more perceptive than I realized.

Now Wade scoffs. "Come on, we're talking about Jack."

His response makes me giggle. I stretch out my legs and cross my ankles.

I start to say something but then I can't seem to find the right words. The silence hangs between us, but it says more than words ever could.

"That bad, huh?"

I know I'm being selfish right now because Wade has a lot going on, but it feels like my chest is going to cave in. More than a year ago when I first met Jack, I thought no strings, no obligations, and I meant it. I would help him write the book, and that would be the end of it. I never thought I would find a connection with someone like Jack, but I did. I felt it when I first met him, my own experiences mimicking some of his, but I didn't know how deep those roots ran until we started working on the book together. Everything about him draws me in, his music, his voice, his eyes, and the way he touches me. I can still feel his touch on my skin, like phantom trails of embers.

These words have been in my throat all morning, threatening to suffocate me.

"I love him," I murmur, maybe hoping he doesn't hear me. I've been in love with him this whole time, I just couldn't admit it to myself because I didn't want it to be true. Now I wonder if I lack judgement, or if Jack is a once in a lifetime gift that you don't give back just because it's a little damaged. There has never been anyone who makes me feel the way Jack does. I don't want to give that up, but... I don't finish that thought.

"Oh, baby girl," Wade says, the emotion thick in his voice.

I don't want to cry.

I hate crying.

Crying makes me feel weak.

So I suck it up and lean over my knees to stop myself and run my hand through my hair, letting it fall to hide my face.

"He didn't say it back?" Wade asks, assuming I've dared to tell Jack and yells, "What a dick!" too loud that I have to turn my volume down because the woman I'm sitting next to gives me an odd look.

"He fucks up everything good in his life," Wade scolds him.

"I haven't told him," I rush to explain before Wade gets even more irritated.

He is uncharacteristically quiet before he says, "And now you're running away." But it's not a question.

"I'm not run..."

"You're at the airport," he interrupts me.

"Because I have to get back to New York for work." I lean back in my uncomfortable airport chair.

"Bullshit, Erin. That's such a Jack move."

"Hey!" I say incredulously.

"I always thought dog's start to resemble their owners, but it's couples too. They start to pick up the bad habits from each other," he coughs.

"It's complicated, Wade," I try to explain, and it's not something I want to discuss while there are strangers surrounding me and can hear every word. I get up from my seat and take my bag with me as I move to the outside aisle and lean against the column.

"Of course it's complicated. It's Jack we're talking about," Wade sounds exasperated. Then his voice softens. "You should tell him."

I sigh. "He's still in love with Mia."

I don't tell him how I waited for him to come home from the studio and found him at the *Lamplight*.

I don't tell him how Jack looked at me last night when he got off stage like he was looking at someone else.

I don't tell him that sometimes I wish I were her.

That I pretend I am her.

I press my hand to my mouth to suppress a cry. This is the first time I've admitted it to myself.

"That does not mean he doesn't have room in his heart for you, Erin. Believe me, I've seen it," Wade says, but I don't know if I believe the same. "You gotta have faith in him."

"I don't want him to have to choose between me or Mia. I can't ask him to give up the memory of her," I tell him.

"You're taking on a burden that's not yours to take," Wade explains.

"What I can do is make a choice for myself."

"The choice that will make you both unhappy?" I can hear the concern in his voice.

I take a deep breath. "I need to take some time to figure that out."

"Does he know how you're feeling?" The moment I tell Jack, he will feel like he needs to make a decision, and I won't do that to him. I would be taking something away from him that I have no right to take.

"I don't know," I say honestly. Deep down he has to know, but I think we are both good at avoiding what is right in front of us.

There's an announcement at my gate that they are getting ready to board. "I have to go, they're going to be boarding soon." I start to put away my laptop while cradling the phone against my ear.

"Erin," Wade says desperately, my name hanging in the air for a beat. "There are some things worth fighting for, and Jack is one of them."

6

Bleeding Music

JACK

Hollywood and Vine is one of the most famous corners in L.A., not only because of Mann's Chinese Theatre, but the stars that line the nearby sidewalks. I can't avoid these ghosts of mine, not here, not on this corner. They stretch like shadows from the sidewalk, taking shape inside my mind. They feed the demons that live within me and bring them to life. If I squint my eyes to the sun, I can see Mia standing on this corner, her dark hair framing her face and that fucking braid hidden within her waves, those hazel eyes looking right at me, and I feel as if I could reach out and touch her. When I blink, she is gone.

It has been over twenty-five years since I played this corner for change, yet these memories make it feel like yesterday. That kind of struggle leaves scars, but it also leaves a roadmap to where I've been so I can appreciate where I am. Life is a series of events that touch you in ways you will never understand until you're ready to look back and really feel them.

Most people go their whole lives not knowing my kind of struggles or reaching the kind of success I have. For me, it was never about the fame; it was always about the music. When you love something so completely, it becomes a part of you, living under your skin, beating in time with your heart until it merges with your soul.

That is what music is to me.

Not being able to finish the album that I started with Mia makes me feel like I'm letting her down yet again. I'm stuck in a tailspin, rolling out of control, desperate to pull myself out… but I can't. Not only am I suffering, but I can see the impact it has on Erin. It's like I'm repeating history, and another person is being caught up in my gravity.

Unfortunately, I can't avoid Bret any longer and I have to face the music, so to speak. Left Turn Records has been my home for my entire career. So I walk past that corner, feeling those memories drag me to a place I don't want to be. I'm already in a bad mood when I walk into the building.

The elevator lets me off on the floor that Left Turn Records occupies. Bret has turned his little indie label from the '90s into something big, yet he's still a champion for the artists he represents. The music industry has changed over the last decade, and traditional labels struggle to compete with artists who are able to record, distribute, and market their own music. That doesn't mean record labels are a dying breed; it just creates more competition and the need for diversity.

I have a feeling this is why Bret is so adamant about meeting with me. I don't often come into this office, so when someone tries to stop me from breezing past the front desk, it doesn't surprise me.

"Excuse me, Sir," a young girl trails after me nervously. "Do you have an appointment?"

I turn around and she nearly crashes into me. "No." I turn back around.

"You can't go back there!" she calls after me.

"Watch me," I say over my shoulder.

"Stop scaring my receptionist." Bret walks around the corner shaking his head and giving the bewildered girl a wave to go back to her desk.

"You know it's hard for me to turn off the charm," I scowl.

"You call that charm?" He steers me down the hall and into his corner office. Wall to ceiling windows provides a killer view of the city, a far cry from his shitty office in West Hollywood back in the day. The style is the same, with posters of musicians and album covers lining the walls.

On his desk is a family picture of him with his wife, Lisa, and their twin boys, Mark and Matt, who are now in college.

There's a photo of Mogo hanging on the wall behind his desk that was taken when we were recording our first album at an old iconic club that was torn down years ago. My eyes can't help but settle on Mia who is looking into the camera, while the rest of us are in the middle of a scuffle. It sums up our dynamic perfectly.

"She put up with a lot, huh?" Bret's eyes follow mine to the photo.

I can't help but let out a laugh, thinking of all the stupid shit we did. "She did." Mia has been on my mind more than anything lately, like a disease that has taken up residence in my brain. I don't want it to consume me, but it already has a hold on me.

I notice the comfortable looking furniture surrounding his glass desk with modern metal accented legs. After closing the door, Bret takes the chair opposite me as I sink into the couch.

"Thanks for sending me an advanced copy of the book, Jack." Bret crosses his ankle over his thigh. He still wears his T-shirt and jeans, and I don't think I've ever seen him in a suit. I'm not a corporate kind of guy. I like my creative freedom, and despite my introverted nature, I like the connection I have with Bret. His label is like a family. He's put up with a lot of shit over the years. I haven't made things easy on him, but he has stuck by and never gave up on me, even though I know he's wanted to, multiple times. "I tried to get ahold of you to say thanks, but you were avoiding my calls." He eyes me.

"I've been busy," I grumble, "but I'm here now."

"Busy in the studio I see." He gets right to the point. Of course, he would know how much time I've been spending there. The studio makes you clock in and reserve the space so they can bill the label.

"A bit," which is an understatement.

"And yet there's no album," Bret says cautiously.

"It's not ready." This is when I look directly into his eyes. I don't know how many times I have to say this to myself, and now to him, in order to get the point across.

"Jack, you've been working on this for too long." He leans forward, frustration creasing his brow. I know exactly how long I have been working on this album.

"I told you I'm not ready to release it," I say with more force to get the point across.

"Jack." His eyes soften and I feel as though he's going to try and guilt me. "I get that this isn't easy, but we need something to offset the cost."

I lean back against the couch, rubbing my chin. I knew when I walked back into that studio and pulled the album off the shelf, I was opening myself up for this type of interrogation. I can't explain it, but it's like the album was calling to me, creeping into my subconscious while I slept.

Although the album is mine, it's actually the property of Left Turn Records. If Bret wanted to, he could release it as it is, but he doesn't do that because he's a decent guy.

"I don't think you do, or you wouldn't be pressuring me."

"You think I'm pressuring you?" He sits back, raising his eyebrow. "Jack, I have let you sit on that album for nearly six years."

I look away. He's absolutely right and I have no excuse, other than my fucking heart has been broken.

"If I were pressuring you, you'd know that having that album sitting on a shelf is costing me money, that every time you take up studio time to do God knows what in there, it costs me money." Bret stands up and walks to the window looking out at the expanse of the city with its art deco architecture giving way to modern buildings.

"So, what you're saying is that if I'm not making the label money, then I'm costing you money?" This album has the potential to bring in a lot of revenue, not only for Bret but for me, too. I get it, but I can't seem to get past this blockage. There's a wall up in my brain concerning this album and I can't seem to chip away at it. I don't know how to explain this to Bret. He means well, but he's not in my shoes.

"If it's money you're worrying about, I'll pay for the studio time myself." My voice is laced with annoyance.

"That's not the point, Jack. The album is done. It has been." Avoiding my questions says more to me than if he answered them. I have known Bret my whole career, he is family, but business is business.

Bret turns to face me, crossing his arms over his chest. His once dark hair has patches of grey along the sides above his ears, and the lines around his eyes are more prominent, especially when he smiles. It's a reminder that we are not getting any younger, and so much time has already passed. I look back at the picture on the wall. We were all just scrawny kids. Mia has been gone for over six years, and I can't help but wonder how much she would have changed in that time.

"It's not." There's something missing, and I'm trying so hard to put together that missing piece. It's right there and I can feel it like a phantom limb, but I can't grasp it.

"You can't let your personal feelings get in the way," Bret pleads, as if I don't already know this.

I stand up. "It is fucking personal, Bret." I look at him from across the room. "It's the last thing I have of hers, of ours." I don't expect Bret to understand, but once the album gets released, it's not mine anymore, and I'm not ready to let go.

"I get that you want to protect it, but she made that album with you. She wanted it to be released." Bret moves behind his desk. "You think you're trying to protect her, but Jack, I think you're trying to protect yourself." Of course, he's fucking right, but I won't admit it. I'll never admit that.

"You fucking spend every minute of the day in a studio, bleeding music, pouring your heart and soul into an album, and tell me you don't want to protect that." I raise my voice. People passing by his office stare in curiously.

"You want all that work to be in vain, Jack? You bled for that album. Mia bled for that album. You don't think I understand that? I've been in this business for three decades." He lets out a breath. "Those are some of the best songs you two wrote since the nineties, and you want to sit on that?" Bret shakes his head in disgust. "Now that's a fucking shame." His palm slaps against the glass of his desk with hard slap.

I want to jump over the desk and grab him by the fucking neck, but my heart knows what he's saying is true. The moment Mia and I sat down to write again after so many years, it was like coming home in the best possible way. We wrote about everything we missed, all the things we hated about each other, the pain, the passion, and the love that we shared for one another.

That is what we put into those songs.

Honesty.

If there isn't anything personal that connects you to the song, then all you have are just words.

I sink into the couch feeling defeated.

"Look, Jack," Bret sits next to me. "I want the best for you. I always have." His voice is full of emotion. "I'm telling you, as a friend, don't let that album collect dust. Let the world hear what you and Mia made together."

Fuck. Fuck. Fuck.

"It's not about the money, Jack. It never was," he reassures me, "but this is a business, and I can't be there for you or the other artists if I based all my decisions on personal feelings."

"I know," I say quietly, "I just want to get it right, Bret." I look at him, feeling more vulnerable than I'm comfortable with. I have to get this right for my sake, and for Mia's. "I have only once chance, and that's it." I feel more determined now.

I know he understands when I see the emotions swimming in his eyes. This is personal for him too. Mia is the crack that resides in all of us.

After a moment of silence, he looks like he's grappling with what to say next. "Go on the book tour. Come back with a clear head," he says, "and then we'll talk."

7

The Chelsea Market

ERIN

The beginning of summer in New York is my favorite time of year. Right now, I'm cruising down the waterfront greenway after navigating through traffic from my apartment. My legs are burning because it's been a while since I've been able to ride. I only have another half mile before I reach the Chelsea Market. The nice weather has lured out other cyclists, making navigating the path a bit of a challenge. I couldn't stay in my apartment on a day like today. My Air Pods are in, and my playlist set to shuffle.

The Chelsea Market on a Saturday is packed. I lock up my bike in the only stall left and hit the hall. There is food from every imaginable continent, and the smell is making my stomach grumble. The problem is that it's hard to choose with so many options. It's still early in the morning and breakfast is sounding really good right now. There's a place down at the end that has amazing bagels.

I used to ride my bike here almost every Saturday. That was when I had a regular gig at *Edge* Magazine. I didn't travel as much, and my schedule was more regular. I pass by other restaurants and fruit stands where people are enjoying each other's company, the chatter loud but not deafening as I take out my Air Pods and place them back in the case that I tuck into my backpack.

I get a glimpse of my reflection in one of the shop windows. My hair is flattened from my helmet and running my fingers through it does nothing. I pull my arm out of one of the straps of my backpack and pull out a *Mogo* hat Jack had given me as a joke. They were tucked away in his closet for God knows how long, along with his gold records that he never hung up.

The line is out the door, but the bagels are worth it. While I'm waiting, I check the emails on my phone. I turned in an article I wrote for *Alt Press* on the production of a charity concert while I was in L.A. The editor had some revisions that I addressed and turned in last night. The magazine was looking to run the article this week to promote the upcoming concert, and I wanted to make sure there weren't any last-minute edits. Among the *enlarge your penis* spam emails, there is an email from my mom. Heat prickles my neck and spreads up to my face. Since I was avoiding her calls, she thought emailing me was the way to get through.

She still lives in Chicago near the lakeshore, in the same Victorian farmhouse style house that I grew up in and couldn't wait to get away from. Even though she is in Chicago and I am in New York, the email seems to lessen the distance. I avoid her calls because I hate the feeling of disappointment I feel after I speak to her. My expectations are always too high, and I get crushed every time, and it's my own fault. I don't open it, not here, not while I am in line waiting for that one small bit of doughy goodness I rode thirteen miles to get. I will still eat my bagel, but I won't enjoy it as much. The line moves up until I'm finally staring down a much trendier, much younger woman, who is impatiently waiting for my order.

I ask for a dirty chai and a garlic bagel with vegetable cream cheese. Joining a half dozen other people waiting for their order, I look for the chance to grab an empty table. Being Saturday morning, the chances are slim.

"Nice hat," the girl standing next me says. She has to be in her early twenties, false eyelashes, dark hair, and a tattoo creeping up her neck from under the collar of her shirt.

I had to think about what I was wearing for a moment before I answered. "Oh, thanks." I touch the tip of the hat to make sure it's still there.

"I love that band," she continues. "Well, they're not a band anymore, but I'm totally into nineties music at the moment," she explains.

"Ah, yes, the nineties," I nod, thinking she wasn't even born yet. God, is grunge music considered classic rock? Lately it seems everyone thinks it's cool to wear a Nirvana, or even a Led Zeppelin T-shirt. Most of them weren't even alive when *Houses of the Holy* was released. I mean, I wasn't either, but I'm not running around with a band shirt on because it was cool.

"Where did you get it? I've never seen any of their merch in *Hot Topic*."

I was at a loss for words because obviously I didn't want to say that Jack O'Donnell gave it to me, right after he fucked me in his closet. A box fell from the top shelf, hat's falling all around us. He picked one up and put it on my head. The thought had me blushing, and I bring my fingers to my mouth to suppress the smile on my face.

"My boyfriend gave it to me as a present," I finally say, because it's not that far from the truth. I did earn that hat though. Was Jack O'Donnell my boyfriend? It's such an understated word for what I felt.

'Boyfriend' seems like an immature label to call the person who makes me weak in the knees with the sound of his voice and the strum of his guitar. Jack O'Donnell is not the lighthearted, simple hand-holding kind of boyfriend. He is the man with ghosts and scars that run deep. He is the man that captivated me with his story and stole my heart.

"Hey, isn't your number 192?" the girl says, nudging my arm and bringing me out of my thoughts.

"Huh? Oh, yeah." I go to the counter and grab my food and drink. I'm still a little frazzled when I turn around to leave so I don't watch where I'm going and run right into someone, almost spilling my drink on them.

"Shit! Sorry." I look up and notice who it is, and almost wished I had spilled my drink on him.

"Erin?" His innocent smile rubs me the wrong way, as if he wasn't a traitor.

"Michael." I give him my best fake smile because I'm a professional, and I can run into an ex-boyfriend, er, boss, and handle it. I haven't seen him since I quit *Edge*, and I'm glad about it. New York is a big city, and even though journalism is a smaller community than one would think, we haven't crossed paths at industry functions or other events.

I forgot that Michael was the one who got me into cycling when I couldn't run anymore because of knee trouble I was having. Cycling is much easier on the joints anyway, and I still wanted to be able to stay in shape. We used to ride to the Chelsea Market on the weekends together.

By the way Michael is dressed in bike shorts and a cycling jersey, I'm sure he rode here too. The fact that his thick dark hair looks windswept and sexy even after cycling just annoys me.

"Nice to run into you," he smiles, "literally." His laugh is a bit forced. I watch as his eyes travel up to my hat and I noticed a tick in his jaw. It's one of his tells that something is bothering him.

"Sorry about that," I wince. What's in the past is in the past. I don't work for him anymore.

My articles have been published in some prominent magazines since I left *Edge*. I shouldn't be feeling self-conscious at all, but he noticed my hat. Back when I first met Jack, I was photographed leaving my hotel with him. No doubt Michael had tipped off the paparazzi of Jack's whereabouts after he sold me out to the tabloids that Amber was in the hospital.

There was a time when I looked up to Michael. He was knowledgeable, had been in journalism for a long time, and I had a lot to learn. We spent time together working on stories, and it felt natural to fall into a relationship with him. He was worldly, smart, good looking. It was good for a while, until it wasn't. The problem with getting involved with someone you work with, is that once it ends, you don't get a clean break. I still had to work with Michael, and although things ended amicably on the surface, I suspect when he found out Jack was in my hotel room, jealousy got the better of him. It doesn't excuse what he did, and in fact, I lost even more respect for him because of it. Seeing him now just brings up those feelings of being disrespected, and my protective nature about Jack kicks into high gear.

"I've seen some of your articles in *Alt Press* and in *Pitchfork*. Really good stuff." He sounds genuine enough.

"Yeah, I get around." After I say it, I cringe internally because I'm letting him get to me, and he's not even doing anything.

Michael chuckles. "Yeah, I guess so," he says, and it rubs me the wrong way. It's one thing for me to say something innocently, but another for him to agree flippantly the way he does.

The drink in my hand, as much as I want to enjoy it, is itching to be poured over his head even more now.

"Is something funny?" I ask, shifting my weight.

He starts to look a little uncomfortable. "No, I mean you're the one that… never mind."

"I don't want to 'never mind'." I narrow my eyes. "What are you getting at?"

"I was just thinking that it kinda seems like a pattern, ya know?" He points to my hat.

I cock my head to the side, clearly a confused gesture.

"No, I don't know." My hand is gripping my latte a little too tight, the ice a cold barrier against my palm. I know what he's implying, but I want him to say it. If he has an issue or an opinion, he should have the balls to say it to my face.

"Look, Erin, I'm not judging, but in this business, people talk, and others can be judgmental." I notice he's not referring to himself, although he is obviously judging me right now. Other customers move around us, order numbers are called from behind the counter, and the chatter seems to move further to the background because I'm trying to focus too hard on what Michael is saying.

"I'm not sure I follow you. Talk about what?" He's making assumptions about me wearing this hat and everything that went down when I quit *Edge,* but I'm confused when he says 'other people might judge'. What other people is he talking about?

"Come on, Erin! I know you're the ghost writer for Jack O'Donnell's book." He's looking at my hat again. "I'd know your writing anywhere."

Wow, so he actually read the book. I want to smack the smirk off his scruffy face with this hat.

"And your point is, Michael?" My heart is beating faster because I'm neither admitting nor denying it to him. I'm a ghost writer for a reason: because I don't want people to know. It's Jack's story, not mine. There is a part of me that doesn't want to be judged when people find out about us, although I know I shouldn't. I can't expect to keep it a secret forever, whatever *it* is.

He pulls out his phone and scrolls through some news apps until he gets to the article he wants to show me. I've always been prepared for pictures of Jack and I to surface, but nothing prepared me for this.

I grab the phone from him to take a closer look. The blood drains from my face and I have to actively concentrate to keep my legs from collapsing. On Michael's phone is a picture of me and Jack making out on the hood of his car in the driveway of his beach house. It's dark and the photo is a little grainy, but that's definitely me, and that's definitely Jack. My stomach is starting to roll, and the caption makes me want to vomit. *Jack O'Donnell seen making out with Mia's ghost?* From the angle and how dark it was, I suppose there is a resemblance, but how fucking dare they print this garbage?! I can only imagine Jack's reaction when he sees this. I hand the phone back because I don't even want to read the rest of the article.

"I'd know you anywhere, especially from the back," he lifts an eyebrow, "but it appears the rest of the industry has not figured out who the mystery girl is, yet. When they do, they'll put two and two together and figure out that you wrote his book. How do you think that will look?"

I think I leave my body for a minute because I don't even remember how the drink ended up on his head. It was inevitable, right? I was itching to do it from the beginning.

Nobody talks to me like that and gets away with it.

Ever.

"Who the fuck do you think you are?" I notice everyone in the bagel shop is staring, and I hear people's whispers and gasps. Michael sputters in shock, the latte dripping from his hair down his face to his shirt. I lean in and say quietly, even though I could care less if anyone here's me, "Just so you know, if I did write that book, I'd be really fucking proud because it's been on the New York Times best seller list for four weeks straight. And as for implying that I got that gig because I slept with him, well, you're the one that sent me out to L.A. because I resemble Mia and you thought he'd open up to me, more so than one of your seasoned writers. So that kinda makes you a pimp." I lean away from him to see the look of shame mixed with anger on his face. "And as for a 'pattern', let's not forget that you were my *boss* at the time, in a position of power. You're fucking lucky I didn't go to HR." I narrow my eyes at him.

"Fuck off, Michael, and go back to your blog and write about the next boy band to make it big. I have better things to do than waste my time on a misogynistic prick like you."

I walk out of that shop devastated that I didn't get to drink my latte, but completely satisfied that it's all over that prick's head. His fucking hair annoyed me anyway. I mean, why does he get to have that sexy wind-swept hair after cycling while mine looks like a flattened rat's nest?

I practically run all the way to the end of the hall and out the doors to where my bike is locked up. I lean against the brick wall of the old meat packing building. I'm shaking from the adrenaline rush. I realize that everything I said to Michael is true. I shouldn't be ashamed to be Jack's ghost writer. His book is on the bestseller list, and I contributed to that. Those are my words, even if it isn't my story. I shouldn't hide from that. Maybe I am the girl who fucked her boss, but if Michael had any integrity, he wouldn't have pursued me in the first place. He wouldn't have sold me out to the tabloids back in L.A. either. I thought it was jealousy about being with Jack, but now I realize it's jealousy about my talent. I don't know why it took me until now to realize this, but I'm glad I finally did.

However, none of this changes the fact that there's a picture of Jack and I during a private moment, and an accusation that I'm Mia's ghost. My problem is not getting involved with Jack while working together, it's getting involved with someone who may not have the capacity to give me what I deserve. Yet I keep coming back for more because I can't get enough of him. He's like a bad drug, making his way through my veins and stopping my heart.

Yet I still want more.

8
You're Not Wearing a Suit
JACK

"You're not wearing a suit," Cash says flatly as I arrive in front of the church. "Fuck." He looks down at his dress pants and pulls at his tie. "If I knew I could have worn jeans, I wouldn't have put this on." He sweeps his hands down his body, clearly uncomfortable in his suit.

"It's a kid getting water dumped on his head." I throw my cigarette on the sidewalk and crush it with the tip of my shoe. "I gotta wear a suit for that?"

"Apparently not." He looks distressed.

Daphne, a good friend from our Mogo days, appears from the entrance of the church and descends the steps. She's dressed up with her hair braided on one side and left loose on the other in long dark curls. It's been a while since I've seen her. When I heard recently about her brother, Aiden's, death, I didn't know how to get in touch with her other than through Cash, since she helps him with the store sometimes. I'm sure he passed along my sentiments, but I'm glad I get to tell her in person.

"I was sorry to hear about Aiden." I wrap my arms around her in a

62

sincere hug. She holds on for a few seconds more before letting go. Considering my history with Aiden, I was still saddened to hear it was an overdose.

So many friends have been lost to suicide or drugs over the years. It never gets easier to comprehend how they gave in to their demons while I'm still standing.

There was a funeral for Aiden in London with the rest of his family, but I didn't attend. With our history, I wasn't sure it was the right thing to do.

"Thank you, Jack." She steps back, her eyes solemn, and she know that I understand what it's like to lose someone close to you. It's a loss I don't wish on anyone. Aiden and I avoided each other in public, and a few years leading up to his death, he stopped attending events. What happened between us was in the past, and I didn't harbor any ill feelings against him. When Mia died, the rift didn't seem to matter anymore. We were young and so stupid back then.

"You're not wearing a suit," Amber says as she walks towards us wearing a pale yellow wrap dress with her blonde hair pulled off her shoulders.

"Why does everyone keep saying that?" I give her an irritated growl.

"Because you're not wearing a fucking suit, Jack!" Amber growls back and rests her hand on her hip. "Tell him, Cash." She nods a greeting to Daphne.

I don't look like a derelict. "I have on a shirt with buttons and a collar," I argue, but my jeans and black converse don't gain me any points.

Amber shakes her head and stops me from talking when she raises her palm to block my face.

A car pulls up and Hayley gets out, wearing black jeans with brown ankle boots and a cream-colored loose blouse. Her hair is dyed an almost grey blonde.

"Really, Hayley?" Amber greets her, and then turns to me. "You are a bad influence."

"I had nothing to do with this." I hold up my hands.

Hayley rolls her eyes in annoyance.

"Do you have a skirt or something in your bag?" I hear Amber ask Hayley as they walk up the steps to the church.

"What's wrong with my jeans?" As Hayley walks past, she gives me a smirk and I know she's not innocent, liking the fact that she's causing her mother distress. I guess the apple doesn't fall far from the tree after all.

I give her a wink back.

"You don't wear jeans to church!" Amber says.

"When was the last time you were in church?" Hayley counters.

"That's not the point!"

I suppress a laugh.

Wade opens the door to the church and stands at the top of the steps looking at all of us. "What the fuck, Jack?" His tone startles me.

"I didn't do anything. I just got here." I say, confused.

"You're not wearing a suit!" He walks down the steps past Hayley and Amber, clearly seeing Hayley's attire.

"Great. This Christening is a disaster," he says, clearly exasperated.

"I told you." Amber motions to Hayley's jeans, and they open the doors to go inside.

"It's not a disaster," I say in a conciliatory voice, trying to calm him down.

"Tell that to my mother-in-law who doesn't like the choice of flowers decorating the pews," Wade complains, looking stressed.

Adam bursts out of the church, rubbing something off his shirt. "I've just been puked on," he announces.

"Why is everyone out here?" He looks up from the puke stain and surveys all of us.

"Where's Dylan?" Wades forehead creases as he looks for his son.

"With your mother," Adam answers. "This is not going to come out," he laments, shaking his head, scrubbing harder at the blotch which is just making it worse.

"We should get back in there," Wade says, "puke or no puke." He gives Adam a peck on the lips before heading back in. "Just put your jacket on." He pats Adam's shoulder as he walks past.

"We better get in there before Wade has a coronary," Adam says. "By the way, thanks for coming." He smiles sweetly at our group.

I look at Cash. "Adam's about to implode," I comment.

"How do you figure?" Cash adjusts his tie again. "Adam's cool as a cucumber. Wade on the other hand, is about to implode."

"Wade's always high strung. It's Adam I'm worried about," I explain, walking up the steps side by side with Cash.

"You two are incorrigible," Daphne says from behind us.

"Wade's gonna lose his shit before the ceremony even begins," Cash counters, which I don't doubt, but if I were a betting man, my money is on Adam. He does not fool me with that sweet smile and nonchalant attitude towards puke on his white dress shirt.

"Ten bucks says Adam breaks down in tears before the priest sprinkles water over Dylan's head," I smirk, walking down the aisle of pews and settling next to Amber and Hayley.

"You're on." Cash shakes my hand as we take a seat.

"What's this about ten bucks?" Amber asks suspiciously.

"Nothing," we say at the same time, sounding even more suspicious.

"Are you betting on something?" Amber gives us a skeptical eye.

"Wouldn't dream of it," I say."The two of you have no empathy." She shakes her head, then she whispers, "But if you were betting, can I put ten bucks on Adam imploding before the ceremony is over?"

I stick my hand out to her behind Cash's head and she gently slaps it as we give each other a secret smile.

"You're both losers," Cash sneers at us.

Hayley shakes her head. "Am I the only adult here?"

"Yes, Hayley. Yes, you are." Daphne narrows her eyes at us as she takes the seat in the row behind us.

Adam's brothers are in the pew opposite us. It's hard to imagine Adam growing up in a household with four brothers. They all look like investment bankers, while Adam, well, he's currently slipping on his metallic blue jacket to cover up the puke stain, his dark hair slicked in a fauxhawk. Wade's father sits in the front pew while his mom is cradling Dylan to her chest.

Maude, Wade's sister, turns around to speak to the person behind her when her eye catches mine. She looks a lot like Wade; dark hair, soft features, kind eyes. I smile at her, and she nods back at me. She sits next to her husband and young daughter, who I met at Adam and Wades wedding. It's still surreal to see her all grown up when it feels like not so long ago, she was flipping off Wade in their garage while we had band practice.

I lean over to Cash. "Why's Dylan wearing a dress?"

"Hell if I know," Cash answers.

"I'm guessing I was never baptized?" Hayley asks.

I shake my head and shrug my shoulders, pointing at Amber behind her back.

"So, when I die, I'm just going to hell? Is that what you're telling me?" She shakes her head.

"Oh, honey," Amber says sweetly, "if that happens, at least you won't be alone." She turns and narrows her eyes at me.

"Wow," I mouth.

Hayley groans.

Wade is up at the front with the priest, and he whips his head towards us, menacing eyes willing us to shut up. I shrivel up in my seat uncomfortably.

"I feel like I'm back in high school," I whisper to Cash.

"You wanna give me that ten bucks now?" Cash whispers back, jabbing me with his elbow.

"It's not over yet, dick," I jab him back.

Wade's mom hands Dylan to him, and he and Adam stand near the baptismal font as the priest welcomes everyone to this special event. A few of Adam's nieces and nephews get scolded by their parents for crawling under the pews. There's a momentary break in the priest's speech, and I can see Wade eyeing Adam as if he's trying to convey telepathically to keep his family in line.

One of Adam's brothers and his wife walk up to the front as the Godparents, and that's when Dylan seems to have had enough. He belts out a bloodcurdling scream, and then something brown shoots out from underneath the white gown and hits the priest square in the stomach. The brown mess slides down his robes and drips onto the floor. Meanwhile, remnants of shit have made their way into the holy water, turning it cloudy.

"I'm guessing they're not gonna use that water now, right?" I ask Cash.

"It's those cloth diapers you insisted on using. They're not snug enough!" Adam's voice echoes throughout the Church.

"Sue me for trying to save the Earth! Not to mention they don't have all those chemicals against Dylan's skin!" Wade is trying to figure out what to do with the mess covering his hands and a crying baby. After searching in the diaper bag, his mom hands him wet wipes, but I don't think there are enough of those to clean up that mess.

"You didn't have to feed him so much right before the ceremony!" Wade argues.

"Now you're calling me a shitty parent?" Adam says in a serious, accusatory tone. I look over at Cash and mouth *did he just say shitty?* Cash turns away from me, trying to suppress his laughter by placing a hand over his face and holding his stomach.

"That's not what I said!" Wade blanches, oblivious to anyone else in the church.

"The ceremony is ruined," Adam says, exasperated.

"You think?" Wade yells back. He grabs the wet wipes from his mom who looks like a deer in headlights at the demonic expression on Wade's face.

"What happens if it's a tie?" Cash manages to get out between fits of laughter.

"This is really hard to watch," Hayley whispers over the back of the pew to me.

I look across the aisle and see Adam's brothers are finding it really hard to keep a straight face. In fact, everyone in the church is either laughing or has a horrified look on their face.

"Let's all take a break," the priest announces, trying to take control of the fiasco. He's so calm about it, making me believe this not the first shit bomb he's experienced. "We can resume after we get this cleaned up." He uses some of the wet wipes to clean up his robes, but then he ushers Wade and Adam to the bathroom located at the back of the Church.

Adam loses it and starts crying. "I've had about 8 hours - total - sleep this month. I don't know when the last time I took a shower was," he wipes his eyes, "and there's this ringing in my ears that might be caused by a busted ear drum," he turns to his mom, "at least that's what Google says." She pulls Adam into a hug but tries to avoid any residual shit that may have splattered on him.

"Oh yeah? Well, I have *shit* on my hands." Wade holds them up in the air, not expressing even a little bit of concern for Adam's break-down. I feel a gag in my throat.

"Make him stop," I whimper to no one in particular.

"I am never having kids," Hayley says.

"Oh, thank God. I'm too young to be a grandmother." Amber wipes her forehead in relief.

I hold my hand out to Cash. "Pay up," I say with a smile.

There's a spiral staircase leading up to Wade's roof where there's a deck and railing. During the day, you can see little bit of the ocean in the distance. Wade and Adam live in a modest two-story house in Santa Monica, not too far from me. It's dark now, and as I cushion my head with my arm, I look up at the sky, so full of stars it almost doesn't seem real.

I never expect anyone to accommodate for my addiction, but when things get too much for me, I have to remove myself. I'm not ready to go home just yet, so coming up on the roof isolates me from the drinks that are being served below.

I hear someone climbing up the stairs, and a few seconds later, Hayley's blonde head appears. She makes her way over to where I am laying on the deck and lays down next to me.

"Well," she starts off, "that was a shit show." We both laugh.

"I wouldn't expect anything less from this bunch."

"What are you doing up here?" she asks.

I let my hand rest on my stomach. "Just wanted to be alone for a little bit."

"Oh." She starts to get up, but I stop her.

"Stay," I urge and she settles back down. "I just needed to get away from the atmosphere."

"You mean the alcohol they're serving downstairs?" Hayley asks tentatively.

"Yeah."

"Is it hard to be around people drinking?" she asks. "I thought..."

"It's not really the alcohol." I save her from having to say it. "It's just the thought of not being able to have what I want. It makes me think of other things," I try to explain.

"So, you want... other things?" she asks with caution.

"Yes," I say bluntly. I'm not going to sugarcoat anything for her.

Hayley gets up from the ground and makes her way to the balcony, looking out as if she can see straight to the ocean. "I don't ever want to be like you."

That's a difficult statement to swallow, even if I can understand it.

"I don't want to have to give up the things I like just because I can't handle them." Those blue eyes of hers look right at me like a mirror, and I can see the shadows lurking behind them.

The voices from the party below drift up to us. I start to say something to her but the sound of the sprinklers kicking on in the grass below elicit screams from guests hurrying for cover.

"You didn't turn the sprinklers off?" I hear Adam yell from out of view. I head over to the railing.

Hayley and I peer over the edge, unnoticed. Bar tables with expensive looking linen and abandoned drinks are now soaked.

Wade is standing in the grass, trying to save drinks and plates, but he finally gives up. "I thought *you* were supposed to!" He starts to laugh like a lunatic, his suit and expensive shoes now completely drenched.

"What are you doing? Are you insane?" Adam walks towards him.

"Absofuckinglutely." Wade places his hands on his thighs, doubled over with laughter, his perfectly coifed hair now hanging in his face in dark strips.

From the mishaps at the church and dealing with a very unhappy baby, I think Wade has finally lost it. After everyone got cleaned up, they soldiered on and got through the ceremony. Everyone was relieved to enjoy food and drinks at Adam and Wade's house.

From the roof, we watch in silence as Adam pushes the wet hair from Wade's face. Gently, he pulls him in for a hug, and whispers something to Wade that makes him close his eyes and smile. I feel as if we are intruding on a private moment. The intimacy pulls something from inside of me that was buried deep. They hold each other, laughing, smiling, and standing in the middle of the lawn with the sprinklers pulsating and spraying water at them as if they are the only two people in the world.

I finally look over at Hayley as she watches them with such rapt attention that it breaks my heart to realize she never experienced her parents looking that way. Amber and I didn't provide her with a good example of what love should look like. This moment right here that we are so absolutely enthralled with is everything she never had.

"They really love each other." Hayley breaks the silence, our earlier conversation abandoned.

I look back down at Adam and Wade as they sway in the grass to the tune of music only they can hear, and it makes me think of Erin. I want to break apart inside.

"Yeah," I sigh. Even though both of them are certifiably insane, I can see how much they love each other. It radiates off them like sound waves. You can't be near them and not hear it. Sometimes I'm jealous because it seems so easy for them, even with all the pressure of having a baby.

"They complement each other," Hayley comments.

I have to agree with her, although Wade is a planner, an organizer, and a royal pain in my ass. Adam is ostentatious, creative, and annoying as fuck. They have at least one thing in common.

"You and Mom did not." Her statement is true and momentarily we can treat it as a joke, but how things were between us was anything but funny.

"Doesn't mean I didn't love her." I did love her. I *do* love her. Just in a different way. She is the mother of my child. That is a bond you can never break, even if you wanted to. We will always be in each other's lives.

"I know that… now," Hayley says softly.

We stand in silence for a minute, and I enjoy her company.

"I wasn't very nice to Mia." Her confession catches me off guard. Some things don't need to be said, and this is one of them. What's in the past is just that, and I don't want Hayley to beat herself up over anything that can't be changed.

I lower my head in frustration, running my palm over the back of my neck.

"You loved her," Hayley states. "I didn't…"

"Not like Adam and Wade." I stop her from saying anything more and lean further against the balcony, digging the toe of my shoe into the ground.

I sigh internally, casting my gaze downward so that my hair falls in my face. I cock my head at her to explain. "It was a selfish kind of love. I didn't care if I hurt other people, or if the world burned down around us."

"Like Uncle Cash," she points out.

"Yeah, like Uncle Cash."

"What about Erin?' Hayley asks tentatively. I allow her to ask about my personal life, even though she doesn't let me in on much about hers. I don't get hung up on that because I'm hoping the more open I am about myself, the more she'll reciprocate one day.

"She wrote your book," Hayley says.

I smile and roll my eyes. "Why does everyone think I can't write a book?" I groan, thinking of Amber's similar comments. "It was a collaboration," I state.

"Erin never came and talked to me." Hayley glosses over my temporary rant. It takes me a minute to understand what she means though.

"I told her not to," I tell Hayley, a stern expression on my face, thinking back to when Erin was doing research and meeting with old band and crew members. She trod lightly with friends and family, at my request, even though she didn't like it. *"You want people to be honest,"* she said to me, *"so I will speak to them alone."* She told rather than asked me. *"What about Hayley?"* I remember our conversation. *"No,"* I said flatly. *"Jack, you can't shelter her,"* Erin said. *"No, she's been through enough."* I told her again, and watched the challenge in her dissipate at my request.

Erin is smart and she knows the business. I respect her opinion, but when it comes to Hayley, I can't compromise.

It's not that I didn't want Erin to meet Hayley, I did, just not about the book. Over the last year, there have been other opportunities so they aren't strangers now, but they are not friends either.

Hayley softens, even though she hates it when I try to be the protective dad. She understands.

"I like her." Hayley looks away from me. "I like the way she wrote your book."

I find Wade in the kitchen, busy putting away leftover food. He must have changed because his clothes are dry, and his hair is fluffed to perfection again. I grab a cube of cheese from one of the trays and pop it in my mouth.

"Hiding out on the roof?" he accuses me like the stalker he is.

"Not hiding." I tilt my head and grab another cheese cube before he covers it with plastic.

"Doing okay?" Wade stops his cleaning to eye me.

"No," I say, "but I'll survive."

"Well, you're lucky you get to escape from this mental ward," Wade chides.

"It wasn't that bad," I say as I lean against the island.

Wade narrows his eyes at me. "Were you at someone else's christening today?"

I laugh. "The kid is all holy and shit now, right? That's what matters." I wave my hand as if to brush it away.

"I didn't even want to have it." He puts a tray into the refrigerator and turns back towards me. "We don't even go to church."

I give him a quizzical look. "Then why put yourself through that torture?"

"Because I have a," he lowers his voice, "monster in-law that wanted it, and because I love my husband. That's why." He snaps the plastic in place around another tray and slides it in the refrigerator.

"Adam is a lucky guy."

"Jack, I'm tired, and I don't need your sarcastic comments," Wade says with exhaustion as he washes a plate in the sink aggressively.

"I'm serious." I place my hand on his shoulder in comfort. Wade might be a little high strung, but there is no doubt that he loves Adam and will do anything to make him happy. That includes having a christening from hell and letting multiple family members from out of state stay with them.

Wade gets a sappy look on his face. "He is pretty fucking lucky, isn't he? Are you ready for the book tour?" he asks, changing the subject.

I groan.

"Jack, you made commitments," he warns me.

"I know, I know. I just hate doing interviews."

"While we're in New York, we have that radio interview and a few live talk shows."

I grumble an acknowledgment.

"Oh, and you have to pick a song that you want to lip sync to," he says absently, while placing a plate in the dish strainer.

"Excuse me?" I say outraged. "I have never lip synced a song in my fucking life!"

"Not one of *your* songs," he snaps. "For the talk show, you know, the skit."

I give him a blank stare.

"The lip sync battle?"

"The what?" I curl my lip.

"The host does these funny skits where you each lip sync a song and the audience decides who is better," Wade tries to explain, but I've already tuned him out.

"Why the *fuck* would I do that?" I shake my head, appalled.

Adam enters the kitchen wearing sweats and a T-shirt, and I have to look twice to make sure it's him. "People are starting to leave." He finally notices me. "Oh, hey, Jack."

"Nice ceremony." I dip my chin to him, but I am rewarded with a glare. I'm sure he thinks I'm getting in a little dig, and he's not wrong. "Great party too," I add, popping a grape in mouth from a tray that promptly gets pulled from my grasp as Wade gives me a warning look.

"Well, thanks, Jack. I'm glad you could make it," Adam says, a little too sweet to be sincere, and then turns to Wade. "We should say our goodbyes."

"Alright, well, I'm out of here too." I push off the counter and hold my hand out to Adam. "Seriously, Adam, it was a lovely day."

"Fuck off, Jack."

I snicker.

"I'll be right there." Wade gives Adam a peck on the cheek and then glares at me.

"Aw, are you going to walk me out, too?" I ask, as he starts to usher me out of the kitchen.

Wade gives me an annoyed look.

"I'll apologize to Adam. He knows I'm just messing with him," I beg. Adam's usually the fun one, but I think the events of the day just sucked the fun right out of him. Wade pushes me out of the door.

9.
Find my iPhone
JACK

I fucking hate interviews.

"My morning's ruined," I tell Wade, who sits next to me in the car on the way to the radio station in the heavy Manhattan traffic.

"Quit whining," Wade says, irritating me even more. My legs are cramped, and I uncross them nervously.

"Couldn't spring for a limo, huh?" I grumble.

"You're like a child." Wade rolls his eyes at me. If I have to be miserable, then I'm taking him down with me.

I shuffle through the pockets in the seats in front of me and then shift my attention to the non-alcoholic beverages in a small cart to my left.

"I hope there's going to be coffee when we get there." I cross my arms over my chest as I watch the city go by. The complimentary hotel coffee was shit.

"Are you going to be like this the entire time we're here?" Wade grumbles.

"Yep, I think I might."

"Just fucking call her!" Wade demands, getting my attention. I'm in

New York and Erin isn't. I look at the clock on the dashboard of the sedan and see that it's quarter to the ass crack of dawn. Erin's probably still sleeping.

"She wants her space," I tell him.

He turns to give me a full-on incredulous face. "Since when do you *ever* do what someone tells you to do?" He slowly turns back in his seat. I remain quiet.

"Like fucking *ever*?" he adds.

I ignore him.

"Just don't pull your 'Jack' shit with her, that's all," Wade says seriously.

"My 'Jack' shit?" I curl my lip.

"Erin is different," Wade states, giving me a stern look.

That's the problem.

"You won't have to worry who will end up with you in the divorce, Wade," I fuck with him. "I willfully hand you over to Erin," I say.

Wade looks at me, offended.

"I'm a giver," I smirk.

We hit a traffic jam and the sedan pulls to a stop. The cars ahead are honking, and I already have a headache.

When I think about that photo of Erin and I in the tabloid, I want to fucking murder someone. In fact, the drywall in my bedroom is being repaired as we speak. I hate to say that I am used to the tabloids writing ridiculous shit about me, but it's the truth. However, it makes me mental to think of how this has affected Erin. She's been quiet, and I don't think it's just because of the photo.

Right now, I'm just trying to get through these interviews.

I can see my reflection in the glass, the image transparent and hazy. Turning away, I knock my knee into Wade's just to annoy him and distract myself.

"How much longer till we get there?" Wade yells to the driver.

"About a block," the driver answers back.

Wade momentarily sighs until the driver adds, "With this traffic jam, could be another hour."

Wade grabs the door handle as if he's going to jump out, and instead of stopping him, I force him out of the car and yell back to the driver, "We'll walk the rest of the way."

As soon as we step onto the sidewalk, traffic starts to free up and the sedan blends in with the flow of cars and turns out of sight.

"I have Ferragamo's on." Wade points to his expensive looking pair of dress shoes with annoyance.

"I have no fucking idea what those are." I start to walk down the street, Wade grumbling behind me.

"When did you turn 80?" I shake my head, watching as Wade struggles to keep up. "How does Adam put up with you?"

At least the weather is nice, but the air smells like garbage.

"Some of us are grownups." Wade assesses me, and I know he's talking about my choice of jeans, Vans, and an old T-shirt. Just because I'm forty er, something, doesn't mean I have to dress like it. Unlike my old bandmate who wants to dress like a mafia henchman every day.

"Don't look at me like that," Wade grumbles as we turn the corner and I see the media building up ahead.

"Like what?" I ask, just for fun.

"Like you're making fun of me in your head." Wade eyes me, and I can't help but crack a smile.

"Wade, I'm always making fun of you in my head." On a serious note, though, "There better be fucking coffee." The doorman sees us coming and opens the large glass doors to the media building.

The program director meets us at the front desk, vigorously shaking Wade's hand and looks at me as I give off the 'don't fucking touch me' vibe. We take the elevator up to the 54th floor. During the ride, I shove my hands in my pockets and lean against the wall. Wade eyes me skeptically as the program director chats with him. The reason I bring Wade is because he likes to talk, and I don't. He's my buffer, and I have the feeling he needed a break.

When the doors open, I push past Wade and his new best friend and head into the lobby. A friendly receptionist greets us.

"Coffee," I say to her.

She gives me an apologetic smile and I'm about to lose it.

"I'm so sorry, but our coffee machine is broken. I can get you some tea though," she says sweetly.

I turn toward Wade with my 'are you fucking kidding me look?' as he ushers me into the studio.

"I will buy you a double cappuccino when we're done," he whispers to me.

"Nobody better speak to me," I grumble.

"It's a radio interview, Jack. They have to speak to you." He's annoyed with me, and I don't blame him. I'm on a tear this morning. It's too early and I don't have any coffee in my system.

The host is sitting at his desk, the mixing board and a microphone acting as a wall between us. There's another desk, almost hidden behind a half wall, where the engineer sits. To the right is a couch with a pair of headphones sitting on the cushion, and next to that is a small area with band equipment. My guitar sits on a stand next to a microphone because I agreed to play a few songs. Although it's so early in the morning, I don't know how my voice will sound.

One of the engineers gets everything set up in the studio. The headphones are a bit snug, but I'll manage. The host has a copy of my book on his desk but there is a huge media poster of the book cover on the wall. I look at that famous photo of Mia and I, and I don't just remember it, I *feel* it. It tears at me from the inside out. It was the moment Mia came out on stage with me to sing *Blood and Bone* after I had broken down and called her for help. My father was dying, and I didn't want to face him alone. She was the only person I wanted with me. The only person I needed in that moment.

"Get over it." Wade catches me staring at the photo and I glare at him. Sometimes he can be an asshole.

We had dinner with the host last night after we got settled into our hotel. He's a legend in this business, and probably the only person I respect enough to appear on his show and promote my book. Not only is he a fantastic interviewer, but he's a music lover and a fan. It was a way for us to get comfortable with each other, and it worked.

The producer brings in a few of my old albums from his personal collection for me to sign.

"Don't bother my fucking guests," the host says through the mic with his booming, sarcastic voice.

The producer looks up like a deer in headlights. "Sorry, boss."

The two bicker back and forth, sounding like an old married couple, while I get settled in.

"Sounds like us," Wade leans over and whispers.

"Never say that to me again!" I glare at him, and he leans away from me, laughing.

The opening music plays inside my headset and then the host introduces me to the audience. For the next hour, I slowly relax into the couch as if I'm having a conversation with a friend, because that's what it feels like. We talk about my old band, *Mogo,* and writing music.

Interviews always irritated the fuck out of me because they asked the same questions over and over again. No one did their research or got to know who they're interviewing, and you can tell most of the time they're not a fan, but this guy, this guy is a fan, and his enthusiasm for the music is infectious.

"*Mogo's* music was so prolific for its time. I mean, it inspired a lot of bands," the DJ says. "You can hear the evolution in your solo albums, but I imagine the writing process is much different."

"Writing solo was very challenging at first," I explain.

"Let's talk about *Blood and Bone.*" He switches gears. "How long did it take you to write that song?" My memory flashes back to that moment in Mia's car, grabbing her leg, the feel of the sharpie against her jeans.

I shake my head to try and remove the memory. "About ten minutes," I say.

"See, that always blows my mind," he says.

"But we refined it over time before recording it," I explain. "While not a complete overhaul, we were able to make it work with the music."

"You wrote those lyrics on a pair of jeans?" he asks me, astonished. It's not common knowledge, but the information has leaked out over the years.

"Yeah," I laugh.

"Probably one of the more interesting items lyrics have been written on," he says.

"You wrote all of *Mogo's* songs with Mia?" he asks.

The subject of Mia is always uncomfortable, and I look over at

Wade who is waiting in another booth, his presence grounding me. Our shared experiences, memories, and grief that never seems to ease, floods the room between us. The host is respectful and sympathetic which is all I really ask for.

"Sometimes you find a partner like Mia to write with and it's like catching lightning in a bottle. You can't replicate it if you tried," I explain. My mind goes back in time when we were all still together. We were working on *Mogo's* second album. Things were so different back then. We were trying to write songs while we were on tour for the first album. We fought, sometimes sitting on the opposite side of the room glaring at each other. We'd do a line of coke, I'd fuck her up against the glass of the superman booth, and we'd make an album.

"How do you get over a loss like that? I mean, it must be hard because such an incredible talent was taken too soon," he says, with as much loss as we all feel.

I take a deep breath because there are no words. "It's simple; you don't." It's a break inside of me that can never be fused back together, and it makes me a miserable person to be around sometimes.

"The two of you recorded an album that never got released." The album that is the bane of my existence.

"Do you think you'll ever release it?" he asks.

There was a push by the publishing company to release the album with the book because they could help promote each other. I was very hesitant to do it, not to mention that it's not finished, and I wasn't going to rush it. If I release that album, it will be because I want to, and not because it would boost sales.

They can all fuck off.

"If it felt right, I would, but I can't see that changing anytime soon." I don't want to mention that I have a massive case of writer's block and can't get my shit together to finish the fucking album. My foot starts twitching nervously.

"We need to take a quick break and when we come back, I want to talk about your book, *In Me, On Me, and All Around Me*, and maybe Jack will play a couple songs for us." I was so engrossed in our conversation that I forgot I was here to promote my book. I can hear the prerecorded commercial in my headset while someone comes into the studio and hands the host some papers and they converse casually.

The producer enters the studio, handing me a cup of coffee. "Sorry about the coffee machine being broken. We had one of the guys get this for you." It smells so good.

"Thanks," I say as I grab the cup from him and take a sip. My eyes roll back in my head.

My knees are stiff from sitting so long and I need to take a piss. We have enough time before the break is over, so I take my headphones off and lay them on the velvet couch and make my way out of the studio and down the hall to where the bathroom is located. The building is full of radio shows, all different genres, and people move about the halls casually, nodding at me in acknowledgment.

I wash up in the sink and feel my phone buzz. I pull it out of my pocket and check my texts, but it's a google alert instead. I have one set up for myself and one for Hayley, because although we talk more now, she still doesn't give me a lot of information about what's going on in her life. It's kinda sad I have to learn about my kid's life through Google.

Recently I set up an alert for Erin. After what happened with being photographed in my driveway, I thought it was best to know what's being put out there. It feels like it's the only thing I can do to protect her, which is not much.

I know Hayley did this on purpose just to piss me off, because the alert is a photo of her on the beach wearing a bikini. It's like she wants me to throat punch a photographer.

"Hey, break's almost over," Wade says as he opens the door to the bathroom. Seeing my expression of utter rage, he looks over my shoulder at the phone to see what has made me so upset.

"Baby girl's all grown up," he says, taunting me. The public seems to have a fascination with my daughter at the beach, but every time I see a picture of her, my dad instincts kick in. I don't want people looking at her like that.

"Shut up," I growl at Wade, and push the phone back into my pocket.

"Get rid of the Google alert if it bothers you so much," Wade says as we walk back down the hallway to the studio.

"Then I won't know where she's at." I raise my eyebrows as if I'm pulling one over on her.

"Are you still paying her cell phone bill?" Wade asks casually.

"Yes." That's what I'm good for.

"You do know how *find my iPhone* works, right?" Wade opens the door for me.

I give him a confused look.

"You're like a technological infant," Wade chastises me. "How did you get the google alert set up anyway?" he asks, as we walk back to the studio.

"Shut up. I just talk on the fucking phone; I don't have time for this other crap." I grab the headphones and put them on my head angrily while Wade laughs at me.

10

Ghost Writer

JACK

"Let's talk about this book, *In Me, On Me, and All Around Me*," the DJ says into the mic with his deep, polished voice. "I understand that was the title of one of the unreleased songs?" It was a song that was difficult to write because it encompassed everything we were feeling over the past decade.

"Yeah, it just seemed fitting. It was one of the last songs we had worked on together," I say nostalgically. I can keep my emotions in check if I try hard enough, and I will not break down in front of this guy.

"What an emotional read. I felt like someone ran me over with a Mack truck when I was done." He laughs sympathetically.

"I know the feeling," I joke half-heartedly with him.

Writing the book with Erin was a cathartic experience. What I realized in writing this book is the underlying pain never fully escapes me. You can't live a life like I have and not have scars, and mine are deep.

"I laughed and I cried," he says. "It's really a book about redemption and unconditional love."

I think about that for a moment. It may not have been my intention, but I think if that's what people get out of it, then I'm happy.

"It's a testament to the bond that you, Cash, and Wade have, because even after everything, you still remain friends." He shakes his head in astonishment. "You can't say that for a lot of other bands."

"I did some really shitty things," I admit as I contemplate the culmination of all my wrongs. "My intentions were usually in the right place," I smile sheepishly. "I don't deserve friends like Wade and Cash, but I think they're stuck with me for life."

"Any chance of a reunion?"

What kind of reunion would it be if you don't have all of the members? Mia always did like watching from the audience rather than being on the stage though.

I laugh. "I don't know about that."

"I understand you had a ghost writer," he says. That's common knowledge, but no one knows who it is, although there have been speculations. I wanted to give Erin credit, but she was being ridiculously stubborn and didn't want to be named. At least I was able to give her a royalty percentage of the sales. After all, she wrote the fucking book. Now I'm stuck doing promotion, under the duress of my publishing company, and everyone knows how much I hate doing press. I realize if I don't promote the book then it doesn't sell as well, and Erin wouldn't get as much money.

"That is true. Writing a book was more difficult than I imagined. I couldn't have done it alone. Besides, my memory is a bit crap. I was high for most of my earlier career." I make light of it, but I feel anything but light inside. People think Rock 'n Roll is glamorous, and they would trade anything for it, but they don't contemplate the dark side, what it does to your life, what it costs you.

"You're not giving anything up, are you?" the DJ jokes with me when I don't elaborate or say who the ghost writer is.

I laugh, shrugging my shoulders, but I'm thinking back to when Erin came into my life unexpectedly. We were both thrust into an intense situation and gravitated towards each other. She was so willing to give up pieces of herself to me, and that is a gift. Erin became my confessional, and I bared my soul to her. Throughout the whole process, I trusted her with the deepest parts of me, some too personal, too sacred, to put in the book. She keeps those secrets locked up inside of her, and I never realized how that might affect her. *Affect us.*

"I don't know what people's expectations are when they read my book. This is the real me, warts and all. Let's just say, I have a lot of warts," I joke.

When Erin got on that plane well over a year ago, she wasn't asking me for anything, but that doesn't mean I am not willing to give. I just don't know how much left of me there is.

"You went to rehab three times," his voice is somber, "but none of that worked." He skates around the reason I got sober, but we both know, and I appreciate his tenderness. I think it's because the last person to make light of my sobriety in connection to Mia's death ended in an altercation. They got a trip to the hospital, and I got a trip to an expensive lawyer's office.

"Everyone likes to think that drug addicts are low-lifes, a drain on society who remind you of the ugliness in the world, but it's a disease." Maybe I sound corny, but I believe every word.

"Rehab only works when you are actually ready to put away your ego and work the program. Being sober is a lifelong commitment, and every day is a struggle," I explain. People like to go to rehab thinking it's a game. They're gonna magically get out after 30 days and be 'cured', but it doesn't work like that.

"Sobriety hurts like a bitch at first, but after a while, the pain subsides. It's the scar underneath that never goes away," I try to explain.

"Is that part of the reason you wrote the book? To help others with addiction?" He leans in and props his chin up with the back of his hand.

"If what I went through resonates with another person who suffers from addiction and they know there's a way out, then I'm glad my story helped them." That is the truth, but I didn't get sober because I'm a fucking angel. I got sober because the one person that I loved more than anything died because of my choices. I could have used that as an excuse to continue to get high, to sink into the depths of heroin's temporary bliss, but I used that indescribable pain to get clean. Being clean is agonizing, and I want to feel every fucking stake to my heart because that's what I deserve.

Getting high would feel too fucking good, and I don't want to feel good.

"You talk a lot about your childhood in the book, and how that impacted your life," he says.

"Addiction was the cause of a lot of the things that went wrong in my life. I can't blame everything on my shitty childhood because I'm the one that made those choices. It's about taking responsibility, and that's really what helped to heal my relationships."

"Are you referring to your relationship with your daughter, Hayley?" As long he's being respectful, I don't mind talking about Hayley.

"It opened up the communication between us," I explain.

"Hayley has a music career of her own now," he says.

"She's very talented." I don't want to speak for Hayley because it's not my place. I'm trying to respect her boundaries and the need to do this on her own.

"Come on, it's in the genes, right?" he laughs. "Seriously though, you must be very proud."

"Very proud."

"You are the only one from *Mogo* that went on to have a solo career," he shifts the subject.

"Yes, that's true. Just because *Mogo* ended, didn't mean that I wanted to stop making music," I tell him.

"What is the rest of the band up to? I see you brought Wade Kernish with you today. For those that don't know, Wade was the drummer in *Mogo*." He waves at Wade who is sitting with the engineer. Wade stands up and gives a salute as if people in the audience can see him.

"Wade always wanted to go back to school, so when the band broke up, he took that opportunity and then worked in the tech industry for a while until he and his partner started their own label." I am incredibly proud of him. "He always was the overachiever out of all of us," I joke.

"And Cash?" the DJ asks. "What's he been up to?"

I try to think of the right way to put this. "He walked away from the music business for a while." I don't want to speak for Cash or tell a story that's not my own, but I can't help but think of how bad things were for a while, how much he floundered after the band broke up, and what brought us back to each other. "But he couldn't stay away from music for long, so he opened a music store in Santa Monica. He's doing really well," I lie for his sake. He is struggling, and not just with his business. When he is ready, I know he will come to me.

"Let's give Cash's store a plug."

I'm sure Cash would love the free advertisement, and it would probably help the business.

"It's *Underground Records* in Santa Monica," I tell the audience.

"You heard it, *Underground Records* in Santa Monica. Go check it out!"

"I want to get back to talking about this ghost writer, which I hear is pretty common, but I'm interested in the process of how that works." He looks genuinely interested and I have no reason to suspect any alternative motive, but I'm always leery of people in this industry. Maybe he's fishing to find out who it is. Honestly, I don't know why people find it so fascinating or why they would even care.

"It's a lot like being interviewed." I motion between us. "Except it's not just three hours, it's pretty much a year-long interview." I raise my eyebrows.

"It's just such an intense story for someone else to take part in. What was that like?"

My mind flips through all the images of Erin like a reel. How we walked on the beach, and I told her things I hadn't told anyone. When we drank coffee together in the café and she told me about losing her brother. All of our late-night phone calls and the frustration that I couldn't reach out and touch her. Her voice on the other end breaking me open. The emails and texts like I was some kind of lovesick puppy. Fuck. I swallow hard.

The sight of her in my bed turning me inside out.

Erin is smart and so talented, and I didn't know her written words would affect me so much. She's not a songwriter, but the way she wrote this book, it's like a love song that breaks you open and puts you back together again. She is the reason this book is on the bestseller list. She is the reason this book got done in the first place. She is the reason I find myself in such a quandary about my feelings. I don't like being vulnerable, but I trust her more than I have ever trusted anyone.

The memories are swallowed up inside of me as I look over at the expectant face of the host and remember he asked me a question, but I can't remember what it was.

"Did you remain friends with your ghost writer?" he asks again.

"Yes, we are still friends. She's an incredibly insightful person, the meticulous detail and fact checking, because let's not forget, I was high most of the time and my memory can't be relied on. Her patience and empathy were beyond what I would ever expect from someone." It's all true because I'm no picnic to be around most of the time. For Erin to listen to me the way she did, without judgement, how could I not respect the hell out of her? "She is the reason this book was even written."

"Your ghost writer is a woman?" The host picks up on my use of pronouns, and that's fine because it doesn't matter. If it were up to me, I would sing it at the top of the Empire State Building what an incredible talent she is. "That makes sense now," he says and I give him a quizzical look.

The producer motions to him that we are running out of time. "I could talk to you all day, but we have to wrap things up. I want to thank you for coming to the studio today and talking with me for nearly three hours. It went by so fast. You're an interesting guy. Before you go, would you mind playing us a couple songs?" he pleads.

My guitar sits on the platform waiting for me, and so I get up and exchange the velvety couch for a wooden stool. I sling the strap over my head and rest the body of the guitar against my thighs.

"Any requests?" I joke.

"I would be honored if you played one of my favorite songs, *Losing You*," he says into the mic. I'm surprised which one he picks because it's not one of my hits. It's an old *Mogo* song from the third album, the album that was born out of betrayal and hatred. I haven't played it in a long time, so I warm up a little with the chords. It was originally meant to be sung with a harmony, but I've played it before with just me.

This was a song Mia wrote, and I fought to keep it off the album because I thought it was too much of a ballad. We were a rock band, and I didn't like how soft it was. Mia agreed to switch up the chorus a bit, make it edgier, and it got released as a single. Sometimes you have to compromise, and it wasn't one of our biggest hits, but it became one of my favorites.

When the song is over, the host stands up and claps.

"Beautiful, just beautiful. Thank you." His voice is so genuine I can feel it in my bones.

"Thank you for having me," I say, feeling eager now to get out of the studio and back onto the street where I can breathe again.

"Listen, pick up Jack O'Donnell's book *In Me, On Me, and All Around Me,* available at your favorite retailer. You can read about Jack's fascinating life, because let me tell you, I was gutted, and I'm usually not a crybaby, but this book got me emotional," he admits with a little bit of joking, but you can tell there's truth to it.

He stands up and comes out of the booth to shake my hand. We take a few press photos and I sign a couple of books for him and the staff before leaving.

11
Huckleberry Finn
ERIN

The table I'm sitting at has a sticky film to it that only dive bars can lay claim to. The air is so muggy and tangible it feels like a blanket on me, even though I'm indoors and the a/c is on. I think it's just Texas; the summer humidity seeps in through every crack, and you can't hide from it. Bodies pack the area in front of the stage, and the bar is filled with excited shouts. Only the sound of a Les Paul drowns out the chatter, and I am in love.

This band has the classic rock melody of *Tom Petty*, but the cool indie vibe of *The Lumineers*, and it's no wonder why they are on the verge of exploding. I can feel it like electricity in the air. Something extraordinary is happening. The lead singer has that emotionally unavailable vibe with a charisma that draws you in. The lyrics are simple yet daring, and his voice is thick with southern charm.

I came to Austin, Texas, to cover a local festival, but ended up in a section of town called Dirty Sixth. The street is lined with bars, but there's something about this one that stands out. It could be the weird demonic gargoyles that line the walls or the life size mural of Betty Page, I can't decide. I've been to a lot of bars, but this one is at the top of my 'bars with character' list. There's something to be said about being alone and listening to a cool indie band that makes you feel alive. This band is my whole world right now, and not even the gargoyle's glowing red eyes, that seem to follow my movements can rattle me right now.

If I believed in fate, that's exactly what happened. This is what I live for, those moments when you feel like you're witnessing history, and it makes the hairs on my arm stand on end. Even if no one in this bar is paying attention, I am. I can hear it in every note, every octave of his voice, but it's not just the lead singer, although he's got talent in spades, it's the guy on the keyboard. It's just the two of them up on stage, but I can hear the soft whine of a fiddle and neither one of them is playing one, which leads me to believe it's a prerecorded instrument on the keyboard. I wonder if he actually plays or if it's just synth. I can't really tell, but I want to know.

A smile plays on my lips, and I am lost. "Can I get you another?" the waitress asks, and I tear my eyes from the stage to look up at her.

My glass is empty, and the ice has already begun to melt. I nod yes, why not? I'll be here for a while longer and I'm not driving. "They're good, huh?" she says casually, lingering at the table. I look back at the stage as they end their set for the night.

"Do they play here regularly?" I ask.

"I've seen them around, but I'm just filling in here. The bar needed extra help because of the festival, and well, I needed the extra money for college," she answers with a smile.

Suddenly it's quiet in the bar as if all the sound has been sucked out, and I can hear everyone talking like I'm in a tunnel. I realize my ears are adjusting to the sudden absence of music and focus back on the waitress. She's pretty and has that flawless skin only girls in their twenties have. I'm only thirty-four, but I feel like youth is slipping away from me. To be honest, I never really felt young. It's that sense of freedom and lack of responsibility that I could never grasp while everyone around me did.

"What are you going to school for?" I ask, because I love a good story.

"Journalism." She smiles sweetly, but internally I'm thinking *what are the chances?* Until she finishes, "Actually, photojournalism."

"Sasha!" A man's voice booms from behind the bar pointing at drinks he's lined up. He doesn't look like the typical Texan, but he wears a pearl snap Western shirt, although the sleeves are cut off. He pulls the battered black cowboy hat from his head to reveal multi-colored hair that falls into his face. He quickly brushes it back with a hand and places the hat back on top of his head.

"Hope I'm not getting you in trouble," I say to her.

"Nah," she waves me off. "He's a pussy cat."

"Is that a tattoo of the TARDIS on his arm?" I ask Sasha curiously.

She smiles. "Don't get me started on his nerdiness. He has the USS Enterprise on the other arm," she finishes with an eye roll, and I narrow my eyes so I can see better but he moves out of view.

"Interesting."

"I'll get that drink for you." She hurries away and I look at the stage where the two guys who were performing just moments ago begin to dismantle their equipment.

I walk over to the edge of the stage where there are a few girls loitering, trying to get their attention because they're pretty good looking and they're musicians, which is a winning combination.

"Hi, I'm Erin Langford from *Alt Press*," I introduce myself. The lead singer stops clipping his guitar case closed. He's put on a black fedora which actually makes him look even cuter and a little folksy. I like it.

"I'm Sawyer." He sticks out his hand for me to shake. "This is my brother, Finn," he continues, pointing to the guy closing the legs of the keyboard stand.

"Wow, your parents must really like Mark Twain." I shake my head, smiling, as I pull out my press pass so they know I'm legit.

Finn shakes his head and laughs. "What's so funny?" I ask.

Sawyer gives his brother a menacing look and I can't help but laugh with whatever this private joke is between them.

"His real name is…"

"Off the record?" Sawyer interrupts, and turns to me for confirmation. His dark hair curls up at the edges of his hat.

I cock an eyebrow, wondering what the big deal is. Lots of musicians use stage names. I mean, Freddie Mercury was born Farrokh Bulsara.

"My name is Milo." I can hear Finn snicker in the background as if he enjoys this way too much. Sawyer, or rather Milo, turns around and Finn stifles his laugh.

"But everyone calls me by my middle name, Sawyer," he explains.

"Because you make them," Finn rats him out.

"I don't make them," Sawyer corrects, rolling his eyes at Finn.

"Still, I think your parents might have a thing for Mark Twain," I say.

"They are mental, but we love them." Sawyer gives me a charming smile.

"Are you able to chat? I'd love to get an interview."

Finn and Sawyer practically trip off the stage to grab a table with me, abandoning their equipment.

"Are you local?" I begin. They both have a Southern accent, but I can't tell if it's Texan or from somewhere else.

"No, we're actually from South Carolina," Finn explains. They look to be in their mid-twenties, but Finn looks like he may be the younger brother. He still has a baby face, and his curly blonde locks are tied at the back of his head in a trendy man bun. Usually I'm not a man bun kinda gal, but it works on him.

"What made you come to Austin? Are you here for the festival?" I ask.

"We were living in New York for the past few years," Sawyer says.

"Our apartment got broken into," Finn interjects.

"They took all our equipment." Sawyer props his elbow on the table, and I can see the tattoo of running horses more clearly on his arm. It's actually quite beautiful and unique.

"We just got fed up with the hustle trying to make rent," Finn continues. "We had some friends out this way and decided to try our luck."

"Crashing on someone's couch sucks, but we're actually making money here playing gigs like this," Sawyer explains.

"I know the feeling," I can definitely relate to the hustle.

"You're crashing on someone's couch?" Finn jokes.

"No," I laugh. "I live in New York. Queens actually."

"No shit!" Sawyer slaps his thigh. "We could have passed each other and never knew it."

"I'm surprised I never saw you at a club there." I went to clubs all the time and I would have remembered them.

"Yeah, that's the thing. We could never get a regular gig except as catering waiters," Finn laughs.

New York is so expensive, and most of the time it felt like I was working just to afford a place to sleep at night. Of course, now I don't have to work so hard with royalties from Jack's book sales. I have the ability to make choices now, and that's a freedom that doesn't come easily.

I dig into the interview with these two talented brothers. Over the next hour we talk about their sound, who their influences are, and what makes them so unique. They even tell me a funny story about how they got their band name, *No Cover,* which is definitely going in the article. They mix folk music with rock, and it blends so well. I'm noticing this more and more, but their sound is different, authentic. I think I have everything I need to write a good piece on them, and I can't wait to get back to my hotel so I can get it down while it's fresh. I look at the clock and see its already well past midnight, but if I can get a draft done tonight, I can flesh it out on the plane back to New York tomorrow.

I gather my things and place them back in my bag. The bar is still open, but I can see the crowd has dwindled, and the young waitress, Sasha, is busy clearing tables. She mentioned she was going to school for photojournalism, and it gives me an idea.

"Sasha!" I call her to our table. If I'm right, she's brought her camera with her to work because the photographers I know have a relationship with their cameras like other people are attached to their phones.

"How would you like to take some photos for an article I'm writing?" I ask her. "You'll get a photo credit of course," I explain, her eyes opening wide as she bounces on the balls of her feet.

"Are you serious?" When I nod, she runs over to the bar and disappears behind the counter.

I turn to Finn and Sawyer. "I didn't ask, but I'm hoping you'd stand for a few pictures, and I can add them to the article," I say. "Final approval from my editor, of course."

As I suspected, they are all too willing, much like Sasha. Any exposure an unknown band gets is great. For Sasha, to have a photo credit in a real online music magazine would be great for her portfolio.

I approach the bar and get the attention of the bartender. "I hope you don't mind if I borrow your waitress," I say to him, not wanting to get Sasha in trouble.

"Just return her in one piece." He eyes me skeptically, but I don't think it's because he's angry, but more that he's looking out for his own.

"I'm Erin," I nod.

"Manic." He holds a large, tattooed hand out to me, and I take it.

"I love Doctor Who, by the way." I point to the tattoo on his arm. He gives me a wink before he walks away to refill someone's drink. A petite woman with the same multi-colored hair bounces behind the bar and gives Manic a peck on the lips before she ducks under his arm to grab a bottle from beneath the counter.

"Not the Bushmills woman!" he grouses as he trails after her.

We spend about a half hour doing a few poses on stage, and Sasha has a great eye to use the exposed brick as a backdrop. Betty Page winks in the background. From what I see so far, they are great, and we exchange information so I can get the photos from her in the next few days.

"I really don't know how to thank you," Sasha says as she shakes my hand, and I can tell that she wants to hug me, so I lean in.

"I'll let you know if any of the photos get used. You won't get paid, but it's a credit, and that's worth more than money for you right now," I explain to her.

"Thank you so much!" she says, putting her camera away.

Sasha's blonde ponytail sways as she shakes both Finn and Sawyer's hands as well, giddy from the unexpected events.

"Good luck, truly. You both are amazing," I say to Finn and Sawyer as I make my way outside to where my Uber is waiting.

"Jon Pertwee!" Manic yells to me from behind the bar, testing my Doctor Who knowledge.

"Peter Capaldi!" I yell back my favorite Doctor from the series and wave a goodbye.

"Fuck all," he laughs and rolls his eyes.

In the back seat of the car, a sense of loss hits me, as if I crashed into a wall because I realize I'm going to an empty hotel room. I've just had the most amazing experience, both intellectually and creatively, but I have no one to share it with. I wish I could talk to Jack, but I need to keep my distance for now.

12

Falling Through the Glass

ERIN

I was in the zone last night, so I finished off the article while everything was fresh. I'm paying for it now because I had to get up early for my flight back home, but it was so worth it. Sasha emailed me the photos this morning which was awesome, and I can send them along with my draft of the article. She was able to do some light editing, but I assured her the magazine would want to do their own touch-ups if they decided to use them and not to worry. She has a great eye, and I can't believe my luck running into her.

Meeting her made me nostalgic for college. For me, it was a time to discover what I wanted to do, and being an accountant was definitely not for me. I thought there was nothing better than working for a magazine in New York, getting into shows for free, flashing my press badge like I was important. It was stable, I had a paycheck, even if I could barely pay for my closet of an apartment, but I was discovering who I was and what I wanted to be. Now, with freelance gigs, I have this freedom and unpredictability I never knew I wanted. Yet, I feel as though there is something missing. I still love the music business and meeting talented artists such as Finn and

Sawyer, but ever since I finished Jack's book, I've had this sense of loss. Covering festivals or showcases doesn't feel as important anymore.

I want to continue telling stories, but this fire inside of me is saying I need to find a different way to fuel it. I'm going back to New York, but in a couple of days, I could be headed anywhere, and that's good enough for now until I figure out what I really want to be doing. I slip in my Air Pods so I can listen to Jack's radio interview this morning. Searching on my satellite radio app, I find the show and tune in while I pack up my things before my Uber driver arrives. I've already missed an hour, but if I want, I can always go back and listen to the entire show. Right now it's live, and this is Jack, so anything can happen.

Jack's early morning voice is rough and gravelly as they talk about his music. I don't know the host personally, but I know he's a huge music lover and a fan of Jack's. Of course, Jack would only agree to do these types of interviews with people he's comfortable with. I used to listen to this DJ when I was younger, and he was one of the reasons I wanted to go into music journalism. He gets people to open up like no one else I've heard.

They are discussing Jack's *Mogo* days and how their music inspired other bands. It makes me think back to the first time I heard *Mogo's* first album and was just blown away with the raw emotion of it. This was a band who knew how to get down into your soul and make you feel every heartbreak and all the angst that went with it. The lyrics meant something, and the sound just got under your skin in the best possible way. In some of the bands I hear today, *Mogo's* influence, as well as other bands of the '90s, is deeply imbedded.

While I am still reminiscing, the subject of Mia comes up and I know this is difficult for Jack. It's one of the reason's he was so hesitant about promoting the book. It's such a delicate subject for someone to pick apart. I think fans will really resonate with all of the raw emotions in the book. Jack didn't hold anything back or romanticize his relationship with Mia. The way I wrote it exposes two flawed people who sparked professionally and personally. Oftentimes they weren't good for each other, but Mia meant everything to him. The way he tells it, she was the one person in his life that really knew him. She was like a mirror, and he could see all of the ugly broken pieces of himself in her, but there is also beauty in the broken.

That's one thing about Jack, he doesn't pull any punches. He describes the process of writing solo, and how difficult it was in the beginning. Maybe no one else picks up on it, but I can hear a slight shake in his voice when he explains writing with Mia was like catching lightning in a bottle. It's so apparent in their songs together, the push and pull, all the angst and the drama; it just blends between the two of them so well. There's no comparison to someone who brings out that much creativity in you. The more I think about it, I realize that is exactly what Jack did for me when I was working on his book.

I was constantly pushing him, and he was constantly pushing back. I told him if he was going to do this book, he needed to do it right. If you are going to write a book about your life, you have to be willing to expose your true self. Even if it's painful. The one subject I yielded to was Hayley. I wanted to meet her, to talk with her about what it was like for her growing up, but Jack said no in a way that stopped me from challenging the idea. I understood his need to protect her, to keep her away from the ugly, exposed parts of himself that he wasn't ready for her to see. I realize now that it was more to protect himself from the truths Hayley might be keeping inside.

When the DJ asks Jack about getting past the loss of Mia and his response is "You don't," I feel another tiny crack develop in my heart. The truth is so simple, it's heartbreaking. The instinct to protect myself is overwhelming. I know the way I feel is senseless, but the part of me that lost my brother knows all too well what it feels like to come in second. I'm starting to feel this more and more lately. Even though I don't want to force Jack's hand to give me more, I deserve better. I just need to ask for it.

My phone chimes letting me know my Uber has arrived, and so I head down into the lobby, having already checked out electronically. The car waits for me in front and the driver helps with my suitcase. I only have the one and then my laptop bag that I keep with me. I think about Sasha and her camera under the bar, and I smile because I seem to carry my laptop with me everywhere I go. A treasured friend I tell all of my secrets and my experiences to.

"How did you like Austin?" my driver asks, obviously noticing my East Coast accent.

"It was interesting and beautiful," I reply and smile, thinking back to the quirky bar where I met Sasha, Finn, and Sawyer, and of course, who could forget Manic, the Doctor Who loving bartender.

I slip my Air Pods back in and listen to more of the interview on the ride to the airport.

The interview switches gears to the unreleased album Jack and Mia were working on before she died. I know Jack has been spending a lot of time in the studio, but he won't talk about it. He goes there to spend time with her, and even though it's irrational, I feel like the other woman in his life. I am worried that he uses this album as a way to keep me at arm's length. I know he cares for me, but he will never love me the way he loved Mia. Maybe that's okay, maybe he's not supposed to. It's something I grapple with internally.

The show cuts to commercial and I look out the window of my Uber to see the Colorado River as we pass over it on the bridge. The phone vibrating inside my bag pulls me out of my thoughts.

"Amazing article," Sandy, the editor from *Alt Press* says as soon as I pick up.

"I'm so glad you liked it." I think of all the work I put into it, staying up late last night. "I have the bones of the article you wanted for the festival, but when I came across these guys, I was hoping you'd take a chance."

"It's different, especially with other media outlets covering the big name bands at the festival. I like the idea of being the magazine who focuses on up and comers." She sounds excited and I'm glad she liked it, because it's the artists just starting out that really need the boost. It's exciting being a part of the beginning of someone's career and watching them rise. There have been a couple bands early on in my career that gave me unfettered access, and now no one can touch them because they've gotten so big.

"I completely agree."

"I checked them out online and you have a great ear. Their sound is perfect for our readers." Sandy has no idea how much I appreciate her compliment. To be recognized in this business for my knowledge of the music industry is everything I wanted, and I'd like to keep it that way. I have come such a long way in my career to be respected. It's hard, especially for a woman in this industry. Putting up with male rock-star's ego, being hit on by sleazy managers, and being mistaken for a groupie more times than I can count.

"I'm so glad you love *No Cover*. I just knew when I heard them that they were perfect. This article could be a real boost to their career, and I'm so glad we get to do that for them together." I smile. Other editors I've worked with don't like to share credit and aren't great at being partners in this process, but Sandy has been different.

"And the photos?" I ask tentatively because I don't want to seem too forward and overstep my place.

"I can't believe she was the waitress at the bar!" Sandy laughs. "The photos are good, and I like putting a face to the band. It gives the readers something to connect with, especially when they are so good looking," she laughs.

"Great! Sasha will be so excited."

"We can give her credit for the photos but that's about it. Do you think she'd be cool with that?"

"I think she'd be more than cool with that."

"I'll email you a license agreement for the photos then."

"Do you have anything else for me?" I ask expectantly. One of the other magazines I've written for is all booked for the summer, so I'm hoping Sandy can use me somewhere. I need to stay busy right now, and I'll go pretty much wherever she needs me.

"Are you sure you don't want to take some time to relax back in the Big Apple?" she jokes. "You've been traveling a lot lately."

"New York will understand." It's true. There is no one back in New York that would miss me, except maybe the stray cat I leave food out for when I'm home.

"Well, if you're sure. I could use another person to cover a festival next weekend in L.A."

Figures, I groan internally. "Is that all you have?" I don't want to be picky, but I wanted space, and the universe keeps putting me right back into the viper's den. Honestly, there's so much more I could be doing than covering festivals.

"For right now," Sandy says. "What is it you're interested in, Erin? I'll make it happen. You're an excellent writer."

"I really like investigative reporting," I tell her.

"Ah, the dark side of music," Sandy teases.

I laugh. "More like industry profiles," I tell her. "Trends, features, something meatier."

"Let me see what I have, but in the meantime, I can send you the details about the festival in L.A."

"Thanks. I'll change my ticket and pick up the festival this weekend." I smile into the phone. I won't have to go back to New York just yet. I can hang out in L.A. for a few days before the show.

Immediately, I send a message over to Sasha that pending final approval, it looks like they are going to use her photos. She messages me back within seconds, over the moon excited. The emoji's and GIFs flashing on my phone in quick succession make me laugh out loud. Meeting Sasha was an unexpected surprise to an already amazing night.

Although challenging, my favorite part of working on Jack's book was the research. It was the pieces of the story that Jack didn't tell or couldn't remember that made it a mystery for me to solve. I could take pieces of the puzzle, stories from other people, and fit them together. Anyone can dictate words and transcript it into a document, but to make a reader connect with the story, you first have to make them *feel*. I was able to accomplish the hard-won battle of making people care about a person who, on paper, they should rationally dislike.

This attention to detail is what earned me the nickname Nancy Drew from Wade. He helped gather a lot of names and numbers for me to contact and set up interviews, gather necessary information for fact checking.

Jack's book is about his memories, his experiences in both his personal life and the music industry. The difficulty with memories is that they are life's greatest liars. They don't intend to be, but they are. Two people do not remember an event the same. In fact, they walk away with two very different experiences, especially when you have an unreliable source, such as Jack. He remembers certain things very differently than his band members. Drugs and alcohol cloud and warp his memory. They make him an unintentional liar. Only when you put the pieces together from multiple sources, you finally get something close to the truth. But truth is an illusion, and it's as elusive as trying to touch the stars.

Jack cloaks himself in the armor of unapproachability, keeping everyone at arm's length. Only those chosen few does he let in, and I'm not certain I am one of those people. I know now it's possible for someone to tell you their life story without ever truly letting you in.

The interview carries on as I slip my Air Pods back in. The subject of Jack's ghost writer is always popular. Jack doesn't care if everyone knows I helped him to write the book. He never hid the fact that he had a ghost writer. It was me who didn't want to expose myself to the kind of scrutiny that was inevitable; the kind of scrutiny Michael was alluding to.

I don't want to be defined by a story that is not my own.

Journalists are supposed to be objective, to look at a story as if you're outside a window looking in. Instead, I fell through the glass and right into Jack O'Donnell's bed. I've been wondering lately how big of a mistake that was.

As we get closer to the airport, the interview turns to the subject of Jack's struggle with addiction. I am reminded that I didn't know Jack as an addict. I only know the Jack in recovery. The guy in the book, the guy I wrote about, is not someone I would want to know. I have no right to judge him, but I do worry about him. We are all flawed, fragile beings who are allowed to make mistakes, and that is what makes us human. Jack has a lot of baggage, and I am not without my own. Our baggage is what made us who we are, what brought us together, and what connects us in ways I can't explain. It's also what makes us vulnerable.

When the Uber drops me off at the airport, I trade in my ticket for L.A. at the check-in desk. Luckily, I am able to get on the next flight, but I have to wait in the airport for several hours which gives me time to explore.

Maybe I should have been an anthropologist because I love to study people, and the airport is the ultimate people watching venue. I only have a small carryon bag, so I pull it behind me as I explore the

Austin airport as if I'm on a Sunday stroll. I've never been in an airport with an actual stage for live music but it's unoccupied at the moment, and I'm guessing it's because it's so early in the morning. I stop to window shop wine stoppers, shot glasses, and oddly, jalapeño jam, which I didn't know was a thing. I pick up a touristy Austin, ATX shirt and shove it in my bag. It might come in handy.

The restaurants get most of my attention and I'm surprised at the variety. I grab a breakfast sandwich and an iced dirty chai from Jo's Coffee and grab a table near the empty stage. I prop my feet up on the chair opposite me and open my laptop. Last night, Sasha sent me a link to her Instagram, but I hadn't had a chance to check it out. I start scrolling and I'm just blown away by her talent. The subject matters are all different, but her unique style is what connects them all. The photos range from student protests on a college campus to a band playing at a club, and then there are some really impactful shots of the homeless youth in Austin. The photos she took of Finn and Sawyer last night were edgy and fun, capturing their personalities so well. I deduce that Sasha is a people watcher too, looking under the surface to bring out the person inside through her photography. Even though I just met her last night, through our text messages and emails, I feel like I've found a kindred spirit. I plan to keep in touch with her, and hopefully she can find a job doing what she loves once she graduates.

In the middle of perusing her Instagram, I get a text from Sasha. Actually, it doesn't seem like it's meant for me. She wouldn't tell me to *fuck off and die a horrible death because I left her homeless with no money.* This does not sound good, so I text her back right away.

> Erin: This is Erin. Are you OK?

> Sasha: OMG! I'm so sorry, wrong person.

> Erin: It's OK, I just want to make sure you're alright.

I wait a few minutes, but she doesn't reply. I set my phone down and stare at my laptop, but I can't concentrate now. I don't want to pry into someone's life, especially when I just met them, but my concern for her overrides my politeness.

I pick up my phone and dial her number. It takes a couple rings, but she finally answers. Her voice cracks and I can tell she's been crying.

"I'm really sorry. I meant to text someone else," she says, apologizing again.

"It's fine. I'm just worried about you. You sounded..." I don't know what to say.

Devastated, I think to myself.

"It's, um..." she hesitates, "my boyfriend. Well, not my boyfriend anymore. It's a long story, but let's just say I'm screwed, and not in the good way."

I've been there and done that.

"I have time if you want to talk." I look at the clock and see I still have about three hours before my flight boards.

"You're just the nicest person I've ever met," she sniffs.

"God, I hope not. That would be really sad if that's true," I joke, trying to lighten the mood.

"Maybe we could meet for coffee this morning," she asks expectantly, and tries to stifle another sob.

"I would, but I'm at the airport on my way to L.A."

"L.A.?" she asks expectantly.

"Yeah, why?"

"You're gonna think I'm totally insane," Sasha says.

13
Lip Sync Battle
JACK

I stand next to Wade in the hallway of the satellite radio studios waiting for the elevator, and I can't help but notice the huge grin on his face.

"Why are you looking like you just ate a canary?" I shove my hands in my pockets.

"You were actually pleasant. I can't believe it. Did someone slip you a happy pill or a magic brownie?" Wade rocks back and forth on his heels until the door to the elevator finally opens. It's only halfway full so we get on.

"I don't know what you're talking about," I say to him quietly as we take a spot at the back.

"There wasn't one F bomb on air. I'm impressed," Wade smiles.

"Fuck off, Wade," I say. "How about that?"

"Aw, now there's the Jack I know and love," he smiles sarcastically.

I roll my eyes at him.

While I'm in New York I have some talk shows I'm taping tonight. My publicist nearly had a coronary when I declined a third talk. There's only so much press I can handle. The book is doing well and what we have scheduled should be good enough to help sales. I have a few other radio shows to do but those are in L.A.

"Look at the picture Adam sent me." Wade shoves his phone in my face. "Adam is trying to get Dylan to try some mashed peas for the first time and he got it all over his face."

Although I really don't want to, I look at the photo anyway. I have to admit he does look slightly cute, but I won't give Wade the satisfaction, so I push the phone away.

"Someone get that kid a napkin," I say. "That's bordering on child abuse. At least give the kid some pudding. He should be properly sugared," I grumble.

"And that's why you won't be babysitting," Wade states as he yanks the phone back.

"I'm devastated," I deadpan.

I'm just barely in my forties, and although it's not old, I can't imagine starting all over again with a baby at this age. Having Hayley young was challenging, but I wouldn't trade that for anything. All of that baby shit is behind me, and now she's a grown woman of legal drinking age, and I don't know how my life has passed by so quickly. I've slowed down a lot. The only touring I've done is to promote this book, and I only travel for select interviews.

I know what Wade is giving up by coming with me to New York, and all I'm giving him is a sour attitude in return.

"You should have brought Adam and Dylan with you on this trip," I offer Wade as we get off the elevator and start walking through the expansive lobby. Wade's expensive shoes click against the tile and echo off the panels of glass that line the busy sidewalk.

"Too long of a flight to bring a baby on. No thank you." Wade shakes his head. "Besides, I have some other business to do while I'm out here, and I wouldn't have had time for them anyway." Wades first love is the tech industry. He likes to find solutions that make life easier for people. He gave up a great career in Northern California to move back to L.A. in order to be with Adam and start their label. Easy decision though, because they have *the life* together. No matter how messy and sleep deprived it is, he's complete. He gets to use his tech knowledge to produce music at the label and help artists.

The car pulls along the sidewalk for us, and Wade opens the door to get in.

"You go ahead. I think I'm gonna walk." I stay rooted on the sidewalk, my hands in my pockets, eyes squinting towards the sun. I'm exhausted, but I don't feel like going back to the hotel. This was the longest interview I've done, and I only agreed to it because I respect the host.

Wade cocks his head at me as if he knows I'm bullshitting him, but right now, that's all I'm doing is going for a walk, nothing more.

Wade steps away from the car and tells the driver to meet us at 30 Rock later today.

"You don't need to babysit me," I tell him.

"As much as I hate being the chaperone all the time, I don't want you to be alone." Wade quirks a grin and I am just blown away at how lucky I am to have a friend like him, even though I'm an asshole most of the time. When I look back at all of the shit that went down, I'm surprised anyone is left in my life. What binds us together is the woven twine of our history, those shared memories of incredible highs and devastating lows.

I walk over to the doorman at the entrance to the media building.

"Where can a guy get a decent fucking cup of coffee?" I ask him.

A couple of blocks later, we're in line at a coffee shop that advertises their milk is sourced from Upstate, and I couldn't give two shits as long as it's from a cow. I order an iced matcha tea with three shots of espresso.

Wade gives me a questioning look.

"Don't fucking judge me," I say to Wade as he laughs and shakes his head. "Blame Hayley. She ordered one for me last time we met for coffee and now I'm obsessed." I mock Hayley with that last word which elicits a snort from Wade.

"Let's just grab a table." I roll my eyes at Wade.

The cafe isn't too crowded and we're able to grab a table outside to enjoy the nice weather. I grab my drink off the counter when the barista calls out my name, and Wade grabs his hot tea.

I cock an eyebrow at him.

"What?"

I look at my drink that's the color of grass with dirt in it and keep my mouth shut.

It's only the beginning of summer and there's a nice breeze. My body relaxes as I stretch my legs. I didn't realize how tense I was.

"Things are good with Hayley?"

"She hates me a little bit less these days," I joke.

"I heard she got picked up for some festivals this summer." He takes a sip of his tea.

I shake my head and smile.

"What?"

"I just don't understand that kind of music," I tell him, because to me, music is using real instruments, a guitar in your hand, the steady beat of drums behind you, a bass to keep the rhythm. Not some mini engineer board with synthetic sounds and bass that could cause a landslide.

"You don't have to understand it to see how good she is, Jack. She has that kind of stage presence that I've only seen a few times in young performers." Wade raises his eyebrows.

"It's a tough business," I sigh. "I just don't want her to get hurt."

"You mean you don't want people looking at your baby girl the way they are."

"And what way would that be?" I lean forward, menace radiating from me.

Wade leans away from me. "She's not a little girl anymore."

"Fuck, you don't think I know that?" I lean back and try to relax. The inkling of a headache is starting, and I pinch the bridge of my nose.

"Do you know her manager?" Wade asks as nonchalantly as only Wade can, and my radar goes up. The music industry is like the six degrees of Kevin Bacon. Of course I know Bobby Hanson. I can feel a low grumble deep in my throat at just the thought of him.

"So, you do know him?" It's more of a statement than a question.

"When I was starting out, Bobby came sniffing around. We signed with *Left Turn* instead and he wasn't happy about it. The guy just rubbed me the wrong way," I explain to Wade. That's the light version of what happened, but I don't want to get into it. I wasn't the nicest guy back then, but neither was Bobby. He was young, hungry, and aggressive. The difference is, I've changed, and he hasn't.

"And I'm sure you had no problem telling him to fuck off."

I pierce Wade with a *no shit* stare.

"We've run into each other over the years, and he's an arrogant prick." Immediately I hold my hand up to Wade to stop him from making a sarcastic comment.

"I'm not saying anything," Wade says as he holds his hands in the air.

"I have heard rumblings about shady deals, but mostly that he's a shrewd businessman with questionable morals." He's not someone I would ever want to work with. The reason I've stayed with *Left Turn Records* my whole career is not just because Bret has put up with my shit, but because he's one of the few decent people in this business.

"It takes every last restraint in me not to throat punch that guy." I have my suspicions about why he signed Hayley. She's talented, sure, but it's the name recognition he's after, and most likely to piss me off. I can't say that to Hayley though. She wouldn't understand, nor would she want to hear it

"I just hope none of its true, that's all," Wade says. "You know how rumors are in this business."

"If half the shit they write about me were true, I'd be in a federal prison stamping license plates wearing an orange jumpsuit right now," I laugh.

"Are you going to tell me what's going on between you and Erin?" Wade interrupts my thoughts.

"Nothing to tell," I say nonchalantly.

"I think you like being miserable," Wade grumbles.

"Thanks for the pep talk, it was enlightening."

"Jack, you deserve to be happy." Wade looks at me thoughtfully, and something just snaps inside of me.

"That's just it, Wade. I don't, and you being okay with everything doesn't help."

"Jack," The sympathy in his eyes makes it worse.

"There is nothing okay with what happened, and everyone acts like I should move on and be happy, well fuck that." I point at him. "You are not me." I slump back into my chair. None of us escaped losing Mia without scars. She's a shadow that follows wherever I go. I'm the reason Mia was on that freeway. If I hadn't fucked up, she would still be here.

"We're all just trying to do the best we can," he sighs.

"Nothing about this book was easy on any of us," I sigh. "It opened wounds." I thought telling my story would expel the demons onto those pages, but it only brought them closer to the surface.

"Sometimes wounds need to be opened in order to heal." What Wade says might be true for a cut on your finger, but not for this gaping hole in my heart.

"When did you become a fucking philosopher?" His answer is interrupted by someone yelling my name.

"Jack O'Donnell!" A fan hurries over to our table trying to figure out how to hold her drink in one hand and her purse in the other while deciding if it's okay to shake my hand or hug me. I hope it's not the latter. Someone might lose an arm, and it won't be me.

"I just heard you on the radio." She's showing me her phone with the satellite radio app open. "I have your book. I can't believe you're here!" She shifts her drink into the crook of her arm and starts fishing around in her purse. People start to stare at us, turning around in their seats to see what the commotion is.

"I'm so sorry, shit, I know it's in here somewhere," she apologizes while shuffling around in her purse, and although it doesn't look huge, she seems to be having trouble finding the bottom.

"It's fine." Wade fills the silence and I glare at him.

She stops and looks down at me. "Gah, I can't believe this." She smiles and then produces my book, and I wonder what else is in her purse that a book was somehow hidden in there.

"I knew it was in there." She produces a pen. "Would you mind signing my book? I can't believe I ran into you. I swear, this is so fucking insane." She lays the book down on the table in front of me and hands me the pen.

"What's your name?" I oblige.

"Erin. You can make it out to Erin."

Fuck me.

I don't look over at Wade because I can already imagine the shit eating grin on his face.

I click the pen open and sign the book for her. *Grab a cup of coffee and enjoy the ride.*

"Thank you so much." She looks at the signature and then hugs it to her chest. We take a quick picture with her phone, which Wade offers to take just to annoy me.

"You're not an asshole at all," she says, and then leaves me sitting at the table looking after her as if she just kicked my dog.

"They used to ask you to sign their tits," Wade snorts.

"You think this is funny?" I shove him.

I check the time on my phone and it's still early so we have plenty of time before we have to be at 30 Rock tonight.

"Let's get the fuck out of here." I stand up, grabbing my drink.

Central Park is not far off so we head in that direction.

My phone chirps and I pull it out of my pocket thinking maybe it's Erin, but it's from Hayley. *Listened to the interview. It was really good. You were actually pleasant.*

I'm always pleasant. I shoot back. Why is everyone shocked when I'm nice? I wonder how much of the interview she actually listened to because it was nearly three hours, and I can't imagine she'd sit through the whole thing.

Hayley sends me a picture of someone rolling their eyes.

I send her a picture of my iced matcha, and I get a smiley face back.

"Is that Jack O'Donnell smiling?" Wade asks.

"Shut up."

"You are definitely not an asshole at all," he says in a mocking high-pitched voice.

"You want me to shove you in the lake?" I joke.

The short text exchange with Hayley has me smiling like a fucking idiot. All I ever wanted was a relationship with her, to know that I didn't completely fuck up her life. I can see she's guarded though, and not just with me.

I feel responsible that she's not careless with her feelings like a young person should be. Being young is about getting your heart broken and feeling every fucking crack with the force of an earthquake. It's only when you get older the cracks become visible like the lines on your face, a badge of honor that you fucking lived and didn't waste a minute of it. Hayley doesn't trust easily, and she's definitely not the one getting her heart broken.

It occurs to me that's exactly what Erin is doing. She's running from me. I'm not going to let her get away that easy.

> Jack: Just finished my interview.

I tap my fingers on the side of my cup waiting for a reply.

> Erin: It was really good. You were... pleasant.

> Jack: I'm always pleasant.

> Erin: Really, Jack?

> Jack: That means I'm in New York.

> Erin: I'm in Texas.

> Jack: That's very convenient.

> Erin: Apparently.

> Jack: Are you afraid of what might happen?

> Erin: Afraid?

> Jack: You're running from me.

> Erin: I'm not running.

> Jack: You can't avoid me forever. I will find you... and when I do...

On either side of me are benches lining the walking path with huge trees leaning inward creating a tunnel of green. As the leaves flutter in the breeze, their shadows create an illusion of the pavement moving ahead of me.

I'm in New York and Erin isn't. When I want something and I can't have it, it makes me want it all the more. If I could get on a plane to Texas right now, I would. Erin has no idea what is coming her way.

14
The Serial Killer Type
ERIN

I 'm in a rental car with a girl I met only last night, and we are driving 1300 miles from Austin, Texas, to Los Angeles, California. If this isn't the premise of a chick flick, then I don't know what is. Maybe I'm being a baby and using this as an excuse to prolong my arrival in L.A. by a couple of days, but I don't care.

I will find you... and when I do...

God I'm an idiot, and really turned on.

Sasha's bag is thrown in the back seat along with my luggage. Her camera bag is up front sitting between her legs. We just left the Quick Trip where we stocked up on all of the road trip essentials, including questionable gas station hot dogs, which I'm sure I will regret later, Coke Zero because I like to eat my calories, not drink them, and Twizzlers because you can't road trip without them.

I pull out onto the highway and settle in. I don't know what I've gotten myself into. If Sasha turns out to be a serial killer, no one will know but me because I'll be dead, but hey, it was an adventure.

She's not a serial killer.

Is she?

I look in her direction suspiciously.

"Oh my God, do you think I'm a serial killer?" Sasha guffaws at me.

"Of course not," I say, offended, and turn back toward the road.

"Look, my grandparents are expecting me in two days, so if I don't show up, guess who they'll be lookin' for." She points at me accusatorially.

"Do I look like the serial killer type?" I ask, my turn to be offended. We really should have addressed all of this before getting on the road.

"Well, no, but I mean people thought Ted Bundy was hot, so, there's that." She shakes her head causing the loose hairs of her messy blonde bun to flutter around her face. I start to laugh because this conversation is so ridiculous. Of course, I don't think Sasha is a serial killer. I wouldn't have agreed to this if I had. I'm a great judge of character; it's part of my job. Sasha is the closest thing I have to a friend, which is really sad because a) I just met her last night, and b) she's at least ten years younger than me.

Well, Jack is more than ten years older than me. Why can't I find playmates my own age?

"How old are you?" I ask.

"Twenty-three," she answers.

"What's your last name?" If I'm traveling two days in a car with a non-serial killer, I need to know her last name.

"Leone."

I forgot to plug my phone back in after we loaded up with road trip items, so I struggle momentarily to get it set back up while maneuvering down the highway. The car in front of me slows down and I have to slam on my breaks eliciting a worried yelp from Sasha.

"Drive much?" Sasha laughs, with her hands braced on the dash.

"Well, no actually."

Sasha turns and gives me a worried look.

"What? I live in New York City," I shrug. "Not much use for cars there."

"Should I be worried?"

"No, I got this," I tell her.

"I could drive," she offers.

"We should definitely take turns," I agree.

We continue down the highway and traffic eases the further away from downtown we get. Sasha is quiet, and from the corner of my eye I can tell she looks sad.

"Hey, I'm sorry. I'm a good driver, promise," I try to reassure her.

"It's not that." She pulls her knees up to her chest. We rented a midsize car, but Sasha's tiny enough for the seat to hold two of her. Well maybe not two, but she has some extra room. She starts to absently pull open her camera bag to check the contents. There are a couple different lenses, chargers and light cubes. "Luckily I had my camera at work with me or he probably would have sold that too," she grumbles.

"Are you going to tell me what happened?" I ask her tentatively. When I spoke to her on the phone at the airport she didn't go into great detail, but I gathered enough information to know that her boyfriend screwed her over and she got evicted from her apartment. She said her family lived in the L.A. area and she was going to go home for the summer. My flight was full. I was lucky to get a seat when I did. I felt sorry for her, and that's when I suggested we drive together to L.A.

I'm all for adventure, and honestly, I need a distraction, but mostly I'm just starved for some company. I agreed to drive two days when I could have flown in four hours, because I Sasha needed a friend and delaying my arrival in L.A. will give me some time to think.

Sasha sighs and looks out the window. She points the camera at something we pass by, and I can hear the shutter click a few times.

"Have you ever been betrayed by someone you loved?" she asks, still focusing her eye into the camera lens.

"Wow, that's a loaded question," I say, gripping the steering wheel. I'm thinking about my parents, my dad especially, and then Michael, my old editor at Edge. I won't even mention my high school prom where my date got high beforehand and then took off a garter belt, with his teeth, from a drunk friend of mine, at the banquet hall of the hotel.

"And the answer is yes," I say definitively.

"We moved in together after dating for a few months because his roommate left town and he couldn't afford the place alone. He was going to have to move back to San Antonio," Sasha confesses. "Tattoos and blue eyes are my weakness," she sighs.

Tell me about it, I grip the steering wheel.

"That's not a good enough excuse to move in with someone, though," I tell her.

"He played drums and had these forearms…" she holds her arms out and clenches her fists to make the veins surface, "you know the ones." She eyes me to make sure I know what she means. "Those drummer veins."

"Mhmm." I mumble, but what I'm really thinking about are the forearms and biceps of a certain guitar player.

"He spent our rent money on band equipment, and to be honest, they weren't even that good." She shakes her head. "Oh, and he fucked my best friend." Her expression softens and she looks to be on the verge of tears.

"I don't want to cry over that asshole!" She wipes her nose with the sleeve of her sweater.

I let her vent while I listen and drive. Sometimes that's all you need when you're sad or pissed off, is to get it off your chest and have someone listen without trying to fix it.

"Fuck Austin!" Sasha screams out the window and I laugh at her audacity.

Inspired, I yell, "Fuck guitarists!"

Sasha turns to me, surprised. "Fuck musicians!" She shoves her fist in the air.

We laugh, able to turn this sad moment into something light-hearted, but I know her pain.

"I have a thing for musicians. Maybe it's daddy issues," she jokes.

I give her a quizzical look. "My Mom was an addict, overdosed when I was a baby.

Never knew who my dad was, but apparently my mom was a groupie so it could have been any number of musicians," she says casually.

"I'm so sorry." At least I know who my dad is.

"It's okay though, because my grandparents are awesome." Sasha smiles, tucking her hands inside of the sleeves of her sweater.

"Maybe not all musicians are bad," I offer. "You father might not even know about you. Have you ever tried to find him?" I ask.

"No," she answers. "My grandparents didn't keep much of my mom's things after she died. There's nothing but some old photos and a journal."

"You'd be surprised what you can find out these days."

"I looked in her journal but there are no names to go by. Honestly, I haven't thought about it in years." Sasha shakes her head.

"Sometimes things are better left undisturbed." I stare at the road, lost in thought.

"I thought Danny was the one, ya know?" she says nostalgically. "Maybe I'm just a horrible judge of character."

"Love clouds our judgement," I tell her. "Makes us believe in people that maybe we shouldn't."

"Well then I was in a fucking San Francisco fog." She puts her face in her hands.

We drive in silence for a little bit, the radio on but neither one of us paying attention.

Austin is now a distant memory as we head west with our sights on New Mexico.

I have too much time to think while I'm driving, and now that I'm invested in

Sasha's life, I can't help but ask. "What about school?" I remembered she has one more year left.

"I'll just have to apply for a dorm," she says. "Or switch schools."

"What made you go to school in Texas?" I ask curiously.

"They had a really good journalism program, but mostly it was because I wanted to be out on my own."

"I can definitely relate to that." I tell her a little bit of why I left home right after high school and moved to New York to go to school.

"Sounds like you have your own daddy issues," she jokes, and I can't help but laugh with her.

"Don't we all?"

"I really do appreciate this, Erin." Her sincerity is apparent. "I wouldn't have had any other way to get back to L.A. if it weren't for you."

"Wouldn't your grandparents have helped you?" I don't want to pry, but it sounded like her grandparents are wonderful people. Surely they would have loaned her money for a plane ticket at least.

"My grandparents are great. They're just kinda strict, and because of everything they went through with my mom, they wouldn't approve of my choices."

"So you're going to tell them you're coming home because you missed them?" I ask, raising my eyebrows.

"Exactly," she smiles innocently. "If there is anything you need, anything I could do to repay you, it's yours."

"Like your first born?" I tease.

She laughs.

"It'll be fun," I reassure her.

Sasha flips the radio to the only station that comes in clear and it's playing Britney, so naturally, we put all the bullshit behind us and sing at the top of our lungs with the windows down without a care in the world.

"Okay, this is a disappointment," Sasha declares, throwing her bag on one of the beds in our hotel room.

"Not one alien or UFO themed hotel in Roswell," she says, opening the curtains that gives us an uninteresting view of a strip mall. "Waste." She shakes her head disappointedly. "And did you see the Auto Zone?" she asks. "It's just way too normal here," she says with obvious despondency.

I'm a bit exhausted from driving for nearly eight hours, so I don't care if the hotel has a spacecraft in the lobby or not. I just want a hot shower and a bed.

"The diner had aliens," I remind her as I grab the only clean shirt from my bag. I knew buying that Austin ATX shirt at the airport was a good idea.

"Pictures of aliens on the menu don't count," she scoffs. "The building should have been shaped like a spaceship or something, but no, it had to be all rectangular and normal."

I hear her unzipping her bag while I'm in the bathroom turning on the shower and laying out my stuff. "They do have a UFO museum," I point out, poking my head out of the bathroom with my toothbrush shoved into my mouth.

"I'm not really the museum type," Sasha says, making a face.

When I come out of the shower, the TV is on and Sasha is lying on her stomach, propping her chin up with the palms of her hands, an empty Twizzlers bag sitting next to her.

On the TV screen is a nature show about lions in Africa.

"There was nothing else on," she shrugs.

"Honestly, I'm too tired to care what's on TV." I pull back the blankets and climb inside.

Sasha grabs a change of clothes and heads into the bathroom.

"The water pressure sucks!" I yell to her.

"Yet another thing about Roswell that can bite my ass!" she yells back.

Oddly, I am riveted to the scene unfolding on the TV. I didn't know that female lions do all the hunting. This fact makes me a bit proud, and I realize females kick ass, no matter the species. Then I discover the males get to eat first and I sit up in bed, appalled. How is that fair?

Sasha emerges from the bathroom with wet hair, and wearing a tank top and sleep shorts that have owls on them. She notices me looking at her shorts questionably. "Owls are my favorite animal," she explains and plops down on the bed, combing through her hair. "I'm sorry I made you drive all the way to California."

"You didn't make me," I argue, propping myself up. "I don't mind. The drive gives me time to think."

Sasha cocks her head, a smile playing on her lips. "I see." She turns back towards the TV.

"What does that mean?" I ask curiously.

"I'm not the only one with relationship troubles," she smiles as if she knows something.

"Why do you think it's relationship troubles?" I ask. I can't believe I'm that easy to read. "It could be work related."

"A stranger does not agree to drive another stranger 1300 miles out of the kindness of her heart," Sasha laughs.

"Hey! I'm kind," I grumble, settling into the pillows.

"If you need to take a road trip to 'think'," she uses air quotes, "it must be something serious."

I roll over on my side, tucking my elbow under my head. She's right, obviously.

"Stay out of my head," I laugh.

"Are you running from something or towards something?" Sasha asks.

"I guess that's the question." I contemplate.

"Oh boy," Sasha laughs.

"What?"

"You must have it bad."

I smile. Sasha might only be twenty-three-years-old, but she's pretty insightful.

I grumble, "So bad."

We both stare at the TV and watch as the lioness jolts into a run with such grace that the unsuspecting gazelle doesn't even have a chance. When she takes it down with the power of an expert predator, I hear Sasha gasp out loud. "Brutal," she whispers.

"Did you know the males get to eat first?" I tell her, proud of that little tidbit I learned.

"The fuck?" she gasps.

I toss the blankets off me because I'm suddenly hot and not as tired as I was a few minutes ago. Am I the gazelle?

I will find you... and when I do... I mean, fuck him.

"What's he like?" Sasha interrupts the silent argument I'm having in my head.

I don't even have to think about my answer and blurt out. "Complicated."

"Oof," she says.

I picture Jack's face, his blue eyes pinning me with their intensity. I can see every broken fracture inside of him, and I wonder, am I enough?

I sigh, propping up my chin with the palm of my hand. "Charismatic." When he wants to be, I think to myself.

"Musician," Sasha says definitively. "Or politician," she adds.

I dissolve into laughter, hiding my face.

"Musician. Definitely a musician." She laughs right along with me

"Occupational hazard," I tell her. Man, I just fell right into that one over a year ago, the minute I knocked on his door.

"Tragic backstory?" Sasha crawls under the blankets and rolls on her side to look at me.

"What musician do you know that doesn't have a tragic back story?" I laugh.

"So true," she sighs.

"So, what's his damage?" she asks.

"Where do I begin?"

"That bad, huh?" Sasha asks, but she already knows the answer.

I don't have any intention on telling her that it's Jack O'Donnell. "Rough childhood," I explain.

"Rotten luck. You can't choose who spawns you."

"Addiction," I'm counting them off in my head. "Absent father."

"Was he the absent father, or was he the victim of an absent father?" she asks.

"Does it make a difference?" I ask, confused.

"Totally, because if he was the absent father then he's carrying around guilt. If he was the victim of an absent father, he's just full of rage," Sasha says as casually as if we were deciding whether we want oranges or apples for a snack.

"Both." I tell her, "And…"

"There's more?" she squeaks.

"He's still in love with someone else." I leave out the part that she died in case that gives away too much. I think that's what I'm afraid of most, that I will never be her. It's a rabbit hole that I don't want to go down, but in the back of my mind, I've already explored that tunnel way more than I want to admit.

Am I running?

Yes. I am running. It's the easy way out. The universe has other plans for me though by sending me to L.A. I could have said no and gone to New York, but I wouldn't have escaped him there either. It's childish, I know. I'm a grown woman, capable of deciding whatever I want for myself, even if that decision is to move on, but I play this statement over and over in my head. Jack is worth fighting for. He is, but I am worth fighting for too.

"What's the problem?" Sasha asks.

"What do you mean? I just gave you the trifecta of reasons," I scoff.

"Is he into you?"

I gulp.

"What are you waiting for?" Sasha takes that as a yes.

"Didn't you just get your heart broken by some asshole musician and now you have no apartment and no best friend?" I remind her.

She looks at me with her soft but intense brown eyes. "Danny was a colossal mistake, but when I'm forty, I'll look back and think of him as the best kind of mistake."

I'm trying to take all of this in. One, when she's forty, okay, and two, the best kind of mistake? I settle into my pillow chewing on that for a minute.

"When it was good, it was so fucking good." She looks like she's salivating. "If I have to go through ten Danny's to find the right guy, at least I'll know what I'm not looking for."

Her words unsettle me. I can deal with all the other baggage, but the elephant in the room will always be Mia.

"Any of your Danny's hold a candle in their heart for someone else?" I ask, wondering how many Danny's this girl has gone through.

She shrugs. "Is this other girl still in the picture?"

"Not really." I don't know how to answer that.

She looks at me with intensity. "Make him forget her," she says emphatically.

Make him forget her.

Just the fact that she knows she might have to go through a bunch of douche bags to appreciate when a real man comes along is next level. I'm thirty-four and I still get pissed when I look back at all the losers that I have crossed paths with, and I certainly don't think of them as doing me any favors.

We are lying opposite each other, the nightstand separating our beds. It's weird because I just met Sasha, but she's already become one of my closest friends.

"I'm not sure if I'm willing to make anyone do anything for me," I tell her. "He should want to be with me because I'm worth being with."

"Truly, you are one of the coolest people I've ever met."

"I don't know about that," I laugh.

We lay in silence for a little while and I think she's fallen asleep but then she says. "He sounds like a fantastic lay."

I nearly choke on my own spit.

"How do you figure that?" She has no idea how true that is.

"The tortured soul of a musician," she winks. "Always trying to prove something."

I grip the pillow tight.

"Anyway, goodnight." Sasha flips over to her other side, and I'm left with a mental image of Jack, making it hard for me to fall asleep.

Thanks a lot, Sasha.

After a while I can hear her breathing even out and I think she's fallen asleep, so I turn the TV back on at a low volume. I flip through the channels and settle on one of the late night Talk Shows. I completely forgot Jack was doing a live appearance tonight. What I see on the screen, I am not prepared for.

I bolt upright. What the fuck is he doing?

I grab my phone and text him.

15
Very Poetic

JACK

"It wasn't that bad," I say to Wade, although I'm not even convincing myself.

I turn back to look at him and see he's doing that pinching the bridge of his nose thing with his fingers.

"I just... I don't even know what to say to you right now." A corner of his mouth quirks up, and I know he's not as mad at me as he claims.

"It's not my fault!" I tell him.

Wade throws his hands up exasperated. "Seriously?" His eyes are big, and I don't like it.

"Geez, Wade, are you gonna be the overbearing Dad?" I joke. "I thought that was gonna be Adam, but you're starting to border on deranged right now." I back away from him, self-preservation kicking in.

We're making our way through the hallway of 30 Rock, and everyone is running frantically from one Green Room to the next as different guests come and go for the shows they're filming tonight. I'm done, thankfully. Filming two talk shows back-to-back is exhausting, and maybe that's what brought on my attitude. Although, some might say I always have an attitude.

"Jack, this isn't funny."

"You should see your face right now." We pass PA's scrambling to get out of our way. My phone rings and I check to see who it is before I answer.

When I pick up, all I hear is Cash laughing. It's more like cackling, so I put it on speaker so Wade can hear.

"Don't encourage him!" Wade yells into the phone as we make our way out of the building to the waiting car.

"This is what fucking happens when I go along with what you guys want. Be nice, Jack. Don't be such an asshole, Jack. Have some fun, Jack," I mock, yelling at both of them.

"Are you fucking happy now?" I slide into the back seat next to Wade who adjusts his suit. I don't know how he can wear that thing all day. It would strangle me.

"I just watched the whole thing. Best TV all year!" Cash says in between fits of laughter.

"You'll never be invited back," Wade chastises, folding his arms over his chest.

"Really? I'm so devastated," I say sarcastically as I roll my eyes at him.

"You're going to give me a fucking ulcer," Wade says, "the both of you!" he yells into the phone so Cash can hear too.

"Ask me to do a fucking lip sync battle again," I grumble, narrowing my eyes as I relax in the back of the car.

Wade has a horrified look on his face.

I can't help but laugh because annoying Wade is so easy. I give him a break and put the phone to my ear.

Cash finally calms down enough to form coherent sentences. Wade eyes me suspiciously as I try to have a conversation without pissing him off even more.

"I gotta go. We're almost at the hotel," I tell Cash and hang up. We don't fly out until the morning because I don't like taking red eyes. I want at least a few hours of sleep. The car pulls up to the hotel and the driver opens the door for us. I give Wade a sly smile.

Wades phone rings and it's Adam calling him on FaceTime.

"I'm almost to my room," Wade tells him.

I push Wade out of the way and jam my face into view. "Good God Adam, have you showered lately?" Adam's hair is sticking out in every direction - and not in a good way. The 5 o'clock shadow on his face is more like a 10 o'clock shadow, and he has a stain on his shoulder that looks suspiciously like throw up.

"Do not judge me, Jack." Adam looks like he's about to lose his shit.

"You have a little something..." I point towards the spot on his shirt, "right there."

Adam mimics trying to strangle me through the phone.

Dylan is making noises in the background, and Wade pushes me out of the way.

"What's wrong with Dylan?"

"You're coming home tomorrow, right?" Adam asks, a pathetic look in his eyes.

Wade nods. "Let me call you when I get into my room," he says to Adam and hangs up the phone.

I know my work here is done tonight when Wade gives me another annoyed look. We enter the lobby and take the elevator to our floor.

"Hey," I stop him before he turns toward his room. "It gets better," I try to reassure him.

"I bet Hayley was never this bad," Wade says.

When Hayley was a baby, I was able to take time off from touring for at least the first three months. I remember the sleepless nights, the feeling of helplessness when nothing worked to calm her, and the stress of wondering if I was damaging my kid for life by making her 'cry it out'. Sleep deprivation can make you feel unhinged, and I know what he's going through, even if it's a distant memory, the impression runs deep.

"She had her moments, Wade." I cock an eyebrow. "Sometimes she still keeps me up at night."

"If I'm being honest, and you better never tell Adam, I used this trip as an excuse to get away," Wade confesses. "I know that's horrible because poor Adam is home trying to calm a crying baby all by himself, but I just needed a break." He looks like he might fall apart.

"It's okay, Wade." I brace both his shoulders and look at him sincerely. "Sometimes you gotta crawl through the shit to see the light."

"Very poetic."

"Eh, I try." I shrug.

We both head for our rooms but I turn around and say, "By the way, your secret's safe with me." I wink.

"But there will come a day when I will call upon you for a favor." I give him my best Brando impression. Wade's smile disappears.

"Noted." Wade walks down the hall to his room as I chuckle.

New York hotel rooms are not at all like New York apartments. My room is spacious and comfortable. The window looks out over Manhattan and the busy street below. On the opposite wall sits a queen-sized bed. Slumping on the edge, I kick my shoes off and reach around my back to pull my shirt off in one smooth motion. The room is eerily quiet, and as tired as I am, I should be able to flop back against the pillows and fall right to sleep, but my mind won't turn off.

It's been a mentally exhausting day. I lie back on the bed and rest my hand against the flat of my stomach. There was a time in my life I couldn't escape the gnawing feeling in the pit of my stomach. Drugs only temporarily eased the pain, but like any pain reliever, it just masks the symptoms, it doesn't cure them. Over the years, I realized that gnawing pain was anxiety.

Like addiction, you have to work at it to keep the claws of anxiety from pulling you under. It's hard to shut off my mind sometimes. I know I need to stop letting the past drag me down, but it's easier said than done, especially when all these memories are forced back into my head. I know I opened myself up to this when I decided to write the book, I just didn't think it would hit me this hard.

I close my eyes trying to relax, but my phone dings.

Erin: You'll never be invited back.

Jack: I'm in mourning over it.

Erin: Was it necessary to get up on the desk?

Jack: Absolutely.

Erin: And the water?

Jack: Can't do Flashdance justice without it.

Erin: Apparently not.

Jack: Where are you?

I'm leaning against the headboard, the phone in my hand, and I'm smiling like a fucking idiot. I like that she's thinking about me, because I never stop thinking about her.

Erin: Roswell, New Mexico.

Jack: Did you get abducted by aliens?

Erin: It's surprisingly normal here.

Jack: What are you doing in Roswell?

Erin: Driving through.

Jack: On your way to...?

It takes her a while to type back. Three dots stop and start as I watch impatiently for her answer.

Erin: L.A.

Jack: Back so soon?

Erin: I'll be covering Summerfest next weekend.

Jack: Hayley is performing there.

Erin: Does that mean you will be there?

> Jack: Do you want me to be there?

> Erin: It's a big festival.

> Jack: I'll take that as a yes.

I WONDERED WHY SHE WAS DRIVING THROUGH ROSWELL IN THE FIRST PLACE.

> Jack: Did you get banned from flying?

> Erin: It's a long story.

> Jack: You can tell me about it when I see you at the festival.

She doesn't answer right away so I drop the phone next to me on the bed, exhaustion beginning to take over as I close my eyes again. I count the number of breaths and each rise and fall of my chest.

The phone chimes and I pick it up to see her answer.

> Erin: Don't be so cocky.

I smile and set the phone back down.

My bare feet are propped up on the railing as I watch the surf in the distance. The clouds have dissipated, and the sky is a clear blue. I got back from New York yesterday and have received a dozen messages from my publicist. She's pissed about the talk show fiasco, which is what she refers to it as, not me. On the other hand, the publishing company has reported an increase in sales. I've been told that I'm not going to be doing any talk shows in the near future, but my book sales are up.

I call that a win-win.

The doorbell rings and I'm not expecting anyone, so I go to the door cautiously. When I peep through the hole, I see Amber standing on the other side of the door. It's never a good sign when she just shows up. This is twice in a matter of a few weeks.

When I open the door, Amber looks me up and down.

"Put a fucking shirt on," she huffs, brushing past me. Her hair is down in subtle waves that flow over her shoulders. She is wearing heels with shorts that go mid-thigh and a billowy blouse.

I grab a random shirt off the back of the couch and slip it over my head.

"Afraid you can't control yourself?" I joke with her.

"You wish, pig," Amber laughs.

There was a time when we couldn't stand to be in the same room with each other unless it was between the sheets. Amber still has an attitude and I still irritate the fuck out of her. I guess some things never really change.

"You must miss me because you keep popping by," I say arrogantly.

"You never answer your phone," Amber sighs. "Do you even know how to use it?" Her voice is laced with annoyance.

"I know how to use it," I say as I raise my eyebrows, and I'm met with a pair of narrowed blue eyes.

"So, you just avoid my calls, then?" She shakes her head. "If you don't like me 'popping by', then next time you'll answer," she counters.

"Noted," I reply.

"By the way, nice stunt on that talk show," she smirks.

"I didn't even use a stunt double," I answer with a smile.

I cross my arms and lean against the kitchen island. "To what do I owe the pleasure of this unannounced visit, again?" I emphasize the last word.

Amber looks around the house that she once occupied. It's clean, but only because I haven't been here much.

"I'm not interrupting anything, am I?" She squints one of her blue eyes at me.

"I'm alone."

"Well, you shouldn't be." Amber drops her purse on the coffee table.

I laugh.

"You've been talking to Wade," I groan, grabbing a glass from the kitchen cabinet and filling it with water.

"Don't you think it's been long enough?" Her expression is gentle. She knows me.

I sigh and take a deep breath.

"So now you're trying to get me laid?" I cock an eyebrow at her.

"I have no doubt you can get laid on your own," Amber eyes me wearily.

"I'm talking about a relationship," she says. "You know, an actual commitment. Sleeping with someone and seeing them again. Possibly even living with them. Maybe even getting married again."

My smile fades.

"It's what adults do." Amber never fails to add an edge of attitude, even when she's trying to be nice. I don't need my ex-wife giving me relationship advice.

"Yeah, I know what a relationship is," I tell her.

"What about that Erin girl, the one that wrote your book?" She knows damn well who Erin is.

"Okay, what is going on? Why are you here?" I push off from the counter and pad into the living room, taking a seat across from her in one of my wingback chairs.

"I'm just worried about you, that's all." She sits down too and crosses her legs.

"Cut the shit Amber," I say lightheartedly.

"I'm getting married," Amber blurts out.

This makes me laugh harder than I have in years.

"What is so fucking funny?" She stands up, anger radiating off her in waves. Amber can be intimidating when she wants to be.

"You're serious?" I straighten myself.

Amber sits back down, pushing her blonde locks from her shoulder.

"Is it ridiculous that someone would want to marry me?" Her face is still incredulous.

"No. I just... isn't it too soon?" To be honest, Amber and I were never compatible, but that didn't mean she was a horrible person. We both had a lot of growing up to do, and having a baby so young when both our careers were starting to take off just added fuel to the fire.

Amber narrows her eyes at me. I can tell she doesn't want me to bring up what happened. I know she's been in therapy and that's attributed to healing our relationship, but for her, it's in the past, and whenever I've brought it up, it didn't go over so well. We are good at avoiding the tough stuff.

"Who is the lucky guy?" I say seriously, but Amber eyes me skeptically.

"If you're gonna have an attitude about it…" She shakes her head and feigns leaving.

"Come on, Amber." I say, knowing that will stop her. "Who is it?"

Amber settles back down. "Do you remember Stephen Ambrose?" she asks me.

Stephen was a boyfriend from years ago when Amber and I were still going through some shit. If I remember correctly, he was a good guy, it was just the wrong timing.

"The real estate agent?" At least I remember what he did.

"Real estate broker," Amber corrects me.

To me, this means he has money. Agent, broker, same shit. He sells houses.

"And he sells commercial real estate," she points out.

"I didn't know you were dating." Not that it's any of my business. I just thought that after everything that happened last year, she would take some time for herself.

"We reconnected last year." She has this dreamy look in her eyes that scares me because Amber never looks dreamy when she's talking about a guy. He must be the real deal.

I can't help but feel protective of her. There is a little pang in my heart because it just means that I wasn't that guy for her, as much as I wanted to be at the time. I thought keeping our family together was important, but I always managed to fuck things up.

"He's a good guy," she reassures me with a smile that reaches her eyes.

"You deserve someone good," I say sincerely. "When's the big day?"

"October."

"That's soon." Summer has just begun, and October doesn't seem too far off, at least not long for Amber to plan.

"Well, not really. We've been engaged for a few months," she says cautiously.

It took her this long to tell me.

"Oh." I look away.

"I just felt awkward telling you," Amber says softly. "I wanted us to be in a good place, ya know?"

"Does Hayley know?"

Amber nods and looks away.

"I'm here because I wanted to invite you in person." She actually looks nervous asking me.

I'll admit, I'm floored. Amber has never wanted me near her boyfriends before. Most of them didn't want me around either. Our history is complicated, and I don't blame them.

I reach across the distance between us and grab her hand. "Just tell me where, and I'll be there."

Amber smiles as she stands up and looks at me thoughtfully.

"I really am happy." A lot has changed over the last year and Amber looks good. Really good.

She eyes my threadbare T-shirt and jeans.

She points to my outfit. "The wedding is formal. You have to wear a suit."

I blanch as I walk her to the door.

"How about a collared shirt?" Because that's a compromise.

"A suit, Jack." She narrows her eyes at me before continuing, "With a fucking tie, too."

My eyes get big. "How about…"

"A fucking suit, Jack. I mean it." She points at me before strutting down the stairs of my beach house. I can't help but notice she still has an amazing ass.

"And stop staring at my ass!" she yells, as I close the door, laughing.

16

Oh, that Axl

ERIN

I'm really pushing through trying to make it to L.A. today, but I don't know if I can drive too much longer. It's only been seven hours since we left Roswell, and I've finally reached Flagstaff, Arizona. We could have made it into Nevada if it weren't for Sasha having me pull over multiple times so she could take photos of random junk piles of cars or abandoned gas stations. She's the photographer, so who am I to judge, especially when I've subjected her to a playlist of obscure bands that rock only my world.

Flagstaff is a small mountain college town with pine trees and rustic brick buildings. When we strutted into town with my rental car that now has more miles on it than my bicycle, the elevation marker says we are at about 7,000 feet above sea level. No wonder the rental car was struggling to gain speed and pass a semi on the way into town. If I'm not mistaken, Denver is only about 5,000 feet, and they call it the mile high city. Flagstaff has an extra 2,000 feet on Denver, yet it has no such moniker. I think they got cheated.

"Who's watching your apartment back in New York?" Sasha asks as I make my way through town looking for a place to park so we can grab dinner.

"No one." Which sounds pretty pathetic. I don't even have a plant that a neighbor needed to water for me. I like to live without attachments. At least, that's what I tell myself.

"What if a pipe bursts or you get a leak or something?" She sounds like a responsible person, and because I haven't really thought of that, maybe it makes me an irresponsible person.

I bullshit an answer hoping this would be true. "It's in a managed building, so if anything happens, the Super will take care of it. He has keys to all the apartments."

"You're not worried he would go in your apartment and jack off to the smell of your underwear?" She scrunches up her nose.

"I want to say that he doesn't use those keys to enter my apartment and sniff my underwear, but I can't be sure if I left my underwear drawer disheveled or not last time I was there." I tilt my head to the side, trying desperately to remember if in my haste to pack, I would have torn through my underwear drawer like a dirty old man looking for an unwashed pair to sniff.

"Do you travel a lot?" She changes the subject, and I'm glad.

"I do now that I'm freelance, but when I worked for *Edge*, I only traveled a few times a year. It always depended on the assignment and the budget," I explain.

I never really thought about traveling before, I was just excited to live in New York. Every day was an adventure trying to learn the Subway system. Queens is a melting pot of its own, and I didn't need to travel far to get such an experience.

"Why do you even have an apartment if you're always on the road? Sounds like a waste of money if you ask me." Sasha props her glittery converse onto the dashboard. Back in Austin when I first met her at the bar, I remember thinking she was a little timid at first, but her true personality is shining right now, just like her shoes.

"I need a place to sleep when I'm not traveling," I laugh as if that should be obvious.

"You could sublet and the rest of the time just Airbnb it," she says, as if it's so easy. Actually, subletting my apartment isn't a bad idea.

"Or convert an old van into your own little camper and you can road trip to any destination with a free place to stay." Her brown eyes light up at the idea.

"I've had my fill of driving, thank you," I reply, shaking my head.

"You could let me drive you know," Sasha pouts.

We left Roswell and Sasha was behind the wheel, but I quickly discovered she liked to sightsee more than pay attention to the road, so I took over.

"I'd like to live, thank you." I teased her.

"I'm starving." Sasha looks longingly at a row of restaurants as we drive slowly through downtown. I pull into an empty spot in front of a small local brewery. We skipped lunch because I wanted to drive a little further so we could make into town, and now I'm starving too.

We grab a table outside, and in the shade it's a little chilly, even for summer. In the distance I can see a tall mountain that almost looks like it has snow on its crest. Downtown Flagstaff is beautiful with its mixture of quirky bohemian shops and a certain lumberjack quality.

We order a local beer and some appetizers.

"When's your birthday?" Sasha asks me.

"July."

"Cancer. Figures." She takes a bite of the mozzarella sticks we ordered.

"What does that mean?" I ask, taking a bite of my own.

"It's like the most compassionate sign. You don't judge, you treat people like family."

I sit back in my chair and chew on that. "Huh. I guess that can be true."

"You don't like birthdays, do you?" Sasha asks.

"It's not that I don't like them. Wait, why do you think I don't like birthdays?"

"Yours is coming up soon, and you didn't seem too enthused about it." She takes a swig of her beer. "There are two kinds of people in the world: people who love their birthday, and people that don't." She crosses her legs as she continues devouring the mozzarella sticks.

"My brother died when we were kids, and after that, it didn't seem right to celebrate my birthday when we would never celebrate another one of his," I confess to her.

Sasha looks up from her drink, her brown eyes full of concern.

"Shit, sorry. I didn't mean to pry like that."

"You didn't, it's fine," I reassure her. "Birthdays have not been special to me in a long time."

Her face is so full of compassion I wonder if she got the horoscopes mixed up."That's so sad. Birthdays are meant to be celebrated."

"When is your birthday?" I ask.

"Not until February," she says. "I'm a Pisces."

I'm not into horoscopes. Not that I don't believe in them, but I just never had the time or the interest to explore any of that.

"Did you at least have good birthdays growing up?" I ask.

"Like a fucking carnival," she smiles. I can picture Sasha riding a unicorn while eating cotton candy wearing an 'it's my birthday' pin.

Down the street from the restaurant is an old hotel. Its brick building is only three stories tall, and the sign is made of monstrous vertical steel lettering, *Hotel Monte Vista* illuminating the darkening sky. The lobby is all red velvety goodness with brass fixtures, and the walls adorned with black and white photos of celebrities from the thirties. The elevator displays a sign that proudly explains it's the original, and also reassures it has been modernized to fit current safety codes. The stairwells are narrow with the steps closer together than what you see in modern buildings. I imagine a tall man would have to duck in order to get through the switchbacks to the next floor.

The hotel does not have a bellman to help us with our luggage, so we drag it into the undersized elevator, closing the accordion metal gate and locking it before we can press our floor number. When we get into our room, I notice the hardwood floors are scratched and scuffed with an area rug in the center. There are two beds opposite two windows that look out over the street below. There is a wood table with two chairs between the windows, and a binder with the hotel's insignia resting atop it.

Sasha drops her bags on one of the beds and makes a beeline for the binder. As she's flipping through it, I take the opportunity to kick my shoes off and flop down on the bed, enjoying my full belly, a beer buzz, and the anticipation that tomorrow I will be in L.A. and no longer have to drive ever again.

"Did you know this hotel is haunted?" Sasha says excitedly.

I immediately sit up. "What?"

"Look at this." She rounds the table and sits down next to me, shoving the binder onto my lap. I flip through the pages and see pictures of celebrities such as John Wayne, Bing Crosby, and even Harry Truman, who have all stayed at the hotel. I notice the page with our room number on it, and scan over the information printed on a card.

"Apparently there's a phantom bell boy." She's just a little too excited about this in my opinion.

"Uh, did you skip over the part about the prostitutes who got thrown out of this very window to their deaths?" I point to the windows across from us incredulously.

"Yeah, but that's not as cool as a phantom bell boy." She raises her eyebrows.

"We passed a Holiday Inn that I'm about 90% sure no one has died in." I tell her, getting ready to put my shoes back on.

Sasha wrinkles her nose. "That percentage might be exaggerated a bit, don't you think?"

She's probably right.

"Are you really that worried?" Sasha asks. "I wouldn't have taken you for someone who believes in ghosts."

"I don't," I say rather quickly. "I want a peaceful night's sleep. I don't want to think about prostitutes being thrown out of windows or phantom bell boys."

"Apparently there's a bank robber who died in the lobby and he likes to ring the bell on the counter," she says with a devilish grin.

"Put that thing away." I grab the binder and throw it back on the table. On second thought, I retrieve it and throw it in the drawer of the nightstand between our beds right on top of the bible, closing it safely inside.

"The book isn't possessed," she laughs, and then grabs her camera.

"You wanna take a walk with me?" Sasha pulls a sweater from her bag. "I saw some cool shops earlier, and I might take some pictures." She puts the camera strap around her neck.

"You go ahead. I need to get some work done." I sit down and pull my laptop from its bag.

"Call me if anything spooky happens," she laughs, and closes the door behind her.

I start researching the lineup for Summerfest and look at some of the bios Sandy emailed me. Most of these bands are new to me because they are mostly the EDM and Trap crowd. I notice Hayley's name on the list. I'll admit I've been following her career a little bit, more because I'm interested in her musically, not because she's Jack's daughter. Okay, that's a lie. I wouldn't know her if it weren't for Jack, and yes, a part of me wants to know her. It's odd to be seeing someone and not know their kid. I know Jack is still trying to repair his relationship with her, so I don't push it. Hayley and I have a causal relationship that's cordial and friendly when we do see each other.

My phone vibrates and I look down to see I have a text from Jack. Little butterflies bang against my stomach at the thought of his sexy smile. I can't help how my body reacts to him, and I like that he's thinking about me. Sometimes distance makes you put things into perspective.

Jack: Where are you now?

He's been keeping track of my road trip. Along the way I've sent him pictures of stupid roadside attractions Sasha begged me to stop at. He would text me back with some random emoji that I don't even think he knows what they mean. I press my finger to my lips to suppress my grin. Just the thought of him sends goosebumps up my arms.

This whole road trip I've been thinking about him and what I'm willing to give up, just to have him. All I know is how he makes me feel when I'm with him, and I block out all of the bad parts because I don't want to see them. I'm putting on blinders because I can't think of a way out of this. Jack will always be Jack, and that's who I fell in love with. This whole time I've been trying to protect myself from Jack when I'm the one I don't trust.

Erin: Flagstaff

Jack: You like?

Erin: It's interesting.

Jack: ???

Erin: Accidentally picked a haunted hotel to stay in overnight.

Jack: There's lots of those in Flag.

Erin: Awesome.

Jack: Can I call you?

I lean away from the phone, horrified, as one does when you're texting, and the other person asks if they can call you.

Jack: Erin?

Erin: Yes?

Jack: I want to hear your voice

The air is being sucked out of the room and I sit here holding my phone, waiting.

When it rings, I pick it up immediately but neither of us says anything. I lay back against the pillows and close my eyes. His shaky breath on the other end runs through my veins and into my belly like a shot of whiskey.

I could fall asleep listening to his breathing, and that would be enough. I sink back into the pillows more, exhaustion slowly taking over.

Jack exhales loudly. We are both at a loss for words but it's as if no words are necessary between us. I picture him cradling the phone to his cheek, his mouth turned up in a lazy smile. I have memorized every tattoo on his body and think about the way his hair covers the tops of his ears.

My lip's part and I'm about to say something when I hear a commotion in the background. Wade's voice breaks our silence.

"It's a disaster!" Wade yells frantically. "Axl broke his fucking leg and now the band can't play at the festival this weekend!"

"Axl Rose broke his leg?" I hear Jack ask.

"No, not fucking Axl Rose, Jack, Axl from *Steel Toe*, the band I manage," Wade's voice is an octave too high to be messing with.

"Oh, that Axl." I can hear the sarcasm in Jack's voice. "Just get one of your other bands."

"I can't just get another band! They're all booked!" Wade sounds annoyed.

"Don't look at me like that," Jack says.

"Like what?" Wade's voice is calmer.

"I'm not filling in!" Jack says.

"Don't flatter yourself; you're not the festival type," Wade says.

"What do you mean, 'I'm not the festival type'?" Jack sounds incredulous. "Have you forgotten *Lallapalooza*, or *The Warped Tour*?"

"Different kind of festival." Wade's tone is laced with annoyance. "Never mind, Jack. I was hoping you could use your connections to help me find a replacement," Wade pleads.

"You're the one with the label," Jack says, dismissing him. "You're telling me you can't find another band?"

"I might know a band," I pipe up, hoping Jack still has the phone close enough so he can hear me.

"Is that Erin?" Wade asks. "Oh, thank God, someone sane!" I hear muffled noises.

"Are they good?" Wade switches me to speaker.

"Goosebumps on the arm good," I tell him.

"Who's their rep?"

"That depends," I say slyly.

"Jack, your girlfriend's gone insane too," Wade yells away from the phone.

"She's not... just give me the phone back." I hear Jack trying to take the phone from him and I dismiss his comment.

"If you're willing to sign them," I interrupt their exchange. It was the perfect opportunity to bring up Finn and Sawyer. If Wade doesn't snatch them up, someone else will. They're too good not to be signed, and with my article coming out soon, there is no doubt labels will take notice.

17
I'm With the Band
JACK

"Just don't tell Hayley I'm here. She'll think I'm checking up on her," I tell Cash as he turns to look at Wade pointedly.

"What? Why are you looking at me?" Wade asks offended.

It's fucking hot, and this idiot is still wearing a suit. Although he has draped the jacket over his forearm and rolled up his sleeves.

"I'm no snitch," Wade scoffs.

We're walking through the backstage area where Wade is meeting up with the band Erin put him in contact with, *No Cover*. When Erin recommends a band, we all take notice. I'm looking forward to seeing them live, especially after meeting them yesterday. Finn and Sawyer are talented and humble. Wade is putting himself out on a limb by booking a band he's not sure has a following, but it's in a time slot on one of the smaller stages that doesn't get much traffic anyway, so there's not a high risk of flopping.

"Besides, you're not here just for Hayley," Wade raises a knowing eyebrow.

"Please, feel free to intervene in my love life yet again," I grumble at Wade, knowing he's referring to Erin.

I watch as people race to erect tents, stages, and unload equipment from trailers parked in the field. It's a clear day, the sky is a baby blue, but my skin tingles with electricity and I can feel a storm coming. I tell myself it's just my imagination, the need to turn something innocent into something foreboding, but the hairs on my neck never lie.

Erin is here somewhere.

Sweat trickles down the back of my neck and I wipe it away, along with my thoughts.

I pop a piece of gum into my mouth.

"Still trying to quit smoking?" Cash asks, as Wade talks with one of the engineers. We take our conversation to the edge of the stage.

I lean against it and look up at the rafters, the box lights now dim but ready for the evening's show. It's been a while since I've performed on a tour like this, but being here, I'm starting to feel the itch. Cash's blonde hair is slicked back, and his aviators hide the nostalgic look I know are behind them. I caught him looking at the stage and the techs setting up. I often wondered why he didn't continue to play after the band broke up. It couldn't have been from lack of opportunity. Cash is one of the most intuitive bassists I know, and I have never played with anyone as good as him.

The atmosphere of the festival reminds me of when the two of us were on stage together, the impeccable timing of his bass matching my voice. The constant switch-ups of songs I put him through, based on the energy of the crowd, never pissed him off. We were on the same wavelength.

The rafter above looks so much higher than it used to, and I don't even know how I could have climbed to the top and hung over the crowd. The stage even looks wider and more intimidating than when I would dive off, trusting the crowd to catch me and deliver me safely back. Those are the things you do in your twenties. You jump without thinking of the fall. I can't imagine doing that now.

"I don't fucking know why," I laugh, shifting my weight, finally remembering the question Cash asked.

"Because you want to be around to see your grandkids?" Cash offers.

"Don't fucking say that." I give him a shove as he laughs at me. "I do not want to think about my daughter being pregnant."

"She's actually older than you were when you had her," Cash points out.

"Don't remind me," I say, rolling my eyes.

"Don't be so fucking sensitive." He rubs his arm while feigning being hurt.

"Did you hear Amber's getting married?" I change the subject, wishing I did have a cigarette right now.

"I heard." He looks like he's about to say something inappropriate, so I stop him.

"Don't fucking go there," I warn.

"You don't even know what I was going to say," he laughs, holding his hands up in surrender. It reminds me of the Cash of my youth, the guy who was class clown, always smiling. He smiles now but it never reaches his eyes, and I know I have something to do with that.

I raise an eyebrow. "Just don't," I warn him.

"Maybe Amber will give Hayley a sibling," he says fast, and starts to back away before he even finishes because he knows I'm about to pummel him.

I take a couple of steps forward, ready to wipe that grin off his face, when I see Adam walking across the stage towards us with what looks like some kind of backpack strapped to the front of his body.

"The fuck..." both Cash and I say in unison as Adam approaches.

What I thought was a regular backpack is actually a baby carrier. Little feet dangle out from the bottom. It looks out of place with Adam's outfit and his hair styled in his usual dark faux hawk. This might actually be the first time he's been out of the house for an event after the Christening fiasco.

"Hey, what's up guys?" Adam smiles, checking to make sure Dylan's face is out of the sun.

"This isn't a nursery," I grumble, just to fuck with him.

"I know it's not a fucking nursery!" he screeches at me.

I might actually be scared right now. Adam's a bit on the wiry side, but insanity beats size any day of the week.

Dylan starts to cry, and Adam's eyes shift down as he strokes the little blonde hairs on Dylan's head. "Now you fucking woke him up!" Adam loud whispers.

"Dude, I think…" Cash starts to say but I give him a pointed look, shaking my head. Cash shuts his mouth and starts to look for someone, anyone else to talk to so he can get away from Adam.

I don't blame him.

Adam switches from unhinged to defeated in less than thirty seconds, and I feel sorry for him. I think lack of sleep is slowly making him more mental than usual.

Adam bounces Dylan to try and calm him, but Dylan's whimpers and cries are starting to escalate. I can't watch this anymore. I reach over and pluck Dylan from his constraints. He has on a white onesie with black lettering that says *I'm With the Band*.

Dylan stops crying as soon as I place him against my chest, and Adam's mouth drops open. Dylan's small soft body fits against my chest the way Hayley used to.

"How did you do that?" he asks, dumbfounded. "Is he still breathing?" Adam cranes his neck to look at Dylan's face, mushed against my chest to confirm.

I slowly rock Dylan in my arms while I gently pat his back. "It's because I'm someone new, that's all," I explain to Adam. "A temporary distraction."

"You want to babysit?"

"No!" I say, before he even finishes his sentence.

Dylan's cool, but I don't really like kids unless they're my own.

My palm is resting gently on Dylan's behind and suddenly I feel something warm.

There's a quiet but noticeable gurgle coming from that direction. Any nostalgia I felt about babies has just been wiped away.

"Here ya go." I hand Dylan back to Adam and he scrunches his nose at the smell.

"Real nice, Jack." He frowns at me.

I wave at Adam as I take off in another direction.

I pass Cash on my way down the stage and wave goodbye.

Right now, the field is deserted. Semi-trucks are parked where people will be later tonight. I think of all of those years on the road by myself, just trying to keep busy so I didn't have to go back to an empty house. The stage was home, the crowd was my family, but the minute the show ended, I did everything I could to stay sober. I thought I could do it all on my own, lie to myself, that all I ever needed was music and I'd be okay. It only works for so long. Instead of longing for the road and isolation, I long for something else now, or rather, *someone* else now.

My car is parked in the worker's lot, and on the way, there are food trucks set up for the workers and artists. From a distance, I see a familiar brunette standing at the coffee truck. She's wearing white sneakers, jean shorts, and a white top. I stand quietly behind her enjoying the view when she steps forward and orders a dirty chai.

"Dirty, eh?" My voice startles her, and she turns in surprise. Her mouth moves into a mischievous smirk. I think about how much I miss her when she goes back to New York or is away on assignment, but I know how happy she is to be a journalist. It is apparent in her articles.

"It means a shot of espresso," she explains, just as she did when I first met her, and it's now a running joke between us. I watch as her lips move in a slow and deliberate way.

"I know," I say quietly, playing my part, just enjoying being in the same space as her.

"Hi." She tucks a piece of hair behind her ear in a nervous gesture.

"Hi." My fingers itch to touch her as if gravity is taking over.

"Holy shit, Jack O'Donnell!" A very enthusiastic young blonde girl startles me as she sidles up next to Erin.

"Jack, this is Sasha," Erin introduces us. Sasha raises her eyebrows at Erin and mouths the word 'wow' at her.

"I love you! I mean I love your music." Sasha stumbles over her words with a wide smile on her face.

"So, you're the road trip partner in crime," I give her a welcoming smile because I know Erin is a great judge of character and she wouldn't have spoken so highly of her if she didn't mean it.

"Guilty." Sasha nervously raises her hand.

"How did you enjoy Flagstaff?" I never got the chance to ask Erin after Wade interrupted us on the phone. Northern Arizona is beautiful, and Flagstaff is not too far from Payson. It's a fun town to visit.

Sasha answers, "It was beautiful. I got a lot of great shots while we were there." She holds up the camera that is dangling from her neck.

Erin makes a noise in the back of her throat and eyes Sasha. "*You* had a great time."

"Oh, come on, it wasn't that bad!" Sasha suppresses a laugh and I look between the two of them, wondering what I'm missing.

"If you call getting choked in the middle of the night fun, then yeah, I had a great time in Flagstaff," Erin answers, annoyed.

"Wait, what?" I ask, confused.

"This one," she points to Sasha, "picks a haunted hotel."

"Yeah, you mentioned that," I say, thinking of our text messages.

"I didn't know it was haunted!" Sasha defends herself.

Erin turns to me. "I'll tell you all about it later."

"Dirty Chai!" The guy calls out from the truck, interrupting us.

"I should get going," Sasha plays with the camera strap. "Meet ya later?" Sasha nods and Erin confirms.

"It was so awesome meeting you," Sasha says, looking as if she wants to shake my hand but isn't sure, and then she starts to... *curtsey*?

"Okay, um... bye." Sasha hurries away, obviously embarrassed.

I turn back to Erin and shake my head, raising my eyebrows. "Did she just..."

Erin shakes her head and waves me off.

I pour myself a black coffee and lean against the table. "How come you never act like *that* around me?" I tease.

"You're not a shiny new toy anymore. I don't spread my legs for aging rock stars past their prime." She cocks her head to the side, smiling mischievously. I want to bend her smart ass over my knee.

"It's a good thing I'm not past my prime," I counter. My gaze travels from her lips to the outline of her bra through her white tank top and over her bare arms as she shifts uncomfortably under my gaze.

I've been thinking about what I want to do to her, for days.

As if she can read my mind, she warns, "Jack."

"What?" I smile devilishly.

I move closer, taking her hand in mine because I just want to touch her. I look down at her fingers linked with mine, the gesture is so small, but it causes a large lump to form in my throat.

"I have to get back," she says without much conviction.

"I'll walk with you." I keep her hand in mine as we walk across the field. She tells me a little more about Austin, meeting Sasha, and their subsequent road trip. I'm content to listen to her voice as I sip my coffee, laughing again about her ghost encounter.

"It's not funny!" she says, as she pushes me, laughing. "I felt something grab my neck in the middle of the night."

"Maybe it was…" I start to say.

"It really happened!" She narrows her eyes at me, daring me to disagree with her.

"I'm sure it did," I raise my hand in surrender.

She changes the subject. "I'm glad Wade could use *No Cover* at this festival because they really deserve it." The way Erin talks about music is enthralling. I can tell how much she loves it in every word in her articles.

"I got to hear them yesterday in the studio," I tell her. "Sawyer's great, but Finn is really talented. He and Wade geeked out over sound equipment that Finn records the fiddle on and plays it back during his set."

"I knew the fiddle had to be real and not synth," Erin says excitedly, as if she won a bet with herself.

"Thanks for saving Wade's ass," I say.

"I'm just glad *No Cover* gets the opportunity. This could be a big break for them."

We walk further across the field, the stages coming into view.

"The editor loved my article, and of course Sasha's photos were great," she continues.

"I liked the way you compared their sound to Tom Petty." My steps match hers. "In the studio yesterday, I could hear the influence."

She stops suddenly and turns toward me. "You read my article?"

"I read all your articles," I assure her.

She blushes and shakes her head like she doesn't believe me.

Not only does she have a great ear for emerging bands, but she's also a champion for indie artists like *No Cover*. How could I not be impressed with her?

"I talked with Sandy at *Alt Press* the other day," Erin says with a serious tone.

I look at her thoughtfully, willing her to continue.

"I told her I didn't want to cover festivals anymore. I need something more."

"You're a talented writer, I know this first-hand. My book is a best-seller because of you," I tell her, not that she needs to hear it from me, but I want her to know how I feel.

"I like writing about music, but I'd like to do more investigative journalism," Erin explains.

"You would be great at that. I remember what you were like working on the book, all of that research, putting together the pieces of my fuzzy memory, talking to the old road crew. You were so focused." I remember so clearly her intense focus, the hyper-vigilance to detail, and it dawns on me. That is the same way I get when I'm working on a song or an album.

"You were like a dog with a bone." I use my hand to mimic a biting dog.

"Well, as much as I like being compared to a dog, I really do have to go," Erin says sarcastically, cocking her head at me.

"You're pretty cute when you're annoyed."

She narrows her eyes at me again. "I really do have to go."

I pull her body close to mine, my hand on her lower back, keeping her in place. I'm not ready to let her go yet. Maybe not ever.

"Jack," she says nervously, looking around.

"I don't give a fuck who sees us." I lean down and kiss her, gently parting her lips with mine. I can feel her resolve fade as she leans into me. It feels as though all of the tension we had before has melted away. We are good together; I can feel it.

When she pulls away, I place my forehead against hers before I release her. Still holding onto her hand as she turns to leave, I stop her "Hey," I smile, "how do you feel about EDM?"

I need to head home and change before coming back for the show later tonight. I started going through Spotify playlists and found there's actually a few artists that I like, and one of them, *Trancelucid,* is playing tonight. I never said I didn't like Hayley's music, I only said I didn't understand it. This is my way of understanding it better.

My car is parked in the lot behind the main stage. I stop to take a look at the enormous setup one more time before I head out. To think all of the hard work Hayley has put in, it's amazing she'll be up there performing tomorrow night. Whether she knows it or not, I am proud of her. I know she's excited for me to see her perform, even though she doesn't admit it. She got me VIP tickets, but I didn't have the heart to tell her I didn't need them.

"Getting nostalgic?" I turn around to see Bobby Hanson standing behind me. Bobby is at least ten years older than me and there's not one grey hair on his blonde head, making me believe he dyes it. He looks like a douchebag wearing a white Henley and black skinny jeans. Just the sight of him gets under my skin.

"Something like that," I say, crossing my arms over my chest.

"This is a little different than back in the day, huh?"

The stages are the same, but the amenities are different. Musicians in the '90s had to beg someone to run to the nearest Taco Bell while these artists have food trucks and catering. Sleeping accommodations? We either stayed up all night or passed out unwillingly in a bush behind the stage. These guys get luxury trailers with king size beds.

"Sure is."

"All these YouTube stars and Soundcloud phenomenon's have it made. Not to mention I don't have to sit through hundreds of bad shows just to find that one gem." Bobby's laugh makes my teeth grate.

What he's saying is true though. We had to work for it, slinging equipment for other bands, playing on the street for some change, hoping to get picked up at a club on the regular, just to get noticed. Bobby was right there in the clubs, trying to build his reputation for finding good talent. He knows what it's like to struggle, but the difference between him and I is that Bobby took those times for granted, and now he screws over his clients to keep lining his pockets.

Now he has his clutches on my kid.

"By the way, congratulations. I heard about the book." Bobby would never actually buy my book, much less read it.

I'm starting to lose my patience.

"What can I do for you?" I'm not interested in making small talk with him. I'm civil because of Hayley, but I can only take so much.

"Hey, just trying to have a friendly conversation, Jack." He holds up his hands with a fake smile as if he doesn't understand why I wouldn't want to talk to him.

"Go have a friendly conversation with someone else."

"I don't know where all this hostility comes from," he says. "We go back a long way."

"That's the problem." I know him too well.

He seems to chew on that. Even though he smiles, it never quite reaches his eyes. Bobby's not as good at hiding his true self from me. He may have everyone else fooled, but not me.

"I wonder if you and Mia had signed with me," he stands casually with his hands in his pockets, "if things might have turned out differently."

My face gets hot, and I don't want to think about what he's implying, because if I do, I won't be able to stop myself. Even though my whole body vibrates with anger, I won't give him the satisfaction of letting him know he's getting to me.

"*Left Turn* did the two of you a disservice," he continues, "giving you all the freedom to self-destruct. The two of you could have been so great." I am about ready to snap. "I keep my talent in line."

I grit my teeth and keep my arms crossed in order to stop myself from strangling him. "Bobby, don't you have something else to do?"

"I figured you'd have a different attitude now," he rocks back on his heels, "especially since I represent your daughter. She's very talented." The smirk on his face rubs me the wrong way. He knows exactly what he's doing, trying to get under my skin. He's succeeded. I am rattled by him and on edge. It doesn't help that I already have self-doubt about protecting my kid in this business and wanting to respect her decisions as an adult.

"Let me ask you this, did you sign her just to get back at me or because you actually believe in her?" I don't expect him to give me a straight answer, but I want to know what he says.

Bobby laughs. "You don't have faith in her abilities? She'd be very disappointed to hear that." It's all I need to know to confirm that while Hayley is talented, he set his sights on her specifically because she's my kid. It's just a bonus that she brings in the crowds and makes him money. He doesn't care about her though, only what she can do for him. I don't like that he has access and influence over her.

I don't dignify that with an answer, instead, I give a defiant tilt of my chin.

"By the way, I see your making the tabloids again." There's a glint in his eye. "It's actually kinda pathetic, chasing a ghost. Whoever that girl is, I feel sorry for her. You going to ruin her life, like you ruined Mia's?"

I slowly lean towards him, taking all of my strength not to punch him in the face. The only reason

I restrain myself is for Hayley. I'm smart enough to know he'll engineer himself as the victim, get in Hayley's ear, and there goes our growing relationship. "Don't fuck with me, Bobby." I look him dead in the eye, "And don't fuck with my kid, or I will end you."

18
I Choose Me
ERIN

"Holy shit, Erin, you are a stone cold gangster! Jack O'Donnell? Like, what the fuck?" Sasha catches up to me as I'm on my way to the main stage.

Her attention is making me blush.

"That is the guy you were talking about, right?" she asks with astonishment.

I nod, trying to suppress the goofy smile I know is threatening to come out. He makes me lose my mind.

"Just wow." Sasha let out a loud breath.

"Do you think he noticed my attempted curtsey?" Sasha cringes.

"I'm pretty sure he noticed," I give her the side eye.

"I'm never gonna live that down." Sasha shakes her head in dismay.

"Nope," I laugh.

We continue to walk.

"I want details," Sasha chirps.

"Later," I promise.

"I still can't believe you were able to get me a press pass." Sasha has a huge smile on her face. "So many amazing bands are here, I'm losing my mind."

I couldn't go to a festival and not invite her.

"Of course. This is such a great opportunity to get your photography noticed." I wish I had someone when I was starting out to give me that extra edge. She's so talented, and I want to do what I can to help her out.

We walk up to the stage where the band *Belvedere* is doing a meet and greet with some VIP fans. Their manager, Artie, is casually talking with Cash, and I'm excited to say hello and see what he thinks of *No Cover*. I haven't had a chance to talk to Wade about them. I tried to stay out of the picture once I made the initial contact because I'm not the one signing them. That's up to Wade and Adam to decide.

Cash notices me approaching and looks our way, but his eyes are not focused on me; he's looking right at Sasha. He tears his eyes away from her, nodding at my arrival and turns his attention back to Artie. I look at Sasha thoughtfully. She's beautiful and sweet, but young. Maybe too young, but who am I to judge? It's not like Cash is the only guy to stare at Sasha. In fact, I've noticed the attention she's gotten all day, but there's something about the way Cash was looking at her that seemed different.

Sasha veers towards the stage to take some shots as I head over to Artie.

"Erin!" Artie, *Belvedere's* manager, takes me out of my thoughts and waves me over. He's an older man with salt and pepper hair and a friendly smile. Artie manages a couple of bands that I covered for a charity event a while back. He's a nice guy, unlike some of the other sleazy managers I've run into in this business.

"Nice to see you again." We shake hands. "Looks like *Belvedere* is doing well." I motion to the stage where his band is taking photos with fans. Cash waits his turn casually next to Artie, before he greets me.

A few years ago when I worked for *Edge*, *Belvedere* was just an up-and-coming band Artie was working his magic on to get them booked into some clubs. I wrote a piece hoping to give them more attention. Now they are playing in one of the most popular summer festivals.

When Cash thinks I'm not paying attention, his eyes travel to where Sasha is kneeling down in front of the stage, taking photos.

"You have come a long way, too," he says to me affectionately. "I read some of your articles."

I can't believe Artie has followed me. It's a huge compliment.

"Thanks, Artie." I can feel the heat rise to my cheeks. "I'm thankful I've had the opportunity to work with some great artists," I tell him.

"Doing a great job, kid." He smiles and pats me on the shoulder. "I gotta get going, but it was nice running into you. You too, Cash." Artie waves and walks off in the direction of the stage.

"I've been dying to ask about Finn and Sawyer." I can't hold in my curiosity a moment longer. I didn't get a chance to ask Jack if Wade was planning to sign them.

"They're really good," he says. "Got down some tracks at the studio the other day. It's looking good."

I know Wade booked them, but I wanted to make sure it wasn't out of pure desperation.

"Makes me happy to see something good happen for them," I say.

"Don't get too excited, Wade hasn't signed them." Cash knocks me off my cloud.

"What do you mean he hasn't signed them?" I say, incredulous.

"Exactly what I said." Cash crosses his arms over his chest.

"I hand deliver you these incredibly talented brothers, and you don't lock them down?" Usually, I stay out of these things, but Wade is making a mistake, and this must be rectified.

"Take it up with Wade and Adam." Cash raises his eyebrows, but not at me. I turn to see what he's looking at.

"Why is she taking pictures of me?" Cash points at Sasha who peers at us from behind her camera.

"Sorry, I'm Sasha." She reaches her hand out and Cash takes it, his grip lasts a beat too long to be casual.

"You're beautiful," Sasha says as she studies him. She motions to the setting sun behind us that casts oranges and pinks into the clouds.

Cash doesn't seem to know what to say. "Thanks?" He cocks his head slightly, confusion obvious in his expression.

"Artistically speaking." Sasha studies his face. "There is a lot going on behind your eyes," she says frankly, as if she's peering right inside of him. I'm not sure I see what Sasha sees. I've known Cash for a while now, and he doesn't let many people in. There are a lot of things Cash wouldn't talk to me about. I let it be because I'm not in the business of exposing someone's secrets. It was Jack's book, not Cash's.

"I've seen her Instagram," I interject. "She takes great portraits."

"I'm studying photojournalism in school," Sasha explains. "I like photographing people the most, but landscapes and anything else interesting is good too." Sasha is more at home behind a camera than she is in front of it, I've noticed. She's more confident behind the lens.

"I work with a local artist who takes photographs of musicians, paints over them and uses them to make screen prints for posters," Cash explains.

"Oh, are you an artist too?" Sasha asks.

Cash clears his throat. "No, I own a record store," he explains.

"That's nice." She looks at him expectantly as if she's waiting for him to elaborate.

"I sell the posters in my store," Cash further clarifies.

"Cash was the bassist in *Mogo* with Jack," I say, trying to help him out, but his eyes fling daggers at me. I stifle a laugh.

"Oh! Jack O'Donnell." Sasha looks over at me appreciatively. "He's amazing."

"Okay, well, I gotta get going." Cash shoves his hands in his pockets. "I have a record store to manage after all."

"Is Daphne back in town?" I ask before he leaves.

"She permanently moved back to London." He has a forlorn look in his eye.

"Who's managing the shop?" I ask concerned.

"No one. I closed it for the day so I could be here." Cash doesn't sound happy about that.

"You need to look into hiring someone," I scold him.

"Daphne just up and left," Cash explains. "Ever since her brother died, things haven't been right with her." He clasps the back of his neck, rubbing it.

"I could help out," Sasha offers, suddenly. "I'm home for the summer, and I have time."

Cash looks at her skeptically.

"I didn't mean to put you on the spot," Sasha says and then bites her lip. "It's just a suggestion. Never mind, it's fine. I'm sure you have it all figured out."

"I can't pay much," Cash says, stopping her from leaving.

"Do I have to wear short skirts or show off my cleavage?" Sasha raises her eyebrows in question.

Cash's eyes get big.

"It was just a joke," she smiles. "I've worked in some sleazy bars in the past." I watch as Cash relaxes.

"Anyway, if you need help, Erin knows how to get in touch with me." She holds onto her camera and peers through the lens at Cash, snapping another photo and smiles innocently.

Sasha looks anything but innocent right now.

The sun went down hours ago. *Trancelucid* is on the main stage performing right now. Heavy bass pours from the speakers in waves, vibrating against my skin. The VIP area is packed, and I haven't been able to find Jack yet.

A platform spans the stage's width, so close to the artists you could reach out and high five them. I peer over and look at the area in front of the stage. Earlier today, I walked across that field with Jack while he held my hand. Now it's a sea of people, lit up, dancing collectively, and it's mesmerizing. A girl next to me, wearing what looks to be a bikini, dances with light whips. Tentacles of bright colors snake around her body as she moves.

From the platform I look behind me, only seeing abandoned beer cups and food tents. In the distance, a familiar form is walking through the crowd, but as he gets closer, I can tell it's not Jack. My skin prickles with irritation, but also with worry. I know he's been on edge lately and that makes me nervous.

I check my phone, but I already know before holding it up, Jack hasn't called or messaged me. I've been here by myself for longer than

I should be. Anger and hurt tells me I should leave and not look back, but my instincts are telling me something different.

Instead of calling Jack, I schedule an Uber and begin to make my way through the crowd. Because of the festival, drivers are already nearby, and I don't have to wait long for mine to show up. When I get to the street, I make sure I'm getting in the right car. I cross my arms over my chest and stare out the window. The lights and sounds of the festival fade into the distance, making way for the city as it comes into view.

This is not my city.

It never was.

I'm trying to rationalize why I keep doing this to myself on the ride over, hoping that when I get to the studio, Jack's car won't be there and there is some other explanation as to why he didn't show up tonight.

As we pull in, the black Audi is the only car in the parking lot, and that familiar ache expands in my chest. I want to understand him, but I fear this is something I can't help him with.

The back door is unlocked, and when I enter the studio, the halls are dark. The sound of my shoes hitting the tiles echoes off the walls. It looks empty, but I know he's here. I can feel it, the hairs on the back of my neck lifting. The lights are off in each room I pass until I get to the end of the hall and turn the corner. It's not the light coming from the room that lets me know where Jack is, it's her voice.

The song is both haunting and beautiful.

My hand is on the doorknob, but I don't know if I can go in there, not knowing if I want to face what's inside. On the other side of that door is the man I am painfully in love with. That same man is teetering on the edge of a crevasse and I'm afraid I won't be able to pull him back or I will go over the edge with him.

When I get the nerve to open the door, Jack is sitting in a chair in front of the mixing board, a notebook lay open on his knee and there's a pencil between his teeth. At the sound of the door opening, he turns to look at me and flips a switch to turn off the song. I find it hard to read his expression, whether he is shocked to see me or if he was expecting me.

He looks strung out or like he hasn't slept. When he doesn't speak, I fill in the silence.

"I waited for you." I stand in the doorway.

He pulls the pencil from his mouth like he would a cigarette.

"Shit, I'm sorry," he curses.

"Jack?" I step forward. "What's going on?" I'm pissed, but something has been going on with him lately. I think for a moment that his erratic behavior has to do with his sobriety, so I give him the benefit of the doubt tonight.

He holds the palm of his hand for me to come to him as if he needs me to breathe, and like gravity pulling me, I move across the room until I am sitting on his lap. His forehead rests against my chest and he breathes me in as he wraps his arms around me. I can't help but run my fingers through his hair tenderly, wanting to make everything alright.

I lean down and place a kiss on the top of his head. His hands are like steel grips on my body, a man holding on for dear life as if I am his life preserver. I continue to brush his hair with my fingers, trying to understand him and willing him to talk to me. Slowly, he brings his lips close to mine, his hands circle my face, fingers wrapping around the strands of my hair as he brushes his lips against mine. It's a tentative kiss, with soft lips, a deep connection coursing through the thinnest of barriers. An intoxicating rush flows through me. His hands roam over my body, grabbing my waist and holding me tight as he deepens the kiss. It's as if he is looking for a way to crawl inside of me. Deeper and deeper I fall, stepping off the edge with him. I feel him unzipping my shorts, his hand stretching the denim material as it slides down between my legs.

I shift away but his fingers skim over the thin material of my panties, sparking a need within me I can't ignore. My hips move to meet him, and I grab his lower lip between my teeth. He groans and I am lost in him.

His fingers dig into my skin desperately. I love it when he loses control. It is the only time he lets his guard down, and I crave it almost as much as I crave him.

The high I'm on won't last. I know this deep down.

I am not making him forget about anyone.

I am only forgetting myself.

The studio comes into focus as I open my eyes. I'm at the studio, not at the festival, and Jack hasn't explained himself to me. The song I heard before I opened the door lingers in my mind.

I am falling over the edge into that crevasse with him, and I fear I will lose myself when he rests his forehead against mine. I breathe him in, the smell of his soap mixed with cigarettes and bubble gum.

"Fuck, Erin, I love you." Jack's words pierce my skin like a knife, sinking deep.

Those words wake me up inside and clear the fog from my brain. I realize I can't do this to myself anymore. I know where this road leads, and I am not willing to give up who I am.

"Stop." I push away from him.

"Erin?" The look in his eyes and my name on his lips break my heart.

"I can't do this anymore, Jack." I stand up and collect myself.

"Can't do what?" he says from behind me, and I sigh.

"Whatever this is." I face him and see the disappointment in his face. He looks like he's barely holding himself together, his life raft gone, and I don't know if it's all because of me. That's the problem.

"This is us, Erin." He motions to the space between us.

Space.

"This is you and me."

Externally, I straighten my back and square my shoulders. "I'm worth more than taking a back seat in your life." Internally, my body is threatening to crumble out from under me.

"I just told you I love you," Jack says in confusion, as if those three words have the power to excuse anything. The angular features of his face seem contorted with the shadows in the room.

I can feel the tears well in my eyes. "When you love someone, you give a piece of yourself away. You don't have any more pieces to give, Jack." It breaks my heart to say it, but I have to.

The confusion on Jack's face turns to realization.

"This is about Mia," Jack says rather than asks. I watch as a wall erects around him, brick by brick.

"Of course, it is, Jack. Look at where you are." I motion to the reel of tape and the photos of Mia on the wall. I'm tired of being silent, tired of putting his feelings before mine. I've been more than gracious, giving him the time he needs to let go of the past on his own, but I can't be silent anymore.

"This is not a place for you to tell me you love me," I explain to him, shocked that he doesn't already know this.

The expression on his face changes from shock to shame.

"When my brother died, the grief consumed my parents. It's all they could feel, and there wasn't any room left for them to love *me*." Saying it out loud is like an affirmation; the feeling in my heart all of these years becoming tangible.

"It's not like that," Jack says, but that's a lie he's telling himself.

"I can't play second to another ghost." I know it's harsh, but it's how I feel.

"I've never compared you to her." His voice is quiet and broken.

"You didn't have to," I quip. "When you look at me, Jack, who do you see? Because sometimes I don't know, and it scares the shit out of me." He backs away from me, running his hand through his hair in frustration and leans against the sound board. I don't know what's going through his head right now, but I wish he would tell me.

"Don't let the tabloids fill your head with garbage," he tells me.

"This isn't about a stupid tabloid photo," I try to explain. "You know when I first realized it?" I ask, not expecting a response. "When I found you at the *Lamplight* playing *Layla*." I feel this profound sadness whenever I think of it because I know when he plays, he's thinking of her, and it is not something he and I will ever share. "*Layla*, Jack. I know what that song is about, and you playing it says way more than you are willing to admit." I shake my head.

Jack takes in my words, and I know they pierce through his armor. It hurts me to say them. His silence is deafening.

"You say you love me but you don't even let me get close to you." He keeps me at a distance. We have a connection, that's apparent, but there's a space inside of his heart.

Jack's eyes swim, emotion burning in those blue depths. I can tell he's conflicted, trapped between the past and the present, and I hate everything about this.

"It's not that simple and you know it, Erin. Don't make this about Mia." He looks as though he wants to reach for me, and I'm afraid if he does, I will crumble.

I love him.

When you love someone, you will do *anything*, give up *anything*, just to have them, even when you shouldn't. There is only so much I can take. Jack is worth fighting for, but so am I.

I don't want to lose pieces of myself that I can't afford to give away.

"You are allowed to love Mia, to miss her. I'm not asking you to choose," I try to reassure him, but I'm so angry my body is vibrating. "But *I* choose me." I bite out the words.

"You don't know what I'm feeling," he says angrily.

"Because you don't tell me!"

"I can't." The anguish on his face is apparent and he slams a fist down onto the soundboard, rattling the notebook.

"You think I can't handle it, but I can," I tell him.

"I don't want to hurt you." His eyes are so full of remorse when he says this, but it isn't enough. Jack paces, his hands running over his face as if to wipe away the pain.

"You're already hurting me. Don't you see that?" I raise my voice.

"Look at what I do to the people I love, Erin." He gestures to me, to this room. This is bigger than just Jack and I. "You want me to tell you that I want to stick a needle in my vein to stop the pain," he bares his arm to me, anguish on his face, "to stop the guilt. You want to see this?" He shows me his shaking hand. "You want to see this side of me?"

"I want to see all of you," I tell him.

"You don't, Erin. Because if you did, you wouldn't want me anymore," he confesses.

"Try me!" I beg him. "Open up to me. Be vulnerable for once, because I fucking deserve that."

I stand on one side of the studio while he is on the other. The space between us might as well be miles. When he doesn't move, doesn't say anything, it is the last straw. I'm giving him an opening to talk to me, and he won't.

"I have to go." I start to walk away.

"I told you when we first met that you couldn't handle my story." His words hit me, hard. "You chose to write it, you chose to know the truth, all of it, all of me," his hands rest against his chest for emphasis, "now you're walking away." He raises his voice, the sound vibrating against my skin. Everything about this breaks my heart, but I have to do what is right for me, for once. I've been put in the backseat for far too long.

It doesn't make a difference if he loves me, because it's not about him or how he feels, it's about me.

I matter.

"You're goddamn right I'm walking away, Jack!" I yell at him. "You didn't show up at the concert, so here I am, chasing after you again, and for what?"

"You don't understand. I just needed..." he starts to say but I cut him off.

"Someone else besides me," I finish for him. "If you're hurting, I should be the one you run to, not her," I gesture to the picture of Mia on the wall.

Jack shakes his head. "That's not what this is." Even he isn't convinced as I stare at him in disbelief.

"Bullshit, Jack," I spit out. "You're running to a ghost, someone who's not even here anymore, but I am. I am right here in front of you! So get your shit together and figure out what you want, because I deserve better."

I can see the tears in his eyes, the tremble of his hands, and the lump in his throat. He is an ocean, rolling in turmoil. I can see he is on precipice, a man on the edge, but I cannot be his anchor.

"You're hurting but that's not an excuse." I take another step towards the door.

"Erin, please don't leave like this," he pleads, moving towards me, and I let him. His face etched in torment as he lays his palms against both of my cheeks. They don't affect me like I thought they would. I know that I am worth more than this, and I want him to see it. I want him to see *me*.

I grip his forearms, not pushing them away, but holding him in place. He breathes into me, resting his forehead against mine. His lips are out of focus, but I can see them tremble with all the pain and need he has pent up inside. He's like a bomb ticking away, ready to explode.

"You want me, Jack?" I ask him, feeling the heat of his breath, the strain of his muscles as he works to hold himself together.

"Yes," he whispers.

"Then fucking earn me." I push him away and walk to the door.

"Fuck. Erin!" I hear him yell as I head into the hallway.

From behind me I hear something crash against the wall, causing me to jump. When I get outside, I slump against the brick wall, my legs shaking, and I pull out my phone. I don't want to leave him like this because I'm afraid of what he might do. He's been pushed too far, but he needed it. It's up to him now. I call the one person I know will be able to help him.

19

Just a Girl

JACK

When Erin walks out the door, it breaks something inside of me. Yet another thing I have managed to destroy. I rest my face inside my palms, breathing in the sweat and cigarettes that permeates my skin. This is why I don't let people in.

I pick up one of the mics and throw it against the wall. The metal collides with drywall and breaks apart, pieces flying in different directions.

"Fuck!" I yell to no one, kicking the chair out from under me and looking around for anything else I can destroy.

There have been a thousand times over the last six years that I wanted to get high. When I think about it, my heart begins to beat rapidly and saliva pools in my mouth, followed by such a deep seeded hate for myself I want to rip off my own skin.

I am tired of fighting it.

Mia was the only thing stopping me all these years, but now all she does is torment me.

It occurs to me that Mia is the reason I can't move on. She is the reason I couldn't make things work with Amber, and now she's fucking things up with Erin. She's like a disease eating away at my organs until there is nothing left of me. It's like the love I have for her has turned sour, congealing and rotting inside of me.

I keep coming back here.

I keep trying to make this album work.

I am drowning in my own sea of recklessness.

I pick up my water bottle and throw it across the room, hitting one of the pictures of Mia, breaking the glass. Tiny shards scatter all over the floor like lethal diamonds.

"Stop fucking punishing me!" I yell at the photo that's hanging precariously on the wall, tilted on its axis, just the way I feel. My guilt has me in knots, and just when I try to move on, to leave the past behind, it grabs ahold of my throat and suffocates me. Mia is all around me as if she never left. The pictures, the album, the jeans... even the fucking dent in my wall. I can't seem to let her go, no matter how much I want to.

It's like I have these ropes around my wrists preventing me from touching and feeling the life that I should be living. Wherever I go, she's the ghost in the room, and I want to exorcise her from my life. In front of me, nestled onto the analogue machine are the reels that hold vibrations of my voice and Mia's voice, frozen in time on those magnetic strips. The only way to edit a reel is to slice it with a razor and attach it to another strip. Once you cut it, there is no going back. It is irreversible.

If I want to exorcise these demons, I will start with the source. I reach for the round metal casing of magnetic tape, and I rip it from its sleeve with utter disregard of its fragility.

"Try to release this fucking album now!" My hands are shaking, and I can barely pull the tape from the wheel, tearing at it and watching as it unravels onto the floor. I take the empty metal wheel and throw it at the door.

"Jack!" I hear my name faintly through the blood pumping in my ears. The pounding in my head is like a jackhammer as I kneel against the floor feeling spent.

Familiar hands grip my shoulders. "What the fuck are you doing?"

I look up to see Cash kneeling in front of me, concern and outrage on his face.

"Go away." I slump back on the floor feeling like I'm going to break apart at any moment. My body is having a physical reaction to my mental state. I am fighting with everything I have to stay in this studio, even if I have to burn it to the ground. There is a small part of me that wants to stay sober because there's not just my promise to Mia at stake. I finally got my kid back, and if I continue down this road, I will lose her and I will lose Erin too.

"What did you do to the tapes?" I watch as he picks up the mangled pile on the floor with a horrified expression.

"What did you do, Jack?!" Cash lifts his eyes, balling my shirt into his fist as he lets the shredded tape fall through his fingers.

"Fuck the album!" I say defiantly, my face inches from his. I can smell alcohol on his breath and my stomach aches.

"Why do you have to destroy everything that is good in your life?" Cash releases me, sadness and disgust evident in his eyes.

I laugh. "You think that's what I do?" I brace myself against the soundboard so I can stand.

"Look at you!" he yells, motioning to me with his hand. His eyes wander over my disheveled appearance. "You're fucking jonesing and you look like shit."

"Fuck off!" He's right, but fuck him.

"You just destroyed the only thing left of Mia." He pushes me. "Why the fuck would you do that?" Tears pool, threatening to spill over, and it momentarily pulls me out of my own head.

"Why do you care about this album?" I push him back, focused solely on trying to figure him out.

A cloud covers his face, and he shuts down. "Fuck off, Jack." He walks away from me. I'm not about to let him get away that easy.

"You keep that record store afloat because you can't give it up either," I tell him. "You're a prisoner too."

"Shut up!" He turns to face me.

"Just fucking burn it down. That's what you should do," I tell him.

"Don't, Jack," Cash warns me.

"The only reason you keep it is because of that mural Mia painted."

I call him out, knowing Mia holds him back too, and I don't understand why he isn't as angry at her as I am. We never talk about it, this elephant in the room between us, for fear that our friendship will come unglued.

Mia will always be the crack in the ice that our friendship stands on. If I push him too hard, the ice will break, and we'll both go under.

Right now, I want to pull him under the water and drown in this sea of misery with me.

"You don't know shit about what I went through, what *we* went through!" He's referring to the life he had with Mia before I fucked it up.

It's true. I don't know anything about what their life was like. It was a topic Mia refused to talk about, so I let it be.

"It's always about you and Mia. You and your fucking book!" Cash turns away from me.

"Now the truth comes out." I bite out a laugh. After all these years, I knew Cash was still angry with me.

"Fucking ego." He runs his hands through his hair in frustration. "Not everything is about you." I can see the turmoil on his face. I'm not helping the situation either because he's right, all I can see is my own pain.

"We had a life, Jack. It wasn't perfect, but it was ours, until you fucking called." He slams his fist onto the table, rattling the empty cups on top.

"You still blame me." It's what I carry around with me every day. I welcome it. I want him to hate me because that's what I deserve. It's as if everyone has gone on with their life, time passing like these wounds are healed, but I can't forget a fucking moment. I am trapped in a spider's web while everyone else is free.

"That's just it, Jack," Cash's eyes swim with emotion. "I don't." He breaks down, his knees hitting the floor, his face in his palms.

I hate everything about this.

"I don't blame you for what happened," he sobs.

It makes me angry. He should blame me. Why doesn't he hate me?

"Fuck you, Cash!" I push him until he falls back onto his elbows. He moves forward quickly catching me off guard and tackles me. I desperately try to grab ahold of him, but his legs are keeping my hands from making contact. He manages to get me in a headlock, keeping me in place, but I connect my knee with his side, and he lets go with a whoosh of breath. I take the opportunity to push him down, but he rolls over and kicks my legs out from under me. I lunge for him, and we wrestle on the floor trapping each other in holds that are futile because exhaustion takes over. I can't fight anymore. Let him beat the shit out of me; I deserve it.

"You think it's easy for me to forgive you, to not *blame* you?" His voice is broken and out of breath. He releases me with a force like a punch. We are both lying on the floor, panting.

"I hate myself more than I hate you." He rolls himself to sit up.

"You should fucking hate me. You should hate me for everything." I push myself up.

"I hate you for destroying those tapes," he points at the reels.

"Why? You have nothing invested in them." I turn to look at him as if something in his face will give me a clue.

Cash is silent for a moment, his chest rising and falling with each breath. He closes his eyes. "When we were together, she wrote all those songs," he turns to me, "they were like messages she wouldn't allow herself to say directly to you." His confession hits me like a Mack truck. "After she left, I wouldn't talk to her. I never gave her the chance..." He trails off.

I understand now. All the things I wanted to say to her but couldn't, I poured into my music. When I heard a song on the radio that someone else was singing, I knew which ones were hers.

The realization hits me deep inside. All this time, I had no idea Cash was waiting for me to release the album, hoping there was something Mia had written, a hidden message for him. Now I'm the asshole that took something away from him, again.

"She wrote a lot of songs. If there was a message in there for you, I didn't know about it." I admit.

"Fuck, Jack!" He swats at the destroyed tape as he stands up.

I look at the mangled mess on the floor and realize that's exactly how I feel. Mangled. It's true; I do fuck up everything in my life.

"What the fuck is it about her? She's just a girl. One fucking girl." I push myself off the ground and place my hands on the soundboard to steady myself.

"She wasn't just a girl," Cash says as he stands beside me.

I hang my head. "I just want to be free."

"You gotta let her go, Jack," Cash tells me.

"I don't know how," I admit.

"You don't want to." Maybe that's true.

I put my head in my hands. "I don't want to let her go."

"You can't have a relationship with Erin if you don't let Mia go." Every word he says is true. I know this deep down. "Erin was right to leave. You know that, don't you?" Why does he make so much fucking sense right now? Erin doesn't deserve this, and I don't know how to make things right.

"How did you do it all these years?" I ask him.

"Anger eats away at you, the same way guilt does," Cash explains. "I don't want to live like that."

"I don't understand." I shake my head. "The store?" If he'd let things go a long time ago, then why does he keep that store open? Why doesn't he move on with someone else?

As if he knows what I'm thinking, he says, "It's not about Mia." He doesn't elaborate, and I won't push him.

Cash is quiet for a moment and then he says, "You like to avoid things," he tells me. "When you keep pushing things down, eventually they bubble up to the top."

"I feel guilty," I confess.

"There are a lot of variables at play. I know this because I thought a lot about it over the years," Cash admits. "She was on that freeway, but it wasn't *you* who was drunk. It wasn't *you* who ran into her," Cash says as he looks at me.

"That's not the guilt I'm referring to." Maybe it was at first, but the pain dulled over the years. Now it's like the wound is ripped open again.

Cash gives me an inquisitive look.

"I fell in love with Erin," I meant it when I told Erin I loved her. How could I ever think that I could hide these dark feelings inside of me from her?

"You're not betraying Mia by falling in love with Erin," Cash explains. I know this in my head, but my heart is telling me something different.

I nod. "I loved two people at the same time before, and it didn't end well."

"This is not the same thing." He's right.

"You have a chance to be happy again. Take it." The pain in his eyes tells a story of something deeper than just losing Mia, something I will never understand.

"I don't know how." I have known brief moments of true happiness, but they slip through my fingers like sand.

"Do what you do best," Cash replies and smiles.

"What's that?" I lift my chin.

"Say goodbye to her in a song." The writer's block I'm suffering from is taunting me.

"Sounds like we both need to say goodbye." I have a feeling Cash's goodbye is deeper than I realize.

The need I felt earlier to get high has been replaced with the need to make music.

"I don't want to fucking be here anymore!" Cash yells at me, throwing the notebook across the room. It skitters across the floor and slides into the wall.

We're both wrecked.

The coffee ran out hours ago, and I think we are going mental from lack of sleep. Cash buries his face in the palms of his hands. His elbows are propped up on his thighs, and although I know how hard this is for him, I can feel it in my bones that this is right.

This is the process.

The creation of something significant is not without suffering.

"I'm not a song writer!" Cash argues, standing to pace the studio for what seems like the hundredth time.

I pick up the notebook and place it on the table next to a dozen paper cups laced with remnants of stale coffee. We've written a few verses, but it's not a song yet.

"That's because you won't let yourself go," I tell him. Writing has always been like therapy for me.

"What the fuck does that mean?" Cash glares at me.

"You gotta bleed." I poke his chest to bring home the point.

"*You* fucking bleed!" he replies angrily and pushes my hand away.

"Every fucking day, dude," I tell him.

"Why do you want to torture me?" Cash asks as he shakes his head.

"Because I need you," I tell him sincerely. He looks back at me, waiting for me to say something sarcastic, but I don't. Cash is my brother. He challenges me, tells me things I don't want to hear, puts up with my bullshit, and I need him. I need him in my life like I need to breathe.

"Write it down." I hand him the notebook. "Write an amazing fucking song and let go of all this shit."

Cash looks at me doubtfully but grabs the notebook and pen from the table.

"You're a fucking asshole," he grumbles. "You know that?"

"Yeah," I smile. "I know.

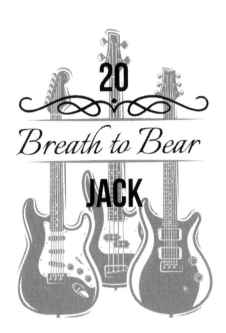

20

Breath to Bear

JACK

As much as both of us wanted to leave, neither one of us does. It's almost as if it's a challenge now, the last man standing. Who can take the most pain without crumbling? I nodded off for a bit, and when I opened my eyes, Cash was holding the pen between his teeth and had a guitar on his lap. I wrote a couple of verses, but they were nowhere near done. Cash was struggling, having never written a song before. Peering over at him, unaware, I can see the focus in his eyes as he stares at the words in the notebook, almost manic, and I wonder if he slept at all.

"Hey, check this out." He motions to me, not breaking eye contact with the notebook, his fingers on the strings, playing around with the melody.

I can see my handwriting on the paper and then below it, Cash's. It looks as though he's scratched out and re-written words more times than the paper can handle, tearing through in spots as if the paper couldn't handle the force of his lyrics. As I scan the words, a smile slowly spreads across my face.

Breath to Bear
Help me breakthrough
Love the torture
I'm going under
The influence of you
Every breath
If you dare
I'm like a martyr
Just a girl, but she's
My breath to bear

There are two verses with a slow build up and then the chorus hits hard and dramatic. The cadence stays strong until the end. I wanted to write a song about two different people trying to break free from the same torture, but Cash took it to another level. If people don't get chills when they hear this, they're fucking heartless, because even I have goosebumps on my arms.

We lay down a very rough track and with every word, every note, it feels like little pieces of Mia are carried away with them, and my chest feels lighter.

"Fucking amazing," I whisper as I hit the last chord.

Cash looks like he might fall off the stool.

"Go get some sleep," I tell him, setting my guitar down. "I'll call Bret to get the engineers in to record soon."

"There's just one problem." Cash looks at the destroyed master tapes on the floor.

I have a lot of regrets in my life, things I did out of spite or anger, and this is one of them. Maybe I can salvage this. I don't know. I do know that when Cash unstraps his bass and looks at me with brotherly love, it's all I could ever need. There's a silent acknowledgment between us that this is what healing looks like. Sometimes you have to confront your demons in order to release them. All along I thought it was writing the book, but I should have known that only the music in my heart had the power to release me.

"Hey," Cash calls over his shoulder as he packs up his gear. "Don't be an idiot."

"When have I ever been an idiot?" I barely have the energy to smirk.

"You need to fix things with Erin," he commands.

I hang my head and pinch my nose, nodding. "I will, when I'm ready." Writing one song doesn't make me the person Erin deserves.

He nods in acknowledgment, understanding etched in the lines on his face.

I look at Cash and I see someone who has loved me at my worst, who loved Mia when I was not able to, and I do not deserve his loyalty, but I will do my best to be his friend.

I think about Erin and everything she has given up for me, and all the things she has never asked of me. Erin shouldn't have to tell me how to love her, I should already know. I haven't done a good job of that. Maybe Erin is right, and I don't have any pieces of myself left to give.

"I just have one more thing to do." My expression is somber.

"What do you need?" Cash asks without hesitation, even though he has already given me so much.

"Nah, I gotta do this myself." Cash puts his hand on my back as we walk out of the studio together. The sun is up and in my fucking eyes, so I pull out my sunglasses.

"It's too fucking sunny here," I say, laughing.

"I like the sun," Cash says as he lifts his leg over the seat of his Harley and hits the throttle. The machine comes to life, rattling beneath him, the sound much louder in the quiet of the early morning.

"Cash," I call to him. He turns to look at me, his sunglasses falling down his nose. "Thank you," I say.

He nods and hits the clutch, shifting into first as he rides off.

I pull my phone out of my pocket. "Bret? I know it's early," I pause to listen as he reprimands me about waking him up. "No, I am not in jail," I say, rolling my eyes at his presumption. "Listen, call the boys, we have a song to record. Book it for tomorrow; I need to get some sleep." In a gutsy move, I say as fast as I can, "By the way, I destroyed the master tapes," and hang up quickly.

I put my phone on silent and shove it in my back pocket and throw the guitar in the back seat of my car.

When I get home, I set everything down in the kitchen. I'm so tired I feel lightheaded. I have unfinished business, but my body has given out on me, and I collapse onto the bed fully dressed, shoes and all. When my cheek hits the mattress, I drift away willingly into the darkness.

When I open my eyes again, my bedroom is shrouded in darkness. I'm still on top of my sheets, fully dressed, sprawled out on my back. It takes me a moment to come back to reality, the gravity of everything crashing down upon me, and my mind takes a moment to catch up. Scratching my head and trying to rub the sleep from my eyes, I head into the bathroom to freshen up.

I look at myself in the mirror. I haven't shaved in a few days and my jawline is rough with stubble. My hair is a bit too long over my ears and it curls at the nape of my neck. I brush my teeth and splash water on my face to wash the sleep away.

I put on a pot of coffee and ease myself onto the stool at the kitchen island, my face in my hands, elbows propped on the granite. I let out a cleansing breath, and think about our song, about Cash, about Mia, and especially about Erin.

I know Erin is scared, and she has every right not to trust me with her feelings. I don't make it easy on anyone, and the thought of losing her haunts me. I was so scared to let her in, to tell her what I had been going through because I thought it would hurt her, but I already accomplished that. Now it's time to fix things, to be the man worthy of someone like Erin.

Lust can sometimes disguise itself as love. It consumes you, drives you mad, turns you into a person you can't look at in the mirror. I loved Mia; we had a bond that was so strong we couldn't see past it. We didn't want to see the truth that was right in front of us. Sometimes you can love someone to the point of madness. It becomes corrupted, a black mold growing out of control until it's too late. I would have burned down the world for her and I nearly did. Falling in love with Erin made me realize that love is not meant to destroy; it's meant to create.

I wanted to *create* a world with Erin and that's when I knew I had fallen in love with her. It happened so easily that I didn't recognize it until I'd seen her in the studio and all I wanted to do was to drown in her, to hold onto her as if she were a buoy in the rolling ocean that was my heart.

How could I so effortlessly fall in love with someone else?

This is why I need to bury my past, because if I don't, it will consume me, and I will lose Erin for good.

I pour a cup of coffee, walk out onto the patio and down the steps to my backyard. The bistro lights have turned on, illuminating the chairs I have set up around the firepit. It's a nice clear night and I can see the outlines of people on the beach, the distant sound of street music on the boardwalk, and the smell of a nearby barbecue.

I throw some lighter fluid on the moist wood to make sure it burns good. I hit the flint of my lighter and the wood immediately catches fire, causing tall orange flames to send embers into the night sky. The flames die down to a soft glow until the whole piece of wood is engulfed and pulses with heat.

I walk back into the house, passing the dent in my wall that I can't ever seem to fix, and I know where I need to start. I head into the bedroom and pull open my dresser drawer. I stare at the jeans, blinking away the fear and the remorse. I pull them out, the black writing now faded and barely legible. They are soft to the touch, and I clutch them in my hands as if they will disappear. I recount all the times I have stood here, bringing them to my nose and wishing they still smelled of her.

I tuck them under my arm, taking them outside with me. As I sink into the chair, I lay my head back and close my eyes. I begin to form a mental picture of her; dark hair surrounding her face, the braid hidden inside the waves, and those hazel eyes always seeing right into me. Her slender wrist rises causing a stack of bracelets to chime together as she tucks a stray piece of hair behind her ear. I can start to see the freckles on her face, dotting the bridge of her nose and fanning out to her cheeks. Her smile, making me feel monumentally loved, like no one has ever loved me before. I can see the understanding in her eyes, telling me that it's okay to let her go.

My cheeks are wet with tears I didn't even realize had escaped my eyes. In all these years, I have never cried for her, fearing if I did, I wouldn't be able to stop. It's okay to cry now.

I have gold records and Grammys that I worked my ass off to get, but the one possession that matters most to me in this world is clutched to my chest right now. It's all that mattered to me back when Mia and I first moved to L.A. When that shitty-ass van was stolen, I thought we would never see these jeans again.

Somehow, they found their way back to us, and it was a fucking miracle. I took it as a sign that we were meant to be together. In my mind, I can see her wearing them, sitting on my front porch and looking devastatingly beautiful and broken. My dark angel. If I try hard enough, I can still smell her in the fibers, vanilla and patchouli, but I know it's just my imagination.

In between shaky breaths I whisper a goodbye, but I feel in my heart that even if I didn't say it out loud, she would still be able to hear me, "I will always love you, but I have to let you go." I can't live in the past anymore. The memories I have are in my head and in my heart, not in these jeans. Keeping them in my drawer won't bring her back. It's not preserving her memory; it's only stopping me from making new ones. I crumple the time-worn material in my hands and bring them to my lips and then I let go.

Each spark that flies into the sky carries a memory with it. My fingers wrapped around her ankle, the way the sharpie bled into the denim, the words I wrote, coasting into L.A. on fumes, playing my guitar on the street corner, living in the squat, performing in clubs, the day we got signed by *Left Turn*, and the day I found out I was going to be a father. This is the path I walked, and those memories are my foot-prints upon this Earth.

Mia made an imprint on me that can never be removed, but that doesn't mean I can't move on and try to be a better person for someone else.

21

Sweet Home Chicago

ERIN

"Hey, I'm glad I can repay the favor," Sasha says, as she lays out a blanket and pillow for me on the spare bed.

When I arrived at Sasha's grandparents' house, I didn't expect it to be so stately. It's not that it's a mansion, but it's the sprawling acres that impressed me. She described it as a ranch, which made me think of a few tumbleweeds floating by in a dirt backyard. I did not expect horses, sheep, and a chicken coop, against the backdrop of the Sierra Nevada's.

I try to hide the pain behind my eyes as I lay my bag on top of the mattress, but I didn't have anywhere else to go. After I left Jack, I didn't want to be alone in a hotel room. I felt bad about disrupting Sasha and her grandparents in the middle of the night, but they were very nice about it.

I haven't booked a flight because I think I'm afraid to leave.

I'm tired of being alone.

"Thank you," I tell her.

"If you want to talk about it, I'm a good listener," Sasha says as she sits on the bed opposite of me.

"Do you ever feel like you were meant to cross paths with someone for a reason?" If I hadn't run into her at the bar, I don't know where I would be right now. I wouldn't have had the adventure I did, or made such a wonderful friend.

"I do," She answers, looking at me thoughtfully.

"I don't want to be a pain in the ass," I laugh.

"Please, I made you drive 1300 miles, so that makes me the bigger pain in the ass," she laughs.

"Oh, and let's not forget that you got me the gig of a lifetime at that festival. I have so many awesome photos." She pulls out her laptop and starts to flip through them.

She tilts the screen so I can look with her. There are shots of the empty stages and some with engineers setting everything up. I like the candid shots she took of some of the artists doing meet and greets with fans. The shots of the nighttime shows are the most vivid. She managed to capture the chaos of the crowd, the emotion of the music, and the passion of the artists. The candid shots of Cash though are the ones I linger on the most. I think she's right; he is beautiful, and I can see it so clearly in her photos.

She flips to a photo I didn't even know she took of me and Jack. We are standing close to each other near the coffee truck. Jack is looking down at our hands linked together. Sasha must have taken the picture before she reached us. I peer down at my own hands as if I expect to see our fingers intertwined, but they are empty.

"I'm sorry," she says as she clicks past the photo.

I push my back against the headboard.

"I thought I could be enough for him," I say. "But I'm not." I shake my head.

"I shouldn't have said what I said," she starts to say, "about making him forget her." Her expression is somber. "I didn't know it was Jack. That was insensitive. I was a big fan of Mia's. She was so talented."

I wave her off. "Don't be silly," I tell her. "You didn't know."

"It was insensitive either way."

"He told me he loved me," I whisper as I turn towards Sasha.

"Wow."

"It should have made me happy," I tell her. "But whenever he's upset, instead of running to me, he runs to her." Her presence is all over that studio.

"Do you love him?" Sasha asks, causing me to look in her direction. Bracelets dangle from her wrist, banging together, making music.

"Yeah." I nod. I am so in love with him, scars and all. I think I love him because of his scars. All of that pain and guilt make him who he is. That's who I fell in love with.

"He's not a bad person," I say, more to convince myself than to Sasha.

"I hate to think that people are truly bad or good," she says. "They just make choices. Sometimes people just don't make the right ones."

I like the thought of that.

"What are you going to do now? Go back to New York?" Sasha asks.

"No." I shake my head. In this moment I know exactly what I need to do. I turn my phone back on and book the next flight to Chicago.

I am standing at the lakeshore with the wind whipping my hair around my face. It's summer and the air is humid, but the breeze is a promise of a coming storm. In the distance I can see the Chicago skyline, the unmistakable architecture rising in bold modern and gothic patterns. Boats rock back and forth in their slips as joggers use the path that lines the shore.

The nearby lighthouse that I used to visit as a kid, peeks out from above the trees. The beach is packed with people, and the sound of an ice cream truck nearby is enticing. I let out a long breath and close my eyes, taking in the smell and the sounds. So familiar, yet so distant. My heart feels heavy, full of emotion that I have a hard time breathing.

There is nothing like coming home.

I take a seat on one of the benches in front of the shore, watching as the water breaks over the huge man-made concrete boulders. In front

PAULA DOMBROWIAK

of me are the murky waters of Lake Michigan I once thought was an ocean. My younger self would argue that because you can't see the other side, it was a logical conclusion.

I have not been home since I left for college fifteen years ago, and until right this second, I didn't realize how much I missed it. I was busy trying to make a name for myself, earn my place as a journalist. Home had been tainted for me, the innocence removed, and the nostalgia lifted. My heart is heavy and full with this long overdue homecoming.

Chicago is the third largest city in the United States, but there is something slower, kinder, and more serene about the Midwest. It doesn't feel as harsh and unforgiving as New York does.

Over the last fifteen years, I made excuses to my mom about why I couldn't make it back for the holidays, and eventually, she stopped asking. Our relationship has been strained for a long time, and that's partly my fault. Harboring hateful feelings all this time hasn't done me any good.

To be honest, if I'm upset about Jack not dealing with his past when I'm guilty of the same, it makes me a hypocrite. I have to be willing to let the past go in order to move forward.

I don't like the person I have become because of it.

There is no good time to confront your fears, there is only *a* time. As much as I'd like to sit here longer, I know if I don't go now, I may never have the courage. I collect my things and stand up, taking one last look at the skyline before heading back to my car. I pass by the now empty fountain that I used to run through as a kid on a hot summer day. My rental car is parked on the street, and as I approach it, my phone vibrates.

When I look at the screen, I see it's a message from Jack's publisher, technically my publisher too. They contact me from time to time with offers to be a ghost writer for other projects, but I keep turning them down. I'm done writing other people's stories. That goes for covering festivals and charity events.

I'm burned out.

Thankfully, I can afford to take some time to figure out what I want

186

to do next. Jack's book is doing well, and royalty checks come in regularly. It feels weird to take money from a book that is not my own, but until I figure out what I want to do, I have to take the money.

Right now, I need to be here and figure out my own shit.

22

Master Tapes

JACK

"What do you mean you ruined the master tapes?" Bret asks, questioning whether I'm fucking with him or not.

Cash is standing to my left, and I'm hoping to get some moral support, but he's cowardly looking the other way. I shrug sheepishly at Bret's question because I can't bring myself to speak.

"Are you fucking with me?" Bret asks, and then he starts to pace which is never a good sign. I can't be sure, but I think some of his hair turned grey right in front of me. At least the one's that haven't already turned grey.

I stare at my feet because I know this is bad. This is so bad, and I can't even come up with an excuse. This is the last recording Mia ever did, and I don't think it can be salvaged. I know I've fucked up in the past, but this is by far the worst. I've already beaten myself up about it and so has Cash, but in a way, I feel we were able to make something good come out of it.

Bret stops pacing and through my lashes I can see he's rubbing his chin as if he's trying to think of what to say to me. I shift my weight and start to open my mouth, but he stops me.

"If you open your fucking mouth right now, Jack..." He doesn't finish the threat, but it still causes me to close my mouth.

The studio still looks like a hurricane hit it. Cash did me a solid and collected the remains of the master tapes before Bret arrived and discarded them. The rest of the recording band is waiting in the lobby. No doubt they can hear the tongue lashing Cash and I are getting right now.

"Look, Bret..." I start to say because I never do as I'm told.

"Is he fucking talking right now?" Bret addresses Cash who looks very uncomfortable. "Please tell me this idiot is not talking to me!" he yells.

"Fuck!" Bret raises his arms and walks away. I can hear his feet stomping down the hallway. Oddly, I feel like I'm back in school, getting reprimanded for not turning in my English assignment, except on a whole other level.

I look at Cash who shrugs at me sympathetically.

"He seems pissed," I say, scrunching up my nose, trying to deflect from this terrible moment. It's all I can do to stay sane.

Cash shakes his head. "Don't fuck with him right now."

"What?" I shrug innocently, but internally I'm reeling.

I hear footsteps coming back down the hallway and Bret enters the studio, still pissed.

"I can't fucking believe the two of you," Bret says, standing in front of us, his legs apart and his arms crossed over his chest.

"I didn't..."

Bret cuts him off with a glare, and Cash shuts his mouth like a little kid getting falsely accused of something.

"I've put up with a lot of shit from you," he points directly at me, "destroyed guitars, *expensive* guitars," he emphasizes, "trashed hotel rooms, bailing your ass out of jail..." he continues, counting with his fingers.

"In my defense, it was the '90s. You haven't had to bail me out of jail in a decade," I try to explain, but Bret is having none of it.

"Is this fun for you?" Bret asks, and I'm not sure if it's rhetorical or not. "Do you like giving me an ulcer?"

Now that question is rhetorical.

"Do you know what an ulcer is?" Bret asks, and I hesitate to answer. "It means my fucking stomach is bleeding." He presses his palm to his torso just to make a point. "You make my stomach bleed."

I'm not really sure how I'm supposed to respond to that, so I shift my weight uncomfortably. Cash is absolutely no help right now. Technically he didn't do anything, but just being here, he's guilty by association.

"Bret," I say cautiously, holding my hand up defensively and I say the only thing I can in this moment. "I'm really sorry."

I start to pace, rubbing at my face and once again feeling the effects of my actions. "I can't take it back and I don't really have a good excuse, but let me try and fix this," I plead.

"How? How can you fix this, Jack?" he asks. "Can you take a mangled pile of tape and splice it all back together again?" he yells, before taking a labored breath.

"Do you have a magic fucking wand that I don't know about?!" he roars.

"For the record…" Cash turns to Bret, "I had nothing to do with the master tapes being destroyed."

Bret gives him a blank stare as if to say he doesn't care in the least.

"Just wanted to make that clear," Cash says and steps away, sheepishly.

Bret closes his eyes, pinching his nose and sucks in a deep breath.

"Well, it's a good thing we backed up those master tapes onto digital a few years ago."

We just finished laying down the track for the new song. I can't believe Bret made me think we had lost all of the songs. I would have strangled him had it not been my fault in the first place. He made a good show of it and effectively made me feel even shittier than I already did. I suppose I deserved it. I'm just glad the album is still intact, and now we can finally finish it.

The back-up band we recorded the song with is excellent. I've used them on several of my solo albums, and they have even gone on tour with me. What I'd like to do is be able to play this live, with both Cash and Wade, although we'd have to convince Wade to do it.

Once Bret calmed down, because he really was pissed that I destroyed the tapes, I could tell he was listening with his critical ear. I trust his judgement, and he was able to provide some good feedback. We made a few tweaks, and the song is even better than we'd hoped. The first run through, I watched Bret from behind the glass as he smoothed the hairs down on his arms.

I wanted to punch the fucking wall in excitement at seeing how much this song affected him. The only thing better than writing a song with Mia, was writing these lyrics with Cash.

Knowing you affected someone with your words and your music is a powerful thing. I never had that growing up. I didn't know my worth. My fans provided that for me, and I will never forget that. No matter how much of an asshole I am, I will always appreciate my fans for allowing me to live my dream.

I lean against the brick wall of the studio and light up a cigarette.

"I thought you quit," Bret states as he exits through the studio's back door.

I take a drag and then knock the cherry off with my shoe.

"Old habits die hard," I say, looking straight ahead, and squinting towards the sun.

I can hear Bret take a swift intake of breath before he speaks, almost as if he's getting up the nerve. "Cash told me what happened."

I lean further into the brick, bracing the flat of my shoe on it for support.

"I'm just glad I didn't completely fuck everything up," I say.

"Don't you think I know you well enough by now to always have a backup plan?" Bret says with a teasing tone.

I hang my head and chuckle. I should have known that Bret would not trust me with the only copy of the album Mia and I made together.

"I'm ready to let this album go now," I admit, and turn towards him slightly to get a glimpse of his face.

"It's a good thing, Jack," he says with encouragement.

I know this. It took a lot longer than I thought it would to get here. As usual, I left a path of destruction in my wake. Namely Erin.

I shouldn't have told her I loved her the way I did, not here, not in this space that is filled with the memories of Mia. As much as I wanted to be with Erin, my past kept getting in the way. She deserves all of me and nothing less. This song is everything I needed to say and more. It's the only way I know how to say goodbye to Mia.

"Mia was someone very special," Bret says. "I've never met anyone like her, and I doubt I ever will."

Bret seems to be lost in thought, looking out past the parking lot to someplace down the street only he can see. "I think this album is a way for all of us to say goodbye."

None of us have been unaffected by the loss of her grace, her talent or her presence.

"Do you have everything you need to finish the album?" I ask.

"Nothing more I need from you. I can have the engineers finish the mixing without you if that's what you want," Bret offers. "Do I need to be worried?" he asks, a concerned look on his face.

"Not anymore," I say and turn to leave.

"Where are you going?" Bret calls after me.

I turn around with a smile on my face. "I need to be somewhere else right now."

23

Gail

ERIN

I'm standing on the front porch of my childhood home, and I have so much anxiety that my body is literally shaking. Perhaps this was too much for me, but if I don't go through with it now, I will never be able to move on. I make my finger hit the doorbell and hear the chime ring inside the house; the sound bringing back childhood memories.

I force myself not to look at the huge evergreen tree in the front yard or the cobwebbed space beneath the front porch, because I am not as strong as I think I am.

Gail opens the door, and for a second, I don't think she recognizes me. I wouldn't be offended because I have not seen her in person in a very long time.

A part of me wants to run into her arms and feel her protective hug around me, but I am scared that it won't be received how I imagined. Hugs feel like a distant memory, almost as if they never really existed. How can you miss something if you don't even remember having it in the first place?

But a part of me does.

And that's what hurts so much.

"Hi, Mom," I say, and give her a small smile.

"Erin?" She looks at me critically as if she has to make sure it's really me. "Erin," she says again, this time it's not a question. I can see the conflict in her body language and on her face because she wants to hug me, but she's not sure what to do.

Gail is slender like me, but taller by only an inch. Her brown hair is cut short and layered with soft highlights to cover the gray. Her eyes are the same as mine, a soft brown, but her face is more angular. She always looked younger than her actual age, but the crow's feet around her eyes make it hard to hide now.

"Look at you. You're so beautiful." Her voice cracks as she tries to keep in her emotions. "Come in, come in." She steps aside so I can enter the house.

The foyer has the same wood paneling that I remember, even the large rectangular mirror opposite the door hasn't changed. I catch a glimpse of myself in it and I am shocked to see this older version, expecting to see the child that had to stand on tippy toes to reach it so long ago.

The living room furniture still resembles the eighties. Even the velvet tapestry above the brick fireplace is the same, which hung in my grandparents' house before I was even born. It's not a family heirloom or a treasure of any sort, but here it hangs in the house I grew up in, with no significance that I can remember. Gail leads me through the swinging door into the kitchen, which is still painted a lovely shade of yellow. We sit down at the breakfast nook and stare at each other for a moment.

"Can I get you something to drink?" she offers. "I can make you some tea." She always offered me tea when I had a cold. The little girl inside of me yearns for that kind of nurturing now.

I nod, and then peer out the window to the backyard. The grass is out of control, but aside from that, it's the same. The detached garage faces the alley, and I wonder if it still smells like gasoline. A part of me wants to go find out.

"What are you doing in town?" Gail asks as she puts the kettle on the stove and grabs two cups from the cupboard. "I wasn't expecting you." Of course, she wasn't expecting me. I haven't been home since college.

"I..." I stop short of answering and collect my thoughts before I speak again. "I wanted to see you."

She stiffens at my confession. "It's been a long time," she says, pulling the tea bags from the container and placing one in each cup.

Taking a deep breath, I try to refocus. "I know."

The water doesn't take long to boil, and the tea kettle whistles, the sound jarring.

Gail grabs the kettle off the stove and brings it to the table, along with a crocheted potholder I remember as a child. She pours our tea and sits down opposite me, studying my face as if trying to decipher me.

"I'm glad you came," she says, her smile is genuine.

Taking a sip of my tea, I ask, "How have you been?" I blow on the hot water to try and cool it down before attempting to sip it again.

Gail loosely intertwines her fingers together, twitching her thumbs. "The Russell's moved a few years ago."

Their faces are fuzzy, although I know they lived a few houses down from us.

"The neighborhood has changed." I noticed while I was driving in that some of the houses have been renovated. A lot of the smaller shops I visited as a kid have been replaced with big chain stores. "When did they get rid of the viaduct across the street?" I ask. That must have been a major project, redirecting the train.

"That's been gone for years." There's no mistaking the edge to her voice.

I look down at my cup of tea, the steam barely visible now. My fingers grip the cup tightly, using it for support.

"How have *you* been doing?" I ask again, because I want to know how she is, not the neighbors.

"I'm fine, Erin." She purses her lips and stands, busying herself in the kitchen by rinsing out the tea kettle and wiping down the counter.

"*I've* been doing great," I emphasize because she hasn't bothered to ask about me.

Gail whips around holding the rag in her hands. "Erin, you don't return my phone calls or my emails, so I don't know what you want from me." She sounds exasperated which rubs me the wrong way.

"Oh, I'm sorry, does it hurt your feelings to be ignored?" I scoot out of the bench seat and stand in the middle of the kitchen.

"Erin, stop it." Gail turns away from me, gripping the countertop.

"Stop what?" I ask, letting my arms hang at my sides.

"Let's not bring up the past."

Growing up, she never wanted to talk about anything. Not about Ethan, not about the fact that my dad stayed on the road longer and longer when he should have been home. She wasn't there for me when I needed her the most, and certainly not when I was an impressionable teen looking for someone to love me. This isn't just about the past.

I want to be able to look at my mom and not feel resentment.

"Sometimes the past is important," I say, approaching her at the sink. "Did you know I felt invisible?" I ask.

"Erin," she laughs nervously, "you're being dramatic."

She's being dismissive to my feelings, maybe to protect her own.

"We never celebrated my birthdays," I continue.

"You had birthday parties," she answers, narrowing her eyes at me. "Remember the clown?"

"That was before Ethan died." Gail blanches at the mention of his name.

"You were too old for parties. We didn't think you wanted them." These are just excuses.

"How would you know what I wanted?" I raise my voice. "You hardly ever came out of your room, and when you did you weren't present."

She balls her fists, hurt in her eyes more than anger. "I was mourning the loss of a child!" The devastation on her face is almost heartbreaking.

"I was mourning the loss of my brother!" I counter. "And I needed you!"

"You don't understand, Erin," she snaps, gripping the counter.

"Because I don't have kids?" I lean against the counter and look at her.

"Did you come here just to tell me what a shitty mom I was?" She doesn't allow me to answer. "You don't think I know I've made mistakes?" The hurt she's feeling is palpable.

"I lost a child, and then I lost a husband, Erin. I hope to God you never have to go through what I have." She closes her eyes and turns away from me.

"I lost a brother and a father," I say back to her.

We are at an impasse, and there is no clear winner.

"Your pain isn't worse than mine, it's just different," I explain. I watch as her shoulders relax in quiet resolve.

"I just wanted you to know how I felt." I thought it would ease my mind, put to rest these hateful feelings I've had all these years, but all I really want is for her to acknowledge my feelings.

Gail covers her mouth with the back of her hand. Her eyes are swimming with tears threatening to spill over.

"There are a lot of things I feel guilty about," she whispers and chokes back a sob. I want to hug her, but I don't. "I can't change the past." I want to tell her it's okay, but I can't. This is a pattern for me, to make excuses for other people's behavior and forget about my own.

Instead, I wait for her to continue, give her the space she needs to formulate her words, to make the decision to open up to me on her own.

"He was my baby," she chokes out.

"I was your baby too," I challenge her.

"You were so strong, Erin." She finally levels her gaze to me. "You've always been so capable."

"I shouldn't have had to be," I tell her, my voice firm.

"I couldn't see past my own grief…"

"To see me," I finish for her.

"Erin." Her soft voice breaks something open inside of me. "I'm sorry."

"That's all I have ever wanted to hear," I say, blinking back my own tears. Those words don't have the power to change the past, but they do have the power to shape the future.

I take a step forward because that is the direction I want to move. I wrap my arms around her and press my body to her. She feels different, a foreign entity, and it's as if I am discovering her for the first time, but it feels good.

My mom wraps her arms around me tentatively at first, as if she's afraid, but once she does, her arms are like vipers threatening to suffocate me.

"I'm so sorry, Erin," she whispers into my hair.

"Thank you," I say into her hair.

"I should have said this a long time ago." She pulls away from me, wiping at her eyes. "I'm just glad you came to see me." She gives me a weak smile.

There is a patch of dirt where the grass never fully grew in because that's where we always set up one of those plastic pools in the summer to cool off in.

Gail stands beside me to rinse her dish. I took her to the grocery store this afternoon and we bought ingredients to make tomato soup and grilled cheese. She cooked the noodles to put in the canned tomato soup while I buttered the bread for the grilled cheese. Neither of us is a fabulous cook, but we know how to use a can opener and make something our own.

"I could never get the grass to come back in," she says, reading my thoughts. "Remember Charlie, our yellow lab?" she continues, and I nod. "He was in that pool more than you kids." There is sadness mixed in with the happy memory at her use of plurals. She doesn't mention Ethan directly for the same reason I don't tell people I had a brother. Memories can have the power to break us.

"I miss him, too." I turn to look at her, my hip resting against the counter. We should be able to talk about him to one another. That's a start.

"I've been going to therapy," Gail confides in me. "That's why I've been trying to get in touch with you lately."

"Oh," I say in surprise.

"It's new," she explains.

"I'm glad," I say sincerely. I don't push for details. When she's ready, she can tell me about it.

She takes both plates and washes them in the sink, placing them in the dish drainer.

After a minute, she takes my hand and leads me into the living room. "Tell me about your job," she says, as she sits opposite me on the couch.

The question is so simple, but it means so much. We settle in and I tuck my legs under me, resting my elbow on the arm rest and begin to tell her about my life. She listens intently, taking in the pieces of me that I so desperately wanted her to see.

"You wrote a book?" she asks, surprised, after I tell her about working with Jack.

"Yeah." It is the one thing I am most proud of. "It's doing really well too." Secretly, I track where it is on the bestsellers list, knowing that I had a part in it, even if it's not my own story.

"I'll have to read it."

I stifle a laugh thinking of my mom reading Jack's book. I can't imagine.

She yawns and I look at the clock above the mantel, not realizing how late it is.

"Are you staying the night?" she asks expectantly.

"Do you mind?" I left my luggage in the rental car, unsure of what to expect.

"Of course not. You can sleep in your old room," she offers.

After we lock up downstairs, she walks with me upstairs to my childhood bedroom, which is down the hall from hers, but my feet carry me to my brother's room which is situated in between.

Gail stands behind me as I lean my head against the doorframe. The twin bed sits against the wall, a baseball patterned comforter draped over it, but that's all that remains of him in this room. I turn towards her, my mouth open.

"I packed it up a while ago," she explains. As if she knows what my next question is, she says, "It's all in the basement, along with your father's things."

I look back into the room, not sure if I am relieved or sad that all of

Ethan's belongings are now collecting dust in the basement. Growing up, his room was like a shrine. A sad museum to what could have been. Ethan was in our lives for such a short time, but losing him has affected all of us so profoundly.

"That must have been hard," I say to her.

"It was necessary," she says.

"I'm sorry you had to do that alone," I offer.

"I'm sorry you had to do a lot of things by yourself." She gives me a weak smile.

"Mom," I smile back.

She touches my face and looks at me with understanding. "You are so beautiful." Her smile warms me.

24

Fireflies

ERIN

The basement is dusty and smells like mold. I sit cross-legged, sifting through the boxes of my father's things. I've gone through the ones with his old clothing, even lifting a shirt to my nose to see if it still smelled like him, and I was sadly disappointed when it didn't. Some of these things can go to charity, but only when my mom is ready.

I woke up early and brought my coffee down here. I'm not sure what I'm hoping to find, but I'll know it when I do. I don't bother looking through the boxes that are labeled with Ethan's name because I already know what's in there. There wasn't enough time for him to accumulate anything near like what my dad has. Ethan's belongings are Lego's and action figures, posters, and old little league trophies.

I'm certain it was more difficult to pack up my brothers belongs than it was to pack up my dad's. Therapy seems to have been good for mom, and being able to pack up his things is a step in the right direction.

The past is the past, and we can't change that. I won't ever get my childhood back, and for that I am sad, but I'm tired of hating her. I'm tired of resenting her. Being angry is so easy; forgiving is the hard part. This isn't about her anymore; this is about me.

I hear footsteps on the basement stairs and my mom comes into view. She's holding a cup of coffee and carrying a plate of biscuits.

"It thought you might be hungry too." She sets them down on the wooden workbench next to me and leans against it.

"Thanks." I grab one, my stomach growling.

"Find what you were looking for?" she asks. Her eyes still sleepy, the brown hues picking up the light that filters through the half windows of the basement.

I set down an old photo album and shake my head. "I'm not sure what I'm looking for," I admit.

She takes the photo album and flips it open to a wedding we all went to before my brother died. She snorts a little looking at the pictures. "This was my cousin Lucy's wedding." She points to a picture of a woman in an awful looking white wedding dress. The dress clings to all the wrong curves, but she has a wide toothy grin. I try to stifle my laugh as I notice the groom is wearing a powder blue suit with a ruffled white shirt.

"I remember this... vaguely," I say, memories of running through a church and playing hide and seek under the pews with some of the other children play out in my mind.

Looking through all this stuff, I'm hoping to find something that will help me understand my dad. He was someone who would read us bedtime stories, play his trumpet for us, barbecue on Sundays, and fill our little play pool with water for the summer, but I don't know him as a person.

I try to hold onto those good memories, but the ugly one's creep in. After Ethan was diagnosed with Leukemia, it was like he was afraid to come home. I always thought he was strong, standing 6'2" and broad shouldered with a thunderous laugh, but he wasn't strong enough to watch his child go through treatments. He wasn't strong enough to hold his wife while she cried. He wasn't strong enough to look me in the eye anymore, maybe afraid to wonder what Ethan would have looked like, as I grew.

I put these expectations on him that weren't fair, and just because he wasn't strong enough, doesn't make him a coward.

I pull out an old record and flip the sleeve over, finding his name on the back. "Did he always want to be a musician?" I ask.

My mom smiles while she nods. "He was playing at a club in downtown the first time we met." I like that she can smile thinking of him now, helping me to understand that it wasn't all bad.

"Do you remember the club's name?" I ask, feeling myself go into interview mode.

She scrunches up her nose, tapping her fingertip against her lips while she thinks. "I don't. I'm not even sure it's still there. So much has changed downtown over the years." She shrugs.

I pull out a box full of old Polaroids and photos of my dad playing at various venues and sift through them. These photos are all pieces to a puzzle that I find myself wanting to put together. In another box there are more, and I come across one with my mom and dad posing in front a building, the name *Jazz Showcase* lit up behind them.

"Is this it?" I ask, showing her the photo. They looked very young, possibly in their twenties, which is when they first met.

She takes it from me, inspecting the photo. "Could be." She hands it back to me. "We went to a lot of clubs."

I take a sip of my coffee and place it on the floor beside me, letting my glasses fall back onto my nose.

"Why such an interest in all of this?" she asks, curious. She's taken a seat on one of the rusty stools next to the workbench, her feet halfway in her slippers, absentmindedly bouncing it against her heel.

I put the picture back in the box and set it aside, along with some of the other things I'd like to go through more.

"Do you remember me telling you about the book I helped to write?" I ask her, referring to the conversation we had last night.

"Yes, that musician you mentioned," she says as she smiles at me.

"I would like to write a book about Dad," I tell her, nervous for her reaction. I'm not sure if she would think this is a good idea or not. Maybe she wants to move forward, having packed away all these memories, not wanting to be reminded of them again. Writing this book would mean bringing up a lot of those memories, and not all of them are good ones.

Her face is contemplative as she assesses me. "I think he would have liked that," she says.

"What would you like?" I ask.

"It's not about me, Erin, this is about you, and if it makes you happy, then I'm behind it."

I let out a breath, the ache in my chest lessening. I realize I want her to be proud of me.

Writing Jack's book gave me the opportunity to do something I really love, but Jack's story wasn't mine.

This story *will* be mine.

The night air is thick with summer humidity, and the front yard is slowly blanketed in darkness. I pull my knees to my chest as I sit on the front porch and rest my chin against them. It's been a really long day, and my body and mind are heavy with emotion. The street is quiet except for the distant sprinklers clicking on in a neighbor's yards.

I've spent most of the day in the basement, rummaging through my father's boxes. There are so many pictures I'd never seen before, other famous jazz artists I didn't know he was associated with. He's played on a lot more albums than I knew about. I also found old newspaper clippings, one in particular featuring him as an artist at the *Chicago Jazz Festival* in 1999, which was only a few years before he passed away.

I plan to take a lot of these artifacts back to New York with me, but most of it I'll have to ship. I texted Sandy, my editor at *Alt Press*, and told her about my project. She offered to do whatever she could to help me. She has been so supportive of my career, and she's a good friend. It's not that I don't like writing for music blogs, but it's time to do something for myself.

I already started an outline with the information I have on hand, but there is so much more involved, like tracking down old band members, speaking to producers and engineers. I told Sandy I will reach out to her when I'm ready. Right now, I want to write it for myself, and when I have a first draft, I can contact the publisher I worked with for Jack's book. I don't know if they'd be interested in small time Jazz musician, but I'll keep my options open.

After everything that has happened over the past few days, I feel emotionally wrecked. Right now, sitting on this porch, I want something I can't have. He's two thousand miles away and I have no business wanting him, but I still do.

I miss him.

Even after everything, he is the person I wanted to call the most when I decided I was going to write a book about my father. When I found my brother's old worn-out baseball cap, the one he wore at his championship game, I broke down on the basement floor, and the only person I wanted to hold me was Jack.

Neither one of us is perfect and we each have our own baggage, but when he is the only person I think of when times are tough, that tells me something. I always relied on my intuition when it came to interviewing people. My intuition is what drew me to Jack in the first place. Even with all of his flaws, Jack is worth fighting for.

One by one, fireflies flicker on and off, illuminating the darkness in the yard before me. They move about like tiny floating lanterns in a sea of darkness. They never flicker on in the same place they start. I watch them in fascination as I lean back on my elbows on the step above me. The chipped paint scrapes against my skin.

As if life is giving me the nudge I need, my phone starts to vibrate in my pocket. Looking at the screen, I'm not surprised to see Jack's name displayed. My heart beats faster at the thought of hearing his voice. I've done a lot of soul searching this past week, because even though I've asked Jack to work out his own shit, I needed to do the same. Coming home has made me realize how much of my past has affected me, causing the insecurities I've had with Jack.

I pick up the phone and place it next to my ear. "I'm glad you called," I say softly.

"Oh yeah, why's that?" he says in his gentle but deep voice.

I'm trying to keep my shit together right now because hearing his voice is breaking something open inside of me. I've done a good job of not losing it so far, but Jack calling seems to give me permission to let my walls down.

"I had a really tough day." My voice comes out broken.

"What do you need?" Listening to his breathing on the other end of the phone is comforting, almost as if he were here.

I'm not ready to talk about it, and not on the phone. "I just want to talk about something else."

"What are you doing right now?" He allows me to change the subject.

"Watching the fireflies," I say, as they dance in front of me.

"Describe them to me."

"You've never seen fireflies?" I ask as I wipe my nose.

"I grew up in Arizona and lived in California most of my life." He chuckles and I forget that fireflies are a Midwest thing. At least that's the only place I've seen them.

I sigh into the phone. "It's like each one has a light switch that someone is turning on and off." I don't know how else to describe them. I'm sure Jack knows what a firefly is, he's just never seen one in person.

"Why do you think they do that?" he asks.

"I don't know." I've never thought about it before. I'm sure there's a scientific reason for it, but I like to make up my own version. "Maybe they've lost their way and they're trying to find each other." Maybe Jack and I are like these fireflies, trying to find our way back to each other in the darkness.

Jack sighs into the phone and says, "Maybe they're trying to light their own way home."

"I like that much better." Smiling, I watch them with a whole new fascination.

On the outside, Jack is all sharp edges, rough and weather beaten, but when he allows me to see the soft insides of his heart, it is the most beautiful thing I've ever seen.

I let out a big sigh. "I wish you were here." This whole time I've been the one running, and Jack has never stopped fighting for me.

"Erin." His voice is no longer just on the phone, and I look to the end of the walkway. Jack is standing in front of the gate, and for a second, I think I might be imagining things. Maybe I've really lost it. When he moves the phone from his ear and lifts the side of his mouth in a shy smile, I drop my phone and walk purposefully towards him. Seeing him causes me to unleash every emotion I've been so desperate to hold in. The fireflies make way as I pass through them to get to Jack. My body crashes into his like a wave crashing into the shore, my emotional baggage drifting away with the tide.

"I was hoping you would say that," he says into my ear as he wraps his arms around me, strong and unyielding.

His shirt collects my tears, and I can feel the wetness spreading through the fibers, moist against my cheek.

"It's okay," he whispers to me, the palm of his hand heavy against my back.

He holds me, not asking questions, because somehow, he knows exactly what I need. I take a deep breath to steady myself, my body shuddering against him.

"They're beautiful." His chest moves under my ear as he speaks, and I look up at the fireflies still blinking in the front yard. I continue to grip the back of his T-shirt as if it's my anchor while I turn to look at them.

They remind me of the best parts of my childhood. I feel Jack kiss the top of my head, letting his chin rest there for a moment as we watch the fireflies together. One by one, they disappear and then reappear.

We walk to the front steps, his hand in mine, and his thumb rubbing against the back of my hand.

"I can't believe you're here." I'm still stunned. He tends to show up when I least expect it.

He moves his hand to my face, brushing away my forgotten tears. I probably look a mess, but I don't care. All I care about is that he's here when I needed him the most.

"Where else would I be?" His smile could melt ice cubes.

"Jack, how did you…" I stop myself from wondering how he even knew where I was when I remember I had talked to Wade a couple days ago. Jack's smile confirms what I was thinking.

"I was hoping you'd want me to be here." He squeezes my hand. "I

PAULA DOMBROWIAK

would have been here sooner, but I had a few things to take care of."
The sheepish look on his face warms me. I know we didn't part on
good terms at the studio. Despite my feelings of taking a backseat in
his life, the fact that he is here right now means so much to me.

Jack looks good, better than when I last saw him. He looked so lost,
so broken, but now… he looks content as if a weight has been lifted.
Whatever happened after I left must have ended well. It gives me hope
that we can move forward

I am drawn to this lighter, happier Jack, and like a magnet's pull, I
move forward, connecting my lips with his. When he kisses me back, I
feel a rush of endorphins flood through my body straight to my heart,
and it hurts. But it hurts so good.

"Erin." He pulls away to look at me, his hands still holding my
face. His gaze pierces through me, right down into my soul. "I see
you."

Those three simple words hold all the meaning in the world for me.
I start to feel tears pool in my eyes again, but I won't let them spill
over.

"When I look at you," he grips me tightly as if wanting to transfer
the sentiment deep into my muscles, "I see only *you*."

I swallow hard.

"You *affect* me," he breathes into my hair, his lips close to my ear as
he whispers, "When I fuck you, I want to make it last." His voice softens, "That is why I don't let you take control."

A shiver runs down my body and I feel the heat of his breath leave
my face as he pulls back to look at me. My eyes are wide, and my pulse
is racing. This is what he does to me, and I lose myself in him every
time he's near. I never thought or imagined I might make him feel the
same way.

I let my forehead fall forward, resting it on the bulk of his chest and
breathe him in. My fingers grip his shirt, pulling the material tight into my
palms as if I am desperate to keep him close to me. The palm of his hand
rests at the back of my head, and it's all I've ever needed from him. I don't
know what the future will hold for us, but I will not give up on us. Nothing
worth this much is ever easy. If it were, it wouldn't mean as much.

Jack is worth fighting for.

I am worth fighting for.

Taking a deep breath, letting my nose fill with the scent that is uniquely his, I pull back so I can look at him. Words don't come easily in this moment, although normally I am full of them. Luckily, Jack is intuitive because he fills the silence, changing the heavy subject we both need a break from.

"This is the house you grew up in?" His gaze shifts behind me to the front porch.

I nod, taking a peek at the two-story Victorian farmhouse.

"Will you tell me about it?" He takes a seat on the step, pulling me down so I can sit between his legs. I rest my arms against his thigh, my head feeling heavy.

"What do you want to know?" I ask.

"What is your favorite memory here?" He smiles, his eyes alive with genuine curiosity. It's not the clear blue of his eyes that draws me in; it's the way he focuses all of his attention on me, as if I am the only person in the world.

He listens.

I take a deep breath. "My little brother and I would catch the fireflies in the summer on a night like this." It feels good to talk about Ethan, to share the memories I have with someone.

Jack looks out at the yard. There are less fireflies than before, but the remaining ones still blink, lighting up the darkness.

"How would you catch them?"

"We would take glass jars and hold them up, trying to get the firefly to go inside and then close the lid as fast as we could," I explain. "They were like our own little lanterns."

"We would try to see who could get the most in one jar," I laugh, thinking of Ethan and I racing around the yard, losing more fireflies in the process of trying to trap others in the jar.

"Who won?"

"Neither of us," I laugh, thinking of Ethan's floppy brown hair holding a jar with a huge grin on his face. Everything was so simple before he had Leukemia. Once he was diagnosed, everything happened so fast. Our world was tipped upside down and was never the same again.

"What else did you do?" Jack brings me back to the present.

I look around the yard. There are so many memories I could pick from, but the huge evergreen tree on the side of the house is one I love the most. "In the winter after a big snowstorm, we would pile up the snow around that tree and make a fort."

"Looks like a good place to hide," he says in his low, gruff voice.

"It was." I look at the tree nostalgically, remembering how it felt like our own special place. "The snow and the thick branches blocked out the wind."

"You have some really good memories here." He drapes his arm around me, bringing me in close so he can kiss the top of my head. I realize that it wasn't all bad, and I wasted so much time focusing on the hurtful memories instead of the good ones.

"I do," I reply, nodding in agreement.

The front door creaks opens and Gail steps out. "Oh, Erin, I didn't realize you had company. I was just coming to check on you," she says in her quiet, frail voice. Her eyes light up at the sight of Jack.

We both stand and Jack keeps an arm around my waist, holding me close to him. "Mom, this is Jack O'Donnell," I introduce him. "Jack, this is my mother, Gail."

"Oh, what a pleasure." She holds her hand out to Jack, a huge smile on her face. "You're the man my daughter wrote a book about," she says proudly, looking from me to Jack.

"The pleasure is mine," Jack replies as he shakes her hand. He is gentle and polite with her.

"Come in, come in." She opens the door wider for us to enter. Jack and I step inside my childhood home together, something I never thought in a million years would happen.

25

You're Staring

JACK

I took a big chance showing up in Chicago to see Erin. When Wade
let it slip where she was, I knew where I needed to be. I still have a
lot of shit to work out, but I couldn't stay away any longer. She could
have told me to fuck off and she'd have every right to, but she didn't.
I've never wanted to be a better person for anyone in my life.

I discovered there were a lot of things we both had to work
through. Erin getting a chance to make things right with her mom is
something I never got to do with my father. Seeing her childhood
home and meeting her mom helped me to realize that I'm not the only
person in this relationship with baggage.

I would have been comfortable staying the night in Erin's old
bedroom, but she insisted we get a hotel room. Looking at her now, I'm
glad we did. I don't think that twin sized bed would have been able to
handle all the things I want to do to her.

My hair is still wet from my shower, and I prop my head up with
the palm of my hand to avoid the pillow getting wet. From the
doorway of the bathroom, I notice Erin admiring the view while she
brushes her hair.

She's wearing those tiny sleep shorts that show off her legs, and I can see the pinpoints of her nipples through the tank top she's wearing. Her gaze starts from my scruffy chin, down to my chest and stops just before the waistband of my boxers.

"You're staring," I smirk.

She presses the hairbrush to her lips trying to hide her smile. "Yes," she admits, "yes I am."

She abandons the hairbrush and crawls across the bed towards me, catlike, her hair hanging in her face, and I reach out to push it back to see her eyes. Just the sight of her causes my stomach to tighten.

"You're thinking too much," I say, noticing her contemplative expression, the way her brow furrows.

"How do you know I'm thinking?" she asks, pursing her lips.

"You get this little crease on your forehead when you overthink things." I press a kiss to her forehead.

"Stop doing that." She pushes me away, flopping down on the bed next to me.

"Doing what?" I laugh, rolling over on my side.

"Reading my mind," she says, clearly exasperated.

"I'm not reading your mind, Erin," I chuckle. "I just know you."

She doesn't realize how much I watch her when she's not looking, not just reveling in her beauty, but dissolving in the gentle beat of her heart. I know every part of her intimately, but it's the part of her I can't see that I know best.

"You bounce your leg when you're nervous," I tell her just as she purses her lips. "You pucker your lips when you don't agree with something." Her lips part as she narrows her eyes at me. "You tuck your hair behind your ear when you're uncomfortable." She stops herself from doing that very thing right now, causing me to smile. Because I like to see her cheeks get red, I say, "You make these little noises when you..." She puts a finger to my mouth to shut me up. I take a bite causing her to squeal.

I look at her thoughtfully. She's curled up on her side next to me. Her hands are tucked under her head and pieces of wet hair stick to her check. Erin has the most expressive eyes. They are a soft brown, reminding me of autumn days in Payson. They darken like a rolling a storm when she's mad and lighten mimicking a sunrise when she's happy. God, I love it when they turn a golden brown in the sun.

"I know I've fucked up a lot," I say. "I'm not the man you deserve but I'm trying to be, and I'll keep trying as long as you let me." It's hard for me to admit, but for her, I would do anything. "I love you, Erin. I shouldn't have said it when I did before, but," I bite my lip to stop the emotions bubbling up inside of me, "I am so fucking in love with you."

She pins me with a look that makes my blood run hot. "I love you, too."

"I don't deserve it." I am a man who does not deserve what she is giving me, but I want it. God, do I want it. "But I *will* earn it."

"Jack?" She gives me a sweet expression, her lips parted, and her eyebrows furrowed. "Shut up and kiss me." I don't hesitate and roll her over on top of me, wanting the weight of her body to push me further into the mattress, and kiss her. When she pulls away, she gives me a heated look as I let her take control, giving myself over to her. I don't know how long I will be able to last, but if giving a little bit of myself to her is what I need to do to prove to her that I am all in, that's what I'll do.

Her body hovers over mine, pressing against me in such a deliciously sweet way that I can't help but move my hips to meet her. Her fingers trace the tattoo on my chest as she drinks me in with those autumn eyes, making my belly quiver with need. Her hair flutters around my shoulders as she leans over to kiss me, lips soft and gentle. I love the way her hair feels between my fingers as I move the longer strands away from her eyes so I can see her.

She pulls back and slowly lifts the shirt over her head, exposing her breasts. Her nipples are tiny pinpoints of the lightest pink, her skin puckered and begging me touch them. It takes all my willpower not to run my thumb over their hardness or take them in my mouth. Instead, I watch her, my gaze travelling from her swollen lips to the lump in her throat and the rapid pulse at the base of her neck. Every move she makes, from the graceful lift of her arm to the arch of her back is pure eroticism. My stomach tightens in response. The trust she has in me is a beautiful thing.

PAULA DOMBROWIAK

Her hand slowly travels down my chest as if she's memorizing every line, every scar, until she reaches the waistband of my boxers. I watch in rapt anticipation as she bites her bottom lip and moves off me just enough to pull them down. She then pulls her own shorts off in a slow and seductive way that makes me want to rip them off her. I can't help but close my eyes, tipping my head back into the pillow, overcome with sensations as she takes me in her hand and guides herself down on me. My hands grip her hips, fingers digging into her skin, pulling her further onto me because I am not a patient man.

My emotions are tangled up in the feel of her, not only the sensation of being inside her, but the pattern of her heartbeat as it quickens and slows with every movement and every touch. Every nerve is on fire begging for release, to possess her, to own her, to give in to this feeling that I am about to fall off the edge of a cliff I didn't even know I was standing on. To let go.

It's because it's her.

It's because I am in love with her.

She moves, rolling her hips, fingernails digging and scraping against my chest that is almost my undoing. I want to flip her over, to sink inside and fuck her so hard right now, but I restrain myself. Her lips curve into a seductive smile as she rides me. She's driving me mad, and she knows it. I reach for her, and she brings her mouth to mine, suppressing my moans. I kiss her deep, digging my fingers into her ass, urging her to move faster. I'm so close to the edge and I can't hold out much longer, no matter how hard I try.

She's not giving in, pushing back against my palm on her ass, and I can feel her smile against my lips.

"Erin," I growl against her lips, slipping my tongue inside. She grinds against me and it's maddening. This pressure inside me is building and building with nowhere to go.

I move away from her lips, hungrily kissing across her cheek, down her neck and push her up so I can run my tongue across her nipple greedily. With the palm of my hand, I cup her breast and clamp my lips down around her. She moans and whispers something that I can't make out. Her breathing is erratic, soft moans escaping from her lips as she runs her fingers through my hair and along my scalp.

"You're not playing fair," she whispers between breaths as she starts to move against me faster. My hand travels from her breast and down to her core between us. Her fingernails scrape against my scalp as she grips my hair tighter, moaning louder.

"Just fuck me, Jack," she bites out. It's all the confirmation I need to flip her over, causing a sharp yelp to come from her lips. Her eyes are heavy and she squirms under my gaze as I hover over her, ready to give her what she wants.

This woman lights me on fire and turns me to ashes every time.

With her legs wrapped around me and her heels pressed firmly against my ass, I sink into her with impatient thrusts. There is nothing sweeter than watching her climax and it sends me over the edge, falling apart in a tangled mess at her side.

"Tell me again," she requests, as if she hasn't taken enough from me already, but I can't deny her anything.

"Fuck." My curse like a sigh. "I love you, Erin," I whisper against her lips.

"I'm never going to get tired of hearing that," she says.

"I will never get tired of saying it."

"I love you." Her words vibrate against my neck and down into my belly.

26

For Cash

JACK

" A re you sure you want to do this?" Erin asks for the hundredth time. I laugh because she seems more nervous than I am.

We left Chicago yesterday, taking whatever direct flight was heading into Phoenix the soonest. I rented a car to drive the two hours into Payson. My emotions are running high at all the familiar sights and memories that come with being here.

"When was the last time you were here?" Erin asks.

"Not since my dad died."

"Do you ever feel homesick?" Erin shifts in her seat to look at me.

I sigh because I don't really know the answer to that. "There are parts of me that do and parts of me that never want to see this place again," I explain. "I never felt safe here unless I was at Wade's or with Amber." I give her an apologetic smile. "I know it's uncomfortable to hear that," I say, but she looks at me thoughtfully. In high school, Amber was everything I thought I wanted. She understood me, made me feel wanted, like I was worth something when I felt so unwanted at home.

"You loved her. She was your high school girlfriend." She smiles at me with understanding. There's no jealousy or judgment in her gaze.

Silence fills the car but it's okay.

"There's nothing here for me anymore." I give a weak smile. "Cash, Wade, Amber, and Mia were my home. So no, I'm not homesick for Payson." I take her hand in mine.

My childhood home was destroyed a long time ago, shortly after my father passed. The city took control of the land and cleared it. The house was in such disarray by then, and it made way for a new home to be built on the property. There's no use driving past it, and I wouldn't want to anyway. That house does not hold any power over me anymore.

Cash's parents moved to a retirement community in the valley years ago. Wade's parents downsized once Maude left for college, and they live on the outskirts of town now.

There are pictures in my book of Payson, providing visuals of certain places that were special to me, one of them being the gas station where I wrote the lyrics to *Blood and Bone* in Mia's car. We passed it on the way into town, and I couldn't help but think of the journal I lost so many years ago in those woods, part of the earth now. It seems so appropriate now.

"Erin, I'll be fine," I tell her.

"But what if it's not?" Her face contorts in anguish. She's worried about my mental state, triggering me into wanting to use. I finally confessed to her how I've been feeling this whole time. It's not something I'm proud of and it was hard to admit to Erin because I didn't want her to think any less of me.

I will always struggle with addiction, and certain situations make it harder, but I know with the support of my friends and Erin, I don't have to do it alone

"If it's not, then I'll deal with it," I shrug.

"*We'll* deal with it," she corrects, narrowing her eyes at me.

I confirm with a smile.

I cut the engine of the rental car and look out the window at the house I never thought I would see again. It's stately columns and large front porch look as intimidating as the people who live inside. The wind blows fierce as clouds close in, mimicking the storm building inside of me.

When Erin and I were working on my book, she wanted to visit Payson, Arizona, where I grew up. It would help her to visualize the places she was writing about, capture the feeling more authentically. She also wanted to meet Mia's parents, interview them. I was adamant they be left alone; not wanting to open old wounds because I knew my book would cause them enough grief. I was not their favorite person while Mia was alive, and I am definitely not their favorite person now that Mia is gone. I did send them a copy of the book, but I have no idea if they even received it. They never reached out to me afterward, but I didn't expect them to.

When Mia died, I respected their decision to take her ashes home with them, even though it tortured me not to have something tangible to visit or hold. Perhaps that's why I held on so tight to the things I *did* have of hers.

It would have been impractical to have her buried in L.A. Fans can sometimes be disrespectful. No matter how hard we would have tried to keep the location of her grave private, there was always the reality that someone would find it. Her parents would rather have her with them. I couldn't bring their daughter back to them, but I could let them take her ashes if that brought them solace. I haven't spoken to them since Mia's memorial over six years ago. They were distraught, angry, and heartbroken, as we all were. This was their only daughter, and I could not imagine a pain worse than that.

They were shocked to hear from me after all this time had passed, and it was one of the hardest phone calls I'd ever had to make. I could have just talked to them over the phone, but I needed to look them in the eye. Seeing them was important to me for closure. It was the last thing I needed to do to say goodbye. Mia would have wanted us to find some kind of peace with each other.

It's not lost on me that over eleven years ago, I was sitting in a car in front of this house, reluctant to leave Mia because I wasn't sure if I would ever see her again. I needed her to help me face my father who was dying, and she needed to try to repair the relationship with her parents. I had no idea at the time that she would show up on my front steps wearing those jeans.

Erin and I exit the car together. The walk to the door is the longest walk I've ever taken, but I don't hesitate to ring the bell, announcing my arrival. I've been ready to do this for a long time.

Camila Stone opens the door, her face a mask of politeness, but underneath, I can feel her disdain for me. Her resemblance to Mia is unsettling because they could not be more different. Mia was not just a woman; she was a force of nature.

"Jack." Camila looks from me to Erin. "Come in." She holds onto the door as if she's ready to slam it in my face at any moment, but then releases it enough so we can enter.

"Jack." Darren Stone appears beside his wife and looks from me to Erin.

"This is Erin Langford, the writer I told you about who worked on the book with me." I motion to Erin and Darren shakes her hand.

"Nice to meet you," Erin says sweetly.

"We can talk in here." Camila's words are clipped as she leads us into the sitting room, obviously eager to get this over with.

On the way to the sitting room, there is a parlor on the right with a grand piano. I can't imagine Mia ever sitting behind it, playing. She never belonged in a place like this.

We sit down on the couch opposite Camila and Darren in the formal sitting room. The wainscoting and stripped patterned wall-paper remind me of old Victorian homes. To my left is a large fireplace with whitewashed brick accents.

On the mantle above the fireplace sits the urn, decorated with an ornate pattern that is very unfitting for who Mia was. The sight of it is unsettling because I don't feel a connection to it like I thought I would. It's almost as if it could be a vase waiting for someone to place flowers inside.

On either side of the fireplace are built in bookshelves, the beautiful spines of hardcovers fill the shelves. That is why my book sticks out so awkwardly, just as much as I do in this house that is more like a museum than a home.

"You received it?" I ask nodding towards the bookshelf.

Camila looks at Darren and he speaks up. "We did." His brow creases. Darren is a tall man with dark hair cut close and parted to the side. His thick eyebrows are expressive sitting above grey/blue eyes with a square, impressive jaw. Under different circumstances, I can imagine having a friendly conversation and listening to his deep, boisterous laugh. I can tell he wants to move past this awkwardness we have created for ourselves, but Camila is unmoving in her disapproval of me, like a rock.

"I don't know what you expect from us, Jack," Camila says sternly. "We read your book, but it doesn't change anything." She shakes her head, her dark hair fluttering around her shoulders. I didn't expect them to like my book or understand it. In fact, I thought that they would hate me even more, learning the reason why Mia was on the freeway when the accident occurred. I think I wanted them to hate me; that's why I sent them the book. I wanted them to hold me accountable. Now, I just want them to know how sorry I am.

"Then you know what happened that night." Camila's eyes change color with the threat of tears, and that may be the only thing in common she has with Mia. "I'm sorry," I say with all the sincerity I can muster.

"You think you can send a book as if knowing what happened that night would make us feel better?" Camila tilts her head, her lips pursed together in restrained anger.

I shake my head in response.

"Now the whole world knows," she says with sad eyes.

"That wasn't easy for me. None of this is. I thought it was time to talk about it," I try to explain. Meeting Erin and after everything that happened with Amber, it felt like the right time to open up the wounds, clean them out, and piece myself back together again.

"It doesn't bring her back." Darren cuts off Camila from saying anything else. His tall frame rises from the couch and Camila stands with him.

"I know that," I reassure them. "I wanted to come here and see you because I've been thinking about her a lot lately," I try my best to explain. "I was hoping…"

"You thought coming here would make *you* feel better, just like writing that book?" Camila points at me in anguish.

"It wasn't my intention to upset you." I feel Erin's fingers wrap around my forearm. She's been silent the whole time, but her touch gives me strength.

"You never seem to have bad intentions, but look what happens!" Camila's eyes, so much like Mia's hazel, flash a watery green.

I scratch the back of my head, trying to think of what to say. She's not wrong. I know this.

"I can't live my entire life regretting what happened," I say. "I thought coming here would help us all move on." There is more I want to say but I don't think they want to hear it, at least not now. Maybe someday.

"Move on?" Camila bites out. "My only child is gone. Do you know what that's like?" I wince at her words thinking of Hayley. I don't ever want to know what that kind of loss feels like.

"I don't," I admit. "I've spent the last six years with regrets and hating myself." I shift my weight, looking at Darren's sympathetic eyes and Camila's accusatory ones. She's in the same loop I've been in the last six years, weighted down with so much anger.

"There are so many things I wish I had done differently, but loving your daughter was not one of them," I explain. "I don't want to live like that anymore. She wouldn't want that for any of us."

"What do you know about what my daughter would have wanted for us?" she says angrily. "You're the reason she left in the first place!"

"Camila, please," Darren says, trying to calm her down. "That was a long time ago. Mia made those decisions…"

"Because I was suffocating her." Camila raises her voice, looking at Darren incredulously.

"Jack, maybe this wasn't a good idea." Darren turns towards me and pleads.

"I'm glad it was so easy for you to move on." Camila looks at Erin's protective arm looped through mine. Erin doesn't move or loosen her grip.

"That is where you're wrong. It wasn't easy. Believe me, I know."

Erin's words collide into me like a wrecking ball. None of this has been easy, on Erin most of all. She's the innocent bystander in all of this.

"We should go," I say, realizing I'm not going to get what I came for. I thought maybe they'd be able to forgive me, but I realize I don't need them to. The hard part was coming here in the first place, and I said what I needed to say. I am sorry for all the pain I caused them, but I can't change the past. Mia made her own decisions about coming to L.A. with me all those years ago, and she never regretted it. Not for a single second.

"This is my adventure, and the songs are my way of writing home to my dad," Mia had told me once. *"This place is full of stories waiting to be told."* And she got to tell a lot of stories through her music.

"I think that's a good idea." Camila walks us to the front door.

"I am sorry."

Darren looks at me sympathetically, and I think at least that's something.

"You shouldn't have come, Jack," Camila says. "Whatever you are looking for, you're not going to find it here." She shuts the door.

I stand a few seconds more on the porch, noticing the flowerpots on either side of the door. There is a swing at the other end between two columns, facing the forest across the street. I wonder if either one of them are able to enjoy this view.

"Jack?" Erin squeezes her hand tighter around my arm and I realize she hasn't let go of me since we left the sitting room. "Are you okay?"

I was prepared for this. They're not ready to let go of the past. I only feel sorry for them. All this time, I've beaten myself up internally because I thought I needed to be blamed or even hated. Wade and Cash have given me the gift of forgiveness. Being forgiven used to make me feel worse, but now I realize that forgiveness is freeing. My body feels lighter because I'm not carrying this weight around with me anymore.

"Yeah." I place a hand to her face and look into her eyes to reassure her.

"They think if they forgive me, they're letting go of their daughter," I tell her, "but it's the exact opposite."

"Let's go home." Erin nods taking my hand as we descend the steps.

From behind, I hear the door creak open. Darren slips out, chasing after us. "Jack?" He stops us at the bottom of the porch.

"The wounds are still so fresh, even after all these years," he explains, "but I did want to thank you for sending us the book."

"Erin wanted to involve you when she was helping to write it," I look to Erin at my side, "but I thought it was best to leave the two of you be," I explain.

"Better to ask forgiveness than permission." Darren offers a small smile.

"Something like that." Even if I had reached out to them, it wouldn't have changed anything I put in the book. I tried to keep their anonymity as best I could.

Darren momentarily looks back at the house. "I don't think you understand how hard this is on Camila," he pauses. "She blames herself."

"I do understand." More than he knows.

Darren's eyes soften towards me.

"I wanted to give this to you." He holds a notebook out to me. "When Mia came to stay with us," Darren's face looks pained, "after she and Cash separated, she left this in her old room." I take the faux leather notebook from him, the strings still tied, keeping its contents safe.

"We found this on her bed after she went back to L.A., but neither of us read it. When we called to ask her about it, she said to just leave it in her room," Darren explains. "We forgot about it until she..." he trails off. "Camila couldn't bear to look at it, and when I started to skim through it, I knew it wasn't meant for us to read."

Darren points to the notebook now in my hand.

"I think it was meant for Cash," he says, surprising me. "We've tried to reach out to him, but..." he trails off again. "Would you give it to him for us?"

I had no idea Mia's parents tried to reach out to Cash. It's not something Cash would have told me about, but I'm still shocked. Perhaps Cash was too angry after the divorce and wanted to cut off all ties with her family. I honestly don't know what kind of relationship he had with them. Better than mine, I guess.

I hold the notebook gently in my hand as if the leather would disintegrate under a less tender grip.

"Jack?" Darren stops me from leaving again. He momentarily hangs his head and stares at the ground as if he's contemplating what he's going to say. His eyes meet mine and there's an understanding between us that can't be explained. "I know you loved her." Darren looks from me to Erin, and I can feel her grip on my hand tighten. "It's none of my business, but I'm glad to see that you are okay." Not that I need their permission to love someone else, but it's nice to hear.

I smile and nod. "Thank you," I say sincerely.

Sliding being the wheel, I notice I'm still clutching the notebook.

"Jack?" Erin's sweet voice cuts through the silence. The wind is getting stronger, and the clouds loom in the sky ominously. I remember how the summer monsoons come in fast, especially in the high country, and have the potential to cause a lot of damage. The car shifts with the battering of wind.

I set the notebook on the console between us, my fingers running over the worn leather. "Yeah?"

I put the car in gear and drive up the road, not wanting to leave, but not wanting to be in front of this house anymore. There's a hiking path not far from here that runs along the rim. It doesn't take long to get to the dirt road that leads into the gravel parking lot. It's a popular spot, but today there are only a few cars parked, most likely because of the weather.

"Why do you think she left that at her parents' house if it was meant for Cash?" Erin crosses her legs as she rests her head against the back of the seat, turning towards me.

"Maybe she didn't want me to find it or read it." I say, remembering after I dropped her off at her parents, I thought I would never see her again, only to find her on my front porch a couple of weeks later. I often thought about that over the years but we never talked about her parents or Cash. She left Cash for me, or maybe their marriage was already over by then. I don't know.

"What are you going to do with it?" Erin asks.

There is no doubt in my mind. "I will give it to Cash, and he can make the decision if he wants to read it or not." As much as I don't want to re-open wounds, especially after what we went through writing that song, I can't keep this from Cash.

Erin narrows her eyes. "I'm not going to read it," I tell her just as the sky opens up, dumping large droplets of rain on the car that sounds like rocks hitting the roof. Thunder booms in the distance, and I see a flash of lighting between the trees.

Erin looks around nervously. "Is this safe?" It has been a long time since I've been in one of these storms and Erin has never experienced it before. It can be scary, especially with the rain coming down so hard and the wind causing it to hit the car sideways. The ground is so hard there's nowhere for the water to go, causing flooding.

"It'll pass." I take her hand. "It's best if we wait it out here."

Mia always liked the rain. She missed it when we lived in California. I never did. I'd like to think that if there is a heaven and Mia is watching, she conjured this storm to remind me not to fear the storm because the rainbow is not far behind.

Erin looks outside the car again to where the wind grabs the fragile trees and pulls them at an angle. Coming to Payson was a last-minute decision and I don't have any plans past this, but the thought of Erin getting on a plane back to New York causes my chest to constrict.

"Don't go back to New York," I say, chewing on the inside of my cheek as I stare forward through the windshield.

My jaw is set in determination and I let out air through my nose.

"What does that mean?" Erin asks.

"Fuck, Erin," I tip my head back, resting it against the seat cushion and closing my eyes. "You don't have to ever go back."

"Are you asking me to move in with you?" I can hear the smile in her voice.

I tilt my head to the side so I can see her. "Yes."

She frowns and says, "No."

"What do you mean, 'no'?" I lift my head in surprise.

"I like my apartment," she says.

"You hate your apartment," I tell her. A smile widens on her beautiful face. "You're fucking with me, aren't you?" I ask her.

She laughs and I reach over the console to grab her as she tries to escape me with nowhere to go. I capture her lips playfully while the sound of thunder awakens the forest around us. Erin smiles against my lips as she runs her fingers through my hair. I rest the side of my nose against hers.

"I don't want you to move into my beach house," I say against her cheek. She pulls away with a look of confusion.

"I want us to find our own place together," I explain, before she smacks me.

Erin smiles and practically climbs over the console to kiss me. I grab her and pull her all the way over on top of me while trying to push the seat back as far as I can.

"I'm guessing that's a yes?" I ask, laughing against her mouth between kisses. She nods furiously, grinding into the already hardening bulge in my pants.

"You better behave yourself," I warn. "I have no problem fucking you right here in this parking lot." I bite her bottom lip eliciting a moan.

The rain has slowed to a trickle, the parking lot now more visible through the windshield. Cars are pulling out of their parking spots, and I realize we are not alone.

"Shit." Erin slides off me, slumping into her seat like a scolded child. She runs a hand through her sexy, tousled hair and levels me with her golden-brown eyes.

"Take me back to the hotel."

I start the engine and put the car in reverse as fast I can.

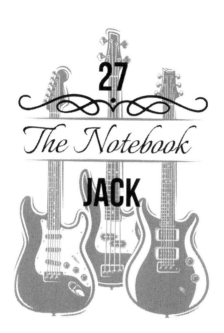

27
The Notebook

JACK

I 've been carrying this leather notebook around with me for a few weeks now. Ever since Erin and I got back from Arizona, I either didn't have the chance or the heart to give it to Cash. The longer I wait, the harder it gets. Now it's just going to be even more awkward giving it to him. Erin is wrapping things up in New York, and I'm left to deal with this on my own. I drive into Santa Monica to Cash's shop, *Music Underground*, because that's where he always is. When I pull up, his bike is parked out front where he likes to keep an eye on it.

The bell chimes when I open the door, and I roll my eyes at the cheesiness. I stop myself from reaching up and flicking it off the top of the door. Cash walks out from the back room and stops short with a withering look when he realizes it's just me.

"Is that the way you greet your customers?" I tease. "No wonder it's crickets in here every time I come to visit." I move towards the counter and lean over the glass casually, the notebook tucked into my back pocket.

"You're not a customer," Cash says flatly.

"I might buy something," I say, offended. "You never know." I glance around the shop and settle on one of the new guitars he has propped up in the corner.

"Did you just come here to make fun of my store?" he asks, moving behind the counter, trying to look busy by rearranging something in the display case.

"No," I say offended. "Can't a guy come and visit his best friend?"

"Jack, with you, there's always an ulterior motive." He narrows his eyes at me.

Well fuck, he does know me too well. I'm a chicken shit and decide to ease in to giving him the notebook. I stride over to the display with the posters he got from that artist and grab one.

Placing it on the counter, I say, "I came to buy this."

Cash flips it around to face him. "You came to buy a screen print of Debbie Harry?"

I snatch it back from him. "Erin likes her," I say indignantly.

"Ah," Cash says as he smiles.

"What is that?" I point to the stupid grin on his face. "What's going on with your face?"

"You are so whipped," Cash chuckles.

I spin away from him on my heel. "Shut the fuck up."

"You buy a house with her and now you're buying Debbie Harry posters."

"We haven't even moved into the house yet."

He's not wrong. Erin liked the idea of waking up to the sound of waves in the morning, and living in the Venice house wasn't an option for me. We needed a fresh start, so we settled on a house in Malibu. What can I say? I want to give the woman what she wants. If that means I'm whipped, so be it.

"What are you doing with the Venice house?" Cash asks while I look at the guitar display. A long time ago when Amber and I were married and we bought that house in the hills, I thought about turning the beach house into a studio. That could still be an option now, but I'm not ready to make any decisions right now.

"Not sure yet," I sigh. The Venice house doesn't hold just memories of Mia, it was where Amber and I raised Hayley. Sometimes it's good to hold onto things.

"Where'd you pick this up at?" I hold the old Washburn bass in my hands.

"Came in with some items I got when that old shop on Kent closed down." Cash takes it from my hands. It fits like a glove against his body. He looked so at home when we recorded the song together, like he actually missed playing.

"You should start playing again."

Cash sets it back on the stand. "Yeah, maybe," he says, far too casually to be casual.

"Hey." I nervously follow him back to the register and reach into my back pocket, placing the notebook on the counter in front of him. It's like ripping off the band aid, do it fast and it won't hurt as much.

He looks at it curiously and then his expression darkens as he realizes what it is. He knows it's Mia's in the same way I do, even if it hadn't been handed to me by her father. The flimsy ties cannot contain what is hidden inside. Its contents sing to him.

"What is that?" he asks, leaning away from it, yet knowing damn well what it is.

"You know what it is," I say gently. "*Whose* it is," I clarify. He's not fooling anyone.

Cash moves his eyes slowly from the notebook to meet my gaze.

"I didn't read it," I answer the question in his eyes.

"Where did you get this?" His eyes lower back to the notebook.

"Mia's father gave it to me," I admit. "He thought it was meant for you."

"That was nearly two weeks ago." Again, he's staring at the notebook, his shoulders tense and I study him, wondering what he's thinking.

"I wasn't purposely trying to keep it from you," I try to explain. "There was never a right time."

After looking at the notebook critically, Cash picks it up and throws it across the room. It hits the wall with a thud and drops to the floor insignificantly.

"Why can't she just leave me the fuck alone?" Cash says angrily.

"Maybe you need to read it and find out?" I sympathize with him.

He shakes his head and leans over the counter, momentarily closing his eyes.

"Do you know why I don't sell this shit hole?" His voice is muffled by his hands cupping his face.

I stand in silence.

"It's not why you think," he says cryptically. "There are things you don't know about me, Jack. There are things you don't get to know." The sadness in his eyes unhinges me.

I know Cash had a whole life with Mia, a life that I am not privy to, nor should I be. When Mia came back to me, she made me promise not to ask what happened between her and Cash. I have never broken that promise and I never will.

I look past Cash to the mural with its blues and greens mixing together like the ocean. I used to look at it with fondness, even though it wasn't even my memory, only because it was another tangible piece of Mia left behind. Now that seems like such a selfish thought.

"Wanna go surfing?" I ask out of the blue.

He looks at me dumbfounded. Neither one of us surfs.

"Have you lost it?" Cash furrows his brows.

My phone vibrates in my pocket. It's a number I don't recognize so I shove my phone back in my pocket.

"Remember when you first came to L.A.?"

Cash cocks his head at me. "Let's not go there," he pleads, embarrassed.

"We borrowed a couple of boards," I continue.

"Please stop." A smile spreads on his face as he speaks.

I can't help but laugh as I recount the story. "You were trying to impress that girl, the one that worked at the shaved ice hut."

Cash shakes his head, laughing.

The phone vibrating in my pocket again interrupts our conversation. Annoyed, I pull it out to see the same number. I start to shove it back in my pocket again, but at the last minute I make the decision to answer.

"It's Beck." Her voice comes through the phone and instantly all the hairs on my arm stand on end.

"What's wrong with Hayley?" I say instinctively. My heart moves up into my throat.

"She'd kill me if she knew I called you." I want to reach into the phone to shake her.

"Beck, tell me what the fuck is going on!" I urge her in a not so polite way.

"I'm outside Bobby's office building," Beck hesitates. "He tried to do something to her." I don't wait for her to continue before I pull the keys out of my pocket and head out the front door.

"What's wrong?" Cash follows me.

"Bobby fucking Hanson," I growl.

I hear the click of the door being locked and a few seconds later, Cash's bike comes alive with a deafening roar. He peels out of the parking lot behind me.

28

Deja Vu

ERIN

"**A**re you sure you don't want to sublease my apartment?" I ask Sasha, cradling the phone to my ear as I push a couple of boxes into the corner of my apartment. They are filled mostly with clothes or personal effects. As I look at the few boxes I do have, it's kind of depressing. There's not much, not that my apartment would allow for me to be a pack rat, but it just goes to show how little I made this place my own. I used to think living in New York was exciting, making it on my own even if I struggled. Having a closet sized apartment was part of paying your dues.

Will I miss listening to Journey on repeat for hours? No.

Will I miss waking up to the sound of the garbage truck every Tuesday morning? No.

Will I miss this shitty little apartment? Maybe.

"I enrolled in UCLA for the fall," Sasha announces excitedly.

I drop the industrial sized tape dispenser on a box. "What?!" I practically yell into the phone.

Sasha chuckles. "I don't want to go back to Austin," she declares. "I have one more year left, and I can do most of my classes online anyway."

I suspect there are other reasons she doesn't want to go back to Austin, but I don't say anything.

"Plus, I got an internship at *Alt Press!*" she practically yells into the phone. "The pictures I took of *No Cover* and the ones from Summerfest got some attention," she says proudly.

"Shut the front door!" I jump up and down.

I have no doubt Sasha will do great. Sandy is an awesome editor, and I know she will treat Sasha right.

"You're amazing," she says. "If it weren't for meeting you, none of this would have happened."

"I'm so glad everything worked out," I smile into the phone.

"What are you going to do with your apartment?" she asks.

I'm leaving all of the furniture, my loveseat, table and lamp, the TV hanging on the wall, and my bedroom set, for whoever subleases my apartment.

Not that I don't trust my relationship with Jack, but I've always been on my own and my instincts always tell me I should have a backup plan. I'm just not ready to give up my apartment altogether. Subleasing is a compromise, and it gives me the little bit of security I need.

"I'll find someone to lease it." Apartments, even the most disgusting, rattiest ones, go quick, and even though I'm in Queens, my proximity to the city makes it very desirable. The rent is slightly less than in Manhattan, and it's in a good neighborhood.

"My offer still stands," Sasha says quietly into the phone.

I laugh. "I think one road trip with you was enough. Besides, I'm mailing all my boxes to my new house in Malibu and catching a flight home." The word 'home' feels heavy on my tongue. I've referred to my apartment as home, but it never really felt like it. It was a place I stayed when I wasn't traveling or working. The lack of personal items here leads me to believe that I never really thought of it as permanent anyway.

When Jack and I left Payson, we went back to L.A. and started looking for a house right away. It was overwhelming to say the least, but we found the perfect house. I insisted on using some of the book money, so it felt equal between the two of us. Although meager compared to what it actually cost, I still felt like I was contributing.

I knew the minute the real estate agent showed it to us that it was our home. Situated on a bluff overlooking the ocean, the house is magical. It's not too big, but there's enough rooms for guests and an office. I've already started imagining how I would decorate my office, which is just one of the perks to having a home bigger than a closet.

It's the perfect location for privacy, and close enough to the studio and *Left Turn Records* offices. Jack is working on refining the album and the song he and Cash wrote together. I can work from anywhere, especially if I'm taking time off to write my dad's biography.

"Well, if you change your mind, you know where to find me," Sasha says, bringing me out of my thoughts.

I smile into the phone, and we say our goodbyes. I have a feeling I'm going to be seeing a lot more of her anyway, especially if she's going to be attending UCLA. I tape up the last of my boxes and label them. Someone will be by to pick them up for mailing. I look around the apartment, surveying it for anything I left behind, but find nothing.

I flop down onto the couch, exhausted, when my phone rings again. It's from a number I don't recognize, but I pick it up anyway.

"Erin?" A familiar voice asks, as if she doesn't know it's me.

"Amber?" I ask tentatively. She has never called me before, not even when I spoke to her about the book. We're not friends, but we are civil to one another, so this must be a good sign if she's calling me. "How are you?" I ask politely.

"This isn't a social call," she says harshly, but then everything that comes out of her mouth sounds snotty whether she means it to or not. It's just Amber, so I roll my eyes.

"Is everything okay?" I start to get impatient

"Not exactly," she says.

"Okay, Amber, I don't have time for this. What's going on?"

"Okay, wow, that's aggressive."

"Amber?"

"Okay, okay. I just wanted to let you know that Jack is in jail." She drops the bomb in one rapid-fire breath.

"What?!" I yell into the phone. I've only been gone a couple days to finish packing things up in my apartment and all hell breaks loose.

"He's been arrested for aggravated assault," she says, as if it's no big deal.

"What happened?" I'm in shock. "Who?"

"I'm not his personal assistant," Amber huffs, and if I could strangle her through the phone, I would.

"And I don't talk to journalists."

I sigh. "You do realize that I'm not going to write about this?" I ask. "He's my..." What do I call someone that I'm living with? 'Boyfriend' doesn't even begin to describe what Jack is.

"I wouldn't do that," I clarify.

"All I know right now is he got arrested for attacking Bobby Hanson at his office." She's no help.

"Wait, why are you the one calling me?" I ask. "Wade's usually the family gossip." He likes to be the one in the know.

"Wade was arrested with him," Amber says. "And Cash, too." I don't think I can be more shocked but I am, although this is not the first time the three of them have been in jail together.

"What the fuck?" I flop down onto my couch. This ought to be a good one.

"**D**oes this feel like deja vu to any of you?" I scrunch up my nose and peer at Cash and Wade who are sitting on the bench in the holding cell next to me.

Wade turns his gaze in my direction. "Probably, because this *has* happened before." He rolls his eyes at me.

I look to Cash. "Nineteen ninety..." He presses his finger to his temple thinking.

"That fight with our hotel security!" I say excitedly at remembering the detail. I nod my head. "Good times." I bring my arms up over my head and link my fingers behind my neck.

"Seattle?" Cash cocks his head.

"No, that was in Michigan," I correct him.

"Michigan was when we got kicked out of the restaurant," Cash offers.

I shake my head. "I don't remember all of us being in jail in Michigan."

"That's because only you got arrested," Cash points out.

"Fuckers left me to rot." I shake my head, turning away from him.

"Is this funny to you?" Wade stands up and paces the small cell. "I have a kid," he moans.

"We know," both Cash and I say in unison.

Wade pierces us with a menacing glare, and if weaponized, we'd both be dead right now.

I stand and walk over to the bars, wrapping my hands around them. He's right, this isn't funny.

A few moments later, I feel Wade standing next to me.

"That asshole is going to get what he deserves," he reassures me.

I didn't have time to think about what was happening. It's only now that I realize Cash must have called Wade on his way over to Bobby's office, because I sure didn't. Now we're all in jail, and I don't know what's going to happen.

"I should have done more to protect her. I knew what he was like, and I did nothing." I grip the bar tighter, mentally chastising myself that once again, I let my kid down.

"You didn't know everything he was capable of," Wade says as he places a hand on my shoulder. "It was just rumors," he says sheepishly.

"I just can't help thinking that I failed her." I hang my head.

"*We* failed her," Wade says. "Hayley's always been special to us, you know that. From the minute she was old enough to join us in the studio, she was like our little groupie."

"Don't call her that," I grumble.

"You know what I mean."

"I get it." I push off the bars.

Beck was in the lobby when I got there. Hayley had already left. All I saw was red when Beck described to me that Bobby had tried to make a move on Hayley in his office. When he wouldn't let her leave, she panicked. Luckily, a secretary walked in on them, giving Hayley the opportunity to get out of there. Even though Beck knew Hayley would be pissed, she told me anyway. She didn't want that asshole to get away with anything either.

I have a newfound respect for Beck now. She's not the spoiled rich party girl I unfairly dubbed her as. She's a good friend to Hayley.

"The thing is, I knew enough." I turn to Wade in anguish. "I should have done something sooner." Wade's soft brown eyes look back at me with sympathy, but it doesn't make me feel any better.

I scratch my head and return to sit down on the concrete bench, putting my head in my hands as I lean over my thighs.

"He's not getting away with anything," Cash tries to reassure me.

"So why are we in here and he's not?" I throw my hand up in the air in frustration.

"What's that saying?" Cash turns to Wade for help. "Revenge is a dessert you can eat cold?"

"Best served cold," Wade corrects him, rolling his eyes.

"Well, I don't fucking know!" Cash says, annoyed.

"What is taking Adam so long?" Wade paces.

Cash slumps further into the concrete bench.

"Worried no one's going to come for you?" I give Cash a little push.

"Fuck off, Jack," he sighs.

"I think we all know no one's coming for me." I lean back.

"Hayley will get over it," Cash says, trying to make me feel better, but it's not working.

"Fuck," I complain as I rub my chin. "This is gonna be all over the tabloids."

"Maybe it won't be that bad," Wade offers.

I pierce him with a gaze as if to ask, 'are you stupid?'

"What you should be worried about is Bobby suing you," Cash says as he leans over his thighs.

"Not helping, Mr. Sunshine," Wade interjects

Cash mockingly mouths the words 'Mr. Sunshine' at Wade, but I ignore them both.

I stand up. "I don't give a fuck if he sues me!" I shout angrily. "He touched my fucking kid!" I can feel the anger bubbling up inside of me again the more I think about it.

"If it's any consolation, I got in a good punch before security came," Cash winces.

"I had him in a headlock." Wade mimics wrapping his arm around a phantom Bobby.

"That was me you had in a headlock you idiot!" Cash says as he rolls his eyes at Wade.

I smile, laughing a little. Security was quick to break up the fight. If I had been smart, I wouldn't have shoved all the shit off Bobby's desk making a scene before I had the chance to reach across and grab him.

"Hayley's lucky to have you two idiots for honorary uncles," I chuckle, shaking my head. "Or unlucky, depending on how you look at it." I cock an eyebrow at the pair of them.

The room becomes quiet, only the sound of footsteps echoing of the walls as someone nears the cell. The room to the holding cells opens and an officer calls our names. We stand up expectantly, looking at each other. Someone must have bailed us all out at the same time. My guess is Adam finally got a sitter and made his way down here.

From experience, processing bail takes a long time. It's not like the officers have an incentive to move quickly.

After being let out of the cell, the officer walks us down the hallway, and as soon as all the paperwork is done, we exit the building to the street.

"Wade!" Adam sees us and runs over to pull Wade into a hug.

"Thanks for bailing me out." I reach out my hand to shake his, but he pulls me in for a hug instead. "I only bailed out Wade and Cash," he tells me once he let's go of me, a sympathetic look in his eyes which is telling.

Behind him, I hear the familiar click of heels on the concrete sidewalk and groan. Erin's in New York packing and she doesn't wear heels, so I know it's not her. My worst nightmare is coming true, again.

"What the fuck were you thinking?" Amber points at all of us, placing her hand on her hip and piercing us with a look.

I hang my head. Fuck.

"We need to get back to Dylan. The neighbor is watching him." Adam says sympathetically and pulls on Wade to leave.

"The Morrisons?" Wade asks horrified.

"I was in a hurry, and I couldn't very well bring Dylan to the police station with me," Adam says annoyed.

"They have gnomes in their front yard!" Wade gives me a wave before he starts to walk away, arguing with Adam. "Fucking gnomes!" I hear his exasperated tone as they walk past Amber.

"Those fucking vultures are going to have a field day with this," Amber shakes her head at me.

I know Hayley won't appreciate the unwanted attention, but I'd do it again in a heartbeat.

"I know," I say.

"There were better ways to handle this," Amber says. "Smarter ways." She levels me with a knowing look. I'm not known for making smart decisions.

"He deserved it," Cash pipes up.

"You can leave now, Cash," Amber narrows her eyes at him.

"Leaving." Cash offers me a small smile as he makes his exit but then stops abruptly. "Um, I don't have a ride," he realizes as he furrows his brow.

"Take a fucking Uber!" Amber hands him a Ziploc bag with his personal effects. He snatches them and hurries down the sidewalk.

"You never think about the consequences!" Amber admonishes, shaking her head, not missing a beat. Behind her, I see a familiar blonde head bobbing as she hurries down the sidewalk towards us. The blood drains from my face.

Hayley stops short of reaching me, anger etched on her face. All I can think about is the fucker's hands on my daughter and I see red. I clench my fists.

"I told you to stay out of my business!" she yells at me, and I wince. "You can't just barge into someone's office and beat the shit of them!"

I sure as shit can and I did. I take a deep breath, taking whatever anger she throws my way.

"I didn't ask you to get involved!" Hayley huffs. "I don't need you to protect me either." Her blue eyes swim with emotion. "Despite what you think, I can take care of myself."

I start to open my mouth, but she stops me. "You're such an asshole sometimes!" she states before crashing into me. Her arms wrap around my torso, and she presses her face to my chest. It's a familiar feeling but so foreign at the same time, because she hasn't hugged me in a very long time.

Tentatively, I wrap my arms around her, placing the palm of my hand at her back and gently pressing her further against me. I've missed this so much.

"Thank you," she whispers in my ear.

I look over Hayley's shoulder at Amber. She places her hand to her chest and gives me a small smile. I smile back at her and then close my eyes, savoring the feeling of my kid giving me a hug.

"I would do anything for you, kid." I dare to press a kiss into the top of her head.

29
The Wedding
JACK

My nerves take over as I stand in the chapel's dressing room, pulling at the collar of my shirt.

"I look stupid in this thing," I complain, trying to straighten my tie.

"You look fine," Cash says as he assesses me. "It's me that looks stupid." He unbuttons his suit jacket.

Cash is wearing a maroon suit jacket with black lapels and matching black slacks. The dark colors are offset by a white button-down shirt. His blonde hair is slicked back, and he's actually clean shaven. Clearly, Amber scared everyone with threats of balls being cut off if we didn't look presentable for her wedding.

"I know you didn't shop for that yourself," I tease and wink at him.

"Sasha helped me pick it out." He looks at himself in the mirror again for the millionth time.

I eye him.

"Don't look at me like that."

"I didn't say anything," I smirk.

"She's helping me out at the store while she goes to school. That's all," Cash is quick to retort, and I leave it be.

"Hey, you two, quit looking at yourselves in the mirror. Show's going to start soon." Wade enters the room all smiles and comfortable in his black tux.

"I'm not, I mean I am, but, oh fuck off, Wade," I stumble. "Shit, why am I so nervous? It's not even my wedding."

"Whoa there Johnny Cash, you're not gonna lose your lunch, are ya?" Adam saunters in wearing an electric blue suit jacket with black lapels. His dark hair is spiked to perfection.

I look down at my black on black tux and think, shit, I do look like Johnny Cash.

"*The Mirage* called and said you're late for the magic show," I tease, my mouth quirking up in a smile.

Adam mocks me. "Late for the magic show, fuck off."

"Do you mind if I get a picture?" The photographer leans into the already crowded room. We all cock our heads and give him a fuck off look, just as the flash goes off. He disappears quickly before anyone can get ahold of him.

"We should get going," Wade says, hooking his thumb in the direction of the main chapel down the hall. He takes Adam's hand in his and a nostalgic look passes between them. I think they are the only people who actually like weddings. Meanwhile, I feel like I'm experiencing hot flashes in this tux.

Cash turns to me before he leaves. "Are you coming?"

"Yeah, I'll be right there. I just want to fix my tie," I lie, wanting to take a moment for myself.

The last wedding I went to was Adam and Wade's. Generally, I don't like these types of events; too many people, too many things to remember. I'm out of my element.

"What the fuck, Jack? You're gonna make me late," Amber complains as she stands in the doorway, hand on her hip.

"Wow, Amber, you look..." I can't seem to find my words. The old Hollywood style satin wedding dress fits her well. I don't think I've ever seen her look this beautiful, or this happy.

"Stunning?" she teases.

She stands back and takes a good look at me. "You clean up real nice, Jack O'Donnell." She nods her approval.

"Are you sure you want me to do this?" I ask with concern. "I tend to fuck things up, ya know." Amber's dad passed away a few years ago, and she thought it seemed fitting that I should be the one to give her away.

"Don't back out on me." She points a finger at me in threat.

I step forward and hold my arm out for her to take. She smiles at me, giving my bicep a firm squeeze. We have come such a long way from where we began, and I like this Amber much more. Especially since I don't have to send her anymore alimony checks.

I can hear music playing as we walk down the hall and stop in front of the big oak doors. Once they open, there's no going back.

"You sure you want to go through with this? Because my car is parked out front and we can hop in…"

She stops me by placing her hand over mine.

"Thank you, Jack." She gives me a genuine smile and then leans in to give me a peck on the cheek. There is a real love between us.

The organ begins the wedding march, and the oak doors open. Everyone stands as I walk Amber down the aisle. I know it seems weird or even inappropriate, but since when have we ever given a shit about what anyone thinks? This is how we do things in our family, and fuck anyone who doesn't like it.

When the priest asks, 'Who gives this woman to be married,' I say, "I do," as I choke down my emotions. Fucking weddings.

I give Amber a kiss on the cheek and hand her over to Stephen, who is looking at Amber the way a man who is head over heels looks at a woman. I give Hayley, who is standing next to her mom, a wink. She smiles back at me and takes Amber's bouquet.

In the front pew is Amber's mother and her sister, Rachel, who is glaring at me. I raise my eyebrow to her arrogantly as I take my seat next to Erin.

"Do you have to taunt her?" Erin whispers, humor in her voice.

"She can eat dirt."

Erin suppresses a laugh.

243

E verything is pink, grey, or white in the ballroom, which suits Amber perfectly. Soft music plays in the background while me and the boys get set up. I have to admit, I'm excited Wade agreed to play.

This is a one-time only *Mogo* concert for Amber's wedding. We haven't played together since the '90s. I promised Amber I wouldn't stage dive or try to hang from the lights that dangle from the ceiling.

Wade does a little drumbeat to warm up and get everyone's attention. Guests have already arrived, taking their assigned seats or mingling by the bar. I turn towards Cash, who looks odd wearing a suit with the Washburn strapped to him. Although, I look just as odd with my black tux and my old Fender. Amber was so elated I wore a tux she didn't even notice my black chucks, although I'm sure she will at some point, and I'll catch hell for it later.

"Has it come to this?" Cash says to me before we start. "We're playing weddings now?" He chuckles.

I pull the pick from between my teeth. "It appears so."

Amber and Stephen are ready to enter the ballroom, and the wedding coordinator motions for me to start the song. I look over at Cash and nod as he stands close to the mic. "Please welcome, Mr. and Mrs. Ambrose!" All the attention is diverted to the doors of the ballroom as they swing open, and Amber and Stephen stroll in. I'm supposed to play some stupid pop song, but when do I ever do as I'm told? I give Amber a wink and say, "Congrats, babe." Wade starts the beat to *My Sharona*. While I'm singing, the wedding coordinator tries to get my attention, using the universal sign for 'cut', like this is a movie set.

I'm Jack O'Donnell. I play whatever the fuck I want.

Amber shakes her head as she walks by, a huge smile on her face. She's used to my antics by now, and I have taken advantage of her good mood. I think she's just happy that I'm in a tux. I can do whatever I want now, and she wouldn't be pissed. Well, almost anything.

Amber and Stephen start dancing and the guests join in. I jump around on stage like I'm twenty years old again, but I know I'll pay for it tomorrow.

It's not lost on me that this is the first time *Mogo* is playing without

Mia, either on stage or in the crowd. I'd like to think she's watching and smiling at us right now. I know Cash feels it too when he looks over at me as we sing the chorus into the same mic. There's nothing like having your best friend on stage with you. It feels like coming home in the best possible way. Life is like a circle; you always end where you begin.

"Thank you," I say into the mic as the song ends. We wait for the crowd of partygoers to settle down as we get ready for the next song.

In the back of the room, I see Erin standing near the entrance watching us, amusement on her beautiful face. The sight of her takes my breath away, and not because of the dress she's wearing. It's just her, making my heart beat faster. I like it when she watches me play.

Everything in my life can be summed up into songs, like a playlist. When I look at Erin, I hear only one. So, I do what I do best and speak to her through my music.

"This one goes out to you, Erin." Looking directly at her, I start playing the chords to Stevie Ray Vaughn's *Pride and Joy*, whaling on this Fender with everything I have. It only took a couple chords for Cash and Wade to understand and roll with it.

I watch as Erin puts her hand up to her mouth to hide her shy smile and shake her head at me. God, I don't want to ever live without that smile.

Before the song even ends, I jump off the stage, pull the guitar strap over my head and walk straight to her. In seconds she's in my arms and I lift her up to kiss her, pressing my mouth to hers as if my life depends on it.

"How did you know I love that song?" she says when I finally release her.

"It's the song that plays in my head every time I see you." I hold her close to me, not wanting to ever let go. I'm making a life with this woman, and I know it won't be easy, but *she* is worth fighting for.

ERIN

"Father of the bride sits over there." Cash points to the long table set up for the wedding party.

"Fuck off." Jack waves him away and takes his seat at the table. "I'd rather sit at the kids table." He raises his eyes at Cash and laughs.

Sasha watches all of this with wide eyes and amusement.

"Where is the rugrat tonight?" Cash asks as he rests his arm over the back of Adam's chair, waiting for his reply.

Adam turns his gaze to Cash, his electric blue suit jacket glaring under all the lights. "My brother and his wife have him for the night."

"Wow, and neither one of you are hyperventilating," Cash teases, eliciting a glare from both Adam and Wade.

"Adam, can you turn off your jacket? I'm gonna go blind." Jack raises his hand to his eyes.

"Fuck off, Jack." Adam shrugs out of his jacket and lays it on the back of his chair. "I was warm anyway," he tells Wade in a huff.

"The real wedding band is pretty good," I say, tapping the toe of my heels to the tune. I don't wear high heels often. I'm more of a casual kind of girl, comfortable in a pair of jeans and a T-shirt, but it's nice to have an occasion to get dressed up for. Not to mention how much I like the way Jack looks at me in this dress. I feel wanted.

"I'm insulted." Wade clutches his heart and fakes being offended.

I giggle. Maybe this *is* the equivalent of the kid's table.

"You guys were pretty good too," I reassure them.

I didn't realize how hungry I was until the waiters start dropping off plates of food. I opted for salmon because I'm not much of a meat eater, but everyone's dish of steak or chicken looks just as good.

I take a bite of my salmon, and at the same time, I feel Jack's hand on my thigh under the table. I look over at him coyly and he smiles at me as his hand moves the material of my dress to the side so he can feel my bare skin.

My fork drops against the plate making a clattering noise as Jack's fingers move up my thigh and slide over my panties. I'm already aroused by the way Jack has been looking at me all night, fantasizing about taking him in the banquet hall's coat check room. With so many people at the table, it fills me with excitement. I never thought something like this would turn me on, but I can't help myself when it comes to Jack. Instead of feeling dirty, he makes me feel empowered.

I grab my fork and shove in another mouthful of salmon, but it doesn't quite stifle the moan escaping my lips as his fingers slide inside of me. I can feel the wetness dampening my panties already.

"Maybe I should have gotten the salmon." Wade's comment interrupts my thoughts as he looks at my plate innocently, and then gives his chicken an unexcited poke. I nearly choke on my food, eliciting a low chuckle from Jack. I am fighting the need to close my eyes and tip my head back. Just as I'm about to, he removes his fingers from inside me.

I whip my head in his direction, upset with the disruption, but he doesn't acknowledge me. Slowly he slips a finger inside his mouth. Heat floods my face as I watch him.

"Mm, mine tastes really good," Jack smirks.

"You're supposed to use your fork," Wade chastises him, completely unaware. "Quit acting like a caveman."

"Great," Hayley startles me from behind, "I get stuck at the boring table." She points to where the wedding party is enjoying their food with no shenanigans.

It's been a long day and I wasn't even the one getting married. Weddings are supposed to make you sappy or nostalgic, but I was neither of those things. It's not the wedding or the piece of paper that I'm after, it's the life that comes after. It's what I already have with Jack at our Malibu home. Not only do I get to wake up to the sound of waves every morning, I get to wake up next to Jack.

"Come sit with us then." Jack motions for Hayley to take his seat as he stands up. Sasha scoots closer to Cash who looks uncomfortable at the close proximity, to make more room at the table. I'm not sure what's going on between the two of them. She's started classes and I haven't been able to ask how that's going. Plus, she's been interning for *Alt Press* and working at Cash's record store. I don't know how the girl does everything. Hoping to have some time to catch up later, I focus my attention on Hayley who looks so beautiful in her Maid of Honor dress.

The off-the-shoulder soft pink satin compliments her. I've been to some weddings where the bridesmaid dresses are just hideous. Amber chose well, and I shouldn't have expected anything less. She does have great taste.

"Where will you sit?" Hayley looks reluctant to take her dad's seat. Hayley and I have gotten to know each other better these last few months and I have loved seeing her and Jack connecting. It makes the book I'm writing about my dad all the more bittersweet. Seeing what they have together, even after all of the bullshit, makes me ache for what I could have had with my own dad if he were still alive. In a way, writing this book is my way of reconnecting with him.

Jack looks around and sees an empty chair at the next table and drags it over. No doubt, the unsuspecting guest who got up to use the bathroom will come back to no chair.

"You can't do that," Wade pipes up, "there's a seating chart!"

Jack chuckles low in his throat and shakes his head as if Wade just said the stupidest thing in the world.

He lowers himself into the chair and sits just as the waiter comes over to refill drinks.

"How are you liking Venice?" I ask Hayley.

"I love it," she beams.

I understood when Jack didn't want to sell the house in Venice Beach, although it wasn't for the same reason I was subleasing my apartment. Not because he couldn't give it up, but because it had so much history. He thought about turning it into a studio and that's still an option someday. Hayley was looking for her own place, and it made sense for her to move in. After everything that happened with Bobby, she didn't finish out the rest of the tour and needed a quiet place of her own to figure out what she wanted to do next.

Jack was relieved when Beck moved in with her. He didn't like the thought of Hayley living alone. The story about Jack assaulting Bobby was in the tabloids, and paparazzi were hounding Hayley more than usual.

After Jack got arrested and I found out what happened, I called

Sandy, my old editor at *Alt Press*. I was betting Hayley was not the only victim of Bobby's. I provided whatever information I had, and my hunch was that there was more to it than just sexual harassment. Sandy wanted me to start investigating, talking to the secretary, putting out feelers for any other artists that had been victimized by Bobby, but I told her I couldn't be the one to write the story.

I wanted to bring down Bobby Hanson and make him pay for preying on young female artists, but I couldn't be the one to do it. It was a conflict of interest because this was Jack's daughter, and I didn't want anything to compromise the investigation. Sandy gave it to one of her senior journalists.

I couldn't expect her to keep me in the loop for fear it would get leaked and give Bobby a chance to spin his own story, but I've gotten enough information to believe he's going to get what's coming to him. As much as Jack hated it, he played along with not fighting the charges of the arrest. Court cases take forever in L.A. County, as well as any lawsuits Bobby filed. When the story breaks about his dirty deals and assault accusations, none of this other stuff will matter. I'm just counting down the days until it does.

I can feel it in my bones that it won't be long now before we hear something.

I am brought out of my thoughts by the sound of Jack's laughter. I didn't catch whatever was funny, but I love to hear Jack laugh, almost as much as I like to hear him sing.

The band is playing soft instrumental music while everyone eats.

"Would you like to dance?" Jack holds his hand out to me.

I take it and he leads me to the dance floor. We are the only two people since everyone else is still eating. Jack takes me in his arms and holds me close as we move to the music. It reminds me of a time not too long ago. He danced with me in his house to music only he could hear. Except this time, I can hear the music too.

"You are so bad." I shake my head at him, burrowing my nose against the side of his neck, thinking about his hands on me under the table. I breathe him in, smelling bubble gum and cologne. He's been pretty good about not smoking, but occasionally I catch the familiar scent on him.

"You like it when I'm bad." He swings me around and dips me, pressing a kiss to my collarbone.

I can't think of a better place to be than in Jack's arms. Maybe his bed, or rather *our* bed. I'll never get tired of saying the word *'ours'*.

Looking back at the table, I can see Amber has made her way over to greet guests. Adam's arm is stretched over the back of Wade's chair, and they lean into each other. Cash looks to be telling a story that has everyone in stitches as Amber reaches over and playfully smacks his arm. I'm so glad to see Hayley laughing too after everything she's been through.

I can't think of a better table to be at, or better friends than the ones sitting around it. I had friends growing up and some close work friends, but none of them have ever felt like family. That is what these people have become to me.

Family.

The song ends and we stand together in the middle of the dance floor.

"So now what?" he asks, a mischievous look in his eye. I think I have everything I've ever wanted.

"You invite me into the coat check room?" I raise my eyebrows suggestively.

Jack grins.

Epilogue
JACK

"Wow." I think my mouth just dropped to the floor. I never thought I would say that Erin could look sexier with clothes *on*, but this dress was made for her. The slit up the side gives me a view of those killer legs, and in heels they look even longer.

"I take it you like?" Erin smiles coyly at me.

I take a step closer to her, letting my fingers touch her bare shoulder and travel down her arm. "I want to see what this dress looks like on the floor," I whisper against her ear.

Erin swallows hard.

"Jack," she laughs, "we're going to be late."

"Fuck the Grammys." Seriously, I don't need one. I just need Erin.

"You can't skip the Grammys! You're performing." She takes my hand as we exit the house and climb into the waiting limo.

The limo hits traffic as soon as we are out of Malibu.

I cross and uncross my legs several times. "This is the longest car ride I've ever been in," I groan.

"Stop complaining. You're like a child," Erin scolds me, crossing her legs and effectively distracting me.

"That's not the first time I've been called a child," I say defiantly.

"I believe it," Erin replies as she rolls her eyes at me. "There's no reason to be nervous." She places a hand on my knee to stop it from bouncing.

"I'm not nervous." We both know that's a lie. "Fuck." I run my hands through my hair.

"Hey," Erin places a hand to my cheek. "You can do this." She searches my eyes for acknowledgment. I take a deep breath and nod.

When the limo pulls up outside of the Staples Center, I can hear the crowd from inside the car. Security surrounds the limo and lines the roped off area where fans are waiting.

"Are you ready for this?" I ask Erin. It's not our first public appearance, but it's the fucking Grammys. There's no going back now.

"I go where you go," Erin says, and I take her hand to help her exit the limo.

"I will follow that ass anywhere," I say behind her, tempted to give it a smack, but I know the photographers are already taking pictures. Erin would be pissed if there's a photo of me smacking her ass on the cover of *Entertainment Weekly*.

"Asshole," she scolds me and laughs. I like the sound of her laughter. Cameras flash in our faces as security leads us past the crowd to the red carpet. Reporters wait to interview celebrities and musicians as they pass by. The area is thick with people, and we wait our turn.

Cash, Adam, and Wade are here somewhere, probably waiting for us inside.

"Jack? Do you have a moment for some questions?" A reporter stops us on the red carpet.

She doesn't give me a chance to say no before she bombards me with questions.

"This is the first time you'll be performing with your old bandmates, what can we expect?" She shoves the microphone in my face.

Mogo is performing the song Cash and I wrote, *Breath to Bear* tonight, because it is up for Best Rock Song of the Year, along with Album of the Year for the album Mia and I made together. We have a special dedication planned that has been under wraps. Only the producers of the show are aware.

"A good fucking show," I say, knowing full well they can't air that answer.

"You're nominated for Album of the Year," she says. "How does that feel?"

Real fucking original. "Be nice," Erin whispers in my ear, knowing I'm already annoyed with this woman.

"Great." I smile sarcastically.

"We should get inside," Erin interrupts sweetly and tugs on my arm to move us along. "Thank you." She waves over her shoulder.

Lots of musicians I've known over the years mill around, chatting with each other and with reporters. I make pleasantries, and now Erin looks more nervous than I was.

"This is exciting." Erin tugs on my arm, noticing that we are standing behind Turn it Up. "Shit, tell me you know them. Can you introduce me?" Erin asks, expectantly.

"Why are you getting all fangirl? You're around musicians all the time," I ask.

"No one as big as Turn it Up. And, well, their lead singer is..." She doesn't finish her sentence, realizing she was once sent to interview me.

I cock my eyebrow at her. "Don't you think one Jack is enough for you?"

Erin barks out a laugh and then demurely covers her mouth.

"You're being a grump," she teases.

"I don't like crowds." I fidget because I'm wearing a white button up shirt that I'm not used to. At least Erin didn't give me shit for wearing my leather jacket and black jeans. It's the Grammys, not a funeral. I've worn enough suits this year.

Erin shakes her head and laughs. "You're just nervous."

While we wait our turn to enter the building, I discreetly run my fingers along her bare back.

"What are you trying to do to me, Jack?" she smiles and whispers in my ear.

"You're so fucking sexy in this dress. I can't wait to get you out of it." I run my nose along her ear and flick my tongue out alone the sensitive outer edge. She smells like flowers.

Erin turns to me, a mischievous look on her face. "I want to see what you look like on your knees." Her cheeks flush a pale pink, and she has no idea how much I would love to oblige her request right here. As cameras flash around us, my balls tighten in response to her request.

"Can I get you to turn this way?!" A photographer calls out, distracting me from my X-rated thoughts. I oblige and turn Erin to face the camera, putting my arm around her waist.

I lean towards her, my lips close to her ear as the photographer takes a few photos. "Don't call my bluff because I will get on my fucking knees for you right here on this red carpet." Erin sucks in a breath. I have no shame when it comes to this woman. She turns me on with just a look, lights me on fire with just a touch, and I would do anything she asked of me just to get a taste of her.

The crowd in front of us disappears and we make our way towards the entrance.

The host for the evening is standing in front of the podium, the screen behind him displaying a photo of Mia. She looks so young and full of life in that picture, it makes my heart constrict. He introduces the chairman of the Rock 'n Roll Hall of Fame who walks out from the side of the stage. Cash, Wade, and I are waiting in the wings to be called out on stage to perform.

The chairman speaks into the mic. "The Rock 'n Roll Hall of Fame is honored to receive this extraordinary piece of history tonight which will be on display in the Cleveland Rock Museum." His gaze stretches out to the crowd of musicians watching the screen. "I have come to learn that when inspiration strikes and there isn't a piece of paper to be found, song lyrics can be written on many odd things. In fact, the lyrics to some of the most famous songs have been written on napkins, toilet paper, on the back of a grocery receipt, and even an envelope, but I must admit, this is the first time we've ever seen lyrics written on a pair of jeans." The audience chuckles. "The story behind these jeans is an incredible tale of things once lost finding their way back again. We are incredibly humbled and excited to be able to put these jeans on display." The screen flashes to a picture of the jeans with the lyrics to *Blood and Bone* written on them, preserved behind a glass display at the museum.

I admit, I wanted to burn them, to exorcise them from my life but that doesn't serve any purpose. When I reached out to the museum, they were more than willing to accept the artifact.

Wade gives my shoulder a squeeze, a gesture of pride and strength for us both. I look over at Cash who seems contemplative and solemn. It's a huge night for all of us, but not without memories that bring about great emotion.

"It is my pleasure tonight to introduce Jack O'Donnell, Cash Morgan, and Wade Kernish, here to perform for you a new song, which, by the way, is up for Best Rock Song of the Year." Thunderous clapping greets us as we walk out onto the stage. My guitar is handed to me by one of the techs who also leaves a mic stand as he runs off stage. Cash clasps the strap to his bass, and behind me, Wade situates himself behind the drums.

I search the crowd for Erin who I find standing in front of our seats not too far back from the stage, a huge smile on her face, and she's clapping proudly. Next to her are Mia's parents, Darren and Camila Stone, while Adam smiles from the other side of Erin. I'm glad Mia's parents agreed to be here tonight in order to witness the dedication and be a part of the celebration their daughter inspired. After Darren handed me the notebook when I last visited them, I realized they are healing on their own time. Camila just needed a chance to see the person I have become, in part because of her daughter. I strive to be a better person, to learn from the past, and look towards the future. There is an understanding between us now, in order to heal, we first have to learn to forgive.

Emotions are running high tonight, and not just because of *Mogo* performing for the first time professionally together without Mia, but because of everything this album represents.

I take a deep breath.

"Thank you!" I yell into the microphone. Security has opened up the pit in front of the stage, letting fans pile in. They gather close to the stage and yell back.

"I'd like to dedicate this song to Mia Stone who can't be here tonight but is always with us." I tap the place on my chest that contains my heart.

I start the first few chords of *Breath to Bear*, the slow melody syncing with Cash's bass, my voice is somber, mimicking the feel of the lyrics. When we get to the chorus the tempo picks up, hurried and dramatic. Cash's voice comes in raw, and it's like an explosion of emotion. The lyrics represent our struggles, our love, and our friendship that has endured more than most. If love teaches you anything, it's how to heal, and that it's okay to let go of your anger and forgive.

"Jack, I'm so proud of you!" Erin hugs me as I stand backstage where she joined me after our performance.

I didn't want to take my seat just yet, needing to decompress and get away from the crowd. The show is still going on, and we can hear announcements through the speakers. I lean into her hand that she's placed on my cheek. We were able to slip behind the stage where engineers are running around, changing equipment, and building out platforms for the next performance.

Sweat still drips from my forehead and I use the bottom of my T-Shirt to wipe it away. Erin's eyes focus on my exposed stomach a few seconds too long to be casual.

"You're staring," I chuckle.

"Yes, I am." Her eyes are like golden brown orbs in the stage lights.

"Come here." I smile against her lips.

For once, I am able to let myself be happy without feeling guilty. All of the pain and struggles I have had to go through in order to heal is worth it. It's not Erin who healed me, but she allowed me the grace to heal myself.

My hand travels down her back and cups her ass. "Jack," she giggles into my mouth, looking around at the almost empty corridor we are standing in. I can't help but stare into her eyes as if I can see our future laid out ahead of us. When I kiss her, it feels different. Like forever didn't exist before, but now it does.

I let go of her and watch as she presses her swollen lips together. Slowly, I kneel down in front of her.

"What are you doing?" Erin looks around nervously, urging for me to stand up, torn between her lust and the embarrassment of getting caught.

"You said you wanted to see me on my knees," I smile at her devilishly. We are in a secluded area of the stage, but someone could come our way at any moment. I like the sight of looking up at her from my vantage point. Her legs are so close, I could run my hand up her dress, slip my fingers inside that thong I know she's wearing, and press my mouth to the wetness that I know has already started to gather.

Her belly moves with each breath against the silk of her dress.

"Yes, but not here," she whispers. I can tell she's actually contemplating letting me go down on her backstage at the Grammys. It wouldn't take much convincing. She pretends to be the angel with those innocent brown eyes of hers, but she gives in to the devil on her shoulder and loves every fucking minute of it.

Instead, I have other plans for her.

I reach inside my pocket and pull out a tiny black velvet case.

"Holy fuck!" she yelps, pressing her hands to her mouth and shaking her head.

"I haven't even asked yet," I laugh, loving her reaction.

"Shit, shit, shit." She covers her mouth, the tears now spilling over and onto her cheeks.

"I never thought I would ever get married again. Hell, I never thought I would fall in love again." I take a deep breath. "Erin, the moment I met you, you ignited a spark inside of me that slowly spread through my veins until every inch of me was on fire." I clutch the box in my hand, suddenly nervous. I've never been at a loss for words, but my mouth is having a hard time conveying what is in my heart. "You're my slow burn." I open the box revealing a ring that I agonized over buying. I only hope she likes it. "Will you marry me?"

"Jack," she whispers, shaking her head, the words forming on her lips but barely audible. "Yes, holy shit, yes." I've never heard Erin swear so much.

Cheers erupt around us from people I didn't even know were there. The announcement of the next award coming from the backstage speakers drowns out their congratulatory voices.

"Album of the Year goes to..." There's a pause before the name is revealed. "Jack O'Donnell for *Resurrection!*"

"Jack!" Erin grabs me frantically, "Jack, that's you!"

It takes me a minute to realize what's happening.

"I don't give a fuck about the award." I realize I hadn't gotten the chance to slip the ring on her finger and do so quickly. She looks down at her hand, mesmerized by the diamond catching the light from the spotlights above.

"Are you sure?" She looks up at me sincerely.

"Don't ask stupid questions," I quip, claiming her mouth as she laughs against my lips. She tastes like the ocean, and I want more. Much more. I could have waited until we got home so I could take her to bed, leaving this dress in shreds on the floor, but when do I ever do anything the easy way?

"Let's go home." I pick her up and sling her over my shoulder. She yelps and giggles in my arms.

"Jack!" One of the producers interrupts us. "You need to get on stage."

I turn my head slightly, still holding Erin in my arms. I don't *need* to do anything. Right now, all I want is to take my fiancée home so I can get her out of this dress.

I narrow my eyes at this unsuspecting little shit as I walk away.

"Fuck off!"

AUTHORS NOTE: Have you ever wondered what happened during the ten year gap in Blood & Bone? Read Mia's story in **Bonds We Break**, book 3 in the Blood & Bone Series. Mia promised herself to one man, while still in love with another. You know how Mia's story ends but it's everything in between that matters most.

If you are looking for a happy ending, you won't find it here. It is not necessary to read Bonds we Break in order to read Cash's story in Bound to Burn, book 4 in the Blood & Bone series.

Read on for an extended sneak peak at **Bonds We Break** book 3 in the Blood & Bone series.

Don't worry, the whole Blood & Bone gang is back to see Cash Morgan finally get his happily ever after. Cash has been burned in the past and closed himself off to love, that is until a much younger, pink glittered Converse wearing, free spirited photographer comes dancing into his record store. Watch this grumpy ex-rock star meet his match and fall hard in **Bound to Burn,** book 4 in the Blood & Bone series.

Read on for an extended sneak peak at **Bound to Burn,** book 4 in the Blood & Bone series.

Don't forget to check out the bonus material of Jack & Erin's wedding.

BONDS WE BREAK PREVIEW
BLOOD & BONE SERIES BOOK 3

The Whiskey is packed, and the boys are in the dressing room getting ready. I feel as though I don't belong. This is not my show, this is not my band, and I don't like the possessive way Keelin is always holding my hand and touching me. What once felt so good is slowly making me uncomfortable, and my stomach clenches in knots.

"You should totally do a number with us," Rob mentions again, even though I shyly declined earlier. We used to mess around on tour and even crashed their show once for fun. The fans loved it.

"She doesn't know our songs," Keelin interjects, and I look at him incredulously.

I don't want to perform, let alone with them, but Keelin's objection raises my hackles. I almost want to do it just for spite.

"Sure you do. We could do that one from the old album," he snaps his fingers, "Taking the Fire." His excitement seems to rattle Keelin. "That's the one you used to crash our show and jam with us." Thinking about all of those fun times makes it hurt even more that it's over.

"We didn't rehearse that," Keelin argues, and Rob shrugs, but he's still looking at me expectantly.

I narrow my eyes at Keelin and he backs off.

"Up to you," Keelin caves, but I can tell he's still against it. In fact, he is dead set against it, and I think I know why. He feels threatened. Now I get why he wanted me in his bed so badly; It's because of who I am. He thinks he's dominating me, proving that he's the lead singer now. Holding my hand is like pissing on his territory.

"Get your asses on stage!" someone yells as they walk by the dressing room door. The band piles out and I follow, but when they get to the stage, I veer towards the floor. I make my way in between the mass of bodies, glad to be distracted. The sound of a drumbeat sparks chaos in the crowd, and the noise drowns out the noise in my head.

I can hear Keelin speak to the crowd, causing another eruption of cheers. Heat rises from my neck to my face at the sound of his voice, and I think about Bret in the limo, Keelin on the beach, and then Jack in New Orleans... which started this whole fucking mess to begin with.

These men want to own me, possess me, or hold me down, but I was never meant to be tamed. I catch Rob's eye from the crowd and give him a nod. A smile spreads on his face and he leans over to tell the security guard to let me up. Rob is being a troublemaker, and I kinda like it.

After the first song, Rob switches up the chords and launches into Taking the Fire. Keelin gives him a menacing look. I walk through the crowd and the security guard helps me up on the stage. I stride across the platform and take the mic from Keelin. The angry look on his face only fuels me further.

Rob smiles mischievously as Keelin moves to the side of the stage, no longer having a place as front man for the band. I launch into the song and the crowd lets loose. I'm still wearing my soiled skirt, my legs are bare, and I'm wearing my combat boots. The oversized *Ruin* shirt is tied at my waist, leaving a smooth patch of my belly exposed. My dark hair flies around my face, getting tangled in the process.

It's a cacophony of sound, bodies, and hands feeding me. I eat it up as if I am starving. I use every inch of the stage, my body emphasizing the music and I lose myself. My voice is rough as I belt out the lyrics, Rob singing harmony. I don't have anything to prove to these men, and I am no one's doll to dress up and pose.

I don't look for Keelin but I know he's seething on the side of the stage because I just fucking owned his band and this crowd.

The song ends and the adrenaline courses through my body, but I'm spent. I collapse on the stage, letting the microphone drop from my hand and roll to the side. Hands reach out for me from the pit and sweat coats my skin. Rob reaches out a hand to help me up with a huge smile on his face. He knows the truth, and so does everyone in this club.

I own this stage.

Rob makes a dramatic bow as everyone is clapping and yelling. I make my exit, intending to get as far away from this place as possible, but as the crowd parts, I see him... the only person to ever own me, but not anymore. Still, my body reacts and my heart pounds in my chest. L.A. is a big city but the music industry is small, and we all swim in the same fishbowl. I knew I would run into him at some point, I just didn't think it would be tonight.

Not now, and not like this.

Not after that performance.

The look in his eyes is feral, possessive, and recalcitrant.

"Mia." My name on his lips fills my veins with venom, a poison so lethal that if he says it again, I may not recover.

I stop in front of him, my chest heaving, and all I feel is despondent.

"Fuck, you are a force of nature," he says to me and I want to catch on fire.

Ready for Mia Stone to break your heart? Read **Bonds We Break** on your favorite storefront today.

Read on for an extended preview of **Bound to Burn**, book 4 in the Blood & Bone series to get a sneak peak at Cash Morgan's happily ever after.

BOUND TO BURN PREVIEW

BLOOD & BONE SERIES BOOK 4

SASHA

The back storeroom is mostly an open space with shelves for storage and an adjacent office. The door hangs open giving me a view of the old rustic wood desk inside. A computer sits amongst a pile of papers haphazardly strew over it's surface. Past the desk, hanging on the wall, are dated band pictures.

What I know of Cash is that he was in a band with Jack when grunge was at it's height but when they broke up he bought this record store and has been running it ever since. Judging by the decor, it hasn't been updated since either but it adds to the vintage feel, especially with the light blue and white checkered tile.

For the better part of the afternoon I go through each box, separating out the damaged albums. The records themselves are still in good condition but the sleeves are either ripped or soiled, making them unsellable.

I hold a *Sublime* album in my hand, flipping it over to admire the artwork. Going through the albums, I've gotten to see the evolution of cover designs over the decades, and wonder what it was like to photograph such artists as Bob Dylan and Mick Jagger. I had a taste of that at the music festival but it's not the same as working with someone in a studio having your concept come to life in unexpected ways.

My grandparents have a collection of old country albums and a record player but it's been years since they've used it, the dust hiding it's original sheen.

Cash has been quiet up front aside from when customers have come through and by the sound of their familiarity, must be regulars. There are long stretches of silence and I'm used to the chaos and constant interaction of working in a bar that being back here by myself is lonely.

"So, you used to play bass," I say loud enough so Cash can hear me.

"What?" He pops his head around the corner.

"You used to play bass?" I ask again.

"Yes," he mutters.

"What kind of bass?" I ask, trying to keep the conversation going.

"I thought you said you weren't musically inclined?" He asks.

"I'm not."

It's a warm summer day and I push the stray pieces of hair from my neck. "Do you mind if I prop open the back door?" I ask.

Cash walks down the hallway towards the back door and shows me how to prop it open by pushing what looks like a piece of parking block to keep it from closing. "It can get pretty stuffy back here."

He looks around at the boxes I have piled up appreciatively and then heads into his office shuffling paper around.

"What did you mean when you said you should be?" He asks, absently.

"Huh?"

"Earlier when I asked if you played. You said you weren't musically inclined but you should be?" He makes a face.

"I'm pretty sure my father was a musician," I explain while stacking up a few more albums and shoving one of the boxes to the side with my foot.

"You don't know?"

"I never knew him," I say, shaking my head. "For all I know you could be my dad," I tease, tossing another album on the unsellable pile.

I'm met with silence and for a minute I think he might have left or passed out, so I peek around the corner of his office door and look at him.

I am met with stormy grey eyes. "I am not your father," he says definitively. It was a joke but he's cute when he looks uncomfortable, especially when he rubs the back of his neck.

"How do you know?" I tease.

"This is not even remotely funny." He crosses his arms over his chest showing off the corded muscles in his forearm and the ink that travels under his sleeve. He tosses his head to remove a few unruly blonde strands off his forehead.

I lean against the doorjamb suggestively. "You were in a rock band. I'm sure sketchier things have happened," I muse.

"I didn't go around knocking up random women," he says, clearly irritated.

I shrug defiantly as if I don't believe him. Just looking at him, if he was even a fraction as good looking when he was younger, as he is now, no would have stood a chance.

"If I were you I'd be worried about getting fired on the first day." He slides sideways past me through the doorway and heads back down the hall to the front of the store.

From behind him I say, "Not when my dad owns the place."

He stops and spins around.

"You're how old?" he assesses me from where I stand, his eyes roaming over my body, to my face and I swear my nipples harden. "Early twenties," he ventures a guess.

"Almost twenty-four." I square my shoulders as if that would make me appear older. For some reason twenty-four seems twice as old as twenty-three even if that's not logical.

"Twenty-three." He levels me with that same steely stare that runs bone deep, making me shiver. "Then, not possible."

Now I'm intrigued.

"How so?"

"Well, for one, I was going to college in Arizona around that time and when I came out to L.A. I was too busy trying to survive on coffee and french fries," he explains.

"French fries?" I ask, wondering what is so special about fries.

"They were cheap and you could share," he clarifies and then disappears around the corner, leaving me wanting more.

"And?" I prompt him, cocking an eyebrow.

"What do you mean, and?" I hear him grumble. "It's not like I had access to a regular shower so having *relations* wasn't exactly on the menu."

I imagine him using air quotes around the word 'relations'.

"Relations?" I giggle uncontrollably while ripping open another box. "I'm not five, you can say the word sex."

"No."

"Why not?" I huff.

"Because your my employee and I don't even know why we're talking about this," he says exasperated.

"You were trying to explain how it's not possible that you're my dad."

"Stop saying that." He pops his head around the corner meeting my gaze.

"Dose it make you *that* uncomfortable?" I laugh.

"Obviously." He draws out the word and I can't help but notice how his eyes drops to my lips and I subconsciously lick them.

"Why?"

"Can you just finish going through the albums?" He motions for me to get back to work and to make him happy I start on a new pile.

While I continue to work, I can still hear him moving around up front, the banging and shuffling of merchandise making it clear he's irritated which I feel bad about. I didn't think it would upset him that much. Maybe he won't ask me to come back after this but I hope that's not the case. I kinda like it here.

I busy myself by methodically shuffling through the boxes, and hold up a Carly Simon album. My fingers glide over the smooth surface of the artwork admiring Carly's high cheek bones and soulful eyes.

Something about Carly Simon makes me think of my Mom and I feel the need to explain myself.

"I don't know much about my dad except that he came to the house once looking for my mom but after she died he never came back looking for me." I say, casually flipping another album over.

It's quiet for a few minutes before he speaks and it's as if he's talking to himself and not me. "Sometimes people use sarcasm to hide deeper issues." He leans around the wall so I can see his face.

"Are you saying I have daddy issues?" I ask, haughtily.

"Were you ever a stripper?"

I huff, "No," and shake my head.

"Then I'll venture to guess that your grandparents did a good enough job raising you to make up for not having a dad." His head disappears.

I narrow my eyes even though he can't see me.

"That's a bit sexist," I challenge.

"Oh yeah?" He says.

"Saying that all strippers have daddy issue," I grumble while effectively mocking him only because I know he can't see me.

"Sue me."

There's a long period of silence but I don't feel like the asshole anymore. I sit and stew but the heat in my cheeks dissipates just as quickly as it rose. I hope I don't get fired before I've even officially started.

I appear at the front and hop up on the counter letting my feet dangle. Cash looks over at me incredulously but he doesn't tell me to get down or go back to work.

"I'm just taking a break," I explain and study him as he goes back to flipping through his phone.

Blonde hair falls onto his forehead and my eyes travel down his strong nose to his lips. Stubble peppers his jawline, the kind that you want to rub your cheek against like a cat wanting to be petted. I think I visibly salivate as my eyes travel down his arms, biceps covered in ink, and I watch as the muscles flex as he scrolls through his phone. He wears a graphic t-shirt, a punk band I recognize but don't know well, and jeans that fit tight, cut open at the knees. That's not even the best part about him. He must sense that I'm staring at him and looks over at me with those stormy grey eyes and all the blood rushes out of my limbs feeling as though I could fall off the counter.

"What are you doing?" I recover by leaning over to get a better look.

"Looking at guitars for a client."

"Oh," I say casually.

He notices me still watching him and moves the phone from my view like I'm invading his privacy. When he walks away, I look after him sadly but take the time to survey the store. Posters cover the front window blocking out the light. In the middle of the store are two columns, each decorated with stickers of bands and other random things. The records are sorted alphabetically and placed in stained wooden bins that people have written on over the years. There are all kinds of names and drawings on every surface of the wood. Along one of the walls are bins that hold CDs and a rack for cassettes. If I thought people didn't by records anymore I'd be shocked if anyone bought cassettes.

Behind the register is a set of iron stairs that I wonder where they lead but what is most interesting is the beautiful mural painted on the wall in front of me. The multidimensional blues and whites remind me of being inside a wave. It's fitting for the area being only a few blocks from the ocean.

A few moments later, Cash returns and hands me a bottle of water which I take gladly.

"It's too quiet in here." I look around and spot an old record player. "We should put on one the records." I suggest jumping down from the counter and racing to the back spotting just the one I want.

When I get back up front Cash is waiting for me, cocking his head to the side. "How about this Guns 'N Roses album?" I hold it up between us.

With a disgusted look on his face, he says, "Never will a Gun's 'N Roses album be played in my presence." He leans back over his phone.

I pucker my lips. "That's odd but I'll take the bait. Did you get into a tiff with Axl Rose back in the day?" I joke sarcastically.

"We had a moment." He doesn't look up from his phone.

"M'kay, I'm just gonna put a pin in that." I tuck the album under my arm.

Cash turns his head towards me, his hair falling onto his forehead again.

"Next time I'll train you on the register," he offers.

I can't help the smile that spreads on my face. "Does this mean I get to come back?" I ask, giddily, figuring today was my test and I failed miserably. Not only do I need this job but I'm beginning to like the company.

"Yeah, if you park the attitude," he says but I have a feeling he doesn't mean it.

"Yes da..." he gives me a warning look, "boss," I correct with a smile.

"And wear more sensible shoes next time." He points to my ankle boots which I have to admit are not the most comfortable even if they are fashionable.

I click my boots together. "Yes, boss." I have a feeling he doesn't like being called boss either but it's better than dad.

"Follow me," he walks down the hallway and I dutifully trail after him.

Kneeling over the damaged boxes he starts sifting through one and pulls a couple out.

"This one is a must listen to on a record player. Do you have one?" He asks me, holding a *Credence Clearwater Revival* album.

My mouth finally catches up to my brain. "Yeah, my grandparents do." I move over to where he stands and look at the pile he's creating.

"This one," he holds up the *Led Zeppelin IV* album and I narrow my eyes, "is better on vinyl." He slaps it onto the pile.

I start picking through the rest of the albums he's stacked up for me, *Eagles, Steely Dan, Steve Miller Band, Tom Petty* are all one's I know and love.

"*Grand Funk Railroad*?" Holding it up in front of me I scrunch my nose. "I have never heard of this band."

He snatches it from me. "Underrated but they will blow your mind." He taps my head with the album and then hands it back to me. I could listen to him talk about music all day. He is animated and full of life, so different from the grumpy boss I have worked with up until now

"Now we are getting into the good stuff." He seems to say more to himself than to me as he pulls out a few more albums.

I lean in close as he holds them up. *The Kinks,*" he tosses it on the top of the pile, *"The Ramones, Dead Kennedy's, INXS…"* he inspects one of the albums and tosses it back in the other pile. "Eh, I was never a fan of *Buzzcocks*, but *The Cure…*" he pauses inspecting the album, "is life."

"Did you know any of them?" I ask, excited. "Like personally?" Sounds like he has some really great band stories.

"I don't kiss and tell," he says with a secretive smile and my eyes suddenly focus on his lips.

I look away to the pile of records in front of me. "You're giving all of these to me?" I ask, confused.

"You said you liked Classic Rock but consider the rest as part of your training." He winks at me causing heat to rise into my face. I watch as he walks down the hall leaving me alone again.

Read Bound to Burn *on your favorite store today!*

BREATH TO BEAR BONUS SCENE

CONVINCE ME
EIGHT MONTHS LATER
Erin

My office looks out at the ocean, the blues and greens tempting me away from working. I prop my chin on my hand and look back down at the photos laying across the desk. Absently I pick one up and look at it. It's a picture of my dad holding me as a baby. He stands outside of a brick building with a smile on his face as I reach out to grab onto the scruffy beard on his chin. I never knew my dad with a beard. He was always clean shaven as far back as I can remember. This picture, this man with a beard, is foreign to me. There's so much I didn't know.

My laptop is open, and I begin to type. It's more of a stream of consciousness at this point, getting all of the details down so I can organize it later. I've pitched my book idea to several publishing houses, providing an outline and rough draft, but the interest just isn't there for a musician who is mostly unknown and obscure, such as my father. Even with the knowledge that I'm the ghost writer for Jack's book, it may have opened doors, but the fact still remains, Cole Langford is not a big name in the music business.

Even if I haven't found a publisher yet, I haven't given up. I continue to write this book because it's all I can think about at the moment. The hundreds of pictures I've looked at, old band members I've met and spoken to, only fuels the fire within me. I'm discovering my history; I'm reconnecting with my father and it's a beautiful thing. Even if no one reads it or appreciates it, I know I won't regret it.

"I don't like waking up to an empty bed." Jack's rough voice comes from behind me. I turn to see him standing in the door frame, faded jeans pulled up with the fly yawning open, sitting low on his hips.

"Eyes up here." His voice is full of humor as my gaze travels up his bare chest and finally settles on his beautiful sleepy blue eyes.

"Don't be so cocky," I smirk at him, beckoning him to come closer and he obeys.

His body leans against the large wooden desk beside me and he places a cup of coffee in front of me. My senses awake at the smell, but it's not just the coffee… it's Jack. His presence, his smell, his touch as he brushes a finger across my shoulder causing the silk material of my robe to slip further down.

"What's wrong?" he asks me and I look up at him. He can tell I've been on edge lately, distracted even.

"Everything's happening so fast," I confess.

He gives me a small smile, but I can see the worry behind his eyes.

"Here I thought I'd be the one to have cold feet." Jack gives me a sympathetic look.

He's not wrong. I've never been married before but Jack has, and it left a sour taste in his mouth. Up until today, everyone, including me has been tiptoeing around this wedding, waiting, watching for Jack to flip out and do something stupid, but he hasn't. There's a calmness about him that unnerves me. Maybe it's because I don't trust this easiness with which we have fallen into this life.

"I'm not having cold feet," I'm quick to explain, putting my hand on his leg. "It's just all this planning, all the pressure, the guests…" He presses a finger to my lips and I don't finish my sentence, but the thought remains. I'm usually the one that fades into the background unnoticed; the people watcher, not the one other people are watching. The wedding is tomorrow, and I may be freaking out a little bit.

Jack kneels down in front of me, turning my chair so I face him. With his blue eyes intense, he says, "All you have to do is look at me waiting for you at the end of that walk." His hands are on my thighs, gripping me, grounding me. "That's all that matters. It's just you and me, Erin." Then he adds, "Everyone else can just fuck off."

I laugh, surpassing the tears that are threatening to bubble up. His soft smile steadies me, and I keep my gaze locked on him as his hands move up my leg, pushing the silk robe to the side. He places soft kisses to my skin as he gently pulls on the tie, letting it fall open, exposing my bare stomach, my already hardening nipples. The way he looks at me, as if I am something to be worshipped, is a heady concoction unlike any glass of whiskey I have ever tasted. I suck in a breath when he grips the edges of my panties and slowly pulls them down. He scoots me further to the edge, licking and kissing his way up my inner thigh. The stubble on his jaw, rough against my sensitive skin, a delicious mix of plea-sure and pain.

I watch with unbridled lust as he buries his face between my legs. The sight of him moves and rocks me to the point of no return. I let my head tip back, pressing into the leather chair, moaning while I grip the arm rests. His mouth owns me, his tongue pulling me to the edge, and I fist his hair between my fingers, panting. He lifts my legs to let them rest on his shoulders, causing my thighs to open farther for him. He takes my pleasure so easily, a gift I am oh so willing to give. I am taken to a place so high, it's almost painful. I rock my hips to meet the cadence of his mouth, chasing, willing, *commanding* me to give him all of me.

I want to give him everything, to split myself in two, exposing the most vulnerable parts of myself and place them into the palm of his hands. The ache is so sweet my chest hurts, and all he has to do is move his hand up to my breast, taking my hard nipple between his fingers and like a switch, I light up, tumbling and falling into that darkness that swallows me whole.

Gentle kisses and hands that hold and caress, bring me back from the void. I am breathless, sated, and treasured, as Jack holds me in his arms, kissing my forehead, my cheek and then my mouth.

"Is this how you convince me to marry you?" I smile against his lips.

A low chuckle escapes his mouth. "Is it working?"

"Yes." I let out a slow moan as he kisses me again, loving the feel of his stubble against my chin.

"You know you're supposed to wait to fuck me until the wedding night," I say to him.

"When have you ever known me to do what I'm supposed to?" Jack says, the sound of his zipper opening further causes my body to react, heat flooding to my core once again.

THE REHEARSAL
ERIN

The wedding planner arrived just after I'd gotten out of the shower. Luckily, Gail was outside making sure the tables and chairs were set up. A catering truck was backed into the driveway, and trays of food were being carried out and placed into the kitchen. The anxiety that had been wiped away this morning was now starting to return.

I look out towards the path that leads to the beach and know that is the path I will be walking to meet Jack at our little altar on the sand. Chairs are already being set up, getting ready for tomorrow. The beach has been blocked off so people can't get through. Security has arrived and been stationed nearby in case overzealous fans get foolish.

In my bedroom, hung up on the back of the door encased in a protective wrap, is my wedding dress. I stare at it, imagining the silky material wrapped around my body. It's simple but elegant, and fits me perfectly.

"It's not going to bite," Gail startles me with her comment.

"Shit, I didn't hear you come in." I clutch my chest and smile at my mother. Her hair is pinned up, but the wind from outside has caused little pieces to fall around her face making her look younger. She looks so happy, her skin glows.

"I'm sorry I startled you." She smiles at me and then looks back at the dress. "Is everything okay?" She asks me, concerned. I take a seat in the chair next to the armoire, and Gail takes the one opposite me.

The bedroom is spacious with large glass doors that open leading to a small patio with a wooden railing. From here I can see the arch being assembled and the lights being hung up on the patio. A dance floor is being erected, and sound equipment is being brought in.

"It's just very overwhelming," I confess to her.

"Just relax. That's what I'm here for." She places her small hand on top of mine. "You don't have to do a thing."

"It's not just that," I tell her. "I don't like attention." I shake my head thinking of all those people that will be here tomorrow.

"Afraid you'll trip on the way to the altar?" Gail offers a small joke to lighten the heaviness in the room.

I shake my head and laugh, although now that I think of it, I'm not terribly proficient at wearing heels. "It wasn't meant to be a big wedding, but the guest list grew out of hand," I explain.

From somewhere inside the house, I hear Amber giving orders. "You don't store the cold food next to the hot food! It's catering 101! Where are you going with those lights?" I hear a tray crash.

"For God's sake, if he's so easily startled then maybe he's in the wrong business." Amber's haughty tone floats into the room. "Excuse me, but I am not scary!" she yells back at someone.

The familiar click of heels on the wood flooring nears, and Amber appears in the doorway. "I swear, if you want something done right, you have to do it yourself." She places a hand on her hip with a withering look. Her blonde hair falls around her shoulders in waves.

"What are you doing here?" I ask, surprised. The rehearsal dinner is not until tonight, and I check my watch to confirm it's barely noon.

"I came to help." She gives me an indignant look as if I should know that.

Amber's gaze turns to my mother who gives Amber a pleasant smile. "Why don't we get you back to the kitchen so you can finish setting up?" Amber says to my mother who looks at her, confused.

"Amber, this is my mother, Gail," I explain, narrowing my gaze at her. Amber plasters an apologetic smile on her face.

"Gail, this is Amber, Jack's ex-wife," I explain, noticing Amber's discomfort at my choice of introduction.

"Nice to meet you," Gail says politely.

Amber smiles and nods at her. The minute Gail turns back to me, Amber shrugs and mouths to me, 'she looked like the help.'

I shake my head and laugh.

"What are you doing in here anyways? Shouldn't you be at a spa or something?" Amber inspects my hair and nails. "You do have someone coming to take care of that, right?" She looks up at me.

"I'm perfectly fine." I pull my hand away.

"I'll leave you two to catch up. I need to get back outside anyway." Gail stands up, giving me a knowing smile. She's much more perceptive than I give her credit for. This is all new to my mother, this house, these people, getting to know Jack, but she's handled it better than I ever imagined. She's been such a great help taking some of the pressure off me that I almost don't want her to leave me alone with Amber.

I give her a pleading look before she exits the room, but she leaves anyway.

Amber and I stand in the middle of the bedroom, and I can't help but be self-conscious of the adjacent king size bed, making this moment even more awkward.

"Maybe we should go somewhere else," I suggest.

"Good idea." Amber turns and I follow her down the hallway.

"Are you sure you want to go through with this?" Amber asks sarcastically, but there's a hint of something genuine in her tone. "Jack is a handful."

I laugh. "I'm sure."

Amber stops me in the hallway, her face serious and sincere. "He looks happy," Amber says. "It's weird." Her tone has a hint of humor. "He was never like this with Mia, ya know." The mention of her name doesn't cause me jealously or make me uncomfortable. She pauses for a moment. "You make him a better person." The blue of her eyes sparkles like the ocean as they fill with tears.

"You're not going to cry, are you?" I joke, but knowing exactly what she means. Some people you can love to the point of madness, your mirror image reflecting back all of the ugliness within you. Jack may have loved Mia, but that doesn't mean they were good for each other. That's what Amber means.

"Fuck no," she scoffs and continues down the hallway.

There's a ruckus in the front room and I hear Wade's voice. We turn the corner and almost smack into him.

"What are you doing here?" He demands, pointing at Amber.

"I can't leave this fiasco up to Erin. She needs to relax," Amber explains. "Can't you see she looks stressed?"

I lean away from her.

"Look, I'm the gay best friend, so step aside." Wade loops his arm in mine and directs me outside.

"Fuck off, Wade," Amber says from behind us.

We make our way through the garden and out to the entrance of the beach. Wade pulls off his shoes and slings his jacket over his arm.

"You can back out anytime. My car is parked out front," he hooks his thumb in the direction of the front of the house, "although, I do hope I didn't get blocked in. A van was pulling in behind me. We may need to hijack someone else's car," he says with amusement, but I have no doubt if I wanted to bolt, Wade would be steering the wheel.

"I don't want to back out." I grab onto his arm again as we walk onto the beach. The breeze is refreshing, and the sand is warm under my toes. This is what I love most about living in Malibu.

"Have you met Jack?" He pierces me with a look to drive home his point.

I laugh. "Stop it." I pat his arm and urge him to keep walking.

"It's going to be beautiful, Erin," he reassures me. "Adam's bringing Dylan later after he wakes up from his nap."

"He's going to make the cutest ring bearer." I squeeze Wade tighter as the cold of the water hits my feet.

"Don't tell anyone yet because it's not finalized, but when we adopted Dylan, we had the opportunity to keep our name on the list to be contacted if Dylan had any siblings in order to keep them together." Wade can't contain the smile on his face, and I think my heart might just bang out of my chest. "The agency contacted us, and it seems Dylan's mom gave birth to a little girl. She would be Dylan's half-sister."

I throw my arms around Wade and hug him fiercely. "Oh my God, that's amazing." Realizing he hadn't said if this was something he and Adam wanted to do, I school my expression and step back. "Is this a good thing? I mean, assuming you want her," I say.

"I just can't imagine Dylan having a half-sister out there somewhere and not being able to grow up with her." His eyes are misty as he explains.

I nod. "Two kids under the age of two," I say, shaking my head. "Are you going to survive?" I tease.

"Babies aren't easy, and even though Adam and I struggled, I would do it all over again. Plus, we're not getting any younger." His expression turns soft, and it's as if he can see right through me.

I sigh.

"What about you, Erin? What do you want?" He doesn't specifically ask but I can tell what's on his mind. I'm ten years younger than Jack. Having a baby is something I should want.

I shake my head. "Not everyone wants what you have, Wade."

"You're not just saying that because you know Jack has made it clear he's done with all that, and I quote, 'baby shit'?" Wade eyes me. He knows Jack better than most people do.

I can tell Wade is trying to assess me, but there is nothing to assess.

"You have a beautiful family that is about to get bigger and I am so happy for you, but it's just not something I want for myself," I try to explain to him. "Not all women want or need babies." I used to think there was something wrong with me because I could appreciate other people's kids, but I didn't get an ache in my chest seeing a pregnant woman lay a protective hand on her swollen belly or get misty when someone let me hold their newborn. I realize now that it's okay not to want kids, and there is nothing broken about me.

"Does this mean you don't want to ever babysit?" Wade pouts.

I laugh, knowing he gets it. "I will babysit anytime, but just don't expect Jack to like it."

"Like what?" Jack's voice says from behind me.

I turn to look at him and squint my eyes at the bright sunlight. It bursts behind him, hiding his face from me, but I feel this pull, this calmness, knowing he's near. That's the effect he has on me, especially with all this chaotic energy about the house. I only have to remember that this is about Jack and I.

"Where have you two been?" Wade points accusatorially at both Jack and Cash, who stands beside him.

"We had to go pick up the tuxes," Cash offers with an annoyed grin. These boys do not like wearing formal attire, aside from Wade, who seems to be made for them. I prefer Jack casual with bare feet, rumpled t-shirt and worn jeans, but when he wears a suit, he could burn down a room.

"What's this about something I'm not going to like?" Jack asks again.

"Erin just volunteered you to babysit Dylan," Wade jokes.

Jack scoffs. "I'll watch the little shit for you, but I can't guarantee he won't come home knowing a few new words."

"Okay, *you're* never babysitting," Wade narrows his eyes.

"That's how I get out of babysitting," Jack whispers to me, loud enough so Wade can hear.

"You joke, but I fucking swear Dylan's first word is going to be 'fuck' from hanging around the two of you," Wade points to both Jack and Cash, and we all stare back at him dumfounded. "Oh, fuck off." He crosses his arms over his chest, and I laugh.

"Are you sure you want to marry this fuck?" Cash points to Jack.

"Why does everyone keep asking me that?" I laugh, throwing my hands up in the air.

"Who is everyone?" Jack says loudly, turning his gaze to both Wade and Cash menacingly. "I swear, if she leaves me at the altar because the two of you scared her away..." He doesn't finish his sentence because I shut him up with a kiss.

Jack leans his head against mine, cupping my face. "What was that for?"

"Because I love you," I tell him.

"Are you sure it wasn't just to shut me up?" he chuckles.

"That too." I smile and kiss him again.

"Why the fuck is everyone standing around?" Amber calls from behind us. She makes her way in the sand hopping on one foot to pull her heel off. "Fuck, I hate sand," she scoffs.

Jack lowers his head and shakes it. "Who let her in?" he says sarcastically, and Amber whacks him in the arm with her purse.

Gathered around the table are Adam, Wade, Cash, Hayley, Amber, Gail, and Jack. The sight of everyone I love in one small space is overwhelming. I've been an emotional wreck all day, but now, sitting at this table, raising our glasses to this wonderful meal, the fading sun warming our faces and the sound of the ocean, I'm complete.

Tears threaten to spill over, and Jack squeezes my hand. In that small but powerful touch, I know he is feeling the same way. It's these people who have slowly embedded themselves under my skin and into my heart. I don't know how I ever got so lucky to have these people in my life, but here they are. They are the family I always wanted after being lonely for so long. I want to bottle them up and put them in my pocket for safe keeping.

"Don't forget about the time Jack climbed up on that rafter. We all thought that was it, he's gonna die this time," Cash's jovial story pulls me from my thoughts.

"You thought you'd finally be rid of me." Jack reaches across the table to try and smack Cash, but he dodges him.

"I hope you can all learn some manners by tomorrow," Amber scolds them.

"Where's Stephen?" I ask Amber, having forgotten to ask her earlier why her husband didn't join us today.

"I thought it would be nice to just have us; one last night, the old gang," she says nostalgically. I watch the way she looks at Jack and how he looks back at her. There's love there. Not the romantic kind, but the friendship kind. They care for each other so deeply that it warms my heart.

"Plus, he tells the most boring stories," Hayley jokes.

"He does not," Amber retorts.

"The percentage of growth in L.A. over the last ten years is riveting conversation," Hayley says as she lifts the glass to her lips.

Amber settles into her seat. "Sometimes boring is good," she says, peering over her glass at Jack. I'm not sure I share the same sentiment. I've had boring my whole life. I'm ready to start living.

THE WEDDING
ERIN

The sun sinks behind the horizon, giving the illusion it's dipping into the water. The clouds are flocked with bright oranges and reds. I don't think I will ever get used to how beautiful this is.

"Hey," Jack says, as he takes a spot next to me on the sand.

"Hey you," I knock into him, smiling.

"What's going on with you?" His voice is laced with concern.

After dinner, I took a walk on the beach to clear my mind, let everything sink in while the staff cleaned up. Everyone moved onto the patio, telling more stories and laughing loudly.

"Nothing's wrong." It's the truth. "Everything is so right." I rest my cheek on my forearm and look at him.

"How are you?" I straighten my head, remembering that I haven't really checked in with him. He seems so calm, and my insecurities don't let me trust in this moment.

"Are you asking if I'm having second thoughts?" he asks, creasing his brow.

I nod my head.

"Not a chance," he responds.

"You've been married before and that didn't work out," I say to him. It's not the first time we've talked about it, but I need reassurance right now.

"I wasn't married to you," he says, so simply and so purely that it sends a shiver up my spine. I kiss him, wanting to feel close to him, that spark, that need, because he is telling me everything I need to hear right now.

"What's really going on with you?" He knows me too well.

"Everyone is here that I love, and tomorrow feels like a show." As soon as I say it, I feel awful. That's not what our wedding is. It's about Jack and me, but with so many guests, most of whom I don't even know, it makes me wish we would have eloped.

"I wanted to give you a wedding you deserved, the wedding I should have had." I lean my cheek against his shoulder, and he wraps his arm around me.

"All I need is you, and everyone at that table."

Jack stands up, pulling me with him. "Then that's what I'll give you." He pulls me along the beach, back towards the house.

"What are you doing?" I laugh against him.

"We're getting married tonight," he smiles.

"We can't cancel the wedding tomorrow!" I say indignantly, thinking of all the planning, the money, the guests. It's insanity. "What about all the guests?"

"Fuck the guests, Erin. This is about you and me." He motions to the house, to the sounds of laughter coming from the garden. The arch is assembled on the beach, lights are strung and lit. The garden is lit up like fireflies winking at us, and I grab onto this hand, squeezing tight.

"You would do that for me?" I whisper, reaching up to kiss him.

"I would do anything for you," Jack says with such conviction it sends a wave of desire from my toes right to my head.

My lips meet his in a soft caress, the connection and the fire coursing through me. It's the burning desire I have for him that fuels me as he deepens the kiss. My body bends to him, circles around him as if we are one, and once again, I become lost in this safe little bubble that is Jack and I. He catches my hand before it reaches his crotch.

"Ah, ah, ah, you have to wait until the wedding night," he teases, devilishly.

"Where the fuck have you two been?" Amber scolds us, and I laugh into his mouth before pulling away.

"Amber, assemble the troops. We're getting married," Jack says.

"Of course you're getting married! That's why we're all here." As soon as she says it, the rest of our friends file out of the garden to see what the commotion is about.

"We're getting married tonight," Jack explains, squeezing my hand.

"Have you been drinking?" Amber purses her lips and scrunches her nose.

"This is not a drill." Jack claps his hands together.

Amber looks to me for confirmation and I nod.

"You heard the idiot, they're getting married tonight." Amber gathers Cash, Wade and Hayley into a huddle, barking commands.

My mother steps out of the group and gathers my hands in hers. "What do you need me to do?" she asks.

I look at Amber who is giving orders. "Help me with my dress?" I ask her.

"We don't have a priest!" Amber shouts. "You can't get married without someone to officiate."

"The minister won't be here until tomorrow," I tell Jack with a worried look.

"Someone could get ordained online," my mom suggests.

"Who wants to become an internet priest?" Amber barks.

"You don't actually become a priest," Wade clarifies.

"Perfect! You can get ordained since you already know so much," Amber points at him. Cash chuckles and Wade gives him a menacing scowl.

"What?" Wade guffaws. "I don't know how to marry someone!"

"Luckily, Gail here seems to know how to get this done." Amber links her arm with Wade, and they follow Gail into the house.

"Are you sure you want Wade to marry you?" Cash asks.

I look at Jack, a silent agreement between us. "I can't think of anyone better," I say.

"Don't think you're getting out of wearing that tux," I poke Jack in the chest. "You too, best man." I point towards Cash.

"Pictures, we need pictures." I look at Cash, tilting my head in a silent plea. There's only one other person I wish were here tonight, Sasha. She's not a wedding photographer but I can't imagine getting married without her here. I don't know what's going on between her and Cash, but they need to put whatever it is aside for this one night.

"I'll call her," Cash slumps his shoulders as he turns and leaves, raising the phone to his ear.

"Help me with my dress?" I ask Hayley since my mom is busy getting Wade ordained.

She's all bashful smiles as she watches Jack and I, and then nods her head.

"It's like junior high all over again," Adam says, deflated. "Last one picked for basketball."

"Shocker," Jack deadpans.

"Fuck off, Jack." Adam says to him, as Hayley and I hurry into the house.

I can't believe Amber pulled it off, but the garden and the walkway are lit up with strings of lights following the path to the beach. I stand on the threshold of the planks that lead down to the archway where Jack stands, waiting for me. Next to him is Cash, and at the center is Wade, now an ordained minister. He'll never live that down. Sasha captures a picture of me standing next to my mother and Hayley.

"You look absolutely…" Gail can't finish the sentence she's so over-whelmed with emotion, as she squeezes my hand. "I wish your father could be here to walk you down the aisle," she adds, with just as much emotion.

He is the missing piece to all of this, but I carry him with me in my heart. I took the picture of him holding me as a baby and tucked it into my bra strap. I think about Ethan and what he would have looked like in a tux. He'd probably be hating it just as much as the rest of the guys. It brings a smile to my face.

"I'll see you down there." Gail leaves me with Hayley, my maid of honor, who hands me the bouquet of fresh pink roses with baby's breath and fresh greens.

I take Hayley's face in my hands, so overcome with emotion for this beautiful young woman who has embraced me into her family. "Thank you," I tell her.

Hayley smiles, her blue eyes sparkling in the fairy lights. "Make him happy, Erin. He deserves it," she tells me with a spark of protectiveness over her father that warms me to the core.

"Every day," I promise, as I release her.

I smile at Sasha as she snaps another photo. "Thank you for coming on such short notice," I tell her.

"Anything for you." She squeezes my hand and the song *Work Song* by Hozier plays. It's perfection.

Hayley turns her head back to me and winks before she starts walking down the wooden planks. From my vantage point I watch Jack, unnoticed, as he adjusts his tie and then smooths his palms against his slacks. His nervousness is endearing, and the look in his eyes as he sees his daughter coming down the aisle almost undoes me. I don't know how I'm going to keep it together.

Sasha has moved down the aisle to be ready to take photos once I appear, leaving me here alone. I am on the precipice of what is to be a monumental moment. I always thought getting married was just a piece of paper, but it is so much more. I thought I'd already given myself to Jack, but getting ready to walk down this aisle, I realize I haven't even begun to do so.

I take one step onto the wooden plank, coming into the view of everyone. My bare foot connecting with the rest of my life, I look up to see Jack and only Jack. The gravity of his stare propels me forward, and in his eyes, I see *everything*.

I see a future of mornings with Jack handing me coffee as I lean over the wooden balcony to watch the waves; passing each other in the kitchen with a peck on the lips; Jack, interrupting me while I'm working, spreading my thighs so he can nestle between them. In the evenings, I see myself crawling into bed, Jack waiting for me, his hand outstretched ready to pull me in so I can curl against him.

Slow it down
Slow it down
Slow it down
Because I don't want to miss a thing
I'm alright with a slow burn
So I can rest my head

And give you this ring

The evening is quiet, only the waves providing background music. It's just me and Jack out on the beach, watching as the moonbeams dance on the water. The party ended hours ago, and everyone's gone home. I don't know what time it is, but I know it's late. I can feel it in my bones.

My dress is flared out around me, my knees bent and drawn into my chest. Jack is barefoot, his slacks rolled up around his ankles, his jacket discarded long ago, and his shirt is pulled open.

Perfection.

"How does it feel to be Mrs. O'Donnell?" Jack smirks.

Uh oh. "I hadn't planned on changing my name." I cock my head to the side, looking at him with amusement.

"When did we decide this?" Jack asks.

"I decided that it was best to keep my last name for professional reasons." Langford is my father's name, and I am my father's daughter. I check to make sure the picture is still tucked away in my bra strap.

"Hmm, then how will people know you're mine?" His arm circles me possessively while his lips hover over mine.

I raise my hand between us to the diamond on my left hand. He smirks, humor on his face as his hand slides up the silk material of my dress unzipping the back. The material opens for him like a door leading inside of me and I arch towards him, pressing our bodies together.

"We'll talk about it in the morning. Right now, I want to fuck my wife." He dips his head to me and crashes his lips on mine like the waves crashing against the shore, and he lays me down onto the sand.

Slow it down
Slow it down

Breath To Bear

Slow it down
Rest your bones
Come with me
I'll give you everything
Take my hand
And when the fire burns out
My love for you will never end

BREATH TO BEAR SONG LYRICS

By Jack O'Donnell and Cash Morgan

Heartbroken, finding my way
I'm tired of lying, she's just a girl I say
To myself over and over
Like a prison
I'm doing time and I'm not really living
Only room for one
And I don't wanna be alone
There's too much violence
In this silence

These chains
My guilt
Take me under
This crown that I built
Ruin me
Leave me lonely
You know you own me
I'm gonna let go, I'm gonna let go

Help me breakthrough
Because I love the torture
I'm going under
The influence of you
Every breath
If you dare
I'm like a martyr
Just a girl, but she's
My breath to bear

I felt a heartbeat

She was in my arms
Tell me baby
When it's over
You're pushing me away
And I'm sick of trying
Tired of lying
That everything's okay
When there's nothing left to say

Give me something
Cuz I'm dying
I'm losing myself over you
But I'm coming down now
I got lucky
When I broke free, why can't you see

Help me breakthrough
I love the torture
I'm going under
The influence of you
Every breath
Is getting harder
I'm like a martyr
She is, oh she is
My breath to bear

BEAUTIFUL LIES PREVIEW

CHECK OUT THIS NEW STANDALONE NOVEL

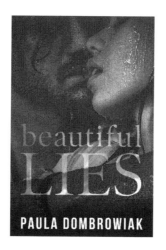

Enjoy a preview of this reverse age gap, one night stand, opposites attract, steamy romance.

T he electricity in the air from the impending storm crackles against my skin as I walk down to the corner. When I reach the end of the block I take a turn onto Southern, following a group of college students to Danelle Plaza. Each step feels like I'm moving back in time because the plaza is exactly the same even if the businesses that have taken up residence have changed. Everything is new, the auto parts store, a smoke shop, and thrift store but not the *Tap Room*.

The same white brick facade and weathered aluminum awning with the distinct white lettering, *Yucca Tap Room*. The entrance is still covered in bold, bright artwork with arrows leading you in as if you could ever miss it. The bouncer takes one look at me and waves me through, not even bothering to card me. I'm not twenty anymore, which is the last time I was here.

It's dark and loud, with people moving from one room to the next. The same L shaped bar with a stained wooden counter sits in the corner. Mirror's line the wall with shelves of liquor illuminated by backlighting and the tv screens above the bar lists all the local beers on tap. I manage to squeeze my way in and get the attention of the bartender.

He's a young guy, nice looking with a dark beard shaved close and black t-shirt with the bar's emblem on it, a green mountain with gold lettering, *Yucca*, across it, and the words *Tap Room* below it.

"What can I get you sweetheart?" He calls out over the noise.

This isn't the kind of place you order a martini in.

I look over the list of beers displayed on the tv screen above and it's a bit overwhelming.

"Blueberry blonde?" he asks, raising an eyebrow at me.

"Excuse me?" I ask.

"That's what she's drinking," he points to a young blonde wearing a pretty sundress at the end of the bar holding a beer glass with something purple in it.

I slide my eyes back to him. "Do I look like I drink grape juice..." I pause, looking for a name tag.

"Gael," he says, looking me up and down and then cocks his head to the side with a smile. "You look like you could put Putin in his place," Gael laughs and turns around, leaving me confused.

A few moments later he returns with a tall glass of dark ale and slides it in front of me. I'm not that much of a beer drinker but the way he's looking at me, it's as if it's a challenge of some kind.

"Not Today, Putin," he says, pointing at the beer and I raise a questioning eyebrow. "Russian imperial," he clarifies.

I laugh. "Oh Gael, you are good," I say and take a sip. "Whew." It's a heavy mix of dark chocolate, coffee, and *very* ripe fruit. I wipe my mouth with the back of my hand.

"You like?" Gael leans against the bar top with a smug expression.

"This'll definitely put some hair on *your* chest, Gael," I say, making him laugh.

Placing a couple bills on the bar top, I take my beer with me as I leave to explore the rest of the bar.

The restaurant is busy with every table now taken, and a line forming to get drinks. It's not just a college bar like it was back in my day, there's young professionals from the nearby businesses that have sprouted up over the years, older folks that probably live in the nearby neighborhoods, and I suppose people like me who are looking for a little nostalgia.

The arcade at the back has been expanded. Pinball machines and other vintage games line the wall. The retro sounds of buttons and levers fill the space mixed with the music from next door and people talking. I don't feel so out of place in my t-shirt, cut off shorts, and sneakers. It's too hot for anything more and everyone else is just as casual. Georgie would have been right at home in her scrubs but in a way I'm glad she didn't come. It gives me time to explore and contemplate the girl I was before I had Noelle.

On the other side of the restaurant I wander into the bar's live music venue. A sultry *Steppenwolf* song seeps into the bar as the singer's deep timbre voice screams the lyrics into the mic. Making my way closer to see the band on the riser, a thick crowd stands at the front of the stage. Tables frame the room but none are empty so I lean against one of the wooden columns at the back, content to watch life teeming around me as if I'm in the center of a tornado just waiting to be swept up.

The *Tap Room* is the kind of place you can lose yourself in and that's exactly what I intend to do.

I can't help the smile on my face as I take a drink of my beer, letting the perfect mix of sweet and bitter coat my throat. Remembering this place like it was yesterday, my college roommates and I would sneak in with our fake IDs, often staying until last call. Rules were a little looser back then but I imagine some still get away with it. We were young and we owned the dance floor and held court at one of these very tables. In fact, I think these are the same fucking tables from twenty years ago.

Now, I own the boardroom, instead of owning the dance floor. I may have grown up but I'm still the same person at my core.

I'm just seeing things through older eyes.

The humidity curls the hairs at the nape of my neck and I wish I had a hair tie to offer some relief. Trying to cool myself off I settle for leaning my cheek against the cold glass of beer and it feels good.

Through the thick of the crowd I look towards the stage and lock eyes with the singer on stage, a pretty face to go with that pretty voice. Pieces of dark brown hair stick to the sweat on his forehead and I watch as his mouth practically swallows the mic with lips that look soft and perfectly kissable.

What is it about musicians that make them so goddamn sexy? I wonder to myself. Is it the poetic nature of writing lyrics, the vulnerability of being up on stage, or the romantic notion of being untouchable?

Maybe it's the prospect of so much passion transferred from stage to the bedroom.

He's all jagged edges, tattoos, ripped jeans, and definitely not age appropriate for me. Old enough to drink, but just young enough to make it hurt. My whole body feels hot as he continues to stare at me. Maybe it's the beer or the stifling heat but his eyes seem to follow as I make my way around the room. Caught staring back, it's as if he sees my thoughts when the corner of his lip tugs into a knowing smile. It's impossible for him to know that I am imagining what kind of lover he would be - selfish or generous, relentless of fleeting, but his smile says otherwise. Maybe for one night I can be someone else and that makes the prospects endless.

Finishing the rest of my beer, I set the empty glass on a nearby table before slipping into the restroom so that I can breathe. While waiting in the short line, I look at all the writing on the walls and on the sides of the stalls. It's a typical dive bar bathroom but I thought after all these years they wouldn't have painted over the writing or replaced the stall doors.

As I wash my hands and look at myself in the mirror I notice my hair has gone limp and any makeup I had on has long since melted off. I run my fingers through my hair trying to salvage the volume but it's no use. As soon as I reach over to grab a paper towel from the dispenser, I see it. Written in black sharpie.

SW + LK

Twenty fucking years and they couldn't have painted the walls? I shake my head and drop the used paper towel into the garbage can.

What was I thinking coming here? I ask myself. Relive some part of me that has been buried twenty years deep? I'm forty-three years old for fucks sake.

This isn't me.

I don't look back.

I don't have regrets.

Because every decision I've made in my life since him has brought me here, to the person I am today. I'm successful whether my hair is styled or my makeup is perfect. Better yet, I am successful because he isn't in my life anymore.

I push open the bathroom door and walk through the bar, slipping between the crowd and find myself on the street. There's a gust of wind that travels down the long strip mall. Everything is dark, all the other stores closed for the night. I close my eyes, inhaling deeply, and smell the rain.

It's coming.

The city hibernates all year waiting for the rain to penetrate the hard shelled soil, breaking it open, and once it does, everything comes to life. Muted browns shift to deep reds and gold.

A lightning bolt stretches across the sky and the wind picks up, blowing the hair from my neck and cooling it. I walk down the block on my way back to my car, passing a darkened record store when I hear a voice call out behind me. "Hey."

Without even turning around, I know it's him, the singer with the velvet voice and the kissable lips. The wind continues to blow like a freight train down the block picking up the edges of my shirt and blowing my hair across my face. Turning around, he stands on the sidewalk, looking every bit as delicious as he did on stage. Waiting for him to look around me, to the person who's attention he was really trying to get, but he just stares at me the same way he did in the bar.

Caught in the web of his brown eyes and kissable lips, I'm unable to move.

The silence is broken by the sky opening and dumping heavy sheets of rain, plastering my hair to my face and my shirt against my body, in less than a minute. Moving towards me, with each step closing the distance between us, my pulse quickens and I can hear the blood rushing in my ears. When he reaches me, his hand grips my waist, guiding me into the alcove of the darkened record store, taking us out of the rain. His hand never leaves my body and the heat from it makes me shiver.

Water drips from his hair onto his lips and down his chin. In the dim light of the alcove with only the street lamp to illuminate his face, I see the green flecks in his brown eyes as he searches mine. They pull me in like a magnet, intense and beautiful. My palms press against his chest slowly gathering his shirt between my fingers. All while my heart is pounding in my chest because this is a man I don't know but he drew me in the minute I laid eyes on him in the bar, as if he was a tiny piece of my past that'd I buried long ago.

Maybe it's the wind, the way it wraps itself around us, pushing us together rather than pulling us apart, I feel as though this is a chance I need to take. How many times in the last eighteen years had I truly taken something just for myself? And how many more times in my lifetime will I get a chance to choose something for myself?

In the small space between us, a question lingers in the air.

Can I kiss you?

Wanting it and doing it are two different things because once I cross that line, will I be taking a step backwards? Looking at his beautiful rain soaked face, I know the answer.

The reach is slow and tantalizing as his lips move dangerously close to mine. Hesitant and seductive, heady and dangerous, I brush my nose along his, feeling his breath against my lips before taking a taste. His kiss is like a shot of bourbon, sweet and smooth with hints of caramel and vanilla with no burn, and no regret. My back hits the wall of the record store, as he steps forward, deepening the kiss. My body comes alive like the desert reacts to the rain.

His hands slip underneath my shirt, skimming along my back before moving down to draw my leg around his waist. Pressing his hips further into me causes an ache deep in my belly that spreads between my thighs. It's the kind of ache that draws out all reason, collapses any hesitation, and makes you feral for more.

I don't know this man.

I have never seen him before in my life.

But there's a long dormant beast inside of me that stretches and unfurls, awakened by his kiss.

It's wild and reckless like the monsoon happening around us but I can't seem to stop myself.

If I feel this way with just a kiss.

I can only imagine what it would be like to take this further.

The problem is, I don't want to just imagine it.

In this little dark corner of Mill Avenue, hidden in the alcove of the record store, safe from the rain, I feel more alive than I have in a very long time.

Read **Beautiful Lies** now on your favorite storefront

ALSO BY PAULA DOMBROWIAK

THE BLOOD & BONE SERIES

BLOOD AND BONE (BOOK 1)

Two days. One Interview. Twenty-five years of Rock 'n Roll. Telling his story might just repair past relationships and ignite new ones.

BREATH TO BEAR (BOOK 2)

These chains that weigh me down, my guilt I wear like a crown, SHE is my Breath to Bear

BONDS WE BREAK (BOOK 3)

To have and to hold from this day forward - to love and to cherish, till death do us part - and these are the bonds we break.

BOUND TO BURN (BOOK 4)

Love has a way of blazing through you like poison, leaving you breathless but still wanting more.

BLOOD & BONE BOXSET PLUS BONUS NOVELLA

ALL FOUR BOOKS IN THE BLOOD & BONE SERIES PLUS A BONUS NOVELLA.

Blood & Bone legacy, bonus novella, give you a glimpse twenty years in the future through the eyes of their children.

This is their legacy.

Already read the series but just want the bonus novella?

Grab it exclusively on my SHOP

www.payhip.com/pauladombrowiakbooks

BLOOD & BONE LEGACY, A BONUS NOVELLA

STANDALONES

BEAUTIFUL LIES

I own the boardroom. He owns the stage. We were never meant to be together, but when somethings forbidden, it only makes you want it more.

A forbidden, reverse age gap romance

KINGMAKER SERIES

A Steamy, Marriage of Convenience, Political Romance Trilogy

She was an escort to the rich and powerful. He was the playboy son of a U.S. Senator. This is the story of their union.

King of Nothing, Book 1 - March 12, 2024

Queen of Ruin, Book 2 - June 11, 2024

State of Union, Book 3 - September 10, 2024

ABOUT THE AUTHOR

Paula Dombrowiak grew up in the suburbs of Chicago, Illinois but currently lives in Arizona. She is the author of Blood and Bone, her first adult romance novel which combines her love of music and imperfect relationships. Paula is a lifelong music junkie, whose wardrobe consists of band T-shirts and leggings which are perpetually covered in pet hair. She is a sucker for a redeemable villain, bad boys and the tragically flawed. Music is what inspires her storytelling.

If you would like a place to discuss only my books, you can join my Facebook Reader Group **Paula's Rock Stars Reader Group**

You can always find out more information about me and my books on my website
PAULADOMBROWIAK.COM

ACKNOWLEDGMENTS

Originally, I hadn't planned on writing a series or continuing Jack and Erin's story. I was content to publish Blood and Bone and leave their story unfinished and up to the imagination of the reader but these two characters refused to leave me alone, especially Jack. I realized that he deserved to have a happily ever after. So, I started writing Breath to Bear and fell in love with Jack and Erin all over again. I hope you did too.

First, I'd like to thank my family. We have been through so much these last couple years, the world being turned upside down by the pandemic. It makes me hold those close to me just a little bit tighter. Thank you for putting up with my absence, my crankiness, lack of cooked dinners and my obsession with showing you funny Tik Toks because that is my love language. Pud, you are my most trusted confidante and I love you (you don't have to say it back). I'd also like to say sorry to my dog, Harley Rose, for neglecting you all these months. I promise I will play with you on the living room floor more often now...until I start the next book.

To my beta readers and wonderful friends, Christina, Daphne, Lizzie, and Lucy, you gal's make me a better writer, challenge me, and support me in the best way possible. Jack and Erin's story is better because of your excellent feedback. Erin got her 'Olivia Pope' moment because of you.

To my editor, Katy Nielson, I am so thankful for this partnership we have created, your attention to detail and your friendship. Thank you for fixing all my homophones. I have a problem, I know, just look at my title.

To my friend, Natalie. Little did you know when you reached out to me all those months ago that you would be stuck with me. Thank you for your friendship, for letting me vent, and keeping me sane. I love your face!

Thank you Michelle Lancaster for such a gorgeous photo. Your Instagram feed is the thirst trap that keeps on giving. To Lori Jackson, thank you for taking this piece of art and turning it into a fantastic book cover. Giorgio Torelli, you are absolutely the sweetest. Thank you for lending your face to once again bring my Jack to life.

A huge shout out to my friend and PA, Erica. Little did I know when I reached out to you in December 2020 asking you to read and review my debut novel, Blood and Bone, we would continue to be on this journey together. Your faith in me as an author is humbling and your love of the indie author community amazes me. Thank you from the bottom of my heart you little Canadian floozy.

To the Peen Posse, thank you for the laughter, the support, and most importantly, the endless sharing of man candy photo's and 'interesting' discussions. We're not called the Peen Posse for no reason.

To all the bookstagrammers, bloggers and booktokers out there who have supported me, shared my posts, reviewed my books, and reached out to me, thank you, thank you, thank you. Word of mouth is huge! Your love of books astounds me, and I am so grateful to be apart of such a wonderful book community. A special shout out to Michelle, Nancy, and Haley. You lovely Bookstagrammers have taken me under your wings and I love being one of your 'girls.' Thank you all so much for the love and support you have given me.

Last but certainly not least, to my readers!!! I can't tell you how much you mean to me. In my heart, I've always been a writer, but you made it real. I am always touched when readers reach out to me to say how much they connected with my characters. I always strive to write from the heart, create characters that are real and flawed, and portray them in the most sensitive way possible. I hope you continue along on this journey with me. Thank you for your support!

Made in the USA
Columbia, SC
06 November 2024

45791928R00188